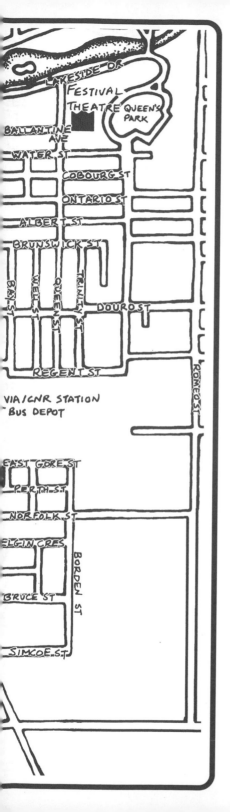

DOWNTOWN
STRATFORD

spadework

Also by Timothy Findley

NOVELS
The Last of the Crazy People
The Butterfly Plague
The Wars
Famous Last Words
Not Wanted on the Voyage
The Telling of Lies
Headhunter
The Piano Man's Daughter
Pilgrim

NOVELLA
You Went Away

SHORT FICTION
Dinner Along the Amazon
Stones
Dust to Dust

PLAYS
Can You See Me Yet?
John A.—Himself
The Stillborn Lover
The Trials of Ezra Pound
Elizabeth Rex

NON-FICTION
Inside Memory: Pages from a Writer's Workbook
From Stone Orchard: A Collection of Memories

Timothy Findley

spadework

a novel

Harper*Flamingo*Canada

Spadework
Copyright © 2001 by Pebble Productions Inc.

www.harpercanada.com

HarperCollins books may be purchased for educa-
tional, business, or sales promotional use. For information please write: Special Markets Department,
HarperCollins Canada,
55 Avenue Road, Suite 2900,
Toronto, Ontario, Canada M5R 3L2

Detective Story and excerpts from *A Household*,
As I walked out one evening, and *Memorial for the
City III* are taken from *Collected Shorter Poems* by
W.H. Auden. Reprinted by permission of Faber and
Faber Ltd.

First edition

Canadian Cataloguing in Publication Data

Findley, Timothy, 1930–
Spadework

ISBN 0-00-225508-1

I. Title.

PS8511.I38S63 2001   C813'.54   C2001-901179-2
PR9199.3.F46S63 2001

HC 9 8 7 6 5 4 3 2 1

Printed and bound in the United States
Set in Sabon

For Matthew Mackey,
whose spade began it all,
and for
the people of Stratford,
with whom I share my daily life.

prologue

For who is ever quite without his landscape,
The straggling village street, the house in trees,
All near the church, or else the gloomy town house,
The one with the Corinthian pillars, or
The tiny workmanlike flat: in any case
A home, the centre where the three or four things
That happen to a man do happen?

W.H. Auden
Detective Story

1

Stratford, Ontario,
Thursday, June 25, 1998

Swirling people. Lights. Music. Enough to make a person dizzy. This was only the beginning. Then you had to get through the doors, hand over your tickets to someone you could barely see in the crush and, after that, find your seat.

Opening night—and nothing in the world to equal it. The audience radiant with expectation—the actors sick with apprehension.

Everyone—as the saying goes—*was there*—all the stars, all the rich, all the Festival Board and staff—the Artistic Director—his assistant—the designer, the composer, the lighting and costume designers, the mass of visiting actors, writers, directors ... And the critics, all of whom were attempting—as always, without success—to maintain anonymity. *Who—me?*

They were somewhat overshadowed by the simultaneous presence of the Governor General and the multiple rumours of visiting actors Meryl Streep, Anthony Hopkins, Vanessa Redgrave, Emma Thompson and Jude Law. (These rumours seldom proved to be correct, but on occasion, some were true.) Nonetheless, the critics meticulously found their way to their aisle seats and stood waiting one by one, still feigning absence, until the rest of their rows had filled.

As always at Stratford's Festival Theatre, the evening began with fanfares—trumpets, applause and the raising of flags.

Because of the Governor General's presence, the national anthem would be played. People would stand—most of them would sing and there would be extensive applause, since the Governor General was an extremely popular figure.

In the midst of all this, Jane Kincaid and her seven-year-old son, Will, made their way to their privileged seats in the orchestra, five rows from the stage, two seats from the aisle. They sat down—stood up—sat down—stood up and sat down again as other members of the audience filed past them, laughing, smiling, excited, lost, apologetic, clumsy, graceful and awkward by turns. Sitting on Jane's other side was the play's director, Jonathan Crawford.

They barely spoke beyond the necessary acknowledgement that they were aware of each other's presence. After the national anthem Jane could see that Jonathan, as was natural, was almost catatonic with nerves, while his masklike expression said: *nothing can possibly faze me—I've done my job— it's over and the rest will be theatre history ...*

Jane Kincaid knew better, but said nothing. She was almost in the same state. Her husband and Will's father, Griffin, would be appearing that night as Claudio in Shakespeare's *Much Ado About Nothing*—and by all accounts, he was sensational and well on his way to stardom. Jane had deliberately stayed away from the dress rehearsal and the previews— wanting to savour the moment with Will.

Like all roads leading to the limelight, Griffin's had been long and arduous. He had begun his acting career at the University of Toronto—on a dare, playing Brick in Tennessee Williams's *Cat on a Hot Tin Roof*. He had broken his leg in a hockey accident and was bored. Since Brick wears a cast on his leg all through the play, Griffin's girlfriend of the moment, who was playing Maggie, the "cat" of the title, had said to him: *why don't you give it a whirl? After all—a person never knows.* What followed was the proverbial story of a duck taking to water. Griffin was stricken as by contagion and almost at once had given up the study of law.

He had gone on to play Brick on two other occasions—in Vancouver and in Winnipeg, which is where he met and fell in love with Jane Terry. They married just before moving to Stratford.

Jane had come to Canada from Plantation, Louisiana, in 1987, seeking work in the theatre as an artist. To her great satisfaction, she had been engaged as a property maker and designer in various theatres and had designed the props for the production of *Cat* at the Manitoba Theatre Centre in Winnipeg. Less than a year later she and Griffin were married, and seven months after that, Will was born.

Now, here they sat—mother and son, their stomachs in knots—waiting for Griffin to make his first entrance. Luckily he was on within the first seven minutes. (Will timed it.)

Jane almost wept. Griffin was surely the best-looking man on the stage—on any stage—and since the play was set in the eighteenth century, his trousers clung to his legs like a second skin and his tunic like a third.

The role of Claudio is difficult, because he must be played as both a charmer and a bastard—a daring soldier and a cowardly lover who denounces his beloved Hero on their wedding day, naïvely believing she has been unfaithful to him.

One minute you'll adore him, the next minute you'll hate him, Jane had warned Will. *Not to worry, hon. It's only a play and Daddy's pretending to be someone else—as he always does at work.*

Sometimes he even looks ugly, Will had said, remembering his father the year before as one of the murderers in *Macbeth.*

Yes, Jane had said with a smile, *but it was awfully hard to believe it was really him.*

Playing opposite Griffin as Hero was a new young actor freshly out of the National Theatre School in Montreal. Her name was Zoë Walker—and she was barely twenty-one. A slight twinge of nervous presentiment rose in Jane's mind when Zoë made her initial entrance off the top of the play.

Oh. I see.

One of those ...

But after a moment Jane dismissed the thought. The girl was remarkably attractive and carried herself like a graceful animal—nervous and shy but outwardly self-assured.

Just right.

The sets and costumes were among the most colourful Jane had ever seen—in spite of the fact that the colours were limited. Everything was red, white and blue—as if denoting empire. But the reds and blues were subdued. Only Beatrice and Benedick wore strong primaries, Benedick the soldier in scarlet, Beatrice the dedicated feminist in Prussian blue— severe, imperial, certain. Hero, the virgin, wore white. Claudio, the junior officer, wore a jacket of pastel blue with red facings and off-white trousers. The Italian court figures were clothed in burnt orange, yellow and a pink that verged on red but never achieved it. Portraits in watercolours, not in oil.

The setting had been transplanted from Italy to Bath—the Bath of Inigo Jones—of spas and terraces, the waters and the baths themselves.

Jane, who at first had been nervous of this interpretation, had come to admire it—principally because it opened so many doors on the way Jonathan had read the play. In England circa 1800, there were even greater social strictures than in Italy circa 1600, which is roughly when *Much Ado* had been written. It was the England of "mad" King George and of the dandified Prince of Wales—the England awaiting the voices of

Jane Austen, Keats, Shelley and Byron. Strictures, yes—and galore—but bursting at the seams.

And so it was with *Much Ado*'s sets and costumes—with the women almost pouring from their cleavage and the men so pronounced in their trousers that a person had to wonder how they contained themselves. As for the sets, the wooden floor of the stage had been transformed with black and white "marble" squares and a terraced effect of curving colonnades. When early in the play the men return from the wars, a scene was played in the baths—all the men girded in towels and shrouded in "steam," poised above the steps that separate the thrust stage from the audience, and stepping down into the "waters."

It was extraordinary.

The play moved on through the convoluted plottings of its leading figures, Beatrice and Benedick, as they tried both to attract and to repulse one another—each claiming they preferred to "remain a bachelor." Jane marvelled, as always, at the brilliance of the verbal fencing and the wit of the dialogue. On this occasion, "B-and-B," as they were known to actors, were played by two of the company's biggest, most popular stars—Julia Stephens and Joel Harrison, who were also paired that season as the Fords in *The Merry Wives of Windsor*.

Jane's contribution to *Much Ado* had been a series of hand-painted "silk" fans which made perfect—if difficult—props for the women in the play. The expert wielding of a fan is not easy. Actors claim they nearly go mad trying to master it. Once having gained control of it, however, they give the appearance of its being a graceful extension of the arm—a web-fingered hand provided as a blessing in disguise to eighteenth-century women.

Jane was proud of what she had created, using the finest netting as her "silk" and painting on it with acrylics—romantic scenes of stolen love affairs set in English gardens, French chateaux and Venetian gondolas.

In the interval, against her will, Jane was forced into encounters with friends, fellow artisans, company members from other plays and strangers. She found all this extremely trying, because she knew that Griffin's "big scenes" were still to come. She soldiered on, however, watching with envy as Jonathan Crawford managed to get to the exclusive VIP Lounge before he was besieged.

She concentrated on Will. She took him outside into the gardens, bought him a hot dog and a Pepsi and herself a glass of wine and smoked three cigarettes with her back to intruders and one hand on Will's shoulder. It was one of those nights when you wished no one knew who you were.

But glorious.

Griffin and Zoë, both relatively unknown, were triumphantly received at the end with cheers of approval and pleasure. (Two days later, a double interview was published with the headline: MUCH ADO ABOUT STAR BIRTHS.)

There were twelve extended curtain calls for the company that lasted almost fifteen minutes. It was everything an actor could hope for, everything a director works for and everything a wife and son could have prayed for. Magic. Will turned to Jane and said, almost as if he himself was a pro: "I bet that was a first for Dad."

Luckily, Jane knew her way around the backstage area and had already inscribed on her mind an indelible map of the route to Griffin's dressing-room.

When she and Will got there, it was already filled with other well-wishers, and when at last they managed to push themselves through to Griffin's presence, they found him sitting stark naked, with nothing but a make-up towel in his lap.

Jane closed her eyes.

What will all these people think?

Then she thought: *well ... as the saying goes, Griff is well-equipped and has never been one to hide his* candle *under a bushel ...*

When he stood up and opened his arms to Jane, all she could do was go in. Still stunned by the audience uproar, she was almost speechless—if not of sound, then certainly of words. Something like *yes!* did manage finally to be articulated—but barely.

Will, in situations where his father was more the actor than Dad, shook Griffin's hand as if they were meeting for the first time.

"Enjoy yourself?"

"Did I ever!" And then: "you were terrific."

"You coming to the party?"

Will looked at Jane.

"Yes." Jane smiled. "Of course he is. He's old enough to make it all the way to midnight. Aren't you, Will ...?"

"Sure. Yeah. Thanks."

Griffin sat back down, spread the make-up towel on his lap again and continued removing his "face" with cold cream and Kleenex. Will was always fascinated by this and stood watching him in the mirror.

Jane went to speak with Nigel Dexter, who shared the dressing-room. Nigel was Griffin's oldest friend in theatre. Half a year older, he was slightly rougher, infinitely tougher and harder to tame. As young men of an age, they made a perfect pair, from a theatrical point of view—their talents both opposite and complementary. In *Much Ado*, Nigel was playing one of the Watch and was riotously funny—impossible to discipline, totally incapable of comprehension and consequently surprisingly loveable.

"That was gorgeous!" Jane said.

"You like?"

"I *adore*. You really are remarkable, my love. I'm just saying hello, now. We'll see you later."

"Yes. With bells on!"

Jane went back to Griffin, kissed him on the lips, reached down and patted him on his naked hip. "We'll see you there. Don't forget to wear your pants."

The opening night party was sometimes held in a private home or in a restaurant, but this time it was in a marquee, erected in one of the extensive gardens that surround the theatre. Cast, crew, staff—all the designers, cutters, fitters, painters and musicians, as well as relatives, friends and visiting theatre folk—to say nothing of the Governor General, her consort and aides and the premier of the province with his wife were in attendance. It was the very definition of a Gala Occasion.

The weather was warm—the breeze was balmy and the night so exquisitely perfect that three sides of the marquee had been left open.

The great cars came and went, depositing honoured guests and other dignitaries. There was unobtrusive music, finger food and champagne, a bar, many different wines, tables to sit at, spaces in which to mingle and, outside, lanterns hung from the trees and, beyond them, the stars—and, in time, the moon.

How could anything be more perfect, Jane wondered. They might all have been in a film—or, indeed, in a play, except that no stage was large enough to accommodate all the wonders of it.

For whatever reason, Griffin was one of the last principal players to arrive. Zoë Walker, Nigel Dexter, Joel Harrison and Julia Stephens were among the first.

Well, Jane decided, *there are two ways to make an entrance. One is to be first—and the other is to come last ...*

She had already had two glasses of champagne by the time she saw Griffin making his way through the crowded entrance. Will was on his second Pepsi.

Jane stood back and beamed.

Unfortunately, in stepping back, she collided with Zoë Walker.

"Oh, I'm terribly sorry," she said.

Zoë Walker made a dismissive gesture. "Not to worry," she replied, and looked away.

Jane persisted. "You're Zoë Walker, aren't you."

"Yes."

"Congratulations."

"Thank you."

"We've never met. I'm ..."

"Do you mind—I'm trying to talk to my friends."

At this point, Zoë Walker turned her back entirely.

Jane muttered: "sure. No doubt we'll meet again."

Then Griff was there.

All, at last, was well.

They stayed until 1:00.

At home, they both put Will to bed, kissed him goodnight, pulled his door half-closed so that Rudyard, the golden Lab, could come and go through the night—and returned to the kitchen.

Jane said: "I vote we take a bottle of red out to the deck and finish the night under the stars."

"I'll second that," said Griffin, pulling off his tie, undoing the collar of his shirt and laying his jacket over the back of a chair.

Carrying glasses, cigarettes and the wine, they made their way onto the back deck, where there was wicker furniture, a gas barbecue and large pots of herbs.

"I've never been prouder to be your wife," Jane said when they were seated. Between the chairs, they held hands.

"Thanks," Griff said—and sighed. "My God, I thought we'd never get here."

"Where? To the deck?"

"No," he laughed. "To this moment in time, where we know something really has been made to happen ... achieved ... After all the years of waiting, the door has opened ... I'm partway through."

"You're all the way through, my darling. *All* the way through."

"Maybe. Certainly to the next stage—whatever it's going to be."

"Well, we mustn't fool ourselves. There are miles to go before either of us feels we've finally made it—but—and it's a big *but*—no one can ignore you, now. No one can forget you. No one can close the door."

"Pray God."

"There's the moon. Just in time."

"You know what I think we should do?" Griff said.

"What?"

"You hear that music coming from the Grahams'?"

"Sure. Lovely."

"I think we should take off our shoes and dance on the lawn in the dew ..."

"I'd love to. I'd love to. Yes."

Hand in hand, they made their way onto the grass, looked up at the moon and the stars and began to dance, cheek-to-cheek.

"Surely we're the luckiest people alive," Jane said.

"I don't see why not," said Griff. "It's our time."

"Yes. It's our time."

"What is this? The music," Griff asked. "I can't remember."

"It's Annie Lennox."

"Oh, yes ... Annie Lennox ..."

The song was "Every Time We Say Goodbye."

heat wave

Who cannot draw the map of his life, shade in
The little station where he meets his loves
And says good-bye continually, and mark the spot
Where the body of his happiness was first discovered?

W.H. Auden
Detective Story

1

Jane was not her real name.

Before she met and ultimately married Griffin Kincaid, she had been—as she was born—Aura Lee Terry of Plantation, a relatively small but extremely wealthy cotton-dependent community in the southern state of Louisiana. Aura Lee's parents—her father now dead—were millionaires many times over. But it had taken countless generations to make them so.

In the 1980s, Aura Lee had "escaped to Canada," as she said at the time, in order to avoid the possessive inclinations of her mother, Maybelle Terry. This was when Aura Lee had changed her name, saying: *I just want to be plain Jane. Ordinary.*

Today, she was shopping for balls.

After work, she drove out to the far side of town, where she was fairly certain she would find what she wanted at Home Hardware.

"Golf balls," she said, going past the check-out counter.

"To your left about halfway down the farthest aisle."

"Thank you."

Monday would be Griff's birthday. His thirtieth. Jane had bought him a new putter on her last visit to Toronto and the golf balls were to be Will's gift. They were his own idea, but Jane had said she was going to the outlet anyway and promised to pick them up. It was also Will's money.

Will was a bright, thoughtful boy—a little too silent,

perhaps, from time to time. Other kids called him *a loner*, in spite of the fact they sometimes rollerbladed together. He preferred books and jigsaw puzzles to communal games—but he was open, not secretive—interested in his surroundings, not withdrawn. He adored his father and also his nanny, Mercedes Bowman, who was a godsend to cats and children. And to Jane.

At the counter again, Jane set down two packages with three balls each and a pair of batteries for a burned-out flashlight.

"Will that be all?"

"Yes, thank you."

Having processed Jane's credit card, the clerk handed her the golf balls and the batteries in a plastic bag. As she signed the bill and retrieved her card, Jane made a silent prayer.

Please don't say: have a good day. *Please don't say that.*

"Have a good day."

"Yes. You, too."

She went to the parking lot smiling.

You can't win, I guess. We're all pretending to be ordinary people here. Which is sad, because we're not. Our lives are too rigidly structured to ever have a good day. *If people were to say:* have the best day you can under the circumstances, *that would be more like it.*

Before going back to the car, Jane glanced at the newspaper vending machines by the exit: *National Post, The Globe and Mail, The Toronto Star* and the *Stratford Beacon-Herald.*

Few indeed, according to the headlines, were having "a good day." The crisis in Kosovo was causing fear and misery to thousands; massacres, burned-out villages and towns, refugees pouring into Montenegro—which could ill afford them—and Milosevic pushing Serbian forces deeper and deeper into Kosovo itself.

The other major nightmare—the unfolding story of President Clinton and Monica Lewinsky—was threatening to bring Clinton down, and though his approval ratings remained remarkably high, his Republican enemies were urging an all-out war against him.

In nearby Kitchener, according to the *Beacon-Herald*, the bizarre rape and murder of a thirty-something single woman was causing a storm of protest against the local police because they had so far failed to produce a single suspect after a two-week investigation.

Crossing the parking lot, Jane thought: *the world, with all its horrors, used to seem so far away. Now, it's beginning to advance on us all—to invade even this beautiful, peaceful town—with its convoy of wars and scandals lumbering down the road towards us.*

Driving along Ontario Street—Stratford's main street, east to west—Jane was acutely aware of the town's history. What had once been a thriving industrial and railroad centre had fallen into the post-war doldrums that hit so many Canadian communities in the late forties and early fifties. Its future was rescued when a man called Tom Patterson had a dream—and the dream took hold. The Stratford Shakespearean Festival came into being in 1953—born in Patterson's dream largely because the town had the name of Stratford and a river called the Avon—just as in England. Stratford-upon-Avon, where Shakespeare was born—and where he died. Now the Stratford Festival of Canada had become the most renowned centre of classical theatre on the North American continent.

The countryside in which the town was situated was one of multiple farms—many of them Mennonite—rolling hills, onetime forests—now woods—cattle-strewn fields, sideroads with separate lanes for horse-drawn buggies and wagons, market gardens, streams, ponds and rivers—principally the Avon—and villages, hamlets and enclaves, none of which approached Stratford in size.

To Jane's right was the sprawling Festival Inn—rather ugly, she had always thought, but the largest motel complex in town, housing some of the thousands who flocked to the theatre every summer.

Shortly afterwards, on her left, was the huge factory whose sign always made her smile. It was a reminder of just how sharply Stratford had once been divided—and, to some degree, still was.

Many of its citizens—bred, born and raised in a basically conservative community—continued to be wary of the world of theatre—of "art"—that had invaded their lives. *Actors are all a bunch of fags*, men would say. *We're guys—guys—and we don't want fags in our bars and restaurants! Why don't they just fuck off and leave us alone?*

The joke was, a very great many of these men were employed in this factory devoted to the manufacture of German ball bearings—and, as its sign proclaimed, the company's name was FAG.

Where do you work? people would ask.

There was no safe answer.

Still, the Festival had become Stratford's most lucrative enterprise, with three theatres sharing ten to twelve plays from May to November each year, and bringing in multiple millions of dollars in tourist money.

As Jane approached the point at which strip malls and suburban business started to give way to houses and gardens, she saw Oliver Ramsay, her "boss"—not a title of which he approved. Oliver was head of the property department, and was walking alone—as always, so it seemed—and carrying a canvas bookbag. Jane knew Ollie well enough to be certain the bag was full of classic film videos, to which he was addicted.

She stopped.

"Where to?" she asked.

"I have to go back to work. Do you mind?"

"Of course not. Get in."

Oliver, who was slight, handsome and perennially lonely, got in beside her and closed the door with a bang.

"Sorry," he said. "But I love doing that. If I slam a door at home, no one hears it."

Jane laughed.

"Terrific day for me," she said. "I got my last window blocked and laid in."

"Yes, I saw."

Jane was making a triptych of stained-glass windows for the production of *Richard III,* which would open in less than three weeks. It had been, so far, something of a nightmare, but now most of the triptych was well on its way to completion. There was just one problem left. A director and a designer may ask for something specific, but the specifics of other people are often impossible to recreate. At any rate, this had been Jane's experience, and she had faltered in finding a face for the figure of Saint George, who was to appear in the windows with his dragon. Of course, the dragon had been no problem. *Dragons never are. Anyone can create a dragon*, Jane had said, *but not a saint.*

"Why do you have to go back?" she asked.

Oliver groaned and sighed. "Swords," he said.

"Ah, yes, swords. Saints and weapons are always the hardest."

"Saints, weapons and breakaways," Oliver said. "The breakaway chairs in *Merry Wives* keep coming back for repair. I think we're going to have to make a new set."

Jane turned down Queen Street, which led to the river, and

then into the parking lot beside the stage door of the Festival Theatre—the largest of three stages, and a structure whose shape was a visual reminder that, for the first few summers, the theatre had been housed in a circus tent.

Oliver got out of the car—and slammed the door again. "Love it!" he said.

"See you tomorrow."

"Maybe. Maybe not. Depends how late I am tonight."

"Sure. In any event, I'll see you at Down the Street on Monday for drinks. Griff's birthday. Don't forget ..."

"Don't worry, I won't. Thanks."

"Take care."

Jane pulled out of the lot and turned down towards the river.

The Avon was like an old friend. It partially went away from year to year, when the water level was lowered in the winter, but it always came back in the spring—and with it, its swans, its geese, its ducks and its gulls. It was a comfort, too, providing a kaleidoscope of colour and reflections, soothing in its slow progress towards its dam and falls and serene as it opened into Lake Victoria, where willowed islands sheltered a world of picnics in the afternoon and lantern light in the evening. Jane came here often, walking down from the Festival Theatre to sit with an illicit paper cup of wine and a cigarette. It was her favourite place in the whole town—but for one other.

The other was the rented house where she lived with Griff and Will at 330 Cambria Street, a house she wanted to call her own almost more than anything else within the reach of possibility—with the exception of another child, if only Griff would agree.

The ownership of the house and the birth of a second child were the only subjects on which they were divided. Griff was cautious—wary of too much financial responsibility before he had firmly established his career. Jane was anything but cautious and far from wary. To own a house in which to raise a family was all that mattered, once you were married and committed to the future.

Still, from Griffin's point of view, she had to admit his concerns were legitimate. It takes a long while for an actor to establish his financial worth, and though at the moment his salary was greater than Jane's, it was by no means grandiose. Jane, on the other hand, had an income. Her father and grandfather had set up an elaborate trust in the hopes that it would last for the lifetimes of Jane, her brothers and sister, Loretta. Which it would.

As Jane turned to drive along the river, she noticed that the Festival Theatre parking lot was already beginning to fill. Carloads of people were streaming up Queen Street, heading for the theatre restaurant and tonight's performance of *The Tempest,* in which Griff would appear as Ferdinand.

She noticed how many American licence plates there were on view. Even from far away as California. Most of the Canadian plates came from Stratford's own province, Ontario.

In the park beyond the parking lot, a display of work by local artists had drawn a crowd, though now—it being almost six o'clock—some of the artists were packing up their paintings and sculptures in wooden crates. Jane had never shown her own work publicly, even though she was a talented and dedicated artist. *Now, I am a professional property maker.* That was her life. For the moment. When they had bought the house and the second child was on the way, perhaps she would consider a small, private exhibition. She had a great deal of skill, but she was too aware of the demands being made on her at the theatre and refused to consider even the thought of *dabbling.* She would wait.

She passed the arena—where the swans, geese and ducks were

housed every winter—and, next to it, the Tom Patterson Theatre, which was presenting *The Glass Menagerie* that evening. The road then led her back up to Ontario Street, where there was a sizable crowd of milling students, who mostly had come from private schools by the busload. One group wore navy blue school blazers, with the girls in grey-and-blue tartan skirts and the boys in grey flannels. They were busy trying to sort out the most likely restaurants for quick service. Smiling at their healthy, happy faces, Jane turned right onto Church Street.

Here was the Stratford she loved the most—a wide enclave of turn-of-the-century houses, both Victorian and Edwardian—some of them built by railroad barons, and others only slightly less impressive, that had been the homes of the upper class until the Second World War, when so much wealth had changed hands.

There were even pillared façades on houses of Georgian design—mansions that had been erected in the mid- to late-1800s. Good taste had run rampant then, if there was money enough to support it. *Good taste, or at least someone's notion of it. Plain grand is what I'd call it,* Jane had thought, *or a bit* piss elegant, *as Griff would have it.*

The area reminded Jane of Plantation, with all its elegant lawns and gardens, porches and trees. It was a kind of paradise for nostalgia, and whenever walking here, Jane was always filled with happy memories of her Southern childhood—those rare moments, collected privately and hoarded from among the darker moments which had made up most of Jane's early life.

Driving towards the intersection of Church and Cambria, she passed the home and office of her psychiatrist, Doctor Fabian. The house of her best Stratford friends, Hugh and Claire Highland, was just two blocks away on Shrewsbury. Claire was a professor of history at the University of Western Ontario in nearby London and Hugh, who was older, had recently taken early retirement from the English Department at Western, in order to pursue his two favourite pastimes, gardening and golf. The house was a classic Ontario stone cottage. Its back screened-in porch looked out over one of the loveliest gardens in town. The impeccably preserved house, plus the summer-long display of blooms that Hugh coaxed from his collection of perennials, had made the daily drive to and from London totally worthwhile.

The thought of these friends was a comfort to Jane. *Right around the corner, the two best people in the world to grow old with ...*

Except that she was only thirty-five and Griff would not be thirty until Monday. Still ... *age happens*, as a Zen master might say. *Be prepared to welcome it.*

At the corner, she turned to the right and, passing Mrs Arnprior watering her front lawn next door, rolled her Subaru up the drive behind Griff's Lexus—a gift from Jane the year he was signed to play at Stratford—and behind Mercy Bowman's ancient Ford Maverick.

Home.

A somewhat battered truck was parked beside the cars, and two men were unloading obviously heavy sacks into a wheel-barrow. Luke Quinlan and his uncle Jesse—hired by the land-lord to create a huge new flower bed. Luke sketched a salute to Jane before heaving up on the handles of the barrow. Then, with Jesse helping him balance the load, he slowly wheeled along the side of the house into the backyard.

Jane could see the labels on some of the remaining sacks: peat moss, sheep manure, enriched soil. She smiled and thought: *how on earth are they going to get all* that *dug into one bed?*

Taking her carryall and the plastic bag from Home Hardware, Jane waved at Mrs Arnprior, went to the side porch, opened the screen door and entered the kitchen.

Griff and Will were both seated at the table, Griff drinking a martini and Will a Pepsi.

Mercy stood at the stove preparing a supper of pork sausages, creamed corn and mashed potatoes into which she had cut four or five green onions.

"Hi, all," Jane said and ruffled Will's hair.

She kissed Griff on the nape of his neck and went to the dining-room for a bottle of Wolf Blass Yellow Label, an Australian wine that was her favourite drink in the world.

Griff was due at the theatre shortly after seven. On performance nights he and Will ate early, and often finished dinner before Jane got home. Tonight, though, she had the benefit of being able to sit with them while they ate and she drank wine.

"Smells good," Jane said, looking over at the stove. She would eat later with Mercy, who usually stayed at the Kincaids' until the evening meal had been eaten and the dishes washed. Then she would go home and feed her four cats.

"What's in the bag?" Griff asked.

"Surprise. Don't ask."

"Okay. Won't."

"Did you get the flashlight batteries?" Will asked. *No batteries—no after-hours books ...*

"Unh-hunh. I'll give them to you later."

"I may be late tonight," Griff said. "Don't bother to wait up."

"How late?"

"Two. Maybe later."

"What's on?"

"Just the usual carousing. Jonathan, Robert, Nigel ..."

"Guys' night out, then."

"Yeah."

"Fine. I'll watch a movie."

"Can I watch, too?" Will said.

"Depends what I can find, hon. I'll go to the store down the street and see what they have."

Mercy said: "you two ready?"

"Not quite," said Griff, lifting his glass. "There's time."

"Suit yourself. You okay, Will?"

"Yes."

"Bring a glass," said Jane. "Sit."

When Mercy was seated and her wine had been poured, Jane looked around the table and said: "I think I'm the luckiest girl in the world. I got everything I wanted."

She kissed her fingers and touched Griff's lips.

He smiled, but his tone was oddly out of keeping with what he said.

"This is beginning to sound like an appropriate moment for Tiny Tim to say: God bless us all, every one."

Jane looked down at her glass.

She was jarred by Griff's seeming dismissal of her joy.

It was not what she had expected at all.

2

Friday, July 3, 1998

By 8:30 the next morning, both Jane and Griffin were in the kitchen with Will and Mercy. Rudyard was in the yard, where Luke Quinlan was already unloading yet more ingredients for the new flower bed.

"Heat's bad," Griff said. He was wearing an open shirt and

rugby shorts. "Woke up at 5:30 and couldn't get back to sleep."

"I think we're in for a siege," said Jane. "While you were in the shower, I listened to the weather forecast and the temp is on the rise by the hour."

Will was eating raisin bran—a favourite.

"There was a tornado in Kansas—just like the *Wizard of Oz*," he told them. "Twelve people dead already."

"Good Lord. I thought the tornado season was over," Jane said.

"So did they," said Will, with a grin.

"You don't need to sound so pleased about it," said Mercy, standing by the stove.

"I just thought it was exciting."

"Not when people die, it's not."

"Damn right," Jane added. She smiled at Will. "Think about it, hon. It could've been us." She was eating yoghurt, which she always laced with apricot jam.

"We don't live in Kansas."

Griffin ruffled Will's hair and winked at him.

"What are you two up to today?" Mercy asked. "This is early for you, Griff. You playing golf?"

"No. I've got a rehearsal with Jonathan and Zoë."

Jonathan? Jonathan and Zoë? Zoë? Jane wondered. Then she put down her spoon and said: "rehearsal? But both your plays have opened."

"Jonathan wants to talk to us about Claudio and Hero. He's like that. You never really finish rehearsing. Not even on the last night, according to people who've worked with him before." He opened one more button of his shirt.

"And you?"

Jane sighed. "On with the windows. Onward, ever onward. Same old problem—the face of Saint George."

"Why don't you just make it Griff?"

Jane laughed. "Griff is no saint, thank you very much—and thank God!" She crossed herself.

"I'll say amen to that," Griff said. "Sainthood is boring. *Bor...ring.*"

"How would *you* know?" Jane asked. "You've never been a saint."

"In my mother's eyes, I was." Griff smiled like a simpering child.

"Oh, well—yes," said Jane. "We know all about *that*. And by the way, don't ever smile like that again. Oosh!"

"You remember Nixon saying his mother was a saint?"

"Who could ever forget it."

"Who's Nixon?" Will said.

"Don't ask," said Mercy, stirring the breakfast eggs.

"American president," Griffin told Will. "Long before your time. A very bad—and a very sad man. You're lucky to have missed him."

"Isn't President Clinton supposed to be bad, too?"

"Some people think so. I don't."

"Neither do I," Jane agreed. "What President Clinton did was merely foolish—what President Nixon did was dangerous and destructive. I'll explain it later, hon. It's complicated."

"Maybe I don't want to know."

"Well, you should. It's important history," said Jane.

"American history. We're Canadian."

"Nevertheless, it affected us all. Besides, Mister Smarty-Pants, I'm an American, born and bred—and that makes you one, too. At least partly."

Mercy set down three plates of scrambled eggs and a plate of toast. The margarine, jam and marmalade were already on the table.

"I hate scrambled eggs," said Will, pushing his plate away.

"No you don't," Mercy said, pushing the plate back in place. "*Eat.*" She went back to the stove, lifted the frying pan and put it in the sink.

"What's got into you today?" Jane asked. "You love scrambled eggs."

"It's hot," said Griff. "It's hot—that's all. Right, Will?"

"I guess," said Will. "It sure isn't cold."

He began to eat.

"When do you have to be at the theatre, hon?" Jane asked.

"Anytime before 10:00," said Griff.

"Good. I'll drive you. I have to pick up some research and my sketchbook. I'm going to bring them back and work here. Can you hitch a ride home?"

"Sure. There's the matinee. I'll probably have lunch in the Green Room and after the show ask Nigel for a lift. He won't mind. He's done it before."

At 9:45 Jane left Griffin at the Stage Door, having kissed him goodbye, and went down to the property department.

Griffin went to his dressing-room, collected his text, smoked an illicit cigarette, put a pencil behind his ear and wandered onto the stage.

Jonathan and Zoë were already there.

"So, what are we doing?"

"We're going to have a chat," said Jonathan. "We probably won't actually rehearse, which is why there's no Stage Management present."

"Okay ..."

Both the actors were mystified, but knew better than to ask questions—yet.

Zoë was wearing a loose-fitting chiton with no waist. It came to just above her knees and was made of pure white cotton. Her hair was tied back with a black bow. She wore no make-up.

Jonathan, as always, wore pressed, well-tailored trousers, a blue striped shirt—tucked neatly beneath a thin leather belt that Griffin found somehow menacing—and leather sandals over bare feet. His toenails looked as if he had hired a professional to give him a pedicure—which, more than likely, he had.

Griffin felt slightly undistinguished in his loose shorts, open shirt and brown loafers without socks. Turning away, he surreptitiously did up two buttons and lowered his shorts so they were not quite so revealing.

Jonathan assumed a position centre stage. "Sit," he said.

Griffin and Zoë sat on the steps leading off left, and set down their already heavily annotated scripts.

"This morning, what I want to talk about specifically is subtext," Jonathan began. "What is *not* written, but implicitly there—the things not said that nonetheless have immense importance to your understanding of how to portray your people—and how we see them ..."

Griffin straightened. Zoë leaned forward, her fingers idly laid on his shoulders. There was genuine affection in the gesture. She and Griffin had become close friends over the past few months and trusted one another absolutely, as actors must who play in any intimate way together.

"We've already discussed, during rehearsals, things like where you have been when you make an entrance and where you are going when you exit. That sort of thing is standard. We all know no one enters from the wings any more than they exit to their dressing-rooms. But more importantly, I want to instill in you both the idea that when you make an entrance, you have no idea what you're going to say—or what anyone else will say—or what's going to happen next. In a play, it is always *now*. *Now*, with absolutely no foreknowledge of *anything*. Nothing of what will happen as a consequence of the immediate. *You know nothing*. And we must believe you know nothing ..."

Zoë removed her hands from Griffin's shoulders and sat on them. Her hair fell forward.

"Obviously, you must learn the text. But you must know it so well—so absolutely—that you are able to *forget* that you know it. Each line you speak must enter your mind in the very same way as anything you might speak in any situation, as yourselves. It must simply be the next thing that occurs to you to say—in the situation you are playing."

Zoë looked up and nodded. "Yes," she said.

Griffin spread his knees.

Jonathan said: "Shakespeare, like any playwright—any writer—was obsessed with certain patterns, certain relationships, certain situations—and repeated them often, sometimes failing to articulate them—sometimes succeeding—but succeeding much more often as he moved from play to play."

Jonathan turned away and lighted a cigarette.

Griffin and Zoë sat forward, tensed. What Jonathan had done was totally forbidden.

When he turned back to face them, he made an expansive gesture with the cigarette and blew smoke upward into the work-light, whose bare beam lit the stage.

Suddenly, it seemed they were in a "scene"—in something being created in the moment—one of untested elements and unrehearsed words.

"You see?" Jonathan removed a portable ashtray from his trouser pocket, opened it and dipped the cigarette towards it. "There is always the unexpected—for which you must be prepared. Is Hero a loose woman? Is she? It would seem so—to Claudio. But how could he possibly have expected it? And Ophelia? Desdemona? What of them? Has Juliet abandoned

Romeo? Are the accusations against them true or false? *We know*—but do Hamlet, Othello and Romeo? Well ... only the playing of the moment will tell. But in the meantime, we must believe in the possibility that Hamlet, Othello, Romeo and Claudio will falter. Because without that possibility, there can be no suspense—and without that suspense, no play. In this instance, in *Much Ado*, the audience already knows that Hero is innocent. The whole situation has been manufactured in order to drive them apart. So—if we already know about the false accusation, where's the suspense?"

"In wondering whether Claudio is going to believe it," said Griffin.

"Exactly. Because we also know precisely how he's going to react if he does believe it—which can only lead to disaster. Tell me what he says."

Griffin said: "he says: if I see anything tonight why I should not marry her tomorrow, in the congregation, where I should wed, there will I shame her."

"Remind me what we said in rehearsal about that speech."

"That it seems heartless—that it reveals something about Claudio that we may not like or want to admit."

"Which is?"

"That he's selfish. That he's childish. That he's ..." Griffin faltered.

"Yes? What? That he's what else?"

"Proud."

"Dead right. Which is where Shakespeare puts the double whammy on him. If pride goeth before the fall, then he's set himself up to trip."

"Yes."

"What sort of pride is it, do you think? What's the source?"

"Well ..." Griffin shrugged. "He comes from a good family, for one thing. He's proud of his name."

"And?"

"And ... I'm not sure. It's just *pride*."

"No. It's more. What does he do?"

"His job?"

"Yes."

"He's a soldier."

"Ah ... *A soldier*. And what do soldiers prize above all else? Especially then—and more, perhaps, then than now."

"Winning."

"Yes. But more. A good deal more."

"What?"

"Honour."

Griffin was silent.

Jonathan said: "honour above all else. Above all else, honour. And so it is his honour—more than his heart—that prompts him to say he will shame her. If Hero has shamed him privately, by making a cuckold of him even before they are married, then he will denounce her publicly—knowing that nothing worse could happen to a woman of her rank and station. In other words, he will ruin her—bring her to ruin. No one would have her after that. No one. What does Hamlet say to Ophelia? 'Get thee to a nunnery. Go!' Always remembering that in Shakespeare's time *nunnery* had two meanings: it was either a place of chastity—or a whore house. Little wonder the girl went mad. And little wonder that Hero 'dies.' The shock of such accusations is overwhelming, when you know that you are innocent."

"Yes." Griffin's gaze drifted. He did not quite yet know where to go with the thought. And then he said: "it certainly does make Claudio more cruel than I imagined."

"Well—he's a soldier. For a soldier, cruelty is a necessity. *And* for honour—the same. It would have been one of the first things he learned as an adult."

"Yes."

"And, by the way, you must learn not to sit like that in those shorts. Put your knees together. And next time you wear them, put on some underwear!"

Griffin closed his legs and stood up.

Oh, God ... What have I done ...?

Jonathan smiled, not unkindly, but with an edge of deliberate finality. "You see?" he said. "Now you know what it feels like to be Hero."

Griffin turned away.

"You mustn't be embarrassed," Jonathan said. "I'm not fool enough to think you were flirting with me. Surely you know better."

"Yes."

"Zoë is strangely silent."

"I'm just trying to make sure that all of me is inside my dress ..."

This broke the tension. Even Griffin had to laugh.

Clever girl, he thought. *I'll thank her later.*

Jonathan butted his cigarette and pocketed the portable ashtray.

"Well, now," he said. "Why did I choose to bring you here alone this morning—just the two of you ... Why not the whole company? Because ... you are young. And I have rarely met two young actors of such promise as you have. And I urge you—both—never to relax your awareness of all the possibilities waiting in the shadow of every word you speak on stage—every word—every gesture—every step you take and every look in every direction. Above all, *listen.* Listen—always listening, knowing you know nothing. If a pin drops, you must hear it. What does it mean? If a fly moves its wings, you must see it. If someone so much as wavers in your direction, you must be aware of it. *Nothing*—nothing that happens in your presence must pass unnoticed. This doesn't mean you must react to virtually everything you see and hear, but you must be aware, so that when reaction is required—or becomes appropriate—it will be in response to everything that preceded it. Some of these things you already know, but I want to re-enforce them. Now—with both *The Tempest* and *Much Ado* running—and running bloody well, I might add—now is a very dangerous time. Perhaps the most dangerous time of all for an actor. Because you can all too easily skip away from the intensity of what you've established. You can become too confident—too certain and too at ease with it all. And an audience always knows. It knows when all of you is not engaged. All right?"

"Yes, Jonathan."

"Yes, Jonathan. Thank you." This was Zoë.

"Now tell me what you're doing today about lunch."

Zoë said: "I'm meeting Richard at Bentley's."

"Richard Harms?"

"Yes."

"I thought you'd given up on him."

Zoë smiled. "No. Not yet."

"Griffin?"

"I was going to eat in the Green Room."

"Alone?"

"Yes."

"Then come with me to Down the Street. It will just give you time before the matinee—unless you have to go home first, of course."

"No. I'd be delighted."

Zoë kissed them both, took up her text and retreated.

"We can go out through the front," said Jonathan, stepping down into the house.

"Lead on," said Griffin and got his script. "I'm right behind you."

3

Friday, July 3, 1998

At 1:15 that afternoon Jane sat at the kitchen table with her sketchbooks and some files of research on the subject of medieval stained-glass windows—including a whole file of various depictions of Saint George and the dragon. This was one of the great advantages of the profession she had elected to pursue: you could do half the work at home.

Now, it was July—and the usual heat wave, so typical of recent summers in southern Ontario. And with the heat, humidity of the kind that forces multiple changes of clothing throughout the day.

Jane felt transported back to the Mississippi Delta. Sometimes she wondered why everyone here did not feel compelled to speak in the accents of her childhood—the accents of William Faulkner's novels and Tennessee Williams's plays. At least Amanda Wingfield had consented to come to Stratford that summer, taking up residence in *The Glass Menagerie* three or four times a week. Where were the others? Why were her friends and neighbours not called Blanche and Alma, Bayard and Quentin, all living out despairing lives on a diet of too much drink and too much poetic speech, wasting away in once proud mansions?

Certainly all the pertinent clothes and accoutrements were in evidence. Ceiling fans, the clink of ice cubes, tall cool drinks in sweating glasses, lazy music drifting from a neighbour's open windows. Loose, unconfining dresses, shirts and trousers. Some days, you never wore shoes—and all days, you tied your hair well back from the face.

Unfettered breasts were *de rigueur* in June, July and August. It was a time of mandatory display; resist it and your body could suffocate. Sales of antiperspirants jumped by twenty per cent. Every household's water bills climbed through the roof. Ninety, ninety-five in the shade, day after day after day.

Still, in spite of the lazy afternoons and sultry nights, it was not the Old South of childhood. Not Plantation, not Louisiana, though similarities abounded. The old houses—which Jane still insisted on calling *antebellum* because so many of them were the very sort of house in which she had been born. Literally. Her grandmother, whose own mother had suffered the *crudity of Yankees* as a child in the late 1860s, did not believe in hospitals. *In hospitals, everyone dies,* she had said, having seen her father die beneath the seemingly sadistic knife of *a N'Yawk doctah!* So Jane was born at home, in her great-grandmother Aura Lee Terry's bed.

And thus, her own name.

On reaching her majority—a word still used back then to denote a person's coming of age—Jane had fled, though quietly, as far away as her money would let her. This brought her into that other culture she had heard so much about during the troubled years of the Vietnam War—that other culture with which America shared its continent, though Americans were the first to declare there was not any culture *up there in Canada*, let alone one by which Canadians could be defined.

Jane had found otherwise. Toronto, Montreal, Vancouver and Winnipeg were vibrant centres of creative activity, where Jane had sought work on arrival. She was an artist of some talent, with which she hoped to find employment in the theatre. And this, in time, she did. Costume design had attracted her at first—and set design—but props had won out. *They're so substantial,* Jane had said. *I love the feel of them in my hand.* And now, eleven years after crossing the border, she was working in Stratford, married to Griffin Kincaid and living in a *post-bellum* house on a tree-lined street in a town of some beauty and much charm. All this was culture enough for Jane, and in it she had flourished.

Well, she now thought, *enough daydreaming. Work. Back to the windows — and that goddamned elusive face ...*

Every morning—every evening—there were the crows. Jane was more aware of them here on Cambria Street than she had been in other places they had rented in Stratford.

"I know we can buy this house, Griff," she said to him that evening after supper. "We must. I so love it here. I haven't been this comfortable in years. Have you? Surely you must feel the same. Here and now—it's the meaning of contentment."

They were seated, final wine in hand, on the back deck. Griff was not playing that evening—a rare occasion, but he seldom played matinees and evenings, back to back.

The crows, about to assemble for the night, were calling from various distances. East—west—north—south. *Here, here—here—come home! Come home!*

Luke, the gardener, was now working alone, Jesse having left for the day. With a fierce concentration, he was wielding his spade to turn the bagged supplements into the new bed. To Griff—and to Jane—it seemed a kind of digging madness.

"The man's possessed," Griff said.

"All the way to China." Jane nodded. "That's where he's headed. He said so this morning. *All the way to China ...*" She smiled at Griff. "Like a child."

"Maybe the flowers will bloom at both ends," Griff said.

"Wouldn't it be nice to think so," said Jane, reaching out to take his hand. "I wish you loved it here as much as I do."

"I do."

"Then why can't we buy it?"

"Because we can't afford it."

"The longer we wait, the more expensive it's going to get. There's no return on all the money we're putting out in rent. And Michael, *the over-charging landlord,* isn't going to wait forever. Right now, he might be content to rent—but sooner or later, he's going to want to sell."

"I know. But ..."

"*I know—but.* You always say that."

"We have to be responsible."

"Owning a house is responsible. It's the most responsible thing you can do, when you're a parent. We owe it to Will. We owe it to ourselves. And there will be other children ... won't there."

It was not a question.

"Sure."

"I've done the math," said Jane.

"Somehow, I knew you would," said Griff. He squeezed her hand and let it go.

"Well, someone has to. It's my job."

"I thought that was Frank Webber's job. We don't spend a fortune on an accountant for nothing. He's supposed to tell us where we are."

"I've already spoken to him."

"Oh?"

"Yes. He says we can swing it."

"I don't want to *swing* anything, Jane-o. I want to do it with absolute confidence. When the time is right. And the time will only be right when my salary matches your income."

"Oh, don't say that. Please don't say that. My income belongs to both of us. To all three of us. I was born wealthy, that's all. I wish you wouldn't hold it against me."

"I don't. You know I don't. It's just ... It's just the way I grew up. A man pays his own way. His own way—and his children's ..."

"Isn't that slightly archaic?"

"Not to me. It's what my father did—and my brother—and it's what I want to do. I expect it of myself. I wish you could understand what it feels like." He took her hand again. "You had to fight your way out of the money-trap," he said. "But we had to fight our way in. Of which I am proud and for which I am grateful. Every advantage, every good thing we had was paid for. In cash."

Jane sighed. Then she suddenly laughed. "There's a song," she said. "You know it? 'Two Different Worlds.' That's us. We come from two different worlds ... and sometimes I curse it."

Griffin smiled. "Jane-o, we have no choice. But there isn't a *different world* on the planet I'd rather have than my own."

The crows were multiplying in the dying walnut tree. For a moment, the only sound was of their settling wings and the creaking branches.

"Foray over?" Jane asked.

"Foray over," said Griff. "You want another of these?"

"One."

Griff stood up, took their glasses and retreated to the kitchen.

Jane said to Luke: "it'll be dark in an hour. Shouldn't you stop?"

"No. I'll stop when I'm done."

Jane cast her mind over Griff. *What is it? What's wrong? Will he never give in—never accept the fact that I've got some money? And after all, it isn't as if I were Ivana Trump or someone. I just have a bit of money in the bank. That's all. Still, he's right about one thing. I know the money will always be there. And he doesn't.*

For Griff, the only money he could count on was what he

made—day by day, season by season. *And—he's a man, goddamit.*

Still, she smiled. He had let her pay for two things: the Lexus—and Mercy Bowman, without whom they would be lost, given their jobs and the fact of Will.

She sighed again. She had to admit that on the subject of the house, a door had closed between them, and she regretted it.

An ambulance screamed its way towards the hospital at the far end of the street. Someone was dying—giving birth— staving off a crisis.

The sun had begun to sink. It was after nine.

Luke was digging deeper.

Jane said nothing. This was how it was done. This was the doing of it—the labour. She thought of Mozart, and the quill poised above the page. Gardens. Music. The doing.

Griffin came back and handed her her glass. Rudyard came with him and sat beside Jane, staring at the crows.

Jane lighted a cigarette and took two deep gulps of her wine. She fondled Rudyard's velvet ears. When she finally spoke, it was a kind of aria, voiced in a curious, vibrant monotone, as if reciting words from an opera on the subject of owning houses.

"It jeopardizes nothing," she began, "if we have a home."

Griffin sighed. She was going to make a speech.

Jane said: "don't do that. Don't just slough it off. Listen to me. Yes—you will always end up having to go where the work is. That's what actors do. It's your job. To *be* there. But it doesn't mean you have to be lost out there, for God's sake. You're still *people*—with *people* needs and *people* orientations. You have to be centred, my darling. Everyone has to be centred, in order to survive. Otherwise you go out into the world and never come back, because there won't be anywhere to come back to when you fail. And you will fail. You already have and you will again. So will I. We know that. Everyone fails in the theatre. That's what it's about—surviving failure. Great Jesus, Griff," Jane laughed, "have I been the only witness to your career? Haven't you watched it yourself? Don't you remember all the hell you've already been through? And dragged me and Will through with you? All those years when you nearly made it and didn't—quite. And guess what, my lover. You always had me to come back to. Yes? *I am your home.* Don't you know that? And where I am, you will always be safe—no matter what happens to you. But if you want me to be here, *need* me to be here—and you do—there has to be a *here* for me to be."

Luke stopped digging and dragged his rag of a handkerchief out to wipe his face and neck.

Griff drank.

"We need the stability, hon. I'm the one who's bringing up Will. And thank God for Mercy. You're *already* not here half the time. And I know that's not your fault," Jane hastily added. "And neither am I—here as much as I want to be—but I'm still the one who has to guarantee that when things go wrong, there's continuity. For *all* of us."

"Jane-o, I don't want a house," Griff said. "Not now. Not yet." He lowered his voice so that Luke would not hear him. "Buying this house right now—given my financial situation—would be a trap. And I don't intend to be trapped. It's too soon. And for me that's the end of it. *It's just too soon.*"

He sank back in his chair.

Jane was devastated.

Was he saying *she* was a trap? The marriage? Will—Mercy—Rudyard—all their beautiful times together ...?

A trap?

Griff stood up.

"I'm going to take a shower," he said. "Then I'm going out."

Leaning down, he kissed her on the cheek.

Jane looked away.

"Okay," she said. "Fine. End of story."

Saying nothing more, Griff took his empty glass and went back into the house. Rudyard stayed with Jane.

I will not ... cry. It's just a passing moment. I won't bring the subject up again. For a while. I should've known better. He's stressed. He's worried about next year—whether he'll be asked back—what he might get to play ...

Nevertheless, she was still upset. In her view, there was no good reason not to buy the house on her own.

Trap be damned. Trap be goddamned.

She would spring it. This way, she could open the door to number 330 Cambria Street, Stratford, Ontario—on whose rear deck she now sat beneath a crown of sleeping crows.

Staring upward, unaware that it was happening, she began to count the stars beyond her tears.

"*Don't,*" she whispered.

But she did—and for a while, she could not stop the flow. It was all too reminiscent of her own escape from the trap of her childhood—her money—her predestined future as the wife of another plantation owner—a mere repetition of her mother's docile hand being placed, palm down, inside her father's—and the consequential torrent of unwanted babies, unwanted social engagements and unwanted privileges. *Welcome to Plantation, Louisiana—home of the Cotton Ball—home of the Cotton Queen and home of the Cottonmouth*—not that anyone ever mentioned the latter. And now, tobacco. Since the 1950s and the advent of hybrid fibres, tobacco had begun to rival cotton as the chosen crop in Plantation, and the money flowed out over the Delta. *Oh, God*—how she hated it all and wanted only to escape. North. Northward. As far away as a person could get from cloying, possessive voices and clawing, possessive fingers—*mine, mine, mine,* her parents had said of their children—their land and their place in the hierarchy. That was when Aura Lee Terry had turned her back, clicked the heels of her ruby-red slippers and become *plain Jane.*

And if you owned your own house—had taken up residence elsewhere—at whatever distance you could achieve—then you were safe. No more clawing fingers—no more cloying demands. Freedom. Freedom from the dead weight of the past.

4

Sunday, July 5, 1998

Today, the heat was at its most killing.

Jane had chosen to sit in the kitchen because of the overhead fan and the open side door. She wore a pale blue cotton dress—one of the four she had ordered from L.L. Bean's Canadian catalogue. Her honeyed hair was pulled into a truncated ponytail, tied with blue ribbons. *Childhood.* Two ribbons—top and bottom.

Green-eyed and well-defined by bones, Jane was neither beautiful nor forbidding. She was, instead, disturbing—provocative. *Who could this woman be, wrapped in all these silent conundrums?* people thought. To relative strangers, it seemed that Jane merely waited in the shadow of her actor husband, their son, Will, and her own profession. She spent most of her hours in her studio or hidden in the depths of the theatre's property department, suspended in time and silence as if, somehow, limbo was where she belonged.

None of this told anything like the true story. Her life was subdivided between the everyday and the extraordinary. And yet—on the street, at work—even with her friends—her expression betrayed nothing.

And today, Troy. Out of nowhere.

Suddenly, there he was. She could not even recall his last name. Just *Troy*—from Plantation High School—*crush*-time. No phone call—no warning. Nothing. Just *there*.

She had been wearing one of the other blue dresses—a darker one, unbuttoned. She had been sitting where she was now, at the kitchen table—her sketchbook open before her—using a bright red polka-dot bandanna to swab the undersides of her breasts and glorying in the fan.

Griffin was playing a matinee. Mercy had agreed to give up her day off and was in the park with Will and Rudyard. Jane had elected to be alone and try to solve the problem of Saint George's enigma.

The doorbell had rung.

Who could it be?

Jane had done up her buttons and gone through the dining-room and living-room to the front door, where there was green-curtained glass. A man stood beyond it, wearing a white polo shirt and white tennis shorts. Vaguely familiar. Short-haired, thick, athletic.

She opened the door.

"Yes?"

The man turned.

"Troy!"

"Hello." Unsmiling. Grim.

"It's been ten years ..."

"Fifteen."

"Oh, do come in. How utterly wonderful to see you."

Now, as she remembered these words and their effusiveness, she cringed. The muscles in her neck and shoulders tightened.

"Whatever are you doing in Stratford, Ontario, Canada? I

cannot believe my eyes!" She let him pass beyond her into the cool interior. He could not have come to see the plays. That was a certainty. Not Troy.

"I came to see you," he said.

There was something vaguely unsettling about this confession. For Jane, it registered, but more in retrospect than in the moment. *Why shouldn't he want to see me? We knew each other all through our childhood and beyond—until I left.*

She had brought him in and offered him a drink. They had talked, but only briefly. On the other hand, he was clearly not ready to leave. He exuded a sense of expectation. What? What of? What for?

She gave him lunch—a bowl of soup—a sandwich. Jane herself had already eaten with Will and Mercy. Now, they had gone to the summerhouse in the park beside the river. This quiet daily moment was a gift of freedom Jane always cherished. Mercy and Will were probably watching Rudyard chase squirrels at that very moment and Jane was alone at last with a rare private glass of wine. Bliss. *Wolf Bliss.* Now interrupted.

My God! Fifteen years! High school, *early eighties.*

Back then, Troy had broken Jane's heart. Not that there was much of a heart to break, she thought now. Life had not been terrific up till then and in many ways she had turned away from it. Shy and thoughtful—tentative—she had been damaged early on. Nothing sexual. Not the usual. It all had to do with denying who you were—her appallingly pretentious and ambitious mother—her equally appallingly apologetic, practically non-existent father—her pathetic sister and brothers, suffering, as she had suffered, from being pushed by their mother in directions none of them had chosen. Too much money, not enough willpower. Too much of the past—nothing of the present. *Money, tradition and lost causes suffocate,* Jane had concluded when she finally escaped the South. She recited this—or a version of it—every two weeks to Doctor Fabian, who was determined to force a confession of personal weakness—even of personal defeat—so that he could introduce her to a liveable future.

Then, along came Troy, first seen on tennis courts at the country club. Even aged twelve, he had a natural gift and a flair for the game. It was in his blood, so it seemed. Having been born with the double blessing of perfect timing and an athlete's strength and structure, he had thought he did not have to apply himself. *Just go out there—play and win,* he would say with that smile of his. After the age of sixteen, this attitude was ruinous. He skipped his professional workouts. Lost his favour—and was dropped. It took two years. Everyone had thought he would win the Davis Cup—Forest Lawn—Wimbledon. But, no. He lost his place in people's eyes—and his grace on the courts. *It is one thing,* someone had said, *to have talent. But you also have to have a talent for having talent.*

Jane sighed. He'd been so beautiful to watch. He took your breath away. She had been fifteen, sixteen—he had been seventeen, eighteen by then. At nineteen—he was gone.

She reached for the bottle and poured another glass of wine, lighted yet another cigarette and counted over the butts already accumulated in the ashtray. Six. Since when?

Since Will had gone for his walk with Mercy. *Dear God. Oh, well. Why not?*

Today, the soup had been good. A particular favourite. Jellied consommé—lemon juice—fresh basil. Tomato and lettuce sandwiches on sourdough bread from Breadworks. And Mercy's favourite—spumoni ice cream.

This had been pretty much what she had offered Troy—not that he seemed to care. He had said nothing, eating as if on automatic pilot.

Afterwards, they had sat in the living-room, where another ceiling fan kept them more or less cool. Jane had vaguely noted how tight his polo shirt and tennis shorts were—as if he had taken up bodybuilding without changing the size of his clothes. He also wore loafers over bare feet, the way Griffin so often did. Strangely silent, in spite of the fact there must have been a story to tell about the intervening years, Troy had watched her during his lunch in the fashion of a man who wanted to speak but could not find the words. Then, all at once, it became clear words were not what he was looking for.

Basically, it happened out of the corner of Jane's eye. An opaque view of an unrecognizable gesture. Movement. He was coming around behind the back of the chair in which she sat and she had thought: *he's looking for an ashtray—or doesn't know how to find the bathroom ...*

That was not it, however. Not the bathroom. Not an ashtray. Her.

When he emerged on the far side of her chair, he had somehow dropped his shorts and kicked them aside.

He leaned in before her and grabbed the back of her head, holding it brutally by the hair. With his other hand, he yanked at his underwear, exposing himself just as the sperm shot forward onto her face and down the front of her dress.

Not a word.

Then he let go of her, fell to his knees and crawled into a corner, where he wept like an abandoned child. The tennis hero of old.

Five immobilized minutes later, Jane had heard Mercy return with Will and Rudyard. Luckily, they entered through the side door. Jane forced herself to her feet and went to the kitchen, where she kept them prisoner with offers of more spumoni, while she pretended to be blotting perspiration and spotting the front of her dress with a dampened dish towel.

For the next few minutes, she could barely breathe—and then, at last, she heard the front door open and close. He was gone. Out at the curb, a car burst into life and drove away.

Mercy looked at Jane.

"Who was that?" she asked.

"No one," said Jane. "No one. Just an old school friend."

She remembered sitting down after that—shaking uncontrollably as she had tried to pour more wine.

Mercy had done it for her.

"Your school friend bring bad news, honey?"

Jane had given a curious, fleeting smile. "In a way," she had said. "An old flame has died." She had touched the front of her dress in the hopes that nothing showed. Then she had added, whispering: "it was all one-sided, anyway. The fact is, I can't ... I can't even remember his last name."

"Sorry."

"Don't be. It's over."

"Sure."

Mercy took Will, who had placed four new pieces in his jigsaw puzzle, for his Sunday afternoon nap—a Terry tradition established in the wake of the multi-coursed lunches attended by uncles, cousins and aunts. When she returned, she found that Jane had opened another bottle of wine. Rudyard had flaked out on the cool tiles beneath the table.

Neither woman spoke. Mercy sat down and fingered a cigarette from her pack, using one of Jane's wooden matches to light it. Kitchen matches. Ever practical. *In case she wanted to burn the house down.* She, Jane and Griffin never smoked in Will's presence inside the house. It was a rule.

"I'm going upstairs," Jane suddenly said and, taking the bottle, she went into the hall—filling Mercy's glass before she left. "I'll wake myself."

"Sure, honey. Go ahead. I'm happy just to sit."

Later, when Griff returned from the theatre, Mercy had told him Jane was lying down with a headache. She debated whether to tell about the extra bottle of wine and the visitor from the past, but she decided against it. Something had happened—none of her business. She was silent. If Jane wanted to tell it, Jane would tell.

Jane said nothing more to Mercy—nothing at all to Griff.

The next morning, listening to the seven o'clock news, she heard of Troy's death in a fiery crash on Highway 401. His last name, so they said, was Preston.

Jane switched off the radio before any further details could be given. She did not want to hear anything more.

Gone.

And never once more mentioned.

Not even to Doctor Fabian.

But he was not gone. At night, for weeks, Jane pondered his fate in the light of her own. She had fled Plantation to seek a life without connections. Troy had apparently fled Plantation in order to close the circle of his desire. Whatever. Desire—lust—connection. And he not only failed to connect, he perished in the attempt.

Perished. What could be more futile? Nothing. But—and Jane could not bear the guilt of this thought—it had not happened to her. It happened to Troy. Two children—running away from the unhappy past—and colliding with the future. One fatally, the other surviving.

Yes?

Yes.

5

Down the Street was a favoured actors' haunt. Both restaurant and bar, where it was impossible to go during the season without seeing several members of the Festival company. Susan, the owner, kept an eye out for tourists who expected too much of the actors, thinking it an opportunity to sit with them or engage them in protracted conversations. Then she would give a smiling reminder: *your table's ready now—just down here.*

The menu was eclectic—part Italian, part Asian, part North American, sometimes even Greek. The chef had all the right skills for this, and was good at judging individual appetites and knowing just how much food to put on each steady customer's plate. The wine was excellent, and there was an exemplary and extensive offering of the best international and local beers on tap.

Down the Street boasted a true Irish bar, with dark polished wood and antique mirrors. A dozen customers and sometimes more could be seated there on comfortable stools. If you chose to, you could eat there. The tables ran down the whole of the restaurant's narrow length, with a raised section at the far end, where windows looked out onto the Avon River. The walls were decorated with theatre posters.

This night, Griff's birthday celebration took place at the front, opposite the bar—using the entire space there as Jane had arranged.

By seven o'clock, the guests had started to arrive—including Nigel Dexter and his wife, Susan Worthington, who was also in the acting company.

Griff had splurged on a pale blue seersucker jacket of a kind rarely seen any more. He claimed it was his *birthday suit.*

"Having seen you in your birthday suit, I prefer the original," said Susie—blonde, full-bodied and blessed with native and captivating charm.

"When did you have that privilege?" Jane asked. "Is there something I don't know?"

"Nothing damaging." Susie smiled. "It happened at theatre school where, of necessity, there was occasional nudity. And to put your mind at ease completely, that's when I first saw Nigel and was swept away. Griff, so far as I was concerned, was immediately passé."

"Get you," said Nigel, giving Griff a playful nudge, "only just thirty and already passé."

"Yes, but get *her*," said Griff, raising his glass to Susie. "And that dress she wears in *Much Ado.* I could go out there in my birthday suit and nobody would even notice. They'd all be looking at Miss Susie's boobs, and wondering how long before they popped out!"

Susie was the first to laugh. She was famous in the costume department as being *difficult to contain. She overflowed the bodice*—as one designer had put it—*like over-risen bread dough.*

Zoë Walker arrived at 7:15 with Jonathan Crawford. She was small as Jonathan was not; he was six-foot-three, Zoë was five-foot-two.

Jane had not forgotten the encounter with Zoë at the opening night party for *Much Ado,* where she had been royally and rudely ignored by the ingenue. *So, what's she going to do* this *time?*

Clearly, Zoë had a future before her, so long as she did not lose her way as too many young actors had, in the tempting worlds of film and television. Griff and Nigel had avoided them like the plague, wanting to be actors more than stars. Stardom might come later, but becoming an actor was first and foremost.

Zoë Walker was definitely ambitious. It showed in her every move—in the way she dressed and in her manner, suitably retiring, but equally ever-present. She had the undeniable quality of attracting light—as if light were the moth and she, the flame.

Jonathan Crawford was in his early forties and already a force to be reckoned with. Canadian by birth, he had made his breakthrough reputation—which was sizable—in New York. There, in his late twenties, he had been regarded as a boy wonder. And it was true—he looked like a boy, with his long angular face, his mournful, arresting eyes and his cascade of dark hair which fell over his forehead in a carefully arranged manner reminiscent of teenage swimmers and tennis players. He had the look of having just emerged from an Olympic pool or a Wimbledon court after winning a spectacular victory. He augmented this image, even now, by wearing dark, loose clothing—beautifully tailored, but always giving the impression of someone who had lost weight and looked all the better for it.

He sat down on Griff's right, shaking the actor's hand and saying: "now that you've acquired thirty years, my dear, there is nothing to say but *onward*. Of which you are entirely capable."

"Thank you, Jonathan."

"I am looking forward to the chance that I might direct you next season in *Love's Labour's Lost*."

Griff looked at Jane.

"Why not?" she said. "You're certainly ready for it, my darling."

She lifted her glass and drank. She had ordered champagne for everyone—a dozen bottles of it.

Zoë Walker said: "you're Jane Kincaid, aren't you. I was afraid you might not remember me. We met on the opening night of *Much Ado*."

Clever girl, Jane thought.

"Yes, of course I remember," she said.

"Would you mind giving up your husband for a moment?"

Jane shrugged. "To what end?" she said, and smiled.

"I've brought him a gift."

"Oh, well then—please."

Jane shifted away from Griff's side and Zoë slid into her place.

She was wearing the classic black dress with spaghetti straps and no decoration except the faux diamond earrings that glistened beneath her dark hair.

She was *altogether charming,* a phrase repeatedly used by critics.

Charming, yes—but dangerous, Jane decided.

"Gift time," Zoë said.

She handed Griff a small package wrapped in starlit blue paper with a wide, silver ribbon. She leaned forward and kissed him on the cheek.

"Happy birthday. Open it."

Griff kissed her hand, said "thank you," and pulled away the ribbon and paper.

Jane watched, careful not to show too much interest.

"Golf balls!" said Griff.

Goddammit to hell ... poor Will, Jane thought, and looked away.

Zoë said: "read the card."

Griff opened it and read aloud: "*just another little something you don't need! Love, Zoë.*"

Jane managed to join in the general laughter.

"Well, then," said Griff. "Joke time! I've got one for you ..."

"Good," said Nigel. "I just hope it's not one I've already heard eighty times." He glanced at Susie. "Sharing a dressing-room—as you well know—you go through your repertoire pretty fast."

Griff ignored him. "How many heterosexual actors does it take to change a light bulb?" he asked.

Zoë giggled. "I have no idea ..."

"Both of them!"

This time, hoots as well as laughter—and then Jonathan raised his glass.

"Good," he said, nodding at Nigel and Griff, "and aren't we lucky. Here you both are ..."

At this moment, Oliver Ramsay arrived with Robert Mayling, each bearing a gift. Robert was the Festival's artistic director—forty-five years old and once an actor. In that capacity, he had enjoyed great success, but at thirty-six had begun to turn to directing. By the age of forty, he had been appointed to his present position and was enjoying even greater success. This season, he had already directed *The Merry Wives of Windsor* and was currently concluding rehearsals of *Richard III*.

"Oh God, Jesus-fucking-Christ," he said, sitting down. "Never, never, *never* take on *Richard III!* There are night-mares enough in life!"

"But we've all been hearing such wonderful things," said Nigel. "Everybody in it is raving."

"Everybody in it is raving, all right. *Raving mad.*"

As if to punctuate this statement, Robert's vodka arrived—unbidden. The artistic director's preferences—and his needs—were well known.

"Now, now, now," said Oliver, who was still on his feet. "It's brilliant and you know it."

"Yes," Jane agreed. "Brilliant."

"Thank God it's Monday. But even so, I've had to spend most of the day with the lighting designer. It's the only chance we have of using the board, thanks to the bloody schedule." Robert drank most of his vodka. "And the bloody unions ..."

He turned to Griff and said: "well—so now you're an old man."

"Getting there."

"I brung you this," Robert said with an exaggerated hillbilly accent. "Gee whiz, kid—I hope you like it."

He handed over a large brown envelope on which was written: *For Griff—with love, admiration and envy. Happy Birthday—Robert.*

Griff laughed.

Inside the envelope he found a photograph of himself, stark naked but with his back turned to the camera. He had been washing his face after removing his make-up.

"Wow!" said Susan, who was delivering Robert's next vodka.

"Looks familiar." Jane smiled. "That's my boy."

"When did you take this?" Griff asked, passing the photograph to Nigel and Susie.

"State secret," Robert said. "I have cameras hidden in every dressing-room. Have to keep an eye on company morals—make sure there's no hanky-panky."

"Oh, sure. But seriously ...?"

Oliver said: "I just came by to give you this and drink a glass of champagne."

He handed Griff a book-sized package done up in festive paper. Paper for a child's birthday party, with balloons and clowns.

Opening it, Griff found two video cassettes in a box—*Les Enfants du Paradis,* the great French classic with Arletty, Jean-Louis Barrault and Pierre Brasseur.

"Oh, my God, Ollie. What a prize ..." Griff was truly overwhelmed, and stood up to kiss Oliver on either cheek. "What a joy. Thank you. Thank you."

Oliver blushed.

Jane handed him a glass of champagne.

"I thank you, too," she said. "I've heard about it all my life and never seen it."

"You will die," said Susie. "It's sensational. Good for you, Ollie."

Oliver raised his glass.

"Happy birthday," he said. "I'll be at the bar."

"If you weren't, it wouldn't be Down the Street," said Griff, and sat down.

"What a dear, dear man," said Susie.

"Yes," said Jane. "I'm lucky."

"How's your window?" Robert asked. "I meant to slip down and take a peek, but the day evaporated with the electricians."

"I'm happy," Jane told him. "Except that I'm having a problem with George's face. I can't quite see it yet, and I don't like the classic models plastered all over my stained-glass research. It's always either too pretty or too harsh ..."

"Hello, everybody. Sorry we're late."

This was Claire Highland, who almost fell through the door, followed by Hugh.

"I was just beginning to wonder if you'd remembered," said Jane. "Glad you could make it."

Room was made for the Highlands, Claire ending up beside Jane.

"Happy, happy birthday, Griff darling."

"Yes," said Hugh. "Happy birthday."

"Thank you," said Griff. "It is."

Jane turned and called out: "Susan—time for more champagne."

From behind the bar, Susan nodded.

"Oh, heavens," said Claire. "Lovely, lovely champagne. How festive."

Claire was of Scottish extraction, causing Hugh Highland to remark, frequently, that she had married him only for his name. Claire's inevitable response was that she had married him for his money—which everyone knew was not true, since they had wed when both were relatively penniless—Hugh as an assistant professor and Claire, his student. The marriage—childless by choice—had proved to be ideal, and included a shared love of language and of the cultures of the past—especially the art of the eighteenth and nineteenth centuries.

Claire was wearing a dress whose colour was best described as mushroom—one of the soft brownish or greyish tones she favoured—with one reservation. *Never admit to beige.* Her colours, whatever they could be called, always did the most for her small stature, her lightly freckled face and her vibrantly red hair. (Jane had once jokingly accused her of applying the freckles daily as perfectly placed beauty spots.) Claire had kept her elegantly stylish hair short for as long as Jane had known her—but at the same time always let it be the badge of her highland ancestry. She loved to repeat her granny's favourite saying: *always remember, you are the child of highland lairds.* Another good reason to claim her present last name. She had been born a McDougall.

Hugh was tall, gaunt and energetic. His hands were rarely still, and during conversation he rose and fell on the balls of his feet as if to gain ascendancy for what he had to say. Before retiring, he had done the same thing while lecturing on modern literature, and had held his students rapt in what appeared to be a dance to the music of words.

Now, Jane introduced Claire and Hugh to Zoë Walker. Claire said: "oh, yes. We saw you in *Much Ado*. You were charming."

Jane smiled. She knew what *charming* meant in Claire's lexicon. It was the same as *interesting*.

"And who have you killed today, Jonathan?" Robert said slyly—filling Jonathan's glass.

Zoë smiled. She had been present on one or two occasions when Robert and Jonathan had crossed swords and she had been fascinated.

Jonathan had wanted a particular actor for Benedick in *Much Ado,* but Robert had said—more than a little point blank—*absolutely not. There is nothing else for him to play. Nothing.*

The given actor, from Robert's point of view, was intolerably mannered and overly British, the latter quality being especially at odds with what Robert regarded as part of his mandate. *The days of hauling in the Brits to play the leading roles are over. I have ended them. This is a Canadian company—and, damn it, I want Canadians. Oh, yes—don't even bother to say it—if we had two roles to offer Paul Scofield, I'd do it in a second. But Scofield is not a* convenience. *He's an artist—and there's the difference.*

End of argument. Jonathan—briefly—had been silenced. Joel Harrison, an actor he could barely tolerate, was given the role. Unfortunately, Jonathan took his revenge by making life hell for Harrison, who—in other people's view—was rather splendid as Benedick, winning much laughter and popularity. He also won plaudits for his playing of Ford in *Merry Wives.* Just what Robert required.

Jonathan emptied his champagne glass, refilled it and then

replied to the question of his way of handling actors. "I am not in the habit of discussing my crimes at table," he said. "But you may find Joel Harrison hanging from a tree tomorrow."

Everyone laughed.

"Anyway," Jonathan said, "I'm off in the morning to Philadelphia—so everybody here will be safe for a while. No more victims—for now." He smiled and drank.

Claire put down her glass and said: "speaking of victims—I confess I watched the Clinton hearings this afternoon. Anyone else?"

"Yes, I did," said Jonathan. "Fascinating. That Tripp woman ... what's her name?"

"Linda."

"Yes ... standing in the witness box and telling all, while the shekels poured down around her ears. And ours. I wonder. Who could one get to play her?"

"Don't tell me you're already making the movie."

"Well—someday, someone will, and I want to be ready to direct it. Pity Jane Fonda's growing old."

"Jane Fonda! As Linda Tripp!" said Claire.

"No, no, no. As *Hillary*."

"I thought you were casting Linda Tripp."

"Well—I'm casting the whole thing."

"Glenn Close plays a wonderful villain," Jane offered.

"True enough," said Jonathan. "Her problem is, she has a chin. Villainess Tripp has none."

"You shouldn't make remarks about people's appearance. She didn't ask to be born without a chin," said Claire.

"Are you taking up her cause, Mrs Highland?"

"Of course not. I detest her. But she can't help what she looks like. Good Lord—I've taught the lives of all kinds of historical characters who were ugly as sin. I've also published articles about them, and no writer I've ever read has equated a person's ugliness with the role that person played in history. Very often in spite of their looks. Think of Sam Johnson. Think of Voltaire."

"Ah, yes, but writers are funny people ... Normally, they save their vitriol for their private lives ... Lillian Hellman, Truman Capote, Mary McCarthy, Ernest Hemingway—that sort of thing. In their plays and novels, however, they dispense compassion, concern and reconciliation. Whereas, in your case, madam, these qualities appear to be reversed."

"Mary McCarthy never wrote a kind word in her whole life. Neither did Lillian Hellman. As for Hemingway—enough said. Your theory doesn't work, Mister Crawford."

"And have you never written a kind word?"

"I can't remember, but probably. Have you ever spoken one?"

Hugh gave a gentle cough and put his hand out.

"Claire? It's party time, remember."

"Yes, dear."

"Maybe we shouldn't talk about Linda Tripp," said Susie. "She seems to be something of a troublemaker in more ways than one."

There was a slight pause in which more champagne was poured, cigarettes lighted and olives eaten.

Then Claire said: "on the radio this morning there was something about a dreadful accident—a man burned alive in his car. Ghastly."

"Oh?" someone said.

Jane looked aside. *Burned alive?*

"If it's so ghastly, Mrs Highland, why do you tell us?" said Jonathan, lifting an olive to his lips.

"It's my job, Mister Crawford, to spread the news. Especially about the past. That's what history is. The news."

"Even the worst of it?"

"Even the worst. It keeps us on our toes in the present. And what is your job? Spreading only the good news?"

"Somebody spin the wheel," said Nigel. "We need *another* new subject."

"Has anybody seen the Branagh *Hamlet?*" Zoë asked. "It's out on video now."

Jane excused herself and went downstairs to the washroom.

On the door of the women's room there was a relief of a female torso. On the door of the Men's, a male torso. On past occasions she had always had to resist reaching out to touch them, but not now. She went straight in, found a cubicle and locked herself in.

Oh, God, what am I going to do?

Nothing. Forget it.

"Forget!" she muttered aloud. And then she whispered: "you have to be kidding. How can I forget? He's dead. He was burned alive. I didn't know that."

Pretend you didn't hear it.

I heard that he was dead, that was all. I didn't need fucking Claire to tell me the details.

Claire is innocent. She didn't know.

Claire didn't know? *I* know! Isn't that enough?

"Jesus. Jesus. Jesus. Jesus."

Jane?

"What?"

You're talking to yourself. Out loud.

"Who cares?"

Someone will come in and hear you.

"So?"

What's wrong?

"How can you ask that? *What's wrong?* Don't be an idiot. Everything's wrong."

Silence.

Jane lighted a cigarette. She was sitting on the toilet lid. Her legs were crossed.

Go back upstairs.

I can't.

Of course you can. Don't be ridiculous.

I can't. They'll know.

Not if you don't show them.

More silence.

Then: *it's Griff's birthday. It's your party. Go back. They think you've come down here to pee. Go back up.*

"I feel sick."

No you don't.

"Yes I do. I feel sick."

Jane stood up, lifted the lid and the seat and threw up into the toilet.

She flushed.

All right, now?

"Yes."

Good. Then wash our hands, rinse your mouth and go back.

"Yes, Mother."

Jane smiled at this and opened the cubicle door.

She returned to the tables, having put a peppermint in her mouth.

"We thought you'd fallen in," said Susie. "Everything okay?"

"Fine."

Jane refilled her glass.

"What are we talking about now?" she asked.

"Old times," said Nigel. "Theatre school. Early hopes. Early failures."

"All the happy stuff."

"Kiddo, you haven't heard the half of it," Nigel laughed.

"Griff as Hyena in *Noah's Ark*—me as Bear—Susie as Wolf. What a riot!"

"I played Hyena in my first year," said Zoë.

"I'll bet that was a laugh," said Griff.

"Oh, *please*," Robert half shouted. "Oh, *please*. Spin the wheel again! Spin it again!"

Jane watched Griff take a sip of champagne. She started to smile, thinking yet again how beautiful he was. The combination of glistening black hair and smooth white skin—the bright intelligent eyes, the heavy eyebrows, the dimpled lips and chin—the attitude—the presence—the man. The *actor*.

She drifted.

She looked down at all the pairs of hands spread out along the table tops beside her.

These people are my closest friends ... This is my private place—my town. It is where I live and where ... yesterday, I was raped. Now, here we all are together. Gathered on the edge—the lot of us—on the edge, waiting.

What for?

"What for?"

She looked up.

There was music.

Someone was singing.

Everyone was staring at her.

"Is something wrong?" she asked.

Claire said: "you just said *what for?*"

Jane looked at her glass. She flushed.

Claire reached out and touched her hand. "I do that, too," she said. "Out of nowhere, suddenly—words." She smiled. "It's usually something I'm writing."

Jane nodded gratefully.

"Maybe you were writing to your dreaded mother ..."

6

Mercy sat in the kitchen, having poured a cooling glass of cranberry juice, to which she added ice. Now she slipped her shoes off under the table and massaged Rudyard's back with her toes.

She smiled. *I know a few good things*, she thought. *No one ever said so, but I do. I can raise four kids, survive a death, keep a memory alive and make a home and lobster salad at the same time.*

Sipping her juice, she thought about Jane. There was a good deal of tension. Something had happened. The death of her old flame? No. There was something more—something deeper—something possibly dangerous—something wanting release, but being held back—suppressed. Something she knew about Griff? Or suspected about herself? What? Illness? A lump? Pray God not that.

Mercy fingered her glass and listened to the night beyond the open door and window. Luke was still out there—digging, digging, digging. It was endless. But tomorrow, he would begin his planting.

Her mind drifted to Monica Lewinsky and President Clinton.

Mercy did not quite know what she made of it. In some ways, she felt sorry for them. Why can't these bloody people leave private lives alone? I agree with Hillary. It's a Republican plot. They caught him, and now they want to crucify him. As for that bloody Tripp woman—taping a friend's private conversations ... parading blue dresses ...

She heard Luke cough and give the shovel a kick. He was done. Mercy went to the door.

"There's beer in here," she said, "and lobster salad, if you want some. Come in."

He mumbled: "sure, thanks," and went to his truck.

"You like spicy things?" Mercy asked.

"To a point."

"There's ginger in it."

"The beer?" He grinned.

"Of course not! The salad."

Luke, with his head down, ate.

He was fifty—or about to be. September. All his life, he had been a perfectionist. He was the family's chosen one, who had tried to keep them all alive—his uncles and aunts—or some of them—and his own parents. Someone had to oversee their survival—so many of them seemed determined to self-destruct. Alcohol had eventually done in Luke's father. His uncle Jesse was manic-depressive, driven by drugs. But hopeless cases deserved a roof, and Luke had provided it for them in the family home. Or had tried.

He never complained of what he had to do. It was what he did—and that was the end of it.

"You want to talk?" Mercy asked.

"About what?"

"About what's eating you. Something is, and it's not that flower bed out there."

Luke set his fork aside and drank some beer. Sleeman—his favourite.

"Runner's gone again."

Runner was Jesse's nickname. He was older only by seven years—more like a brother to Luke than an uncle. He never allowed himself to be medicated—had never even seen a doctor. His drugs were cocaine, pot and, on occasion, heroin, which he got from various local dealers.

"I'm sorry to hear this," Mercy said. "But he was here with you the other day. He helped you deliver the peat moss and sheep manure and all that. I thought he looked fine."

"He was. Then. But he took off Saturday night, soon as I paid him."

"Poor man."

"Yes. *Poor man.* And all that other *social worker shit* ... I'm sick of it—and I'm sick of him. Sorry, but I am."

"Who can blame you?" Mercy shrugged. "Seems understandable to me—after all this time."

"I guess. But, he's my uncle."

Mercy got up and took Luke's emptied plate to the sink. "Why do you call him *Runner?* I've never known."

"Because he's always trying to escape from his demons. God—the devil—conscience. I don't know. He never talks about it—at least, not much. All I know is, he ambles. Shuffles—runs in baby steps ..." Smiling, Luke ran his fingers across the tabletop in slow motion.

"He'll amble back," Mercy said. "Baby steps or whatever." She grinned. "He always has."

"So far."

"You want some pavlova? I made a small one at home and brought it for Griff's birthday, but Jane decided to take him out to dinner."

"Pavlova? What the hell is that?"

Mercy laughed. "It's Australian. Meringue pie and berries—apricots—stuff. Slathered in whipped cream."

"Sounds good. But later."

"You want a smoke?"

"I don't touch it."

Mercy laughed again. "No, idiot. I meant a plain old cigarette."

"Sure."

Mercy sat down. Luke poured beer. They lighted up and sat there. Will was upstairs watching *Star Wars* for the ninetieth time.

Looking at Luke, Mercy thought: *we could be married, the way we get along.*

"Is it Monday?" Luke asked. "I forget."

"Yes. Monday."

"Good. I'll bring the plants over tomorrow. Have it all finished by Wednesday."

Jane and Griff had eaten at the Church Restaurant—just the two of them. Now, at home, Griff was already halfway up the stairs.

"Coming?"

"You go on," said Jane. "I'll be ... a while."

"Suit yourself. Great party. Thanks, Jane-o. 'Night."

" 'Night, love."

He was gone. She was alone with Rudyard, clean dishes, kitchen paraphernalia, leftover lyrics, the smell of her own perfume. She poured a glass of wine, put on a record and locked the side door.

Her instinct told her to prop a chair underneath its handle.

Troy.

She turned lights down and listened. *Con te partiro.* "Time to Say Goodbye ..."

And so.

Chair? Door?

No.

I will not bow to terror. Fuck it.

All he'd have to do, anyway, is break the glass and reach inside.
Except that he's dead.

It was impossible to believe. Not because it was Troy, but because he had spurted "life" all over her face and dress the day before.

Not that he thought of his sperm as life. At least, she doubted that. God knows what it *had* meant to him. That he *could?* That she herself remained, somehow, someone he desired—but could not deal with. That he had always thought of her as a *sperm target*—the way she had overheard other Plantation boys talk about girls—as *targets*—set up to shoot down and take. Blow jobs and hand jobs—that's what they expected of you, then. Most girls going on a date carried wads of Kleenex in their handbags. What was the point of expecting condoms? *No one does it that way any more*, the boys had said, meaning penetration. *A likely story.* Jane could think of three girls, at least, in her time who had to have abortions.

She listened to the singing.

Romanza.

There was no such thing.

She got up and turned the player off. Then, one by one, all the lights.

"Bedtime," she said to Rudyard.

He yawned and stretched and followed her.

Halfway up the stairs, she stopped and looked back into the dining-room at the portrait of her great-grandmother Terry, gleaming in the light of street lamps beyond the windows.

Something is over, Jane thought. *This is a demarcation point.*

Aura Lee Terry looked back.

Yes, she seemed to say. *You have come to the end of privileged quietude. Now, my child, as there were for me, there will be consequences.*

consequences

The rest's traditional. All goes to plan:
The feud between the local common sense
And the exasperating brilliant intuition
That's always on the spot by chance before us ...

W.H. Auden
Detective Story

1

Mercy arrived every morning at seven o'clock in order to let Rudyard into the yard and to prepare Will's breakfast. Most days, except Sunday, Will was up between 7:00 and 7:30. On Sundays, Mercy's day off, he had learned to delay coming down until eight. Mercy had showed him how to deal with the coffee maker for his parents and, of course, he had long been proficient in dishing up his own cereal and juice.

Today was Tuesday.

Griff had another matinee—*The Tempest.*

At 8:00, Luke arrived alone with several plants, including roses, in the back of his pick-up truck. He was ready now to start creating placements.

Jane was in the kitchen by 8:00, though still in her dressing gown. She wanted to leave the bathroom free for Griff, who had a luncheon date—which is all he had said. Nothing about who with or where or why. Just: *I won't be here for lunch.* At 10:00, he came down in his robe and said: "I've just tried to place a phone call and the phone's dead."

"Dead?"

"As a doornail. Try it yourself."

"Did you check the connection?"

"Yep. All intact."

Jane picked up the kitchen phone and dialled Mercy's number. She knew, of course, that no one would answer because Mercy was sitting across the kitchen with Will—but at least it might ring.

It did not. Not even a dial tone.

Hanging up, Jane said, "Thank heavens there isn't an emergency."

"Who says it isn't an emergency?" Griff said. "I have to make this call—*now*—and here we fucking are with the phone done in."

"Somebody murdered the telephone," Will said, clearly delighted. "Who?"

"Gremlins," said Griffin, and shakily poured himself a cup of coffee.

"I like gremlins," said Will. "I have three of them."

"Do you know where they are at this minute?"

"Sure. On the windowsill in my room."

"Maybe one of them hopped down in the night and murdered the telephone."

"Poor old phone."

"Poor old phone. Done in by a gremlin."

"What can have really happened?" Mercy asked.

At that moment, Luke passed the open side door to collect his long-handled spade.

Seeing him, Jane said. "Luke happened." She made a wry face. "Luke and his endless digging. He's cut through the line."

Griff went to the screen. "Luke?" he called. "Could you come in here a minute?"

Luke, already perspiring, came to the door. Clearly, he did not appreciate the interruption. Once he had begun his mapping, he needed to concentrate entirely on the logistics of what he was doing. Jane had watched him earlier in the week as he sat in a lawn chair, pad and pen in hand, beer in a bottle plus cigarette, writing out the names of plants and noting their collective sizes and colours. *Don't speak*, she had decided. *Do not speak*.

"What?" he said.

"The phone," said Griff. "It's dead. Any chance you could have cut through the line?"

"Oh, Jesus." Luke came into the kitchen. "I'm sorry," he said. "Yes, it's entirely possible."

"Not to worry," Jane said. "Just so long as you know where to look."

"You want me to phone Bell?" Luke asked. "I have the number by heart. This has happened to me before. They're supposed to give you a chart—sometimes they even have tags pegged into the ground. But there was nothing here. Sorry."

"Maybe Mrs Arnprior would let you use her line ..." Griffin said. "Unless you've cut that, too."

"No," said Luke. "But no need. I've got a cell."

He removed it from his pocket, dialled and stared at space.

Jane could hear him give the address—the rest was unintelligible—as if he spoke in code. Perhaps he did.

Beep. The call was over.

"Done," Luke said. "Someone will be here after lunch."

"Terrific. Thank you."

Luke began to pocket the cellphone.

"Could I ... use it?" Griff asked. "It's a local call."

"Sure," said Luke. "When you're finished, leave it on the kitchen table. I'll pick it up at break."

"Thanks."

Taking the phone, Griffin moved into the dining-room and then, as he talked, farther off into the living-room.

Jane tried desperately to hear, but Will started prattling to Mercy about what he was reading. Jane had given him *Lassie Come Home* for his birthday and the story had swept him away.

Jane went to the fridge and quietly removed an open bottle

of white wine. *What am I doing?* she thought. *It's barely nine in the morning. Still ... just this once ...*

Will was talking more to the world at large than to Mercy, who sat with her back to Jane. "Did you know," he was saying, "that sheep cough just like people? I found that out last night. Lassie goes inside this sort of cave when there's a storm and she can smell the sheep—she's a sheep dog, you see—and in the dark, she hears this human cough!" Will coughed dramatically. "Just like that. And she thought maybe there was a bad person in there who wanted to capture her again. But she finds out there aren't no people there at all. It was just some old ram ..."

"Aren't *any* people," Mercy said.

Jane drank straight from the bottle—once—twice—three times—four—*four is bad luck to the Chinese*—five. Refitting the cork, she put the wine back in the fridge and drifted towards the dining-room on the pretence that she had lost her matches. They were in her pocket.

In the living-room, Griffin turned away from her.

"Could you try again?" she heard. "Please. It's important."

And that was all. Griff, his eyes on the floor, moved in her direction, and Jane went back into the kitchen.

Who? Zoë? People had said so. Certainly, someone Griff did not want her to recognize. *But who?* There was no one appropriate she could think of, unless it was Robert Mayling. It was not too early for a private discussion of the next season in which, as rumour had it, there were to be good parts for Griff. *Oh, pray God. It's time, after all. He's right on the cusp. And with Alec and Paulie leaving to tackle "the world at large," there would be room now. Room for Nigel and Griff to move up ... Yes, pray God. Time for Griff's Berowne and Mercutio—time for Nigel's Stanley Kowalski ...*

When Griff came back to the kitchen, Jane beamed at him.

"I hope all this secrecy is going to lead to something positive," she said. "I've been hoping for you."

Griff set the cellphone on the kitchen table and warned Will not to play with it. Then he said: "maybe."

"Can't you tell us anything?"

"No. It's too soon. But there is—there will be good news coming."

Having said this, he turned—it seemed, to Jane, more abruptly than he needed to—and went upstairs.

So.

He doesn't want questions ...

At noon, Luke came in and reclaimed his cellphone, took a beer to drink in the garden and unwrapped the sandwich he had brought from home. *Peanut butter and jelly, for God's sake!* Mercy thought. *Kids' food.*

So. Some things you never give up, Mercy decided. *Dreamscapes ... Comfort food. They sustain the past.* There were still a lot of people—perhaps Luke included—who thought there was safety in the past. *Hah!* Mercy knew better. There was nowhere safer than the present, even when it brought rapes in Kitchener, wars in Kosovo and Kenneth Starr. If you keep your wits about you, you just might survive.

At 1:00, Will, Rudyard and Mercy went for their walk in the park. They took *Lassie Come Home* and a Thermos of lemonade.

At 1:30, a Bell Telephone van drove into the drive and was parked behind Luke's truck. A man got out and Jane heard Luke greet him.

For a moment, the man disappeared—gone to inspect the injured line. Four to five minutes later, he came and stood outside the screen door, leaning a spade against the wall.

"Someone?" he asked, knocking lightly on the wood of the door.

"Yes," said Jane. She set down her wine glass and stepped forward. "Can I help you?"

"I am Bell repairman," the man said. "I need cellar. Yes? I come in?"

"Please ..."

As soon as he entered, Jane had to sit down. *They must have sent the wrong man,* she was thinking. *This is a movie star in a ragman's borrowed clothes. Any minute a director and a camera crew will arrive and begin filming ... Real people just don't look like this ...*

She smiled apologetically. "Excuse me," she muttered. "I thought you were someone else," she lied. "Forgive me."

"I'm sorry," the young man said. "I do not mean to frighten."

"No, no, no." Jane laughed and stood up. "Don't even think of it. My mistake. A trick of the light. Plain and simple ..."

Clearly, the young man did not understand her meaning. Given his accent, his English did not encompass what she was saying. Beside which, given his unearthly beauty, what did *plain and simple* mean?

Jane thought: *maybe it's true. Maybe angels really do fall into your ...*

Your what?

Into your garden?

Into your kitchen?

Into your life.

2

That evening, as Jane and Griffin sat on the deck in the twilight, a silence fell between them.

Luke had left the garden hose running, using a sweeping sprinkler whose range was wide enough to soak the whole of the new bed with its fresh plantings. *Turn if off at 8:30,* he had said. *That'll leave an hour before the sun goes down.*

It was now 8:15.

To Jane, the sound and the scent of the running water on the freshly cut grass and the freshly dug earth was comforting. Images of Plantation evenings, with the sound of other people's hand-pushed lawnmowers and of Joshua hosing down their flagstone terrace floated like a mirage above what felt like the desert of the present. And the word *lost*, whispered by a child. *I'm lost ...*

She was sitting on the chaise with kicked-off shoes, a cigarette and a large martini—a triple, Griff had insisted: *the kind you only get at home. No bar would sell one to you.*

"But it's blue," Jane had said.

"Trust me," Griff had told her. "Once you've had one of my new blue martinis, you will never go back to the old kind."

"New?"

"In my spare time, I've been taking lessons in bartending." He grinned and flicked his fingers. "Easy as pie. All you have to have is a reasonable love of drink."

"Oh, sure. Every second bartender in Stratford—to say nothing of Toronto, Montreal, New York and L.A.—is an out-of-work actor. Are you telling me the truth? Are you really ...?"

Griff reached out and patted her hand. "Just kidding, Jane-o. Kidding. The thing is—I get around. I watch. I taste. I savour—or I don't. I had a couple of these the other day. Not so hefty, mind you. But I liked 'em."

"Where?"

"Pazzo. Upstairs. There's a new guy—unbelievable. Best martinis and Manhattans in the world. They call him Shaker. Don't you love it? He practically does flamenco when he's mixing. It's fabulous to watch—and the drinks are to die for."

"Let us pray not to die *of*. What on earth is in them?"

"It's a secret," Griff had said. "Drink up."

Delicious. Odd—but delicious—and somehow ... dangerous. Now, there was silence.

Where does he go in the silences? Jane wondered. *Zoë? Down the Street? And still no mention of who he'd been with. The other night—when was it? Friday ...* She had found him masturbating in the bathroom. He hadn't seen her because his back was turned in the shower. She had silently retreated and gone to bed.

Why that? she had thought.

Why only with himself, and not me? Who was he thinking about? What was his fantasy? Someone from the past? Maybe even Jane herself, eight years ago, when they were first in love? Someone from the present—Zoë Walker? Some unknown, unguessed-at other? Who? *What would Doctor Fabian say? Ask him. That's what. Be direct. Don't hide.*

Then Jane thought: *I beg your pardon? What the hell do you mean, don't hide? I've been left out in the open with no defences, and Griff keeps bombing me with his bloody secret rendezvous. Well—he just may not always be alone in that ...*

"I *have* to hide," she whispered aloud.

Jane turned and looked at Griff.

He was sitting, eyes slitted, staring over the rim of his martini glass at something so distant he barely seemed to be with her.

She looked away. Any minute, she would rise and go down the steps and turn off the hose. Eight-twenty-five.

I have something to tell you, Griff ...

She looked at him again. He was lighting a cigarette. Lazily. *Lazily*. Fingering the lighter, almost fondling it, the way he fondled himself ...

... something you wouldn't even begin to believe ...

She remembered.

"... I need cellar. May I come in?"

They had stood there. Blank. Both of them.

Then he smiled. "The cellar? Please?"

"Of course. It's down there."

Jane pointed to a large trap door in the floor beside the sink and cutting board.

The man nodded, walked over and heaved the door up until it leaned against the utility island.

"There are ..."

"Yes. I see them."

He fixed the door in place by hooking it to a bracket near the cutting board, lifting out the three crossbars that supported it when closed and piling them up beside the opening. He looked down into the darkness and then around at the walls.

"Is there a ..."

"Yes. The switch is ..." Jane pointed.

"Thank you."

He turned on the cellar light, gave her a quick nod and disappeared beneath the floor.

Jane retreated to the table, where she had begun drawing up a list of preliminary details regarding her proposed purchase of the house.

Dear God, it's hot! She wiped away perspiration, absently opening the front of her dress to do so.

Heat.

She blinked at the page, unable to focus on it.

Why?

She felt somehow—what? Somehow what?

Helpless.

He was the most beautiful man she had ever seen. But his beauty was more than physical. There was something else. Something indefinable—the way it was with people who were born to die young.

Jane was still watching Griff as he drank in the first drag from his cigarette. *Drank? Yes. Smoke in the throat is like a martini. Smoking's just another way of drinking ...*

She looked away and tested this theory with her own cigarette: *lips, mouth, throat ... Yes. I drink Matinee Extra Mild Slims—the second-best martini in town!*

Eight-thirty. Jane set aside her glass not yet half drunk, and descended to turn off the hose. The crows looked down, watched her and shuffled. *Don't turn on the yard light,* they pleaded. *The owl can find us well enough as it is.*

Jane had no intention of turning on exterior lights. She loved this evening moment. One more hour and a bit to go.

Walking over the sodden grass, barefooted, she went to see what Luke had planted.

It all looked shockingly inadequate—although she realized, given his meticulous calculations, it would fill out in time—in the months and years to come—roses, flowering shrubs—various kinds of lilies, iris, peonies—and other plants she did not yet recognize. Still, it already smelled like a garden, with its dampened earth and wetted leaves. *Green. Earth. The green earth of where I was born and am ... And ... that young man, smiling.*

Jane looked back at Griff. Clearly, he did not even see her standing there—nor when she returned to the chaise and took up her blue martini.

She closed her eyes and drew a deep breath. It was not a sigh. It was a declaration. *I have something to tell you, Griff.*

She had touched the Bell man. He had touched her.

It was intended, so it seemed. Meant to be. Foreordained.

That's nonsense.

Is it?

Jane thought of Troy. Was that foreordained? The craziness of it—the suddenness—the ugliness. And the betrayal. No. *Not foreordained—plotted.* Determined by someone desperate—someone who had lost control of the wheel of his life. It seemed somehow inevitable that Troy had died the way he had—the car spinning off the road in the throes of whatever it was that tormented him.

She remembered his eyes, filled with loss and anguish. Rage. He had lost everything, even fumbling the last gesture.

I have something to tell you, Griff. Something I don't understand.

"What time is it?"

Jane looked at her watch.

"Eight-forty-two. Why?"

"I'm going out."

"Jesus Christ, Griff. Not again. What? Every night?"

"I told you," he said, rising, "there's going to be good news. Just be patient."

"Yes, sir."

She said this in a mock schoolgirl voice. "Anything you say, sir." She smiled at him, teeth clamped, eyes blazing.

But I have something to tell you ... you bastard! I'm in love with a stranger!

Griff looked at her with brief curiosity. The questions were becoming mutual. *She's up to something. What ...?*

"G'night."

Jane did not reply. Instead, she picked at her dress, looking at the walnut tree—at the battalion of crows.

When she heard the screen door click, she whispered: "goodnight. Go in peace—wherever ..."

Mercy came to the door and spoke through the screen.

"Anything you want? Otherwise, I'm going home. It's 9:15. You okay?"

"Yes. Sure. Absolutely."

"Hotter'n all hell put together," Mercy sighed. "I don't remember heat like this since we fried in '92."

"Yes." Jane turned halfway over her shoulder. "Mercy?"

"Yes?"

Jane subsided—and said nothing.

"You sure you're okay?"

"Yes."

"You want me to stay? I can, if you like. I don't mind."

"No. It's all right. I'll see you in the morning."

"Sure."

"Will in bed?"

"Reading. We're going to need a new book any minute."

"Yes."

"You got something you want to say? You do. I can tell."

Pause.

"No. I'll see you in the morning. Don't forget tomorrow is sheets and towels."

"As if I could forget."

"And ... let's see. I've got Doctor Fabian Friday morning, and otherwise, I'll just be at work all week. Sorry."

"That's okay. I'm used to it. What about lunches?"

"Tomorrow, anyway. I'll try to be home by noon."

Jane listened as Mercy collected her keys and went out the side door. Her car started—shouted: *not that gear! Reverse!*—and backed away.

Day's end.

Not yet.

Jane got up and went inside the house.

She poured the remainder of her blue martini into the sink and opened a bottle of Valpolicella—retreating with it into the living-room, where she turned on the television set and sat in the corner of the sofa.

You're drinking too much, sweetheart.

Leave me alone!

She drank.

A court in Maryland had announced the decision of a grand jury to investigate whether Linda Tripp should be prosecuted for taping Monica Lewinsky's phone calls. Under that state's law (it was where the taping had occurred) both parties must consent. It was a unique moment in American history. Two spiteful women—a president in jeopardy. A whole nation's business sidelined for a sexual liaison. *God—it makes you feel forlorn.*

Jane gave a wan smile at the ceiling. *So—what else is new?*

July 8, 1998.

She closed her eyes. A person could guess the rest. *Guess—yes—but not predict. Could you have predicted the arrival of a telephone repairman ... smiling shyly, in torn jeans and bare knees?*

A man who, just like a gentle, untamed animal, let you touch the back of his hand. The world, it seemed, could still deliver miracles.

3

Thursday, July 9, 1998

Griff did not get home until 2:00. Jane was asleep.

Probably just as well ... he thought. Considering ...

He took his clothes off and crawled into the bed beside her, throwing back the covers and lying there, staring into the dark. First on his right side, facing Jane—who was turned away and also naked—then on his left side—then on his back.

His hand—it seemed inevitably—drifted down to his groin.

You are the world's most desirable man, he was thinking. That had been said to him a few days ago. *You are the world's most desirable man ...*

He smiled.

At least I had the grace to blush.

And then: *what am I getting into? Do I really want what I want so badly as this? As to ...? Oh, God—what am I doing? Why?*

He stopped thinking.

When he came, the sperm flooded over his belly—for the first time in weeks. Not that he masturbated every day, but rehearsals had been a period of reduced sexual desire. Jane had suffered for this. He knew that.

He shifted, now, and dropped his feet to the floor.

Jane still slept.

Rising, Griff went to the bathroom, closed the door and turned on the light. He looked in the mirror, saw the whole of himself and muttered: *I guess it's true.* Then he grinned and shook his head. *Never believe your own publicity, friend.*

Most dangerous thing an artist can do. Once you believe that shit, you become a shit. He had seen it happen—even to the "nicest" people. Kevin, for instance—gone into facelifts and TV. *Please. Kevin is only twenty-five, for gawd's sake—having a facelift!*

He cleaned himself with a damp washcloth.

Finished, he decided he was hungry and went down to the kitchen.

Rye bread—sweet white onion—lemon juice—lettuce—white wine.

He prepared the sandwich, poured the wine and sat on a tall stool by the island.

Next door, Mrs Arnprior's upper lights were on. She stood—a silhouette only—staring at his nakedness from a window.

Griff stood up, exposing himself completely, smiled, saluted and bowed. Then he sat back down.

Bitch. Why do women keep saying they're not voyeurs?

At 3:00, he was back in bed and sound asleep. Jane slowly rose, descended to the kitchen and, clutching her robe at the waist, sat down and finished the wine.

In the walnut tree, one old crow—perhaps the troop's leader—spoke as if from his sleep.

We're lost. The crows and I, Jane thought. *All of us, in the dark.*

Mrs Arnprior's lights, one by one, were extinguished.

Blackness. Black.

No stars.

Nothing.

Nothing.

Nothing.

Not until morning. And in the morning—Doctor Fabian.

Well ... I'll have to say something. I want to. Not about Troy. I won't tell that—but the other—the young man—the angel-man ...

He touched me. I touched him. Finger ends ...

Only finger ends—speaking—saying: I am here. *Are you? Connections.*

And yet, she did not even know his name.

4

Friday, July 10, 1998

Doctor Fabian's house on Church Street was not that far away. Jane could have walked there in less than ten minutes, but she wanted the car to be waiting at the curb when she made her escape. Maybe after this session, she would never go back. It would be too shaming—too intimidating. *There are some things you don't tell.* No one—*no one*—would ever know about Troy but her. But the angel-man was different. This was something she had initiated—something for which she was responsible. It was something she had done, but did not understand. *Where had it come from? What did it mean? I reached out and touched his hand. I reached out ...*

And he reached back.

She sat there, smoking—the window rolled down—wishing she had finished the bottle of wine she had left half-emptied in the kitchen.

She stubbed her cigarette.

I can't go in, she thought. *I can't. I don't want to deal with this. Not yet.*

Yet *can last forever, Aura Lee.*

This reminded her of her escape from Plantation. There had been a time—years ago—when she had dreamed of emancipation but had been afraid to inaugurate it—make it absolute. Aura Lee Terry had always used the word *emancipation* in her thoughts of being free of Plantation and all it stood for—but because she was a Southerner, born, bred and inundated with the notion that emancipation was forbidden, she was forever saying—back then—*not yet.*

Jane reached out and started the motor. Luckily, the Subaru was an almost silent car. So long as Doctor Fabian had not looked out of his front windows, he would not even know she had been there.

I'll go home and cancel.

I'll finish the wine. I'll sleep.

She looked at her watch. Ten minutes left.

Doctor Fabian would understand. She had cancelled other appointments at the last minute—for other more sensible reasons: taking Will to a sports day, an emergency at work, that sort of thing. She would have to make something up.

Because one-way streets were involved in her homeward route, she had to drive around the corner. A long corner—inconvenient when you were in a hurry.

What would she say to Mercy? *I could lie and say he was ill and couldn't see me ...* But she couldn't bear to lie to Mercy. She never had—except in the smallest unimportant matters.

I got cold feet, she could say. *I just didn't want to go today.* Mercy would understand—Mercy, who had endured every aspect of men from rapture to brutality, would understand anything Jane, a mere *blueblood*, had to say. Besides, Jane had to go to work after lunch in order to finish her window—or try to finish it. She did not want the distraction of a Fabian session. Not now. Next time would do. In a month.

Thinking all this, she overshot her destination and went one more block than she had intended.

Where the hell was she?

St. Patrick Street.

She wheeled the car recklessly, almost knocking down an old woman.

Dear Jesus—pay attention.

The only way back was to go along to Erie Street and turn south to Cambria. Halfway there, she stopped.

It was an automatic reaction.

In front of her, tight against the curb, with flashing parking lights, was a Bell Telephone van.

Good God.

Was it him?

Her heart began to race.

She drew up behind the van, but left her motor running.

All I want to do is see him ...

Just a glance, to see that he's alive and I'm not crazy. That he's real ...

She waited and watched.

Her windows were still rolled down. She heard the sound of an opening door, somewhere along the side of the house being serviced.

"Please," she whispered. "Please ..."

A man came out.

He must have been sixty years old, and though he wore an identical utility belt to the angel-man's, he was dressed in neater clothes and wore a cap.

Jane closed her eyes.

Now what? I've just made a fool of myself. An idiot.

Well ... If she went to Doctor Fabian, she decided, at least she would not have to lie to Mercy.

Five minutes later—and ten years older (or so it felt)—she

drove around the corner and parked again in front of Doctor Fabian's.

The house was a large, late-Victorian red-brick wonder—with porches on every side and filigreed gables. Six chimneys, three hideaway gardens, wrought-iron fences and a sleeping dog. Daniel the spaniel, lying on the front lawn in the shade of a sycamore tree.

Jane got out of the car and went to the front door. On a wide brass plate she saw the familiar DOCTOR CONRAD FABIAN—OFFICE AT THE REAR. She had always ignored it. *I'm not a back-door person.* There was, after all, such a thing as pride.

She was facing away, looking out the window.

She did not want to see Doctor Fabian's eyes—his expression—his reaction as she told her story.

Bad enough that she would have to hear what he had to say.

"I have something to tell you ..." she began.

It was like confessional. The curtain parting, the latticework revealing only portions of the face beyond. And the lies—the knowledge, for both the priest and the penitent, that lies were going to be told. But also that certain truths would be unavoidable—weights a person could shed only by confessing the burden of their presence.

Something to tell you ...

"Are you comfortable?"

"No."

She laughed bitterly.

"Am I ever comfortable sitting here? With you? I'm already plotting my escape," she added. "How many steps to the door—how to avoid saying goodbye—how to get past Miss National Enquirer out there at her desk—without letting her know that something wicked has happened. As it always does ... always will. Wicked, wicked me. Jane wicked, you good."

"Nothing can be that wicked, Jane. For one thing, you are utterly incapable of premeditated murder. I know that. I'm certain of it—and aside from murder, there's nothing you can tell me that's going to faze me." He waited. "Nothing. Unless you've harmed someone physically ..."

"No."

"Well, then." He smiled. "Remember that man who fell in love with his pet mouse?"

"Yes. The only thing was, they couldn't have sex ..."

"But they did."

"Please. Oh—*please!*" Jane laughed and waved the notion aside.

"But they *did*—in their way. Guess where the mouse had her nest."

"Do I want to know this?"

"In behalf of your sanity—yes."

"Tell me."

"She made her nest in his pubic hair."

"You're kidding."

"No. She slept there every night of her life."

Jane's inadvertent first reaction was: *how sweet.* But instead she said: "how long did she live?"

"Five years. More or less average for a white mouse." He lifted his gaze. "This disappoints you. I can tell. Happiness and contentment should not last so long between opposites. Yes? You do not care for anything that defies the norm. This we know. And so, you are having an affair with a horse? A donkey? A mule?"

"Of course not. And besides ..." She looked at him. "How do you know what I have to say refers to sex?"

"Well ..." He shrugged. "I can *see* you. There you are. Changed."

Now, Jane turned completely away.

"You have to let me smoke."

"Go right ahead."

"And please, please ..."

"No. Don't even ask. You can have some wine in the kitchen. After. When we're finished. Maybe. But not until then. You know that. We're both professionals."

"But it's so hard. So difficult ..."

"Jane ..." He coughed deliberately. "You're already fortified. I can smell it. Light your cigarette."

"Yes, sir," Jane said meekly—still not turning.

But how? How? How?

Just begin. Just say it. Speak.

"I ..."

"Yes?"

She withdrew a Matinee Slim and lighted it with a match.

"Have you ever ..." she began. "Has there ever been someone so beautiful ... so dazzling that you couldn't look at them?"

"Wouldn't you have to look at them to know it?"

"Oh, yes—of course—but I mean ..." She blew smoke— watched it and began again. "They walk through the door and you see them and ... then you have to turn away. It hurts—it literally *hurts* to look the second time. Has that ever happened to you?"

"Yes."

No explanation.

Jane, being Jane, smiled at this and said ruefully: "you mean, I haven't had a unique experience?"

"Everyone's experience of another person is unique. For

instance, I admire your husband as an actor—I also find him immensely attractive. But I am not gay, thank God—and I mean only *thank God* because I have Allison—without whom I would perish. But the circumstance is common. I mean between what you're proposing and what transpired between Alli and me and what transpired between you and Griffin. I did not marry him—you did."

"Transpired?"

"Good word. *Came to be.* You should use the dictionary more, Jane. It provides a great many answers. *Transpired.* Useful, when it comes to affairs—and I assume that what you have to say may have to do with such an episode."

"Why do you assume that?"

"I've already told you. You are not your usual Southern languid-seeming self, today. Something has provoked you. Greatly disturbed you. And that can only be another man ... or woman, if you will. But I suspect, in your case, a man."

"Yes."

"And so?"

"And so ..."

Jane looked at her cigarette.

"Is there an ashtray?"

"Right beside you. Stop procrastinating. We have only an hour. Less, now. Speak."

Jane leaned forward. The ashtray sat on the table by her right hand—between herself and the window.

The window. The garden. The trees. The sky.

The door.

Escape.

Something has provoked you ... Troy ... something has greatly disturbed you ... the angel-man ... but how does a person say these things?

Doctor Fabian sat back in his chair and tapped his fingers on the desk between them.

Jane knew that was a command.

Speak.

Now.

"Yes. Speak. Me. Jane. Jane speak ..." She laughed—more or less. One note only. "*Me Jane—You Tarzan* ... Yes? Dear Jesus." She put her face in her hand. "I'm getting it all wrong."

Doctor Fabian waited.

Jane fumbled for her purse and retrieved a wad of Kleenex. "Tarzan. Tarzan." She looked away and waved her hand, as if the ape man might be sitting in a tree beyond the window. "He could have been Tarzan," she said. "Naked. He seemed *naked*—even fully dressed. Every vein was visible."

"Who is this?"

"Man. Man. A man."

She took a deep breath and leaned back in the chair—Kleenex in one hand, cigarette in the other

"Luke had cut through the telephone line with his spade—in the garden. The owner is having a new flower bed, you see—perennials, roses—and Luke—you know, the gardener—works for you, too. Well, he'd cut through ... the telephone line. So—someone had to come and repair it ... to put it right ... And he came. This man. This ... *Tarzan*. This ..." She stubbed her cigarette. "This naked angel."

Doctor Fabian set down his pen. No more notes. Notes would come later. He rarely recorded every word his patients said. It was enough to ingest the words and savour them. The summary would come later. Much was private. Always.

Jane Kincaid was a favoured patient. A woman in whom he was deeply interested, being part—as she was—of the theatre world he worshipped. Her husband was an actor—she herself worked in the property department. All her friends were actors, artists, writers—the world he had failed to join as a young man longing to be anything—*anything*—inside the magic circle behind the curtain. And Alli—Allison, now retired by choice, whose career as an actor had been dazzling. But she had wanted life. *Life*. Not imitation. And not the regimen of disciplines under which she had lived for twenty-five years—so little food—so little drink—no love—no lovers—no intervals of leisure in the forward thrust of her career. *I want to be the fat, floppy woman I am!* she had said to him, shortly after they had met and fallen in love. *And you can give me that—all of that, by setting me free!*

Free.

And now, Jane Kincaid and another kind of freedom, if that was indeed what it was. Totally unexpected. Jane, of all people—one of whose central problems was the regime of strictures she had forced upon herself. In spite of the leaning in towards drink, in spite of the overindulgence in cigarettes, she might be capable of giving a master class in personal discipline. Above all, after the advent of Griffin, there had never been another man. Not a hint. Not even of a flirtation. In fact, Doctor Fabian had begun to wonder if perhaps Jane had lost all interest in sex. And, by all accounts, she had mastered the art of balancing motherhood with professional work outside the home, although—at the same time—he was realistic enough to acknowledge her personal income, which allowed her a latitude not enjoyed by the majority of women.

Now, she said: "he came to the door. This man. To the side door—screen door—kitchen. I was sitting there—mid-afternoon—my usual mid-afternoon self... wine—cigarette—blue dress..."

She stopped.

No. That wasn't a blue dress day ... it was the other time ... Troy ... stains ...

Fabian watched her. He made a mental note: *remember the blue dress.*

"... and I guess the gloss of the screen—the glare of it in the sun—I don't know—or the heat—the smoke from my cigarette ... I didn't quite see him—didn't know who he was, or why ..." (*Like Troy ...*) "... and I stood up and said: *come in. Come in, whoever you are.* And he did ..."

She closed her eyes.

"Have you ever seen—met—encountered anyone who was supremely—utterly innocent? *Truly,* truly innocent? With absolutely—utterly no notion of who they are—or of what they possess? An absolute innocent? *Absolute.* That was who stood there. That was this man. *The Bell man. Ding-dong!*" She laughed, not meaning to. "I was flabbergasted—struck by lightning. I sat back down—I had to sit back down because I couldn't stand. Oh, please. It's all so crazy. So unreal." She withdrew and lighted a second cigarette, stubbed the first and continued. "Well ... so there he was. Standing there. Sandy haired. Not greatly tall. Maybe five-foot-nine or ten. Pale, pale, pale—almost white faded jeans—with all these rips and tears—calves, knees, thighs, bum ... crotch, for God's sake—pockets—everything torn—as if he'd wanted to destroy them—kill them, the jeans—because they prevented the world from seeing what they were meant to hide. *Shreds.* Literally shreds. Except—the man wearing them wasn't ... what's the word ...? He wasn't in the least *provocative.* He was not *provoking.* He wasn't saying: *come and look at this—look!* At *me.* He was just ... he was only ... he was simply *there.* Standing in front of me. With no expression. Nothing written ... nothing written on his face. Nothing. Merely ... *there.* As if he'd just stepped out of the shower—and had no towel with which to hide himself ... Nothing. Naked."

Doctor Fabian swung his chair away from Jane. In the garden, a robin sang.

"I ..."

Yes?

"I don't know when, but somewhere—somehow—in time, we talked. I explained my crazy reaction by saying I'd thought he was someone else—and he apologized, for God's sake. *I didn't mean to frighten you*, he said. Do you see? Absolutely innocent. I drank some wine—I offered him a beer. He said: *I'm working.* Yes, I thought: *working.* And then—I don't know how long after that, my hand went out. You see? Like this ... and my fingers ... I reached for him ... that was all. I just reached out and touched him. He was staring at me. No—not staring. *Watching.* He was watching me. And he saw my hand—my fingers—and he stood his ground. He didn't ... there was not a flicker of resistance—nothing. He simply stood there and took—accepted my touch. I might have been a bullet fired by a firing squad. I might have been ..."

She leaned forward, hands clenched.

"I might have been death, for all he knew."

The sound of Miss National Enquirer's computer filtered through the door.

"His skin was so soft—so warm—the warmth of a trusting child—and ..." She stopped. "Why am I obliged to tell this? Why?"

"Because you chose to."

"Yes. Yes. Maybe. Perhaps I had no choice. After all—I'm a good Catholic girl."

"The truth will out—is that it? Otherwise you go to hell?"

"Not hell. Purgatory. And purgatory is worse than hell.

Read Dante. Besides, I've already been there. Remember? Remember Daddy? Remember Mama? Remember my anorexic sister, Loretta? And my lost, emasculated brothers?"

"I wouldn't call that purgatory, Jane. Auschwitz was purgatory. Stalingrad was purgatory. Jim Jones was purgatory. You call a difficult family purgatory? Wait till you get to hell."

"Hell is other people," Jane said. "Someone said that."

"Sartre."

"Well—he was right."

"Hell, dear lady, is not about familial degradation. Hell is payment on demand for something you've never done. Jesus! You goddamned Catholics drive me crazy!"

Jane smiled.

Join the club, she thought.

"And so ... you touched him. *Him.*"

"Yes. On the hand. The back of his hand."

"And?"

"And he touched me ..." She waited. "The same way. Just there ..." She pointed to the place, not allowing her finger to land, as if the place was sacred.

Now it was Doctor Fabian's turn to wait. What had been so earth-shattering about a touch on the hand?

Then Jane spoke again.

"Nothing was said," she said. "Nothing. He did not speak. I did not speak." She closed her eyes. "I could see he had an erection. Why? I mean, *why?* Because he'd touched my hand?" She inhaled—exhaled—and looked again out the window. "His underwear, I knew, was white ... *whiter than white...* what is that? Some kind of commercial ... *whiter than white* and worn ... thin ... thin, like rice paper ..." There was a long pause. Then she said: "edible." As if it might be a separate sentence.

"Edible?" Fabian asked quietly.

"Yes." Jane took a breath. Gulped for it. "I could see it through one of the rips ..." And then: "please," she said. "Let me have one glass of wine."

"No."

"Oh, Jesus ..."

She stood up.

Doctor Fabian put out his hand and lifted his pen. He had not seen Jane in this condition before.

Daniel was in the side yard, now. He must have been moving with the sun, seeking shade as its glare caught up with him. He walked three times in a wide circle and lay down on the lattice-patterned bricks. *Latticed. There's the damned lattice again. Confession.*

The dog was lying, splayed beneath a wooden bench on which someone—probably Alli—had already set some cushions and an unread novel. Such a comforting image of domestic bliss ... The shaded bench, the cool red bricks, the anticipated book, the flowering lilies, the over-arching tree—a maple.

"I've never thought of the penis, erect or otherwise, as beautiful. I've never thought about it at all, if you want to know the truth. Women aren't like that. At least ... Well, they're not. I mean, like men. Other things attract us. Yes? The shape of a man. His waist—his bum—his shoulders. Maybe his hands. Yes. His hands. But the rest is all another kind of aesthetic. A trustworthy smile. A lack of super-ego. A sense of fun. A love—a passion felt for something—anything—beyond himself. For riding a bike or sitting by a lake or books, music—anything. But not his penis. Do you know ... it's the absolute truth. I couldn't begin to describe Griff's penis." She laughed. "He hasn't been circumcised. That I know—but who the hell knows its dimensions? Who the hell cares? It's *there*—that's all that matters. It's there—and it's ..."

"Yes?"

"I was going to say *it's mine*. But I'm not really sure of that any more."

"Oh?"

"Yes. But that's not what this is about. This is about the *other* man. The angel-man—just like Adam before the fig leaf, and suddenly I was Eve." She smiled. "I hadn't even been in the goddamned orchard, Doctor. I hadn't even seen the goddamned apple tree, let alone ..."

"The serpent?"

"Oh, don't be so damned literal."

"It was your image—not mine."

Jane wadded the Kleenex and looked at it in her hand.

"White," she whispered.

"White?"

"Yes. White. And delicate. His skin. His hand. Himself. Fragile. I felt that if I were to touch him again, he would melt away ... I thought ... *dear God in heaven* ... I couldn't help thinking of Monica Lewinsky and her goddamned thong panties and her goddamned blue dress and her goddamned practised knees and fucking Bill Clinton just standing there and letting her undo him—and all the world with him—and all the world watching ... But—he was so beautiful—the Bell man—the angel-man. So clean. So innocent. So ready to have and to lose it all ... But ... That isn't what happened." She drew herself up, as if about to accept an invitation to waltz. "I'm a lady, remember? I'm Aura Lee Terry from Plantation, Louisiana. *Please, sir, your hand, so I might rise to the dance floor.*" She opened the window wider. "That's the kind of thing my mother used to say—and expected me to follow suit. Fat chance."

Daniel made himself into a ball. Perhaps too much shadow had fallen beneath the bench. All at once, he seemed cold.

Jane looked up. High-flying birds were floating there.

She turned her back on the garden view and moved to stand behind Doctor Fabian, where a print of Paul Klee's *Scholar, 1933* steadfastly confronted her from the wall. It was, she surmised, his inner eye—his daily reminder, as he approached his desk, that the world was full of endless mystery and that nothing was known. Nothing. The oval, childlike drawing of a face with tortured eyes and down-turned mouth that told the story of its time—its own time, and this that Jane was in. And Doctor Fabian.

"In my mind, I undid his fly, pulled the cotton of his underwear aside and lifted it down to his knees and... I put him in my mouth."

She touched her eyes with the Kleenex.

"You don't have to finish this," said Fabian, "if you really don't want to."

"No. I don't want to—but I must." She sighed. "It was as though I had been starving. Starving—and fell upon the sight of food. What does it mean? I was voracious. In my mind. In my mind. In my mind, I fell to my knees. I touched the most intimate parts of his body. I tore his shirt so all the buttons fell—like hail—onto the floor. Right now, it's just as if I heard them falling. I wanted him. Naked. Whole. All of him. I pulled his shoes off—I unrolled his socks. I kissed his toes—I licked his thighs—I sucked his nipples. And then ..."

She shrugged.

"Then he asked me how he could reach the cellar."

Doctor Fabian capped his pen and pushed aside his notebook.

"None of this—you understand, none of this happened," Jane told him.

"Yes. I understand."

"Oh, dear Jesus—God in heaven. What has become of me?"

She sat down.

There was a moment.

Doctor Fabian rose and went to the kitchen. He returned with two glasses, a bottle of red wine and a simple pronouncement.

"Good for you," he said. "You said it. You've taken step one. I know you're busy, but after you've finished your windows, I think we should have an extra session. I'll have Bella phone."

Bella was Miss National Enquirer, whose ear even now was more than likely pressed against the door. Or so Jane always suspected.

"In the meantime," Doctor Fabian went on, "I want you to be very clear about one thing. You are not crazy—you have simply returned to a natural state of desire after years of self-exile. Welcome home. *Salut!*"

They drank.

5

Saturday, July 11, 1998

The property department was at the rear of the Festival Theatre. Its multiple windows gave a panoramic view across the baseball diamond to the river. When you stepped outside to smoke, you stood at the top of a relatively steep descent of about eight or ten feet. (Jane, having grown up in the States, had never learned to translate into Canadian metric.)

Each property maker had a personal work area, centred on a long, wide table and shelf-space beneath the windows. It was congenial and private all at once. You could ignore your fellow workers entirely, or chat at will. Somewhere, a CD player was always playing compatible music—nothing that stomped and screamed—and each of the twenty-odd artisans had brought along ther favourites—some of it classical, some of it not. Jane's contribution was a collection of eight discs featuring the guitar mastery of Andrés Segovia—now more than ten years dead, though he played for them almost daily. On matinee days, they could also turn on the tannoy system that allowed them to hear the play of the day, if they wished.

Oliver Ramsay had a child's eyes and hands and a smile that could break your heart. He spoke so quietly that you often had to ask him to repeat himself.

Nonetheless, he was a meticulous taskmaster. You "got away" with nothing. After consultations with directors and designers as they presented their requirements, Oliver would assign the creation of each prop, or set of props, to one or another of his crew. Just as he rejected the word "boss," he rejected the word "staff." *It sounds like a horde of office workers* ... "Crew" was more suitable because the property department was very like a well-run ship on a voyage of exploration. The properties took on the character of specimens collected on exotic shores—and at the end of each workday throughout the winter and spring, crew members would display their individual "finds." Seventeenth-century candelabra, sixteenth-century braziers and torches, fifteenth-century altarpieces and twelfth-century tapestries—these were but a few examples of what had been required for the present season, besides all the normal weaponry, breakaway chairs, dining utensils, "pewter" plates and the infamous "butt of Malmsey" in which to drown the Duke of Clarence—plus the gruesome decapitated head of "a certain political enemy"... an image that could produce gagging, if you had to confront it for longer than three seconds. The head had been produced by Mary Jane Ralston, and there had been much speculation as to the identity of its model. So far, no connections had been made to anyone still living.

Jane's final assignment of the season was the creation of the stained-glass triptych for Robert's production of *Richard III*. It was to open on the 7th of August, just under a month from now. She had long before done all her sketches and preliminary drawings—showing them every two or three days to the play's designer, whose name was Sara Monkton. Sara had also designed the costumes for *Much Ado,* for which Jane had already created the set of painted fans.

Robert had asked that the windows reflect the historical past of England by means of a depiction of Saint George slaying the dragon. The killing itself took up the whole of the central window, while on either side he had asked for separate portraits of Saint George and the dragon before their encounter.

Jane had enjoyed herself immensely doing the research, ordering up a mass of expensive volumes which would end up in the theatre library. She had filled five sketchbooks with drawings, notes and measurements—colour schemes—photographs—reproductions and other references. Then she had settled in to do the actual creation.

On this particular day, she was determined to finish the countenance—*a person couldn't call it a* face!—of Saint George, in all its glory and romantic fervour. It was a countenance for which she had searched high and low, filling more than half a sketchbook with the saint's shining image—and hating every version.

She arrived at 1:45, set her work-bag on the table, took up the sketchbook and some pencils and retired to the hillside with her cigarettes, an ashtray and a wooden chair.

Behind her, through the open windows, she could hear

Mary Jane Ralston's CD of the music from *Les Misérables*.

She sat, lighted up, opened the book and turned its pages.

No—no—no—no ...

Maybe, maybe, maybe ...

No.

She still had come nowhere near.

Now, she turned to a clean page and let her pencil hover above the paper.

Below her, someone had loosed his dogs and a ball had been thrown.

Grass. Dogs. Ball.

Ball. Bull. Bell.

Bell.

Two minutes later, Jane was drawing full out—never pausing once to criticize what she was doing.

When she finished, she gazed at the page, closed her eyes and began, imperceptibly, to cry.

Oh, God. Oh, God ...

It was him. The angel-man.

At 1:30, when Jane left to go to the theatre, Mercy did the dishes, made lemonade, changed her shoes and took Will and Rudyard for their walk.

To get to the park, you had to go to the east, turn at St. Vincent Street and head north. This brought you out on the west side of the park, where a sizable playing field stretched all the way to the river. Mercy, Will and Rudyard seldom stopped there—except when Rudyard spotted a squirrel, in which case they waited for him. He had never yet caught one. *Not yet,* Mercy thought. *Thank God.*

She always carried a bag of what she called "bird-bread" in her satchel—cubed, stale bread for the ducks, swans and geese—plus commercial bird feed, which featured corn and sunflower seeds as well as grains. All this could be dispensed wherever they decided to stop.

Once you had left the playing field behind, climbing over a low barrier to do so, you came to a more formal park area, with paths and trees and benches—and halfway along to the far end, a metal pavilion—or, as Mercy called it, "the summer house." It was somewhat like a gazebo, but it had no sheltering roof and it was of a looser, more free-wheeling design.

She had been to Fanfare and bought a copy of *Treasure Island* to follow *Lassie Come Home*, knowing how voracious Will was for storytelling. In fact, he was so devoted to his books that she wondered sometimes if it was completely healthy. Will would abjure all enticements to backyard lawn tennis or badminton. He and the other boys on the street of his age rollerbladed, mostly in the late afternoon or, on occasion, after supper. But he had few friends he depended on—and seemed by all appearances not to feel the lack of their company when they played elsewhere. In the winter, there was Harry Lambermont from down the street and Mally (his name was Malcolm) Rosequist—also the son of an actor. Together, they would skate at the arena on Saturdays and sometimes go to the movies. But seven-going-on-eight was a bit young to give Will his head entirely, and though both Jane and Mercy tried not to bind him to them in any over-protective sense, they kept a sharp eye and ear out for what he was up to whenever he was not with them.

Theatre children are a breed unto themselves. Their parents, in the eyes of non-theatre children, led grandiose, glamorous, distant lives—their pictures in papers and magazines and often displayed in public venues such as grocery stores, shop windows and restaurants. Questions such as: *is it true your father's queer?* were not uncommon; nor were straight-out statements such as: *everyone says your mum's an alcoholic.* Children have little sense of subtlety when it comes to such matters. All they want to know is: *what's going on where* you *live?* Then they tell you what's going on where they live—often, if not always, with a dollop of melodramatic detail. *Dad threw Mum down the stairs last night*—which meant she tripped.

Theatre children, at home, were of course exposed to unique timetables, curious midnight kitchen meetings, during which voices were raised on questions such as: *how do you* want *me to say it, for Christ's sake?* with answers like: *as if he'd just cut your balls off.* That none of this was about real life had to be established early on—even in the cradle. And consequently understood. And accepted.

Tensions also were sometimes greater than in average homes—tensions based on deadlines or on untold pressures regarding success and failure—either of which could happen overnight. Sundays and Mondays, there would be parties quite unlike the parties in other households. Not that they were "mad carnivals of drink and lust"—as someone had quite erroneously speculated a few years before in the press. They were instead accepted and enjoyed as blow-offs, when performance worries could be relaxed and put aside in favour of food, wine, laughter and good company.

As for Will, he accepted his role as theatre-child with easy grace and solemnity. What both his parents did intrigued him. Watching his father on the stage was always a source of mystery to him. *Where did this other man come from? Why have I never seen him before? Where did he get all that blond hair? Who is that woman he's kissing? And why doesn't Mum seem to mind?* But these were questions that could not be asked. They could not be formulated.

As for his mother, he was seldom admitted to her presence

when she was at work—sketching, designing or painting. He was never allowed in her studio unless accompanied. Otherwise, she locked the door. This worried him. Was what his mother did for a living a secret? Was it something bad? (*Could she be arrested if someone found out?* he had asked Mercy, when he was five.)

But he was proud of them both. They had many good friends, among them people Will liked a great deal—Claire and Hugh, Nigel and Susan, Robert, Oliver and others.

This day—the 11th of July, a Saturday—was what Mercy called a "high, blue day"—a day of cloudless skies and nothing but a gentle breeze.

In the park, as they walked, Will had been silent. Now they were seated on the bench on what they called their "secret island" by the river. A large tree spread its shade around them and Mercy served them each a cup of lemonade. Rudyard went to the river and stooped to drink, spreading his front legs and raising his hindquarters. Where he drank, the incline was steep and he was not so fond of water that he wanted to slide in.

Watching him, Will said: "what's wrong with Mum?"

Mercy looked away and took a deep breath. She capped the lemonade and pulled out her cigarettes and a bunch of Jane's matches tied with an elastic band.

"How do you mean, hon?"

She tried to be off-hand—but she fumbled the first match and had to strike a second.

"She never comes to see me any more before I go to sleep," Will said. "She hardly ever talks. Like today at lunch, she didn't say a word." He looked accusingly at Mercy as if it were her fault and pressed his hands down flat on the bench, making it seem that he was about to rise and walk away.

Mercy said carefully: "she's a bit unhappy, that's all.

Sunday, a man came and gave her some bad news about a friend who'd died. And ..."

"Why didn't she tell me?"

"Well ... she was grieving. Also, it wasn't a friend any of us would know. Someone from when she was at school in Plan-tation—way, way back before our time in your mum's life."

Will thought about it.

"Was she killed?" he said gravely.

"It was a man, hon—and yes, he was killed. Some kind of accident." She added: "also, she's very busy at work, trying to finish up that window she's been making. It's due for some rehearsals in just over a week—what they call 'technical rehearsals,' when the actors get to go on the stage with all the sets and props and things. Also, your dad's birthday party Monday tired her out. You know what it's like ..." She smiled at him. "Not easy, giving a party. Takes it out of you."

"She drinks too much." Will was watching Rudyard through narrowed eyes and Mercy did not like the look of him. Now is when she had to be doubly careful.

She sighed deliberately—giving herself a moment's pause. She drank some lemonade and smoked a bit more before she spoke.

"Well ..." she said, "that's what happens, time to time, when folks are under pressure. Your dad, he overdoes it time to time as well. It's not uncommon."

"You don't do it."

"Oh, yes I do, smarty! Not around you, of course—but in my own time-to-time moments, I've had my way with a bottle of wine or two. Only I do that at home, where only the cats are witness."

Will considered this and then said: "maybe I'll take it up myself. Time to time."

Mercy gave a laugh. The boy was precious smart. He always knew what to say to get at you—or to stand his ground.

"Not sure you'd like it," she said and patted him on his flattened hand.

Instantly, he withdrew the hand and stood up, slowly moving away in Rudyard's direction.

Oh, oh, Mercy thought. *This is serious.*

When Jane returned to the property room, the first thing she heard was Griff's voice on the tannoy.

"*I pray you,*" he said as Jane entered, "*leave me.*"

She smiled and closed the door. The next thing she heard was Griff saying: "*if it will not be, I'll leave you.*"

"Surely you're not listening to that crap again," she said, going to her work table. "It's been running for over a month. Aren't you sick of it yet?"

Mary Jane Ralston, lean and hawklike, looked up from her bead work, the beads made of papier mâché. It was her best talent. The beads were for the oversized rosaries carried by the Duchess of York and Queen Elizabeth in *Richard III.* They were to have the appearance of gigantic pearls, with heavy crucifixes made of faux ivory. Robert had asked that all the props and insignia be oversized and over-weighted, in aid of illustrating the despondency of Richard's victims.

Janice O'Connor, who was Jane's occasional friend, stood up and silenced the tannoy.

"Anybody want some music?" she asked.

There was a general murmuring of *sure, anything* and *no problem.*

Janice put on a CD of songs sung by Annie Lennox, who happened to be her favourite singer.

Everyone settled back to work.

Jane opened her sketchbook and quickly turned to a blank page. She found, inadvertently, that she was hunching over it like someone guarding her answers in a classroom examination. Her forearms encircled the page and her shoulders pushed forward.

Visage. Visage. Countenance. Saint George ...

She closed her eyes and tried not to see the Bell man.

Mary Jane Ralston, two tables behind her and off to one side, noted Jane's posture with interest.

Didn't want to hear Griffin's voice ... she was thinking. *Not the first time, either. Last week, went over right in the middle of the denunciation scene and turned off the tannoy herself. Bam!*

Fascinating.

Is dear, sweet, innocent Jane Kincaid waging war on her husband? An aggressive, self-propelled war? Or some kind of defensive action? Watch and listen. This one could be choice ...

Mary Jane opened her work-bag and took out a small, hard-covered notebook, which she opened and smoothed flat.

Then, she wrote out the date: *Wednesday, July 8th*, after which she scribbled a terse one-liner to herself: *trouble raises its head between Jane and Griff.* She then added: *another woman? Another man? Now,* that *would be interesting.*

Before she closed the notebook and set it back in her bag, Mary Jane riffled the pages, noting other recent entries: *Friday, July 3rd—Oliver still languishing, but who's the object?* And: *Allison—July 3rd—naughty, naughty—work table piled with chocolate bars! I counted eight!* And: *Tuesday, June 30th— Michael back on the sauce. How long will it take? Last time it took a month.*

Oliver, who had seen her on occasion making these notes, watched her slip the little book back into her bag and vowed he would find out what was in it. Truth to tell, though only

Mary Jane Ralston knew the answer, this was not the first of her annotated diaries. Perhaps there had been dozens of others—maybe only a handful. *However many*, Oliver wondered, *what were they in aid of? What is she up to?*

Jane had begun to draw again, obsessively. Soon there was a pair of male legs enclosed in pale ragged trousers.

At the waist, there was a brief indication of a work-belt, pulled taut by the weight of various tools and other accoutrements—a pencil, a pen, a cellphone. The knees of the trousers were torn—as was the inside of one thigh. The cuffs drifted off into sketchy lines that might have been threads—and the crotch showed a fly with metal buttons—one button undone.

Jane sat back.

She completed the shading, using the side of her pencil—shaping the legs and their shrouds as if she was making a visual testament of physical perfection.

Pray God no one will come and look over my shoulder.

She stared at what she had created—numb with silent approval and apprehension.

She ran the back of her thumbnail across her lips.

She raised the other hand to her forehead and shielded her eyes. But it was not the light that concerned her—it was the image it illuminated and the fact that the image appeared to have a life of its own, that another hand had put it there. Another hand and therefore another ...

What?

Another will?

She suddenly wanted to tear out the page, burn it, deny it had ever existed—forget that she had created these legs and the intimation of what lay beneath the cloth—the exposed tension in the groin, the split thigh with its skin and hair—the very texture of its imagined warmth. *He does not exist,* she told herself. *I've made him up. It's all a craziness, like that* movie, Repulsion, *where Catherine Deneuve imagined a non-existent lover so vividly that when some poor, desperate man turned up in the flesh, she killed him because she was afraid of his reality ...*

Jane lowered her hand and traced what she had done.

Eve with her basket, she suddenly remembered, *came to the gate ...*

Or some such words. She had read them years before, but could not remember who had written them, or how the rest of the poem went. She remembered only its lovely, simple portrait of innocent curiosity lingering undecided by the orchard gate in Eden.

Now all at once, Jane herself seemed to stand there, asking the same question. *Dare I go in—where it is forbidden?*

She looked aside, imagining a shadow had passed.

Who?

What?

Only the voice of Annie Lennox answered.

Every time we say goodbye ...

She closed her eyes. *Griff and I were dancing barefoot on the grass ...*

Jane closed the sketchbook.

We went inside and made love ...

She opened and closed a drawer with a bang.

"I'm going home," she said abruptly—stood up and began to assemble her things. "I'll see you all on Monday."

It was four o'clock.

Mary Jane Ralston retrieved her notebook from her bag and wrote, as the door closed: *J.K. went home early.*

Janice O'Connor went to the player and replaced Annie Lennox with Carly Simon.

Mary Jane Ralston tapped her pencil on the tabletop, smiled

her analyst's smile and wrote: *once disintegration starts, it takes no time at all to cripple the victim. If* victim *is quite the right word.* Perpetrator *also occurs. Also* facilitator. *Also* guilty party. *Let us see.*

summer nights

... but when the truth,
The truth about our happiness comes out
How much it owed to blackmail and philandering.

W.H. Auden
Detective Story

1

Every night—except on special occasions such as dinner parties—Mercy went home to her house on Graham Crescent to be greeted with silence—the first true silence of the day. No early-morning alarm clocks, no TV, no radios, none of Will's chatter, none of Rudyard's yelps, none of Jane's tricky questions.

But then, there were sudden moments of loneliness—intrusive, unexpected—when the yearning for Tom would take over and leave her ambushed by regret and sorrow. Even after all the years—now twelve of them since his death—she would be overwhelmed by his presence, as if he were about to walk in from the next room or turn around in bed and lay his head on her shoulder.

Tom had been the love of her life—and, indeed, still was. Her husband, Stan, had left her before the birth of their last child to run off with a fifteen-year-old girl to California. *Well, it's where she wants to go,* he had explained. What the hell was her name? *Lilah. As in Lilith* ... That was in 1968. *Dearie me—thirty years ago.*

Mercy was fifty-three now—still attractive, if somewhat overweight. But she had lost her eye for men, though she was fond of Luke Quinlan. Men were there, that was all—mostly making trouble for women. Or maybe only for women when they could not find men to pick on. That had been her experience—or mostly. Her husband—her father—sometimes her younger brother, Lou.

When you can't beat up the bullies at work, go home and beat up your wife.

Still, Mercedes Corben managed. Stan Corben, of course, had left nothing. He had skipped, plain and simple. But Tom had left her everything he owned, including his gas station on Lorne Avenue—now sold for money in the bank.

When Tom died, she started using his last name. Bowman. *Like an archer.* That's what he had said to her, early on. *Bowman, like an archer*—and he shot her, straight through the heart.

Her children, however—now completely grown and gone—had kept their father's name. On rare occasions, they came home to be with her. They loved her. It mattered to them that Mercy had done her best in their behalf. Two of them—Rose and Stan, Jr.—had gone on to university and at present had decent lives in business and law. Meanwhile, Alice was happily married with three kids, living in Vancouver with her architect husband, Andrew. Melanie ... Well.

Melanie had disappeared. Wilfully—and young. She never communicated. Not with Mercy, at any rate. She was alive—that was a certainty—she just did not want anyone to know where or how. She had always been problematical—complaining—argumentative—sometimes downright obnoxious. She had hated Mercy and Mercy's mother, Martha Mae Renaldo, for working in a restaurant where everyone could see them. All the kids at school knew who they were. The child had never been reconciled to the fact of it. Mercy finally made a difficult decision: not to cut her daughter off, but to let her go. All that had been offered had been accepted without gratitude: *after all, it's free.* In the end, however, Melanie threw all her pretty clothes in a heap and left them behind, along with her CDs, her ghetto blaster and her stuffed animals. She was gone beyond a slamming door—like *that*—like a storm that passed after wreaking havoc.

Sometimes you had to say goodbye. Mercy knew this.

Now Luke had lost Jesse. It was all the same.

When her brother Frank left home, all he said was: *I'm leavin', now*—and that was the end of it. He had been the shining light of Mercy's life—now disappeared. A clean break—and gone.

Rose. Stan, Jr. Alice. Melanie. Their photographs adorned her vanity—all in uniform sterling silver frames she had regretted having to pay for. But she knew she could not stint on them. Not like that. They were her accomplishment. They were her prize for having made it through hell.

Now, what Mercy had was cats. Four of them—each one a foundling. The oldest had turned up barely weaned at Tom's Esso Service Station, where Mercy was working the pumps while Tom plied his trade as a mechanic.

Her first encounter with Tom Bowman had been unsensational. *Downright ordinary was what it was. Almost a joke, it had been so everyday.*

Mercy had driven in for gas in her decrepit 1953 Mercury and Tom had served her. It was summer, as now—though maybe June, not July. *Put out the cigarette, ma'am* had been his opening gambit. Mercy had barely realized she was smoking, she was so instantly smitten. She had never seen Tom before, buying her gas farther north on Ontario and Erie streets most times. This time, however, she had been south of town to St. Marys and had run out before getting home.

Tom was big and muscular. *In a dark alley,* she had told Jane, *you'd turn around and run.* He wore a filthy boiler suit, unzipped perilously close to the crotch. Underneath it, he wore nothing. Nothing. She could see. He was covered in oil and grease and was hardly a romantic figure, though he had a shock of dark hair and white, white teeth and the shoulders of a Hercules.

But that was not it. It was the man inside the image who caught her attention. It was instant.

Instant?

Yeah. Instant. Don't laugh.

God knew how many times she had had that exchange with friends and acquaintances who thought she was crazy, falling for Tom Bowman. Even her mum, who had married a dark-skinned man everyone had said would be dangerous. But her mum had laughed at this and told them: *Renaldo is Spanish, for God's sake! Guys from Spain are only dangerous to bulls!*

Still, there were those who insisted on pestering Mercy with their small-town news about Tom: *after his wife died,* they told her, *he took on downright peculiar. Anyone'll tell you that.* Also: *maybe you haven't noticed, but he don't have women comin' outa every pocket. That's a sure sign he's some kinda trouble.*

But Mercy paid no attention.

She knew what she wanted, knowing what she had already had. There would be a difference.

Over eight and a half years ago, when Jane and Griffin Kincaid had first employed her during the last months of Jane's pregnancy, Mercy had been "widowed" four years since Tom's death. She needed a job and she wanted to be a domestic, no matter what people said. Inspecting her bank statement one evening, she swore she would never touch the savings from Tom's garage and service station. These were for later life, when all else failed—as she knew all too well it always did.

I'm a good cook. I brought up four kids on my own. I'm responsible, respectable and now the gas pumps are gone, I don't want to go back to any damn greasy spoon. A nice home uptown would be a welcome haven, day to day.

She had said to Jane in her interview: *well, I'm all alone now, but for visits all too brief from three of my kids—and I want another family. I need one, to put it blunt. A chance maybe to bring up another child—chance to finance a new car—chance to have some excitement. She had smiled then. I guess your house must be full of famous people ...*

In those days, of course, Griffin Kincaid was still very much a junior actor who often took work outside of Stratford, but Jane Kincaid had money written all over her. *Not that a person has to be too brash about it, but the fact is, there's money there an' you can smell it.* This was Mercy's opinion. And she was right.

At the second and final interview, Mercy had set out her stipulations: *Sundays off—overtime pay after six—gas allowance for family errands. Above all—no uniforms. I got my own workin' clothes an' I'll never make you ashamed of how I look—but I don't wear a uniform. It's a rule. After waitressin', it's something you know you're never gonna wear again.*

Jane had not known where to look, because she had been overwhelmed by a desire to cheer. This woman sitting across the table from her, that summer morning in 1989, was so absolutely certain of who she was that Jane had desperately wanted to shout her approval. *I could take lessons from this woman,* she had thought later the next day. *And maybe I will.* Then she had picked up the telephone, dialled the number and said: *I don't know where else you've applied, but I hope to heaven you're still free.*

Mercy had thought about it—chuckled—and replied: *I wouldn't say I'm free, Mrs Kincaid. But I would say I'm willin'.* She had started work the next day.

2

It was 2:00 a.m.

Will could not sleep.

He had finished *Lassie Come Home* and today in the park, he and Mercy had started *Treasure Island*, but his mind was on other matters. This was a phrase that appealed to him: *my mind is on other matters* ... He could not remember where or how it had caught his attention. Maybe in the book before last, *The Wind in the Willows*. Toad, more than likely, who was always being *distracted*. Another new word.

He turned on his bedside lamp.

Two o'clock.

He must already have been asleep. He could not believe he had been awake so long, having turned the light out at 10:00 when Mercy left.

Four hours.

Maybe.

It certainly felt like it.

Jane had gone to bed while he was still awake—that was for certain. He had heard her coming up the stairs, tripping at the top and swearing: *damn.* He had smiled. *She knows I'm listening, or she'd have said something worse, like* shit *or* fuck ...

I wonder why they think I don't know those words—as if I'd never heard them.

He was hungry—but he was afraid of getting caught making a sandwich or looking for chocolate chip cookies, which were kept in a biscuit box whose lid always fell to the floor.

There was something else down there in the kitchen—something Mercy had brought home this morning from Sobey's. Nachos in a silver bag.

He tried not to think about them—peppery, cheesy and crisp in their package with the mouse in the red sombrero on the outside.

Maybe he could sneak down and get them back into his bedroom without anybody else waking up. Also a Pepsi. If he closed his door, no one would hear him *cha-cha-crunching and cha-cha-munching* like the Nachos Mice on television.

He knew better than to wear his slippers. *They give you away every time ...* Other midnight forays had proved this—the slippers sliding on the stairs or coming off to trip you up in the dining-room.

Using his flashlight and everything he remembered about moving Indian fashion through enemy territory, he made his way into the upper hallway.

Rudyard lay asleep at the top of the stairs.

Now what?

The dog was sprawled in such a way, it would be tempting fate to step over him. *Tempting fate* was another new phrase, gleaned from *Lassie Come Home*. Will considered his chances and had just decided the only way to manage his raiding party was to wake Rudyard up and enlist his help, when suddenly the kitchen lights went on, spilling into the lower hallway like an accusing finger.

Will stood back and crouched by the bannister that ran above the stairwell.

It's Dad, he thought—*and it's after 2:00 ...*

He heard Griff searching for a glass and the sound of something being poured—gin or vodka. It had to be one or the other—they were all his father drank. He waited for the sound of the mixer being added, but nothing reached him, only the glass being refilled, followed by angry whispers and disjointed muttering.

The muttering seemed to be made up only of the ends of sentences: ... *don't understand* and ... *can't be happening* and ... *don't believe it.*

There was a final splash of gin or vodka and the kitchen light went out.

Almost instantly, the lower hall light itself went on.

Will pulled away from the bannister, turning off his flashlight—which up until then had been darkened against his side.

Rudyard was awake by now and, totally ignoring Will, was blinking into the stairwell, his ears erect, his nose at work in the air.

Will could smell a burning cigarette and he heard the fumbling progress of his father making his way to the landing. Afraid of being caught, Will instinctively shut his eyes and hunched his shoulders.

But Griffin came no farther.

Will heard him slump on the stairs and heave a sigh.

After a moment, Will opened his eyes and looked down at the top of his father's head.

Rudyard's tail began to thump.

Griffin looked up and saw him.

"Good boy, down you come."

Rudyard descended.

Griffin scratched the dog's ears and pressed his face against Rudyard's muzzle.

"Ruddy, Ruddy—you'll never know ..." Will heard. "You'll never believe what they've done to me now ..."

Will leaned forward again.

He saw the long ash of his father's cigarette fall to the stairs and almost believed he could hear it land.

Griff slumped against the wall, closed his eyes and drank from his glass. His left hand was still on Rudyard's head. "I just don't believe it," he said, as if to the air. "I just can't believe it. It's so fucking unfair."

Then, all at once, he began to cry.

Will at first was shocked and then numbed. What did it mean—his father so angry and crying all at once?

A door opened off to the left.

Will cringed, though he had no need. He might as well have been invisible.

When Jane emerged, pulling on her robe, she went to the top of the stairs, looked down and said: "for God's sake, Griff ... What the hell ...?"

Griff looked up at her like a confused child—held out his arms and gave a muted wail: "they've taken it all away, Jane-o. All I've got next season is ... *shit*."

Jane went down and sat beside him, cradling his head.

"Oh, my darling. I'm so sorry. How did you find out? What happened?"

"I've lost Berowne—I've lost Mercutio ... Everything I wanted and worked for! Everything I was promised. They won't say who's going to play them, but it's probably that bastard Blyth! Edwin-fucking-Blyth!"

Suddenly Griff raised his voice.

"It's all so goddamned wrong!"

Jane said: "come on, hon. We'll go down and talk. I'll fix us a sandwich—pour us some wine and we can talk ... Come on, hon. Come on. We don't want to wake up Will ..."

They went down all the way to the bottom and Will saw the kitchen lights go back on. He had never seen his father so helpless. Jane had had to lead him by the hand, as if he was blind.

The boy did not listen after that. He stood up and went back to his room.

"Ruddy ...?" he called softly. "Rudd-o ...?"

But his companion had gone. After all, he was Griff's dog.

Will laid his flashlight aside and climbed under the covers. All thoughts of nachos were far behind him. Instead, he wanted only to erase the image of his father stumbling along the hall towards the kitchen. He thought of Lassie, arriving home at last. He thought of Rat and Moley drifting happily through an afternoon on the river. He thought of Jim at the Admiral Benbow, listening to the singing ... *Fifteen men on a dead man's chest—yo-ho-ho and a bottle of rum* ... He thought of Mercy in the park, with Rudyard running on ahead. He thought of coming home tomorrow, where surely everything would be changed and his dad would be laughing again. And his mum would smile at him and put her hand on his shoulder. And Mercy would hand them each a hot dog— *mustard and relish, with onions on the side and fries, fries and more fries.* For supper, a pizza from Pazzo—*hold the anchovies!*—with Mercy's homemade chocolate shakes—and ... *Rudyard will climb back onto the bed and lie along my leg—and I will sing him to sleep the way we used to do—and I ... and I ... and I ... will sleep.*

This way, he slept.

3

Monday, July 13, 1998

During the creation of the new flower bed in the Kincaids' rented backyard, Luke Quinlan had the assistance of his uncle, Jesse Quinlan—Runner Quinlan, to most people—although he

liked Luke to call him "Bro." He was the youngest brother of
Luke's father and strong as the proverbial ox. He enjoyed
manhandling earth and rocks and heavy bags of manure,
cement and organic fertilizer. They were like demons to him,
and he had to best them.

For years, Jesse had lived with Luke in the old family home
on McKenzie Street, but had not always shared the gardening
work. Time to time, he went off into other worlds, where he
tested himself against the forces of a failed education and a
lifelong predilection for escape. As he grew older, he began to
escape into drugs and thievery. That was when Luke began to
call him Runner. A man in flight from a fear of who he was.

And now he had taken flight again.

Luke was sitting on the screened-in porch of the big house,
nursing a Sleeman. It was well after midnight. The crickets
were singing—the frogs were calling to one another and all the
street lamps were veiled with clouds of insects. A dog was
barking somewhere. There was music coming from someone's
garden and the late-night skateboarders were returning from
their fruitless quest for girls uptown. The telltale slap of their
boards as they hit the cement and the gentle *whirr* of their
wheels as they glided past had become the seminal sound of
every summer's night. Watching their ragged silhouettes in
their oversized jeans, their floppy shirts and their baseball caps
in reverse, Luke was put in mind of his own teenage years,
when eight to a dozen lonely boys, himself included, would be
dispersed from their unrewarded vigil on the City Hall steps
with a gentle reminder from Henderson-the-Cop: midnight,
lads. Time to hit the road.

Back then, they called their bicycles "wheels." It was before
the time of mountain bikes, ten-speeds and other fancy inno-
vations. Most of Luke's friends and Luke himself had Saturday
afternoon jobs as delivery boys, bag boys or yard boys whose

winter work was stoking furnaces and shovelling snow. Nineteen sixty-one to sixty-six. Stratford was so utterly different
then, Luke could barely credit it as being a real place. But it
was, and you could survive it if you kept your eye on the horizon. Now, the town itself had survived and there was barely a
trace of its railroad-oriented past.

When Luke was approaching five in 1953, everything had
changed forever. The Stratford Shakespearean Festival was
born that year in a circus tent up on the hill above the baseball
diamond, and *nothing now would ever be the same.* He had
read that somewhere—or something like it—in a poem about
what happens when your lover dies. Not that Luke and Stratford had been "lovers." But he had loved his childhood there,
despite his brawling parents. There was a quietness then to be
found in the woods along the river and the whispering ice
beneath your skates on a Saturday afternoon. These things
were gone—but he found his compensation in gardens.

Luke was fifty now—or would be one month down the
road. Runner was fifty-seven—and yet, a true "little" brother,
small, wiry and broad-shouldered, with bitten nails and
worried, staring eyes.

Whirr—whirr—whirr. Skateboards and the ghosts of
wheels. Youth and its dreadful loneliness. The everlasting
sense of hopelessness and all those asshole adults saying it was
meant to be *the time of your life*—when all you really had was
going home, raiding the fridge—cold pizza, chocolate cake, a
Pepsi—and up the stairs to your suffocating sheets and the
day's fifth jerk-off.

Luke lighted a cigarette.

Now, in his mind, the whole of his father's family slowly
appeared—the way a film sometimes shows the actors in the
cast—the kind of film where everyone is a star, or so it seems.
Leading the parade were his grandparents:

Preacher Quinlan and Mar'beth Hawkes present their children! Ta—dah!

*Huck Quinlan—played by Mickey Rooney—*dead on some highway at the age of forty-two, guiding his beloved eighteen-wheeler down a ramp in fog somewhere. Somewhere—somewhere ... always *somewhere,* never pinpointed, never identified because the rest of the Quinlan family had to travel the highways of Ontario, hither and yon—and had to survive a chance encounter with his ghost, or the ghost of his vehicle—paid for, as life will have it, in blood. Blood, bones, brain and flesh—there being nothing left of him but the crystal of his watch and the melted ruin of his Lion's Club medal ...

*Tom Quinlan—played by Henry Fonda—*tall as Huck had been short—the quintessence of a certain nobility deeply innate, yet inaccessible in both his parents. Still, he was their child—loving them, even now, in all the years of their absence—*Tom the pillar—Tom the father of the Quinlan clan remaining—Tom the beacon—*whose only failing was his inability to understand Jesse's pain—his anguish, his confusion—whatever it was that had driven him to drugs, alcohol and despair. But Tom had taken his own clan with him, far away as Alberta—not a cutting of bonds, but a loosening of ties. He was no longer available for consultation: *over to you, Luke ... Goodbye.*

Thus, Jesse—the youngest—had been bequeathed to Luke, who soon learned, first-hand, a sad lesson: *Jesse knew nothing from birth. He didn't even know he was human—he only knew he was alive ...*

He never connected. He never knew—he never understood he was one of us. He was alone. Always alone.

The litany of family names moved towards its end.

*Becky—played by a seven-year-old Shirley Temple—*even now, aged sixty-eight, the finger still rising up towards the dimple. *Something I can do for you, sweetie ...? Some chicken soup? A back rub? Somewhere to flop ...?*

Jim—Jo—Meg—Amy—Beth, who was stillborn—*Frank* and *Jesse* ... and in the middle, *Mark,* Luke's father—the child with five on either side. He was now dead, along with two of his siblings. All the *Twains* and all the *Alcotts*—one saint and two outlaws—all of them Quinlans. And only one total disaster. *Jesse.* Some other disasters, maybe—but none of them total. Meggy's screwed-up marriages—Jim's unhappy life as a gay man before the time of gay rights—Frank's unhappy gay life since the dawning of AIDS—Jo's frustrated devotion to her namesake's passion for the written word—now in her late sixties and still unpublished.

*No, the rest are not total disaster*s, Luke reflected—knowing how great his affection was for all his aunts and uncles and their struggles—like his own—to become themselves.

Become yourself ...

Quote—unquote: Preacher and Mar'beth Quinlan. Preacher had said it—Mar'beth had stitched it into the sampler that hung above the dining-room's double doors, where all could see it. It was still there, just inside the window that looked out onto the porch where Luke now sat.

Become yourself. The family motto.

And now ...

Jesse.

Becoming himself.

Become himself.

Entire.

Runner.

All right, Runner, where the hell have you gone this time?

He remembered sitting here two years ago, when his uncle had sat with him. That evening, they had both been drinking Sleeman.

Around that time, there was a film whose title perfectly

described Runner's apprehension of what lay hidden inside him: *Natural Born Killers*. Of course, Runner went to see it three times, wanting confirmation.

"One day ..." he had said to Luke back then, "... one day it will happen and I'll do it."

"No you won't," Luke had told him. "You won't because you always know when to run."

Runner seemed to be listening to the darkness around them.

"You want another Sleeman?"

"Sure."

When Luke returned, he saw by the light of the street lamp out beyond the maple tree that Runner's cheeks were wet and gleaming.

Luke handed over the beer and sat down, pushing back inside the shadows. After a minute, he said: "Runner—just tell me. Don't hold it in. What is it?"

Runner bent forward, his dampened face in his free hand. At first, he couldn't speak—and then he said: "I'm scared. I'm afraid. I'm scared." He fumbled his hand in Luke's direction.

Luke took it and said: "tell me. Say it."

Runner, still bowed, had spoken so low that Luke could barely hear him.

"I'm always going to be alone," he had said. "I'm never going to have a friend—or meet a girl ... I don't know how to give. I don't know how to make contact. I don't know how. I don't know how. And I'm lonely—I'm so goddamn lonely. It scares me."

Luke had not spoken after this. He just held his uncle's hand until Runner let go. Still without speaking. They had gone their separate ways to bed.

Three days later, Runner had gone back on coke and disappeared.

He had eventually come home—stayed—worked—and

disappeared again. That was the age-old pattern. It had been this way for years.

Now, Luke listened to the neighbourhood dogs raising the usual alarm that no one ever heeded, as strangers—humans, dogs and cats—invaded other strangers' gardens, seeking whatever it is that people and creatures seek from one another in the dark.

Over on Ponty Street, a woman was being raped, though only she and her attacker were aware of it. Nearby, the dogs had been barking, but the only response was the usual cranky voice from a neighbour's window and a pail of cold water heaved into the night.

Luke sucked on his bottled Sleeman—*the only beer in town.* He hated cans. *Canned beer isn't civilized.*

Poor old Runner. Where would he be this time? Over and over again, the same procedure. Almost a practised routine.

Come back, fall back and come back again.

Luke wondered if he should bother to go and look for him. He was aware of only one or two dealers in town and he knew there were many more. Sometimes Runner would head for Kitchener, London or Grand Bend—just to get out of Stratford and away from Luke's accusatory presence. Not that Luke harangued him. Far from it. He always took his uncle back and got him through withdrawal. But the plain and simple fact that Luke was Luke, and had made it past the family's self-indulgent ills and woes, was like an accusation to Runner. A challenge. A proof that failure could be survived, if you only tried. But trying, for Runner, seemed impossible.

Luke knew how his uncle felt from long experience. He had survived his own parents' appalling demands and the wasted lives of his school friends. But he had chosen silence. Silence and presence. *Say nothing. Show nothing. What you have to do—and all you have to do—is be here.*

4

The afternoon sun was baking the limestone façade of the Pinewood Hotel.

The Pinewood was the favoured residence of visiting stars and other luminaries who came to visit or to work at Stratford, though it was more than twenty kilometres away in the limestone town of St. Marys. It had once been the treasured and pampered home of the nineteenth-century railroad baron John MacCready, whose mark was visible still in the stumps that showed where his line had been drawn between the unruly forest and the manicured lawns.

MacCready was a penniless Scot who had found his way to Upper Canada in the 1850s. He had struggled up through the immigrant heap to the top in twelve short years. It was said he had been born with a silver railroad spike in his mouth and soon enough had talked his way into the ownership of several interconnected railway lines in what, after 1867 and Confederation, came to be known as southern Ontario. In his way, you could say MacCready had been the making of Stratford as the hub of lines coming from far away as Montreal and Windsor. Certainly he was among the first local entrepreneurs to stake his claim in the seemingly bottomless pit of wealth generated by steam locomotion.

Once married and firmly established, however, he chose not to live in the lap of his work. He preferred the ways and the airs of a Scottish laird, and thus he went to St. Marys to build his castle in the pines—his beloved country gardens tended by eight hired hands and his stables filled with a uniform race of greys whose appearance with the polished MacCready landau caused gasps of admiration everywhere they were seen.

But nothing lasts.

The railroads perished.

By the early 1950s, his accumulated fortunes had dwindled and Pinewood was sold—"into slavery," as the last MacCready descendant had put it.

Still, its spirit flourished—and now, its Victorian gardens, Edwardian gazebos and seried ponds had all been restored, while the house itself and its stables had become a thriving hotel, whose restaurant and hospitality were written about in the Sunday *New York Times*, the *Chicago Tribune* and—tribute of tributes!—Montreal's *La Presse*, an unheard-of honour for an "Upper Canada" establishment.

Jonathan Crawford had taken up residence at Pinewood in March of 1998, while beginning his final preparations for rehearsals of *Much Ado About Nothing*. He had chosen a suite of rooms that overlooked the swimming pool, its terrace and the tennis courts. These led the eye away to the edge of the trees, where, out of the sunlight, *one could enter—or so it seemed—a prehistoric darkness under prehistoric boughs in the midst of prehistoric whispers ...* or so he had written in his journal.

From his windows, he could watch the athletic young men who came and went their way, whether actors, audience or simply the idle rich. He was a confirmed voyeur and kept a large collection of photographs, through which he would thumb his way with a bottle of Scotch on a Saturday night or a Sunday morning when all his carefully worded invitations had gone unanswered or been refused.

But this was neither here nor there when Jonathan settled into the business of serious conquest. A desultory desire for a nice young athletic walk-on was one thing—but a concerted campaign to bring *the Chosen* to his bed was quite another.

The Chosen (Jonathan over-romanticized everything but his plays) was always a budding *artiste*—a man, never a woman—of such promise that to miss his advent would be to miss a whole season of wonders. Looking out over the roster of performers on offer in New York, London, Stratford, Jonathan would select—and very often correctly—those who were destined for stardom. And he wanted to be—insisted on being—the one who achieved it for them.

He thought of himself as a sculptor of talent. He moulded his protegés as if from clay—their limbs, their profiles, their vocal talents, their understanding, their emotional responses and, of course, their sexual submission.

His bed was not a "casting couch"—far from it. His bed was a testing ground, where every response was graded on a gauge as harsh and unemotional as a court of law. If you were guilty of a moment's hesitation—a fraction of insincerity or a lack of subservience—you were gone.

That Jonathan had chosen Griffin Kincaid was a fact of which, at first, only he was aware. Even Robert had not twigged. While directing *Much Ado*, Jonathan had been at pains to give nothing away. Consequently, during rehearsals, Griffin had to endure Jonathan's daily frontal attacks and subversive commando raids on *Mister Kincaid's braying voice, his appalling posture, his lack of integrity and his lax intelligence* ... That none of these complaints was based on any but the most superficial of truths was entirely self-evident. But they worked as spurs to drive Griff on.

This way, as March bled into April and April into May and the opening night approached, Jonathan knew—and Griffin knew—that *a definitive performance was aborning* (Jonathan's note, 15th May, margin of director's script). It had all been worth it.

Then came the question of next year's season.

Jonathan was to direct both *Romeo* and *Love's Labour's Lost*. Griffin knew he could have Berowne and Mercutio for the asking. *Who else could be chosen? Eddie Blyth? Impossible.*

In June, some time after *Much Ado* had opened and proved to be a tremendous hit, Griff received an invitation to dine at Pinewood.

Jane was not invited.

The lack of her inclusion was so blatant that Griff had known there would be no explanation. Certainly it was not an oversight. It was pointedly deliberate. Also, it could only mean one thing.

Consequently, Griff had accepted without telling Jane. *But how do you get what you want without giving in?*

The bed was offered.

And refused.

More or less gracefully, Jonathan accepted the refusal—only smiling sadly and waving aside an inconclusive gesture.

Griffin was asked a second time.

The second time—it was now approaching the end of June—though he accepted the dinner, Griff felt compelled to put his case.

He did not hedge. He made no excuses. It simply was not in him to sleep and have sex with a man. He was suitably sorry—even apologetic. He lauded Jonathan's "genius"—he thanked him for what had already been achieved between them in *Much Ado*—but he could not acquiesce to this *sudden and unexpected* invitation. (Griffin threw in "sudden and unexpected," thinking it sounded suitably ingenuous. It did not. It sounded precisely as calculated as it was.)

Jonathan wasted no time in reacting. He never did.

He would have Griffin, or Griffin would pay for it.

He went to Robert.

There were subtle complaints. He hemmed and hawed about

Griffin's range—*a Claudio is one thing*—*a Berowne, another* ... and *while he has the stamina for it, I'm not really certain he has the panache for Mercutio ...*

Slowly, Jonathan's manufactured "reservations" took seed and flowered. By mid-July, Griff had failed to be cast in anything but *lesser roles*—acceptable, but not at all what he had expected or wanted.

Robert had broken the news to Griff after the matinee on Sunday.

Griff was stunned. At first, all he could think was: *why?* Then: *oh.* And finally: *Christ!*

He had not believed it would actually happen.

Surely no one could be so grotesquely demanding that a whole career could turn on a refusal of sexual favours ... But, of course, it happened all the time. *Power is power and those who have it, use it. Simple as that.*

Jonathan had made a final bid just a week ago: *agree, or you're dead in the water.* He was going to Philadelphia—who cared why?—and if Griff had not agreed before he left, the threats would become reality.

And then Luke had cut the telephone line.

That was the end of it.

Jonathan flew to Philadelphia without having heard from Griff. When he returned, he met with Robert—who tried to keep Griff's chances alive, but Jonathan was adamant. They finally agreed that Griffin Kincaid was not quite ready for such demanding roles. They also agreed to wait a month before reassigning them. The leading contender, within the company, was Eddie Blyth. *Edwin Blyth, a rising star, and more amenable to persuasion ...*

Ambition. The old story.

Or at least, one aspect of it.

Now—on Monday—there had been another carefully muted invitation to the Pinewood Hotel.

Griffin said yes.

5

"Where are you going?"

"Out."

"Dear one, I'm not a child. *Out* is not an answer, it's an evasion. Tell me where you're going."

"I have a dinner engagement."

"That sounds like Somerset Maugham. And, considering how passé his world of manners is at the moment, little better than laughable. Am I supposed to ask you *with whom you are going to dine, my dear?* As if I didn't know? As if I'm just another silly, blasé wife who writes in her day-book: *G. to dinner with Z?* It is Z, isn't it? Or is it—as happens so often in Maughamish novels: *din-dins with Claire?* After all, a wife's best friend is always fair game in these tired old stories ..."

"Are you through?"

"I will never be through. Not until you are. I'm strong, Griff. Strong—and you'd better believe it. I don't care how long this moment takes—I am more than willing to wait until it ends. Because it will end. You will end it. And you know how? *You'll grow up.* All of a sudden—*ala kazaam*—there will be an adult!"

Griff was pulling on his trousers, trying not to fall over. One foot was caught in the crotch and no matter how he pushed and pulled, it would not go through to the cuff.

"I could give you a pair of scissors," Jane said—watching him, "then you could cut your way out. Just like hacking through the undergrowth ..." Then she said: "good word, *undergrowth*. Denotes not only nature's subversive entanglements, but a failure of forward movement in the ages of man. Some grow upward, Griff. Others do not. They hang back, wallowing in youth, with their left foot caught in their crotch."

"Oh, for Christ's sake, Jane ..."

"*Oh, for Christ's sake, Jane ...* Is that all you're going to say?"

"Yes. *Yes!* You're becoming a fucking bore. Leave me alone."

"Well." Jane sighed, leaning back against the bedroom door jamb, nursing her pre-dinner wine. "At least that's something I don't need to say to you."

"I beg your pardon?"

Griff at last had managed to pull on the trousers and was now selecting a shirt from the bureau.

"I'm only remarking that I spend a good deal of time alone these days. I'm only remarking that, if I had an opportunity to tell someone—namely you—to *leave me alone*, I might welcome it with open arms. But somehow the opportunity never arises ..."

She drank.

Griff selected his favourite short-sleeved Tilley—blue—and put it on, facing the mirror.

Jane watched him, as if already looking back at someone in the past.

"Who is it, Griff?" she said hoarsely. "I don't care who it is. I really don't. I just want to know."

Griff did not respond, though he glanced at her briefly,

fumbling his buttons and cursing under his breath. He wanted
desperately for this inquisition to end, because he was afraid
that if she pushed him too far he would blurt out the truth.
And the thought—the very thought of the truth—was too
overwhelming to consider.

Jane approached him from behind and put her free hand on
his shoulder.

"I want to know, hon," she said. "I need to know. I have to.
I have a right."

"Why? What difference does it make? You want to play
Claudio to my Hero, go right ahead. Be my guest."

He turned and brushed her hand aside.

"Who says I'm having an affair?" he said as bluntly as he
dared. Having played the outraged, seemingly betrayed Claudio for so long, he knew that nothing makes a fool of a man
like a self-righteous defence. "Who says so?"

"I do," said Jane. "What the hell else can you be up to,
having all these private assignations? And never even deigning
to tell me where, let alone who with. Am I honestly meant to
believe you when you say: *good news is coming, Jane-o! Good
news is on the way!* As if you really were off with Robert
discussing next year's casting. As if this was all—and only—
about your hyperactive ambition? Please—give me some
credit. You don't dress up like this for *me*—let alone for
Robert, unless we're going to a party where you want to over-
whelm someone."

She gestured at his newly pressed shirt and trousers—the
perfect blazer, tailored within an inch of its life to his splendid
(*dammit*) physique. If looks were really all that mattered, he
would win the palm hands down. And he knew it.

"I'm surprised you didn't go for a trim and a manicure ..."
she said.

Griff moved past her and headed for the stairs.

"All you have to do is tell me! Tell me, that's all I ask."
Griff turned.

"Don't raise your voice, Jane-o. You want Will to hear?"

"Jesus Christ! As if you gave a shit about Will!"

Griff descended to the landing. Jane began to follow him.

"The other night on these stairs, you were in tears," she said
to his back. "The other night you were in tears—and you
asked me to help you ... and I did. *I did.* I fucking well did, you
bastard. And now I'm standing here in tears and asking *you* to
help *me*. It isn't much I'm asking, Griff. It isn't all that bloody
much! Just *who* and *where* ... and *why* ..."

The side door closed.

That was the end of it. Nothing.

She heard the car start. The Lexus.

She hovered by the newel post.

Mercy came out of the kitchen, having heard it all but
pretending she had been with Will in the sunroom with the
door closed.

"Griffin leave?" she asked.

"Yes," said Jane, dead-voiced.

"I can whip something up in two shakes," Mercy said, turning back to the kitchen—afraid to see what was written on
Jane's face—afraid to address the obvious.

"No," said Jane from behind her. "I'll take us to Bentley's. I
feel like getting out of here, and it's the only place we like
that's open today."

"Sounds good to me. Will and I played Scrabble the last
hour. He won, of course. Makes a person feel so dumb ..."

"If you were dumb, Mercy, the world would end. You're all
that holds us together."

Mercy sensed an onslaught of Jane's tears, and no matter
how justified they might be, Will must not see his mother that
way. Not now. He had already asked *what's wrong with Dad?*

He's never home ... He also knew there had been an argument on the stairs. And Griff had passed through the kitchen, seen Will in the sunroom and had not spoken. All the boy had heard was a closing door.

"I'll get my sweater," Mercy said. "We can go in my car."

Jane finished her wine and put the empty glass in the dishwasher.

"Who's for Bentley burger?" she said, trying to sound like her usual self.

Will came and stood in the open doorway.

He waited. Then he said: "can Ruddy come with us?"

"No, hon. Sorry. They don't allow dogs. You know that. But he'll be fine. I promise."

All the way to Bentley's, led by Mercy, they sang what used to be Stratford's theme song:

I've been working on the railroad,
All the livelong day!
I've been working on the railroad,
Just to pass the time away ...!

But time, Jane knew, could not be *passed away*. It had to be lived—it had to be endured. It had to be *done*, as in prison. Now, she was *doing time* in a foundering marriage that had become, in its own way, a kind of prison. But whether she or Griff was the warder, she could not tell. The keys, if hers, had been lost.

It was 8:45 of a midsummer night as Mercy's car turned onto Ontario Street and slid into its parking space on the curb near Bentley's, and the nine o'clock freight to Windsor roared through town as if not early, but late.

On the sidewalk, they fell silent. Will went in and Mercy followed, but Jane lingered. The sound of the departing train had taken up residence inside her and its echo would stay with her all through the night.

6

Monday, July 13, 1998

The Pinewood dining-room was more than amply air-conditioned, to combat the stifling heat that still lingered into the evening.

The room was somewhat Edwardian, having begun its life as a darkly panelled Victorian drawing-room of immense size, with a fireplace at either end between rows of intermingled French doors and windows.

When the estate had become a hotel in the early 1950s, most of the panelling had been removed to the present reading-room and replaced with rough-textured plaster walls decorated with various costume designs from Stratford productions.

The tables were spread with white cloths and the mantel-piece sported Inuit carvings of various weights and sizes. These latter were mostly depictions of the wildlife indigenous to the Arctic—wolves, whales, foxes, hares and owls. The collection was priceless and had been donated to the Pinewood in the 1970s by an American collector who thought, perhaps rightly, that it had a chance of being seen and appreciated by a greater number of people than would encounter it in the obscure gallery in Pennsylvania where it had previously been housed.

"All very civilized," Jonathan observed, sitting opposite Griff that evening at a table somewhat removed from the rest—not precisely in a corner, but near one.

"Yes."

"And the food is excellent. I had thought we might share a chateaubriand, if we can agree on how it should be cooked."

"Medium-rare—not too bloody."

"Good. My choice, precisely."

They were drinking Gibsons, which Jonathan had ordered knowing Griff's predilection for gin.

"The bartender here is an expert. I believe he must shop for the cocktail onions himself. Never less than perfect."

"Yes."

Jonathan wore a light summer suit with a blue-and-white-striped shirt open at the neck. He had guessed correctly that Griff would not wear a tie and had not wanted to embarrass him.

"You look extremely well," he said—as if it was an obligation to say so, before whatever else he had to say.

"Thank you."

"So—tell me what's on your mind."

"You invited me, Jonathan. I'm here at your request."

"Does that mean you have nothing on your mind?"

"You know damn well it doesn't."

"Then tell me. I can guess, of course, but I'm not about to say it for you."

"What happened to my roles?"

Jonathan smiled and shrugged. "They took three steps to the right," he said. "I'm sure you know why." He selected a cigarette. "What happened to my phone call? The one you promised before I left."

Griffin explained about the cut line.

Jonathan clearly did not believe the explanation. He lighted his cigarette. "Done in by a flower bed," he said. "I see. Well—at least it's original."

Griff was not deterred. "The parts," he said. "Are you giving them to Edwin Blyth?"

"That question has no answer at the moment."

Griff looked away. He felt helpless, wanting to speak and not knowing how to articulate what he had to say.

"You've never slept with a man, have you," said Jonathan, gazing down as if absently at his fingers spread on the cloth.

Griff said nothing, wondering whether he should lie and say yes.

"I'll tell you how I know you haven't, Griffin. Some years ago, while scouting for actors, I happened to see you at the Manitoba Theatre Centre in Winnipeg. You were playing Brick in *Cat on a Hot Tin Roof*."

"You never told me you'd seen that."

"Why should I? I was intrigued by your good looks and your innate talent, but I knew you weren't ready for my kind of work. Not then."

Griffin unfolded his napkin.

"What's this got to do with sleeping with men?"

"Everything. As you well know, the audience at that play must believe in the possibility that Brick has indeed had sex with his old teammate Skipper. Maggie, his wife, must believe it sufficiently to be afraid that it's a fact. Big Daddy must also believe in it. Otherwise there's no play. What is the word Williams put at the centre? The word at the centre is mendacity. *Mendacity*. The art of lying. But in your performance, I didn't believe for one moment Brick could have slept with Skipper. It was an absolute impossibility. You gave one of those *I'm not queer and you'd damn well better believe it* readings that was unworthy of a real actor. Real actors are fearless, Griffin. If they hide—nothing happens. Your edges were so harshly drawn, there were no open doors. And the essence of

Brick, and of playing him, is the doors he's left open and is trying—and failing—to shut. That information was simply not there in what you did. Which saddened me."

"Well—it would, wouldn't it."

"Don't be snide, Griffin. I was not saying what you think I was. You must learn to listen more carefully. You must learn to hear and to understand the meaning of nuance."

Griff lighted a cigarette and sat back. He did not know how to have this conversation—how to handle this situation. He was too intimidated by Jonathan's power to make or break him.

"It's true," Jonathan said, "I want to sleep with you. But I want more than sex."

"More? What more?"

"I want to teach you how to accept the fact of being desired. An invaluable understanding for both the man and the actor."

Griff waited.

"If, for example, you *were* to play Berowne ..."

Griff looked down at his empty glass and touched its stem with his index finger.

Yes?

If ...

"When it appears that Rosaline is turning him down, every-one in the audience—and I mean *every one*, men and women—must have something more than a little sympathy for him, because they know why she's pretending to refuse him, which is the only thing he *doesn't* know. And every one of us—*every* one of us, as I said—must be thinking: *how can she do this to him, when I would take him in a second?* And in order to achieve this coup, you have to have made us under-stand, if not as an absolute fact, then at least as an absolute *possibility*, that Berowne would sleep with any one of us to get to Rosaline."

"May we have another drink?"

"Of course."

The waiter came and the order was given for two more Gibsons.

"Go on," said Griff.

"You may or may not be aware of how much of his own experience Shakespeare drew on while writing *Love's Labour's Lost*."

"I guess not. In what way?"

"When he was still a young man, he had fallen in love with his patron, the Earl of Southampton ..."

"The sonnets. Yes. So the critics say."

"During one of the great plagues that occurred at that time, all the theatres were closed and people who could afford to, got out of London as far away as they could. It was the only way to protect yourself from contagion."

"Yes."

"To whatever degree, Southampton reciprocated Shakespeare's feeling for him—and he invited Will to his estate in the south, along with a large—or fairly large—number of other young men who formed Southampton's coterie of friends. They made what might be called a 'merry band.'"

Jonathan smiled.

The Gibsons came.

They drank.

"And ...?" said Griff.

"Well, think about it. What happens in *Love's Labour's*? A group of aristocratic young men, who happen to be students, set up an elaborate camp near their university and swear off the company of women in order to concentrate on their studies. Sound familiar?"

"Are you saying Shakespeare thought of women as a plague?" Griff said slyly.

Jonathan smiled. "That's better," he said. "Approach all important matters with a sense of humour."

"Go back to your wanting me to learn how to be desired."

"Desired—loved—wanted."

"My wife loves me."

"True. But you chose Jane—Jane did not choose you."

"She did, you know."

"Perhaps. But only as *women* choose. I have observed, as I dare say you have, that aggressive women in pursuit of men more often fail than succeed. A woman's way with desire is different from a man's. She waits. Men do not wait. They proceed to the object. Whereas aggressive women attack. And no man will accept that. That's what *men* do. Attack."

Griff drank.

"Okay ..."

"It's an invaluable lesson for an actor, for an artist, for a man. Ninety per cent of the men you meet have no idea what it's like to be a woman."

"They don't want to *be* a woman."

"Well—not wanting to be and failing to understand are two different things. I'm not asking you to be a woman. I'm asking you to grow as a man."

Now, Griff looked away. The light beyond the windows had reached that evening moment when shadows begin to fall. Here, the shadows fell from the pine trees and stretched over the lawns like benign fingers reaching for the hotel.

"I've never been had," he heard himself say—as if he were talking to himself.

"*Had* is not the right word, Griffin."

"It would feel like it."

"No. What you mean is—or should mean, pray God—is that you've never given over to someone else's desire."

Griff took another sip of gin—still looking out the window—still not meeting Jonathan's gaze.

"I find it very difficult to believe that no other man has ever approached you," Jonathan said.

"Oh, yes. They have. But ..."

"What happened?"

"I couldn't. So I didn't."

"Because you didn't want to—or because you were afraid?"

"Both, I guess."

"More the latter, I'd bet."

They were still, now—both of them.

Then Jonathan said: "there's nothing wrong with being wanted, Griff. It's not a mortal sin to be desired."

"There was an older boy at school. When I was thirteen. He ..."

Jonathan, too, looked out the window. "Yes. I know that story from both sides," he said.

"And when you were the younger boy?"

"I thought about it. I liked him well enough. After a while I decided to prepare the way."

"What does that mean?"

"It means I did what you're doing now. I considered the consequences and made my choice accordingly. But, of course, I was just fourteen. Not quite the same. Luckily, as I said, he was acceptable. He was seventeen. And you see, I wanted to be wanted. I had only been waiting for the right boy."

Griff said: "what was his name?"

"David Masterson. Why do you ask?"

"I wanted to see if you'd remembered."

"A person never forgets such things. He gave me my freedom to become myself."

Griff now looked at Jonathan.

Jonathan smiled.

"Are you ready to order?" he asked.

"Yes."

"The chateaubriand?"

"Yes."

Jonathan lifted his glass.

"Here's to the future," he said.

They both drank

"Let us say no more."

Griff looked down.

"Yes," he said. "We will say no more."

7

Monday, July 13, 1998

Mercy got home late that night. There had been a murder over on Ponty Street the night before, and everyone was talking about it. The victim was a woman in her early forties who was known for her drug habits and had long been suspected of being a dealer, though nothing had ever been proved.

Her name was Maggie Miller, and from time to time, Mercy had encountered her waitressing over the years—or sitting in this bar or that with people who clearly thought they could take advantage of Maggie's natural generosity. She was always willing—and always able—to buy a person a drink, so long as you would sit with her and let her spill out her troubles. Which were legion: abortions—deserting husbands—runaway lovers—batterings—the lot. If it could happen to a woman, it happened to Maggie.

Now she was dead. Strangled, having first been raped.

Whoever did it got away scot-free. For the time being, at any rate. Just as with the rape-murderer in Kitchener.

Among the young and the single men—and among the straying husbands of Stratford—there was a sudden flurry of alibis.

The radio and TV would not shut up about it. You had to hear it every time you turned around—and then everyone you met had to tell their personal version. *It's as bad as Monica and Bill,* Mercy thought, *the way they push it down your throat ...*

"You should pardon the expression," she said aloud to the cats, and had a good laugh.

As always before going to bed on a summer night, she was on the screened-in porch at the back of the house, looking out over the yard with its meagre flower beds and shady trees. It was small, but she loved it. There were pots of night-blooming nicotiania brought up close to the house so she could smell the blossoms pouring out their scent.

Heaven. Heaven. Heaven-scent ...!

And now poor Maggie Miller ...

And the question: who?

Oh, Lord ... such a long, long way through trouble, Mercy thought, pouring herself some wine from a bottle of Wolf Blass Yellow Label in which she occasionally indulged.

All those years of her own childhood, rarely happy. Her daddy's death—and her mother's. Then her sisters and brothers, gone to the four winds.

And then ...

And then Stan Corben, and the horror story of the next eight years. (They had met and married in 1961.) Mercy learned, if not to laugh at it, at least to smile about it. *Some people land on their feet,* she used to say about her arrival in Stratford and the advent of Stan—*I landed on my ankles.*

At the gas station, there had been a covey of stray cats. Tom more or less tolerated their presence, but once there was Mercy, he welcomed them. *Broken warriors, mostly,* is how she would describe them. Missing parts of ears and tails and one of them, a whole paw. They were old, unloved and homeless, every one of them. Even the females seemed to have been warriors, and more than likely were, having fought their way out of trap-nets, corners and gang rapes.

Mercy had set up a dozen cardboard-box condominiums, feeding stations, water bowls, litter boxes. *Tom's Esso* became known for its cats as much as for his mechanical expertise.

At this point, in 1973, Tom was forty-nine and almost twenty years Mercy's senior. She took the children and went to live with him in his run-down house on Louise Street. This meant giving up the apartment she had loved on Ontario, but she took her furniture and all her household goods along and tactfully got rid of almost everything he had been left by his wife, who had deserted him five years before when their boy, out riding his bicycle in the dark, had been killed.

That was when Tom had begun to drink—when the boy died and his wife left. Then she died. Of devastation, leaving him only a single word written on a photograph of the boy. *Why?* Mercy had been totally unaware of his grief and its consequence until one night, three months after she had gone to live with him. Mystified, she had waited till midnight—five hours after the meal had been ready—for him to return. When he did, he literally fell through the front door and broke his nose on the tiles.

Even now, Mercy kept no liquor in the house. This had to

do with Tom's predilection for it. As if he might return and lay claim to it. Instead, she kept wine and beer. Not that she had ever made the mistake of "forbidding" it. There had been no rules—only hopes and expectations.

The beer was for guests. Since becoming Will Kincaid's nanny, Mercy had begun to cultivate Jane's taste for wine. Wine had not been part of her own growing-up experience. Then, everyone in her parents' purview consumed rye, ginger ale, plus beer. It was *a class thing*, as someone later told her. *Plebes never drink wine—unless they're winos. Then, it's not really wine, it's rotgut.*

Not that Mercy could afford Wolf Blass Yellow Label every day. The only time she bought it was as a birthday or Christmas gift for Jane—or at Jane's request, with Jane's money. But she did experiment, using Jane's "cellar" (a cupboard in the dining-room) as a guide to wines that were passable, but a good deal less expensive. Tonight, however ... *there's been a murder*, she told herself. *Life is short. Sometimes shorter than you think.*

After feeding the cats and cleaning their box, she had opened the "wine-gift-from-me-to-me" and carried it with her cigarettes and a glass onto the porch. The cats had come with her and taken up their favourite places on the cushioned wicker furniture, lavishly washing away the chinned and whiskered remnants of their evening meal.

Mercy was stretched out on the chaise. She sighed happily. A worrying but intriguing day. Now it was over. What remained of it was hers.

Somewhere, three or four gardens along the street, a cat fight began. Gabby and Roly, two of Mercy's younger males, leapt down from their chairs and made for the kitchen. Clearly, they were eager to join the fray.

Luke Quinlan had installed a cat flap for Mercy in the side

door, leading—like Jane's—to a stoop from which she could hang the laundry on the line that stretched from there to a hydro pole in the backyard. Having the flap, the cats could come and go at will during her absence. (Though she cleaned their box every night, there was little need, unless there had been a blizzard or a thunderstorm.)

She heard the flap bang twice, after which Gabby led Roly through the darkened yard. Mercy watched them go—shadow hunters, as old as time.

Next door to the left, someone—presumably Fiona Haney—was playing the piano. Something gentle. Mercy did not recognize what it was, but the melody was contagious. In seconds, she had it memorized and *hummed along*, as people said.

Mercy lighted another cigarette. She loved to see it glowing in the dark. A firefly. Another living presence. She felt like a reflection of Jane—the solitude, the drink, the smoke—surrounded by the past. *I'm an overweight twin image.*

The sound of the cat fight intensified. Rags, the oldest of Mercy's males, crept into her lap. She stroked his scarred head and massaged his ears until he began to purr. Perhaps the sounds down the street provoked memories of past defeats and victories. Rags was Mercy's last surviving physical contact with Tom, who had held Rags the kitten. He had even played mouse-on-a-string with him, pulling a bit of old cloth across the floor for Rags to pounce on. *Oh, dear ... now it seemed like yesterday*—not twelve long years ago.

Next door to the right, all the Saworskis' lights were blazing. Mercy heard running water and words—each cascading from the upstairs windows. Not in anger—not gushing—only flowing in twin streams—two voices, two taps. But not the expected voice of the damaged child. None of his crying. None of his pain. None of his anxiety, so clearly visible when you saw him. There was something he could not achieve—sight?—

hearing?—comfort? He simply railed, so it seemed to Mercy, at the ignorance of everyone around him to whom he reached out with his voice and his arms. How can you tell what cannot be told without words? *Shriek. Howl. Wail.* These were his only means of telling—and no one understood him. Or—so far as his mother was concerned—wanted to hear.

The Saworskis—young and barely one year married—had a three-week-old baby boy whom they had named Anton. The doctors had not wanted him to leave the hospital, but Agnewska, the mother, had insisted.

He's mine and I want him with me.

You can stay, too, Mrs Saworski. That is possible. We can arrange it.

No. I want to take him home. He belongs at home.

But there's something wrong with him, Mrs Saworski—and we need to find out what it is.

No. I will not leave him here. He will die.

Only if you don't let us examine him more thoroughly.

God does not do evil things to children! Doctors do! she had yelled at them.

Mrs Saworski, that was not necessary. We are professionals. We do know what we're doing. We are here to help your son—and you must let us. For his sake—for God's sake.

Do not say for God's sake! *You have no right. The boy is God's and mine and I will take him!*

And she had.

Milos Saworski had hung back, silent through all of this. He did not know what to do. His parental instincts and knowledge were on the side of the doctors—of medicine—of common sense. But he also knew the hysterical nature of his wife's religious views concerning life and death and the rightness of things. She would not be crossed. *God's will above man's. We shall pray.*

Milos was too embarrassed to get on his knees. His parents—like Agnewska's, and Agnewska herself—were survivors of the Russian occupation of Poland. But the Saworskis were nominally Catholic and only mildly political, whereas Agnewska's parents were violent—not to say rabid—anti-communists and hyperactive Jehovah's Witnesses, ranting, tiresome and sterile. Before Anton's birth, Agnewska was regularly seen at the corner of Downie and Ontario streets, displaying her pamphlets, stoically ignoring both the heat and the cold. This was how Milos had first seen her. This was how they had met. He had braved the storm of proselytizing just to meet her.

Agnewska was desperately attracted to him—not only because of her parents' strictures, barring the door against suitors—but because she also thought that in this beautiful young man she had met her first convert. And if she could and did convert him, she could then get him through the door.

There had never been a sizable Polish community in Stratford, but there were enough Poles to form a relatively solid enclave within the Catholic community—and a significant contingent of the labour force. Germans, Italians, Bosnians (most recently), Poles and a very few visible minorities—among them, indigenous Canadians—made up the bulk of the local factory workers. Not so, Milos. Milos worked for Bell Canada as a repairman.

Mercy considered them—the Saworskis—as she listened to their taps and their talk, while Fiona played what might have been background music. Just like a film. *How people fall apart because of an impaired child—starring Meryl Streep and Harrison Ford* ... Any fool could see what was coming—the bitterness, even the hatred replacing the love because of Agnewska's obtuse and unforgiving refusal to face reality and Milo's failure to seize control and act in the child's behalf.

Physically, Milos was beyond well-made—he was virtually the stuff of Greek godhood, but he was not like other handsome men. He never preened or strutted—he never glanced at his reflection in passing surfaces. He was simply there—in his torn, faded jeans, unbuttoned shirt, utility belt and workboots. Clean and presentable, professional, polite and quiet, all the while unknowingly exuding an overwhelming physical presence through every pore. Even Mercy, who had rarely thought of sex since Tom, conjured Milos when she did. He had all the attributes of vibrant sexual maturity—plus the mystery of virginal adolescence. And yet, he was almost thirty.

The distant taps, all at once, were turned off.

"There," she heard Milos saying, "will I go now?"

"But where?"

"Out. I will not be long."

"Please not too late. I do not like to be alone with him."

"I will be home by 12:00—12:30."

"Please—by 12:00. Midnight. Bad things can happen then."

"I will try."

"Do not try. Be here."

Mercy wondered, as always, why they did not speak Polish. She was unaware that Agnewska Saworski wanted only to be rid of Poland and the past and that, in doing so, she had given up her language. To Mercy, such a deliberate sacrifice would have been inconceivable. The past *is*. A person *is*. To learn another language was one thing—to discard your own, quite another.

As for Milos, he had been only partially schooled in English. At home with his parents, as with Agnewska's, Polish was spoken. But his English was formal, even stilted, which Mercy assumed was the result of his native shyness.

She now became aware of the shape of Milos standing briefly in his kitchen, hoisting a beer. She also saw the shape of Agnewska moving from one upper window to another.

The side door opened.

A yard light was switched on.

Milos appeared wearing an unadorned sweatshirt—got into his minivan and backed out of the driveway.

Silence. More or less.

Fiona Haney went on playing. This time it was a song Mercy knew, "Moonglow."

As she listened, she slowly drifted back to the film in which the song had played such a prominent role. *Picnic*. William Holden, Rosalind Russell, Susan Strasberg, Kim Novak. When it was first shown in 1956, Mercy had been roughly the same age as the character played by Susan Strasberg—the book-haunted teenage sister of the beautiful Kim Novak, who fell— as her older sister had—for the sexy, ne'er-do-well vagabond played by William Holden. Mercy wondered if Fiona, too, had a secret curiosity regarding their neighbour in the ragged jeans, who came and went like another kind of vagabond—Eros—an Adonis in disguise, who called himself the *Bell repairman*.

Mercy lay back and smiled at the "Moonglow" memories of being eleven—twelve—thirteen—lost, book-haunted and alone in the wilderness of adolescence—learning how to wear a bra, how to smoke cigarettes and scan the school cafeteria with knowing, unknowing eyes. And always wondering why it was that fifteen-year-old Teddy Carlson had suddenly caught her interest, when barely a month before she had laughed in his face. And her mother had said: *only nice boys, Mercedes. Only nice boys. No Teddy Carlsons. Not in my house.* Mercy had given up eating for two days ... Gone, now—the unforgivable, unforgettable past of parental denial and doors locked at 10:00 p.m.—midnight on Saturdays. Gone—but all too well remembered. With a shrug and a smile.

The Saworskis' side door opened again and banged shut. *What would a midsummer night be without the sound of banging screen doors?* Mercy wondered. *It wouldn't take place in southern Ontario, that's for certain ...*

Barefooted, Agnewska whispered across the twin drives—her own and Mercy's—and came to the porch door. She was carrying Anton, who was asleep, overwrapped in baby blankets.

"I saw your cigarette," she said. "Can I come in?"

How quiet it suddenly was.

The cat fight had ended.

Fiona fell silent. *Is the movie over?*

There were crickets—frogs—the usual. Otherwise, nothing.

At the sound of Agnewska's voice, Rags jumped down from his owner's lap. Mercy stood up and unlatched the door. Eleven-fifteen. She could hear the chimes from her old-fashioned station clock in the kitchen.

"Is there something I can do?" she asked.

"No, thank you. Just to be here. Milos has left me."

With these words, Agnewska entered. Mercy could not help conjuring the future moment, all too predictable, when it could be true.

"I'm not sure I understand," she said—feigning innocence, knowing perfectly well he had only gone for a drink downtown.

Agnewska loved drama. It was part of her over-the-top attitude to religion, politics, love, death and her child. She had a performer's expertise in milking the moment.

"He has gone to return drunk again."

"Oh, I'm sure not. That doesn't sound like Milos at all."

This was true.

"He has gone to drink beer and pick up girls," Agnewska said. She had no imaginary life of her own, but she delighted in providing one for Milos. "He last night stayed away until after 2:00. No matter what he promise, he does not come." Glancing around, she selected a chair and almost sat down on top of Lily, Mercy's only female cat, who had fallen asleep.

"Sit here," said Mercy, giving up the chaise. "You'll be more comfortable with Anton that way."

"Yes."

Agnewska settled Anton in the crook of her arm and sat, stretching her legs.

"What is that you drink?" she asked.

"Red wine," said Mercy. "I can get you something else. Some cranberry juice, orange juice, Evian water ..." Agnewska did not drink alcohol of any kind.

"I shall have wine," she declared.

Oh.

Mercy went back to the kitchen. Rags went back to his own chair.

Wine. Damn her. I'll have to open another bottle. I'm not going to give her my Yellow Label. To hell with her.

In spite of what she had said to Will, Mercy had never really allowed herself to overindulge in drink, but suddenly, having opened the second bottle—this one, Valpolicella—she found herself pouring a secretive glass and throwing it back with a toss of the head that nearly sent her spinning into the sink.

She laughed. Silently. *Mercy Bowman—falling-down-drunk at last!*

She got a fresh glass for Agnewska and returned to the porch. She wished that Fiona would start again. Background music would help her deal with this difficult, off-putting, uncharming and demanding young woman. *Now, I have to play the kindly, older neighbour with a heart of gold.*

Well, I damn well won't.

I've never liked her. Bloody Polack ...

Now, now. Charity. Charity.

To hell with charity. Where the hell is her *charity? Bitch. She's killing that baby. Now she wants my wine—and, doubtless, my sympathy ...*

Mercy poured a polite glass of wine—half-filled—and handed it to her unwelcome guest.

"I have had wine once. At my wedding," Agnewska said.

"Cheers."

"Is that Canadian? *Cheers?*"

"Well—it's actually British, but it's what we say, too. If we were French, we'd say *salut.*"

"So. *Cheers* and *salut.*"

They both drank.

Mercy sat in the one remaining empty chair and lighted a cigarette.

"I wish you would not smoke," Agnewska said. "The boy."

"It's my house," said Mercy—amazed at the words as she spoke them. "In your house, I would not. Here, I do. Besides, we're out of doors." She took a deliberate drag and smiled.

Agnewska set her glass at her elbow and pulled away the blankets covering Anton's face.

"He sleeps now," she said—ignoring the smoke. "Very quiet, most of day."

"Do you never take him back to the doctor?"

"Never. Would kill him."

If you don't, first.

"But shouldn't you know what's wrong with him? At least let them find out what the problem is? It would just be too sad for words if it turned out there was something they could do and it wasn't done. I had friends, once," Mercy went on, "who had a daughter. Beautiful, beautiful child—but all you had to do was take one look at her to see there was something wrong. She had one crossed eye ..."

"What is cross-eye?"

"Where the eyes don't focus together. Her left eye was locked in place, staring only to the right ..."

"Like in movies. They do it so you can laugh."

"Well—I guess so—yes. But this was serious. I wasn't the only one who noticed it. The parents knew, but they kept saying it would fix itself. She was very young, this child—not yet two years old. But nothing was done. They did nothing. Nothing. And such a beautiful child. By the time she was eighteen, the eye was so badly damaged it had to be removed.

"God's will."

"No, dammit!" Mercy flared. "*Not* God's will. Parental stupidity. Pride. That's what it amounted to. They couldn't admit their perfect daughter had a defect—but if they had taken her to a specialist before she was three or four years old, the eye could have been corrected and today she would be whole." Mercy decided to push the argument one last dangerous step. "And bloody hell," she said, "the same could be true of Anton. I'm not going to call you stupid, Agnewska. You're not—but I do have to tell you, I think you're cruel."

"Not cruel. I obey God's will."

"Anton doesn't know anything about God's will!" Mercy hissed, leaning forward towards the young mother. "He's only a baby. All he knows is, there's something wrong. Why should he suffer—*why*—when all you have to do is take him to the hospital and let the doctors examine him?"

Mercy sat back. She poured more wine into her glass and even poured more into her neighbour's glass.

Agnewska said nothing for a moment. Then she looked down at her son and touched his face with her fingers.

"He's sleeping," she said—and smiled. "Is asleep."

"Yes—but not by God's will. He's sleeping because he's tired. *Dead* tired of calling for help and being ignored. I'm sorry to speak so harshly, but I am very, very, *very* concerned about this. God made *doctors*, Agnewska. God made doctors, medicine, hospitals. *Help*. He wants us to help. It's what being alive is about. *Helping*."

"But I am able to help more. I am his mother. I take care of him. What mothers are for. I am doctor, medicine, hospital. *Mother*."

Mercy said: "I'm a mother, too. Four times."

"I did not know. I never see your children."

"Well, the truth is—neither do I. Except now and then. But I love them. All."

"As I love Anton."

"Yes. As you love Anton. But ..."

"Do not say *but*. I will not hear *but*. You do not understand. I am mother, yes, but also I am child. And ... I obey. *No*, they say. *No*. It is God's will. Wait. And so ... I wait."

She looked down at her sleeping baby. "I want ... I want ..." she said. "I want him alive. To live. But ... I am not able. I am not free. I am ... prisoner."

Mercy set aside her glass and went to sit with Agnewska on the chaise.

"May I hold him?" she asked.

"Yes, yes. Oh, yes. Please."

Agnewska lifted Anton towards Mercy's hands.

Mercy held him against her breast, the top of his head beneath her chin. He seemed entirely weightless—merely a fold in the blanket.

"I have not held a child like this for over thirty years," she said.

"He is beautiful, yes?"

"Yes. Beautiful."

Mercy kissed the baby's hands—one and then the other.

Agnewska watched her—tears rising in her eyes.

"I wish you were my mother," she said.

Mercy fought back the tears in her own eyes.

So do I, she thought.

"My mother—my father—never once hold Anton in arms,"

Agnewska said. "Is strange to me. So much love of God—so little love of us."

Mercy smiled.

There is hope.

"Anytime I'm here and you want me to help," she said, "please come. And bring him with you."

"Yes." Agnewska accepted her son and readjusted his blanket. "I will," she said. "I will."

There were lights in the driveway.

It was midnight.

The station clock began to chime.

"There's your husband," said Mercy.

"Yes," said Agnewska, and stood up. "I say to him twelve o'clock, and look how good he is."

At the door, she turned back.

"Thank you for letting me sit and for the wine. Goodnight."

"Goodnight," said Mercy, rising. In her mind, she also said goodbye to Anton.

Agnewska stepped down onto the grass.

The screen door slammed. She crossed the lawn.

"Milos! Milos! I am here! I am here!"

The headlights went out. But Milos stayed inside the van.

He did not want to tell his wife that, this time, he really had nearly left her.

8

When they got home from Bentley's, Jane took a bottle of Wolf Blass Yellow Label into her studio and locked the door.

She put a CD called *Sakura* in her player and turned the volume down. The music was Japanese—fluted and soothing—and somehow reassuring. It was music that had persisted through time, which is what she now intended to do. *Goddammit.*

Then, the Yellow Label. Maybe expensive, but who gave a damn. *I'm grieving and I want comfort ... And there's damn little comfort in this bloody heat wave. Or from Griff.*

She fished in her work-bag for the sketchbook in which she had begun to assemble the angel-man—took it out and, for a moment, closed her eyes before she opened it.

If he *has,* I'm *going to,* she thought as the image of Griff and whoever he might be with raised itself in her mind.

She tried to make a picture of a room somewhere in which he was making love to Zoë Walker. The beautiful black chiffon dress being laid carefully across the back of a chair—her discarded lingerie (she wouldn't dare be seen in mere underwear) had been lifted aside and was artistically arranged at the foot and the head of the bed—*a little here, a little there*—and her stockings—*black, of course*—were doubtless draped over the lamp shade ... *sheer heaven.*

Jane had to laugh ... The whole scene was plain ridiculous. *Bodice-ripper stuff—or, worse,* Nurse Zoë Does Doctor Kincaid.

She opened her eyes.

Where might he really be? And who with?

She poured a glass of wine and lighted a cigarette. *Props for all my* Jane-Seeks-Solace *scenes. Same old props, day in, day out.*

You know somethin', honey chile? You are *becoming tiresome. So? I'm tiresome. But at least I'm visible, not hiding somewhere in the dark. And speaking of tiresome, I'm tired of being lied to. I'm tired of being ignored. I'm tired of this fucking deception and Griffin's pretence that nothing is going on.* That's *what's tiresome.*

She opened the sketchbook.

There he was ...

His face as Saint George.

His torn jeans.

His hands—his fingers—his fly ... all those brass buttons.

She tried to imagine what it would be like to undo them.

Me and Monica Lewinsky ...

I haven't done that since I married Griff ...

But there was a time in the eighties when every girl was expected to perform oral sex—even on a first date. It was supposed to boost your partner's ego, letting him know there was nothing you would deny him. And so she had, along with almost everyone else she knew. *If you didn't do it, you were slotted in with all the other trash.*

Funny how, back then, you were trash if you didn't, not if you did. And if you wanted a condom used, you were just *uptight*— even though AIDS was beginning to show itself. No one had used a condom for years. If you stole your mother's pills or somehow managed to get your own, who needed any other kind of protection? It was passé. Until Rock Hudson died.

The trouble was, ninety per cent of the boys and men you dated thought it was exclusively a *gay disease. Wouldn't catch me friggin' around with another guy,* they would say. And everyone would snigger. *The very idea, Charlie!*

Then young women started to be infected. No one, at first, could figure out why—*unless good ol' Charlie's been lying all along.*

It took two years and more to figure it out. AIDS was everywhere. It was everyone's disease. Even your closest friends could be HIV positive ... *Coralee Haslup ... Rita Mae Coolidge ... Charlie Feller.*

Yes. Even good ol' Charlie Feller—who cared how? It killed him.

She stared at the angel-man's incomplete image.

I want to ... she thought. *I want to. And I don't know why ...*

It was *that goddamned Lewinsky woman*, making everyone think about it and daydream about it. *And want to do it.*

Without condoms.

So?

It's supposed to be the safest sex there is. Long as you don't swallow.

She ran her finger over the pencilled contours of his legs, his arms, his shoulders.

She had already begun to fill him in—to attach the face of Saint George to the neck and the booted feet to the jean-encased ankles. He had become, beneath her hand, a completed man. Finished—but still not whole. Still hidden.

She leaned in over the desk—pushing aside jars of paint brushes, boxes of crayons, bottles of coloured ink and scraps of broken charcoal.

She drew the goose-neck lamp down closer and opened the book to a new page.

Over the next two hours, while the wine bottle slowly emptied and *Sakura* was endlessly repeated, Jane created a nude—not naked—Bell man, as from dust.

As from dust, she said half aloud. *Like Adam.*

What she had done was not unlike the ancient practice of

flaying a prisoner—stripping away not layers of skin, but of clothing. Using her pencils as knives, she cut away his protective covering bit by bit, until—by 2:00 a.m.—he stood before her utterly revealed—innocent as ever, smiling and uncomplaining. *Done.*

May I come in? I'm here to fix the phone ...
And someone's life. And someone's future.
Yes.

Jane had thought she would go to the kitchen and be there when Griff came home—however late it might be. She wanted to catch him unawares. If she could see his eyes, she would know how serious it was.

At 3:00, he was still not home. Nor at 4:00. At 5:00, Jane went upstairs with a final glass of wine, took off her clothes and sat on the edge of the bed.

Why am I naked?

It could matter less.

But I have kept my figure. In spite of the dreadful struggle giving birth to Will, when I thought every muscle in my body had been torn from its anchor, twisted in knots and thrown back at me like so much sausage meat ...

She regarded her limbs as if they might belong to someone else—the Venus de Milo's missing arms—the legs of Aphrodite rising from the sea.

I have nice hands, she thought. *Nice hands and pretty feet, though strong enough to lift my own weight and sturdy enough to stand my ground.*

A woman's hands and feet are the hallmarks of her breeding, Aura Lee ...

Jane smiled, in spite of herself. Maybelle Harper Terry.

Oh, mother, mother—poor, dear remnant of the past. She

shook her head, but Maybelle's birdlike voice continued: *the hands, the feet, the neck and the hair, chile ... No one cares about the breasts but men—forget all that. A becomin', truly attractive woman never puts herself forward. Present yourself to yourself—and long as you are proud of what you see, the world will give its 'proval an' its appabation.*

Mother, the word is ap-probation.

What's the diff'rence? Means the same thing.

All to be a lady.

The instruction was unending.

Your great-grandmother Aura Lee Terry never put a drop o' water on her face nor on her hair. Not one single drop. Not one. Cold-cream concoctions for the face, brushed-through powder for the hair. An' to the very day she died, she had the most beautiful skin and hair I ever saw. Also her fingernails— never once professionally manicured ... Still, always buffed, with shinin' moons and rounded tips. An' just remember, this was the woman who scrabbled in the earth with her three-year-old brother to dig up the family silver from the garden and who spent her pre-marriage years scrubbin' floors, burnin' her hands with acids an' scaldin' water, livin' on God's most inedible, indigestible scraps of pork rind an' dried-out collards an' all the while poundin' her pretty clothes with a stone in the river, so's to make them clean. She was a lesson to us all. An' did not die till the 1960s at the age of one hundred and five.

Yes, Jane remembered. *A lesson, and a hard one.*

Jane had admired but never loved her great-grandmother Terry—however brief their relationship had been. Though her mark on Jane's life was indelible—*stay the course*—her unforgiving, élitist and racist attitudes had been intolerable.

Nice hands and pretty feet ...? So?

And what they accomplished and what they stood for?

And a person's mind ...?

Jane was always driven back to silence at the very thought of Aura Lee Terry. After all, without her, Jane might not even exist. Though she knew this was only a child's justification for silence, she also knew that, but for Aura Lee, she herself would have been born to an ignorant breed of social outcasts.

She sighed.

God, she thought. *What we are forced to carry ...*

"I don't want to be a lady," she said out loud. "I never did. Fuck ladyhood, Mama. And fuck you."

She finished the wine, set the glass aside and swung her legs under the covers.

At that very moment, she heard the Lexus pull into the driveway.

"I'm not here," she said.

And turned out the light.

She did, however, note—before she slept—that Griff had returned at 5:15.

9

Tuesday, July 14, 1998

Standing beside the Lexus, its door still ajar as if to offer him escape, Griff looked over at the kitchen lights left on for his return. He knew he must, but he did not want to go inside. Instead, he gently eased the car door into place and turned towards the backyard.

Above him, the stars still shone but the moon had set. Beneath his feet, the dew had risen. He knew the crows would all be in their place, possibly watching, possibly afraid.

"It's all right," he whispered, "I'm not here to harm you."

He ventured farther towards the centre.

Oh, the smell of it all ... and all my boyhood nights beneath the stars ...

Sleeping bags on camping trips—the canoes upside down on shore, their paddles slung from the slatted seats. *Never leave a paddle where the beavers and porcupines can find it ...* and so the canoes with their burden were always hoisted somehow— a loop of rope—a convenient crook in the branches of a tree ...

You fellows go to too much trouble. All that shit about beavers and porkies is just a myth.

Who had said that?

Ralphie Redlitz, Mister Know-it-all ...

They were twelve.

It was Griffin's dad who had told them about the beavers and porcupines. *They like the salt where your hands have been,* he had said. *All animals like salt, boys, but Mister Beaver has the teeth to do more damage than your average night prowler. All the others do is lick the salt away, but he gnaws it—same as a porcupine.*

Griff made a face in the dark. *Words have a way of ganging up on you ...*

Beaver.

Lick.

Eat.

He put his hands in his pockets. They were cold. His feet were cold. And his nose.

Who cares? I like to stand here—one foot in now, the other in the past, where I was safe.

Safe?

Yes. As houses. Mum used to say that.

He and his sister, Megan, and his brother, Allun. Safe.

Allun.

Never with an "a" at the end, son—only at the beginning.

It was Al who had told him the other meaning of "beaver."
Al, when he was thirteen—voice cracking, hair sprouting
everywhere—sweating, sweating, endlessly sweating—always
in the shower, terrified of how he smelled. Or thought he did.

Cold showers are good for you.

Dad had said so.

Meggy had Mum. We had Dad. We were safe.

Money—St. Andrew's—a great house in Rosedale—a
cottage in Muskoka. Everything.

*Me at centre ice. Me and the five-mile swim. Me as a prefect.
Me as head boy. Me as the lady-killer, aged eighteen ...*

Safe.

The stars shifted.

Or was it clouds?

Something above him had been altered—blurred, somehow.
Obscured.

There was wing noise.

One of the crows left the walnut tree.

Dawn could not be that far away.

Oh, Jesus. What have I done?

*What have I done to myself—and everything I had and
loved? What have I done to it all?*

He looked at the house.

Asleep, as its occupants.

Nobody waited for me, he thought. *I wanted them to wait.
I wanted them to be here.*

Cocksucker.

No. Hey. No. I didn't do that. And I won't. Not ever.

To Griff, it was the ugliest word in the whole language.

At school, *cocksucker* was the ultimate pejorative. Any boy labelled with it was never able to regain respect. Not until he left St. Andrew's, at any rate. In the adult world, they had made their deliberate way—rising above the labels—even embracing the labels willingly—claiming what they called *gay pride* and achieving creative lives of which the rest of the world had thought them incapable. Now, they took up residence in a more accepting world. Or a world that seemed accepting, at its best. *More safety.* This time, in numbers.

Griffin had no qualms about homosexuals. They were all around him, given his profession. He simply did not want to be one—that was all. *And thank God I'm not ...*

And yet ...

And yet what?

Well ...

"I didn't do it," he said out loud, as if explaining himself to the crows, the walnut tree and the stars. "I didn't do it. I only let it be done. There's a difference."

Oh?

Yes.

The lights went on in Mrs Arnprior's kitchen.

Jesus.

What time is it?

He could not see his watch.

Go in.

Yes.

In.

Yes.

Now.

He turned back towards the porch.

He got out his keys.

Since that Miller woman had been murdered, all doors were locked the minute darkness fell.

Griff gave a final look at the sky.

In its eastern reaches, the lift towards daylight had begun. It was time to go home.

Pray God Mrs Arnprior had not seen his arrival at this hour. He would never hear the end of it—all over town.

"Goodnight," he said—as if there was an obligation to speak. And perhaps there was, seeing he had shared the final moments of darkness with whoever else—whatever else—was out there.

Jane had left the bathroom light on. Griff had removed his shoes before entering the house and now went in without a sound.

He needed to urinate.

Urinate? Don't we say pee *anymore?*

He set the shoes in the sink. They were soaking wet and cold to the touch. When he lifted the toilet seat and undid his fly, he found that his penis had shrivelled and was also cold.

Freezing.

Griff had already washed himself at the Pinewood. It had been his father's advice to wash himself with soap and water after every sexual *encounter*. That was his father's word for it. For sex. An *encounter*.

Well.

He did not wash again. Nor did he flush the toilet. He was too tired and he did not want to wake Jane or Will. Or Rudyard. Perhaps especially Rudyard, who would be all over him.

Turning out the light, he made his way to the bedroom, threw off his clothes onto the nearest chair and, lifting the covers, climbed beneath them, glad at last to find a hiding place.

At first, he lay on his back. Rigid.

Jane was asleep, but he wanted to wake her up. He wanted

someone to hear him—listen to him—share his victory ...

I didn't do it, Jane-o, he would tell her. *I didn't do it, I only let it be done ...*

Cocksucker.

He turned on his side, away from her.

Twenty seconds later, he realized he was weeping—but only when he moved his cheek against the pillow did he discover it.

Don't, he told himself. *Don't. Please don't do that. It isn't ...*

He took a deep breath—and slowly let it out as an invitation to sleep.

It isn't what?

He smiled.

I was going to say manly, he told whoever was listening inside him. *And then I thought: that isn't quite the right word. I'll think about it in the morning. I'll think about it tomorrow. After all—tomorrow is ... another day.*

Goodnight, Scarlett.

He slept. Jane heard him. She was wide awake and staring into the burgeoning light.

I'm not going to leave you, Griff. I'm not going to give up. I'm here—and I'm here to stay. Whoever she is, she will pass— but I am anchored. You are my harbour. And I am yours.

disclosures

An enigma always
And with a buried past ...

W.H. Auden
Detective Story

1

He looks so goddamned peaceful lying there, it isn't decent ...

Jane pulled on her robe, turned away from the bed and went across the hall into the bathroom.

Tuesday.

And one of her last working days on the windows. She had to be there by 9:00. The tech dress was less than a week away.

Jesus Christ! His shoes are in the sink!

She lifted them out and set them aside, facing herself in the mirror.

There I am. Dead.

Oh, well. It was worth dying for.

She thought of the angel-man drawings and of how hard she had worked to make him come alive.

Funny, doing something you really need to do—must do— how you lose all track of time and place and how the energy for such moments in life is always there—like a high. Like shooting up with dreams.

For yourself, Jane. Doing something for yourself.

She had been an artist for wages such a long time now, she barely remembered the freedom of choosing her own subject, doing it in her own time, being entirely her own judge.

I want that back.

And why not?

Money. *If I'm going to buy this house, it's going to take a lot of money. Yes—my inheritance fund—but more. Much more. Ingenuity. Connivance.*

She wanted to play it like a perfect hand of bridge. One day—whenever—she would set out all the necessary papers, lay them down like trump cards in front of Griff and Will and Mercy on the kitchen table and say to them: *okay—who wants champagne? We own a house. This house. This one, right where we're standing. Ours!*

She could see their faces. She could see them reach for the necessary backs of chairs. She could see them trying to find the right words. And she herself would open the pre-chilled champagne—Dom Perignon—and pour it out for all the world. She would even put some down on the floor in a water dish for Rudyard! She would kiss them all on the tops of their heads and she would say: *just a little gift from Jane-o—just a wee surprise to welcome you all to a new and perfect world ...*

Who wrote this shit?

There she was in the mirror, pulling back her hair and tying it with ribbons. The real Jane. *The real me ...*

Who writes your lines, Jane-o?

I do. To my grief. In all my life, I've never known what to say when something decent happens. Finally *happens.*

Gosh!

Crikey!

Jeepers!

I mean—I ask you!

She turned towards the toilet.

Look at this, for God's sake. He didn't even flush.

Weren't his parents civilized? Was he?

No, goddamn him—he's fucking all the women in town—except me.

Pushing the handle and watching the water churning in the toilet bowl, she wondered when had been the last time

anything decent had happened. Anything magnificent—
anything shattering.

Will. That's when.

Wee Willie Winkie. She had called him that when he was
born.

Wee Willie Winkie runs through the town,
Upstairs and downstairs in his nightgown ...

Magnificent. Shattering. Life-affirming.

Sleeping now down the hall. A gift.

She washed her face and brushed her teeth and—carrying
Griff's dampened shoes—went back into the bedroom to dress.

Look at him. I could bring in an orchestra and choir, we
could all shout the Hallelujah Chorus *and he still wouldn't*
move a muscle. Not even an eyelid. Oh, my dear one, lying
there at daybreak after a night of God-knows-what—sinfully
beautiful—beautifully sinful ...

The perfect scenario.

What do they call it?

The seven-year itch?

Yes. Except it's been eight years—almost nine ...

And you'd think, from the expression on his face, he'd just
seen the Mona Lisa.

In order to get at her own underwear, Jane had to remove
Griff's clothes from the chair, where he had thrown them in
the dark.

There was a scent. Something new. Cologne. But where? On
what?

Griffin wore only one cologne. One and one only. He had
worn it all his adult life. Guerlain's Vetiver. This was not it.

She glanced at the bed and then down at the clothes. His
shorts were on the top. She lifted them to her nose.

Jesus Christ! she almost said aloud. *They're soaked in it!*
His shorts!

Clean, however, she could not help noting. Every stitch he wore was always impeccable.

Who the hell had been wearing them?

Don't ask.

She threw them aside.

But still—it was a mystery.

A man's cologne.

So.

The plot thickens ...

She slid into her shoes and made for the door.

Who does write your dialogue, kiddo? Last night wasn't even dark and stormy, but two bits, whenever you tell this story—and you will—that's how you'll describe it—unless you pull your poor old fractious mind into focus. Rejoice, at least, that he's here. The sun is shining. There's a brave new world ...

Oh, shut up.

Will and Mercy were already in the kitchen.

"I didn't hear you arrive," Jane said to Mercy.

"Came in like a mouse when I saw how Griff had parked his car. Must have been a party somewhere. You go, too?"

"No," Jane said, without elaboration.

She kissed Will's forehead and caressed the back of his neck.

"Where's Rudyard?"

"Garden."

Jane glanced through the screen door at the Lexus. Curiously angled—as if Griff had wanted to drive across Mrs Arnprior's lawn and had stopped himself just in time.

"I'm off to the theatre all day. I'll eat in the Green Room."

"Okay."

Jane went into the dining-room and surreptitiously placed a bottle of Merlot in her work-bag. She already carried a corkscrew in her purse, against emergencies. The only problem with the Green Room was that you could not buy alcohol of any kind, not even beer. Probably a good policy.

While she stashed the wine, she went on talking to Mercy.

"Might as well take advantage of my absence and give the studio a whizz. It hasn't been dusted or vacuumed in ages."

" 'Cause you're always in there locked up, that's why. A person can't get near it."

"Well, you can today."

Jane returned to the kitchen, rummaged in the fridge for yoghurt and juice and sat down at the table.

"Don't even think of trying to get Griff out of bed," she said. "He doesn't have a matinee today and won't need to go to the theatre till 7:00. You might want to treat him kindly. He was out till quite late."

"Sure," said Mercy.

"He came home just before 6:00," said Will. "I saw him on the lawn."

Mercy looked away.

Jane said: "well, well. Late as that. I didn't hear a thing."

I'll bet, Mercy thought. *You didn't sleep a wink yourself, from the look of you.*

Fifteen minutes later, Jane grabbed her work-bag, her purse and her car keys and gave Will and Mercy a farewell kiss.

"I'm off," she said. "Be good." And then: "oh, look. Here's Ruddy. 'Morning, Dog. Bye, y'all."

The screen door slammed.

"Well," said Mercy, rising to put Rudyard's kibble in his dish, "she seems to be in happy spirits."

Will did not reply. While he ate his Frosted Flakes, he kicked the rungs of his chair with his heels and thought about Long John Silver. *Fifteen men on a dead man's chest — yo-ho-ho and a bottle of rum ...*

Rum was spirits. Someone had said so.

He glanced around at Jane's departing car and tried to think of her as being in happy spirits. But he knew she was not. She was pretending.

About half an hour later, Will went upstairs to use the bathroom.

His parents' bedroom door was open.

The curtains—white cotton—were reaching out for his father's form in the bed—as if they wanted to touch him. The breeze from the open window smelled of cut grass.

Rudyard came and stood beside him.

"Don't go in," Will whispered, and held on to the dog's collar. "We're not supposed to wake him."

Rudyard sat down.

In spite of what he had said, Will went and stood at the foot of the bed.

The covers were mussed and scrabbled—the way his own had been that morning.

He's restless ...

Another new word.

Griffin was lying on his side—his face towards the windows. One arm was lying pressed against the headboard, the other was bent out of sight beneath the pillows. The hand Will could see seemed to be pointing upwards. *The ceiling—the sky? I need to use the washroom, please, Miss Dickson ... Or maybe: I have the answer—look at me ...*

All the familiar gestures of a schoolboy—questions and answers—wanting attention. *Me.*

Will moved closer.

Dad ...?

Nothing.

"Me."

Claire sobered and sat back.

Jane had managed to get the best table at The Belfry for lunch—in a private alcove partway up the stairs.

The Belfry was just the right name. *I've seen a lot of people go bats up here,* Claire had once said. It was a small, if not entirely intimate restaurant above The Church—an overly expensive but popular eating place established by the formidable Joseph Mandell in the 1970s. Once both Church and Belfry were up and running, Joe Mandell had gone on to other things. It was called *the way of the world. Would an actor play the same role for life?* he had said.

Popular with pre-theatre audiences, The Church and The Belfry were even more popular with actors after the final curtain. Especially The Belfry, where you could be guaranteed a certain amount of protection from the public gaze.

Jane had asked Claire to lunch only that morning. *If you aren't free—make yourself free.*

Claire had more than happily cancelled a previously arranged date with someone she did not really want to see, and had waited in front of her house on Shrewsbury, wondering what the urgency was all about, but asking no questions. *This was Jane Drop-everything-I-need-you Kincaid.* There was no denying her.

"We'll go in my car," Jane had said. "I have to collect all my crap from the theatre."

Whatever that might mean.

Now, there they sat—Jane somewhat hastily thrown together—Claire, as ever, elegant in shades of mushroom and pearl—*Darkeyes* sunglasses, no jewellery except her wedding and engagement rings, her watch and a silver buckle. Also a silver Dunhill lighter, which she now flashed.

Watching Jane take the first drag on her cigarette, Claire,

having lighted her own, sat back and said: "okay, love. Your hands are shaking. This is serious."

"Yes."

"Drinks?"

"Yellow Label."

"No cocktail?"

"Yellow Label."

Claire attracted the waiter's attention by raising one finger—something Jane could never accomplish.

"Bottle of Wolf Blass Yellow Label. Mrs Kincaid will start it, and we'll finish it with the meal. I'll have a double vodka martini—no ice—squeeze of lime on the side."

Claire removed her sunglasses and laid them open on the table.

Jane undid her napkin and spread it on her lap. A map without demarcation—nowhere to go and nowhere to leave. Just a desert of nothingness. *This is where I live now,* she thought.

Claire rolled the ash from her cigarette into the cut-glass *cendrier*—a word she rather liked, not knowing why. She hoarded words like a pack rat—*putting them in jars,* she had once said. She and Hugh spent two months every year in France, with side trips to Spain and Italy, all of which had to do with their love of imagery, whether it was expressed in the visual arts or in words. *Language is language—who cares about the origin?* Some words in French, Italian, Spanish were infinitely more beautiful, more appropriate and more precise than their counterparts in English. She cherished them. *Ashtray* was so pedestrian; *cendrier* was elegant, persuasive, graceful. *She rolled her ash into the cendrier ... Yes ...*

The drinks arrived.

It seemed to take forever to get the wine opened. The waiter kept fussing over the formalities—most of which Claire thought were pretentious nonsense, anyway.

"Forget all that," Claire said when the waiter offered Jane the extracted cork. "Fill the goddamned glass."

"Yes, madam."

Claire was watching Jane with a good deal of growing concern.

When at last the waiter had departed, she leaned forward, lifted her martini and said: "don't try to speak just yet—have some wine. We have all afternoon."

She gave a smile, somewhat sadly, and reached out for Jane's hand.

"I can't lift the glass," Jane said. She was frozen. The news of Loretta's death had been the last nail. There was nothing—nothing, so it seemed, to be done but concede defeat.

"Yes, you can," Claire said. "Goddammit, *yes, you can.*" She leaned forward even farther. "Do it slowly. Everything's going to be all right. Take your time ..."

She sat back.

Jane eyed the glass.

When at last her fingers reached and grasped its stem, she closed her eyes.

"Got it?"

"Yes."

"I love you, kiddo. Whatever's going on, you've got *me*—and with me, you've got someone standing by forever."

At last, Jane wept.

Claire stood up and went to the bar.

"Could I have two menus, please?"

"Yes, of course, Mrs Highland."

"Thank you."

Returning down the steps, she handed one of the menus to Jane.

"Open it. I thought you might like somewhere to hide," she said. Sitting, she unfolded her linen serviette—*I know we aren't supposed to say* serviette—*but come on, fellas*—napkin *is gross.* "See what I have in my hand?" she said, and held it up. "One double damask serviette. Nice, eh?"

Jane did not respond. She was wiping her eyes with a Kleenex.

"I ever tell you the time Hugh went to Zehrs and carried six of those No Name yellow packages of napkins to the cashier? Told her he was in a hurry—plonked them down and got out his wallet. We had guests—some of his graduate students— and suddenly discovered we had no decent paper napkins. You know, the big ones—'dinner size.' So the cashier looks at him and hesitates and he looks back and says: *is there a problem?* And she says: *well, I just wanted to be certain, sir. Are you sure you want six whole packs of these? Yes,* Hugh says. *Of course I'm sure. We have guests—and we ran out ... But, sir,* says the girl, *I mean—forgive me, but are* all *your guests women? Are all of them ... you know ... having their period?*" Claire shook her head and laughed. "Poor darling, he finally twigged. *Maxi-serviettes* are *not* dinner-sized paper napkins! God! We laughed about that for weeks ..."

Jane smiled vaguely.

"You've told me that before," she said.

Claire shrugged. "At least I got your attention."

They drank.

"Anybody here we know?" Jane asked. "You can see better than I can. My back is to everything."

Claire gave the restaurant a quick glance.

"Only the dreaded Jonathan Crawford. Nobody else I know."

"Don't let on you see him. If he sees us, he'll be over here before you can say *spit.* Not my favourite, by a long shot."

"Not mine, either."

"He seems to have cut Griff off at the pass over those roles he wanted next season—Berowne—Mercutio. Griff's been a mess since he found out. I hardly ever see him. That's one of the problems I want to talk about ... but ..." She drank. "Who's he with?" she asked.

"No one. There's an empty chair. Table for two."

"What's he doing?"

"Sitting there."

"I hope he doesn't twig. I'm afraid I'd say something."

"Don't. Not worth it. Griff will survive. Jonathan Crawford isn't God. He can't last forever."

"I know that—but Griffin doesn't. He's become a cypher. Blank."

"When did you last see him? Griff."

"Oh, Jesus, Claire ..."

"Come on. Hold on. Tell me when."

"Sunday."

"Three days. Well ..."

"And only then as a body, dead in the guest room, fully clothed."

"Bad as that."

"He doesn't want me to know how he feels—that he's afraid—that he doesn't know what to do. It's plain panic, when you come right down to it. He's a panic-stricken child. The truth is, he wants his mother. He wants to crawl in somewhere safe and be told that none of this is happening to him. And I ..."

"You?"

"I can't help him, Cee. I don't know what to do. I've gone through too much of it. I've watched my brothers doing the same thing—and my sister—Loretta ..."

"Yes. I know."

"How they all fell silent, one by one—stopped having lives altogether and ..." she waved a hand, "turned away, like

people in one of those abstract landscapes called *Infinity*—
with nothing in it but distance—turned away and walked off
into nowhere. And that's what Griff is doing right now. He's
... disappearing. Disappearing over the horizon and I can't get
him back—I can't ... I can't entice him ... I can't tempt him. I
sure as hell won't *ask* him and ... I can't ... I can't ... I just don't
know what to do. I mean, there's Will, for God's sake—there's
Will and me and ... he's leaving us ... all because he can't ... all
because he can't ... I don't know."

"All because he can't grow up," Claire said.

"That's a cruel thing to say."

"Who cares if it's cruel. It's still the truth. He needs a good
slap—a whack—a puck in the face. We *all* fail, for Christ's
sake. Jesus Christ, it took me eleven years to achieve tenure.
Eleven years! Eleven—to become a full professor. So he's
thirty years old and isn't staring down at the rest of us from
the starry heights. It'll do him good."

"You're wrong about that."

"No, I'm not, goddammit. No—I am not."

"I only mean Griff suffers from vertigo." Jane gave a sly
smile.

Claire took only two seconds before she roared.

"Bravo, kiddo. Brav-fucking-o! Good for you."

She poured more wine into Jane's glass.

"Thanks for being here."

"It's my job. Isn't there a song that tells you *that's what
friends are for?*"

"If you start singing that, I'll cry again."

"I promise not to sing."

Claire lighted a second cigarette and, inadvertently looking
up, trying to avoid her own smoke, she saw that Jonathan was
no longer alone.

Jane was watching her.

"Is something wrong?" she asked.

"No," said Claire too quickly. "No. Of course not. Just a bit of something in my eye."

If only ... she was thinking. *If only I hadn't seen that.*

"Maybe we should order."

"I haven't even looked ..."

"Then read, my darling. Read all about it. I don't know about you—but me—I'm starving."

They both bent over their menus.

What Claire had seen was Griffin, all in white, looking as he never had before in her experience of him—boylike, not *boyish*—childlike, not coy. Defenceless. *Pristine—as if he's never been laid.* There he was—Griffin Kincaid—like a model in *Gentleman's Quarterly*, walking along the catwalk, looking only at Jonathan Crawford, who rose to greet him, kissing him on either cheek. And Griffin returned the kisses.

How very French of them, she thought. *How very ... French.*

"When will it be announced?"

"Next week. But Robert has to announce it."

"Of course."

"You satisfied?"

"More than."

"And to eat?"

"Can I pay?"

"No."

"Then I don't know."

Smiles.

"I really did think it wasn't going to happen."

"There you are, then. All settled."

"And all agreed? No arguments?"

"None. They were delighted. It was what they'd wanted all

along. Robert is especially pleased. He thinks you have a lot of promise ..." This was said with deliberate ambiguity.

"You're a crafty bugger."

"I'm not a bugger. As you well know. I have other predilections."

"So I've noticed."

"Don't get cheeky."

"It was just a comment. I hope you noticed I was smiling."

"Yes. But then, you always smile when it's expected of you. One of your better qualities."

Shrug.

"Don't shrug. It's unbecoming. What are you staring at?"

"My wife. She's sitting in the alcove. I can see her back."

"Yes. I saw them come in. Her professor friend waltzed up to the bar and collected two menus. Didn't even see me—by all appearances. Don't like—don't care for the professor friend. Typical academic. A know-it-all."

Griffin managed not to comment on the subject of know-it-alls.

Jonathan tapped his menu.

"You made up your mind, yet?"

"Oh, yes."

"You have begun to smile too often. I meant: do you know what you're going to eat?"

"Yes."

"Well, now. *That* was an interesting smile. One I've never seen before. You must recover its motivation when you come to play Mercutio. He was—if ever there was—a hungry man."

"Indeed."

"Just remember his fate."

"I do. I will."

"I should hope. It was by no means pleasant."

"No." And then: "I think I'll have the steak."

"I might have guessed as much. And rare, no doubt—with blood on the side."

This got no response.

"Are you happy?"

"Yes."

"Do you miss her?"

"Of course."

"Of course. But you'll get over it. It takes time—but success is nothing, if there hasn't been a sacrifice."

"If you say so."

"I know so. What you are facing, now, is a fire I passed through long, long ago—almost twenty years, to be exact. When I left Anne. I thought I was going to die of it. But here I am. You have to remember—the price of all realized ambition is pain."

"So I understand."

"Don't make me laugh. How curious you are. As if you hadn't known it all along. You'd kill your dog, if not your mother, for success. That, too, is one of your better qualities. If you aren't prepared to kill, you have no business aspiring to success. Not on the scale you hope for. If I hadn't seen that in you, I wouldn't have bothered with you. It's in your eyes. It's in the set of your lips. It's in the way you wore rugby shorts to rehearsals so we could all see your legs. And not just shorts— but red ones. *Red.* Also in your seemingly casual habit of greeting visitors naked in your dressing-room. Not an unusual thing for actors with good bodies. I'm sure you can't imagine you're the only one who does it. I've seen dozens—Broadway, West End, Paris—with nothing but an immodest hand towel in the lap, like you—and sometimes not even that. Don't be alarmed at my saying this. I happen to think it's healthy in some cases. If you want to *be there*—be there entirely. If the killer instinct wasn't of such high value to an artist, it would be

obscene. We all know that. It's why we resent the great ones—
it's why we detest their success—because we know that unless
we *go and do likewise*, we will never have what they have and
we want. What we crave. What we *crave* and must have. That
goes a great way on from merely wanting. It's a form of star-
vation. It's Scarlett O'Hara standing in a field of radishes, raising her fist at heaven, choking on her own vomit. The very
image of human deprivation ... Yes?"

"Yes."

"Don't whisper. Speak up. Never apologize for what you
want. So, tell me. Tell me what she says at that point."

"She says ..."

"Look at me. Don't look away. Look at *me* and tell me what
she says."

There was a pause—perhaps of fifteen seconds.

"Yes?"

"She says: *as God is my witness, I will never be hungry
again.*"

Far away, Jane raised her glass to her lips.

"Well said. And well remembered. I wonder why ..." This,
with a smile. "By the way, speaking of ambition, I'm
delighted to be able to tell you that Jacob, my son, has left for
Peru, where he will spend what remains of the summer
inspecting the Inca ruins at Machu Picchu. He's going to be
an archaeologist—and a good one, I think. Highest marks
you can imagine, barring a hundred. This is what they all
have to do before their final year—go off anywhere in the
world and bring home a personal report of a famous ruin. I'm
very proud of him."

"You should be."

The waiter came and hovered.

"Gentlemen. Have you decided?"

"Yes. We will both have the filet mignon. Rare."

* * *

Off at the other end of the dining-room—three steps down—
Jane finished one glass of wine and poured another. Claire had
put her *Darkeyes* back on. She was watching every move the
others made—the tilt of their heads—the intensity of their
conversation—the way the early afternoon light approached
them as if waiting for Jonathan's permission to settle on their
shoulders and the way both pairs of hands were clearly avoid-
ing contact. After all, the world was watching—*and there are
some things we do not do in public.* In spite of the kiss. *What
was that called? The French way of greeting ... beez ... bisou?*
Jane and Claire had ordered the lobster salad, which now
arrived. Jane was not really hungry, but she forced herself to
eat. *Be a good girl ... every bite.* However good it was, she
thanked God for the wine to wash it down with.

"I hope you don't mind," she said. "I know you're supposed
to drink white with fish and seafood, but I find it somehow
insipid at lunch. White is for evening aperitifs. I like it then,
because you can knock it back without feeling the effect too
much. But at noon, give me red."

She drank.

Claire pushed at her sunglasses and tried not to stare either
at Jane or at Jonathan and Griff. She busied herself with lemon
squeezes and pepper. *Never put salt on seafood. You might as
well empty a salt mine into the ocean, for all the effect it would
have.* She glanced at Jane. *Say something.*

"You gone mute?" she said.

Jane looked up as if she had been disturbed in the middle of
a trance.

"No," she said. "Sorry. I was thinking about Zoë Walker."

"Oh, yes. Her." Claire set the pepper mill aside and picked
up her fork.

"I think she's the one," said Jane.

"The one?"

"Yes. With Griff. I think they're having an affair—a fling—whatever you want to call it."

"What makes you think it's her?"

"Because she's available. Because she's ambitious. Because she knows she can."

"Can?"

"Have Griffin. I've watched her. I think she wants to impress Jonathan and thinks she can do it by proving she can seduce him ..."

"Griff?"

"Of course, Griff. Who'd want Jonathan?"

Claire looked away. "Isn't she supposed to be involved with what's-his-face?"

"Richard Harms? She certainly was—but she isn't going to get him—and she knows it."

"Heavily married?"

"Very."

"But not happily. That's what I've heard. Apparently she hates theatre. The wife."

"I've never met her," Jane said. "But how odd of her, if you're right, to marry an actor."

For a moment, they ate in silence.

Claire thought: *she really doesn't seem to understand how ordinary all of this is. There she sits, talking about the fruits of ambition as demonstrated by Zoë Walker, and she hasn't even bothered to understand the extent of her own husband's ambition.*

Some people will stop at nothing, she wanted to yell. *Griff is sleeping with another man! Turn around and look!*

Instead, she said: "do you have any memory at all of the first man you slept with—had sex with?"

"Yes."

"What was his name?"

"Andrew Jackson."

"Is that some kind of joke?"

"No. His name was Andrew Jackson. Named for a hero."

"And was he?"

"What?"

"A hero."

Jane looked up at the flowers on the windowsill behind Claire. *White. Something white.*

"No," she said. "Nice enough at a distance—up close, no hero. Just another batterer."

"That's an interesting description."

"It's what he was. He pounded into me one afternoon, in a field where he'd taken me to look for wildflowers. He might as well have used a pneumatic drill. He's a famous botanist now. Do you believe it? Teaches at Sandford. Drills all the girls."

Jane began to eat again, like a nervous rabbit somewhere out in the open.

Claire tried to make a scene of it. *Man with pneumatic drill, looking for wildflowers.*

"How old were you?"

"Thirteen."

"Jesus."

"I wanted it," Jane said without inflection. "I wanted to get it over with to spite my mother."

Claire pushed her plate aside.

Jane looked at her. "I thought you were dying of hunger."

"I was. But I recovered."

The waiter came and poured more wine. Their glasses were not empty. This infuriated Claire, who hated any kind of officious behaviour. *Next thing you know, he'll ask us if we want dessert—and Jane isn't finished ...*

Hover—hover—picking the bread crumbs off his sleeve ...

Fuck off.

She did not say this—but somehow, he heard it. Or appeared to. He left.

"Why did you ask about the first time I had sex?"

Griff and Jonathan.

"Mind if I smoke?"

"Of course not."

Claire took out a Matinee Extra Light and the silver Dunhill.

"I wanted to know if you could remember," she said, "what it felt like to be a virgin."

"Oh, well. The answer is yes and no."

"Unh-hunh."

"I never thought about being a virgin. I only thought about being pure. Church stuff. Catholic stuff. The only virgin I'd ever heard of was the Virgin Mary—and how's a kid supposed to understand that?"

"I did."

"Yes. But then, you're you. I was me. It meant nothing . So ..." Jane waved her fork. "I wanted what I didn't know. I wanted to ... fill the gap between me and the rest of the world. The *rest-of-the-world* being entirely made up of silent, complacent, confident others who called themselves *grown-ups*—adults. What did they know—what was it they knew that I didn't know—that no one would tell me? I didn't even know it was sex. I just thought it must have something to do with ... I don't know ... with something you were incomplete without." She ate again.

Claire watched her, toying with her own glass, smoking her cigarette, silent.

Then Jane said: "it's true, you know. A person isn't whole until there's another person. After Andrew Jackson, who was fourteen, I guess—fifteen—and out to prove or find his manhood, so-called. There was another boy I really liked. His name was Troy. An athlete. Tennis. But it scared me. Would he be like Andrew Jackson—just another pile-driver? In my childish—in my girlish way, I guess I sort of fell in love with him. But ..."

She laid down her knife and fork.

"... nothing ever happened ..."

She fell into space.

"Jane?"

Jane reached over across the tablecloth and took Claire's hand. Claire's rings cut almost through her skin, but she did not pull away.

"Oh, God. Why am I dumping all this on you? I'm sorry."

Jane withdrew her hand and lifted her napkin—her serviette—to her eyes.

"Tell me. Say it."

Jane looked away. *Pretend it all happened in the distant past ...*

"He came up to see me. All the way from Plantation—all the way from Louisiana. He wanted to ... He wanted to reintroduce himself." She smiled. "He'd changed, of course. So had I. No more tennis for him—no more passion for me. Not for him, anyway. And ..." Nothing.

"Yes?"

Space. The comfort of space. Of being nowhere. Only being—and all that space. Jane thought of telling Claire what had happened—but she could not. She lied.

"At long last, he wanted me," she said, still smiling, "but I turned him down. *I'm married, now,* I said, *to a man I love. But I thank you for your solicitations and your attentions ...* something like that. Words of a real lady, bred, born and raised in Plantation, L'isiana, same as he was."

Claire waited. She knew the story was not over. She drank—

and watched and waited. *Jane Aura Lee is really remarkably beautiful,* she thought. *If sad. But I guess it's partly the sadness that makes her so. Beautiful. Like a Pre-Raphaelite drawing— like a photograph of Virginia Woolf when young. Like the Lady of Shallot, who only wants to see the world, but dares not look out her window. What was the rest of it?* she wondered. *What had not yet been said?*

"He died."

"I'm sorry."

"Don't be. I didn't much care for him any more." When they had finished, Claire could see that Jonathan and Griff were still there. She had already decided what to do if that were the case. She would make sure she and Jane made their exit down the front stairs.

Jane paid. *It's my lunch.*

Claire accepted, said thank you, stood up and took Jane's arm.

"We'll have to go this way. I've got to speak to Marjorie about a reservation."

Jane thought Claire's grip on her arm was a little excessive, but ignored it. She did not turn around. She saw nothing.

Jonathan watched their exit. In Jonathan's lexicon, no one ever *arrived* or *departed*—they always *entered* and made an *exit. Well, well, well ... here's to the ladies who lunch—aren't they too much ...?*

He turned to Griffin.

"What are you doing this afternoon? Anything significant?"

Griff pushed his empty plate aside and absently dipped a finger in his wine.

Raising the finger to his lips, he said: "I don't know. It may be up to you."

Jonathan smiled.

The boy is learning.

Then he said: "you'd better put that finger in your mouth before the wine falls onto your white lapel."

Griffin did so.

"Good for you," said Jonathan. "There's nothing more unforgiving than red wine."

Then he called for the bill.

On George Street, making for Claire's house, Jane saw a Bell Canada van.

Slowing down, she looked to see who it was.

"I have to go to the bathroom," Claire said. "Do you think you could speed things up?"

"Sure."

It was him.

The profile was unmistakable.

He was standing at the rear, getting out or putting away a spade.

Jane's stomach turned over.

"You okay?"

"Yeah, fine."

"You look funny."

"So? That's unusual?"

Claire did not reply. The expression on Jane's face had, indeed, been odd. As if she had seen a ghost.

On Shrewsbury, letting Claire out, Jane said: "thanks for your ears. I'll stay in touch."

"You off to the theatre?"

"Yes. To get all my stuff and take it home. End of the season for me. *Richard* opens tomorrow and that was my last job. I don't mind. It's been a long, hard slog. Now it's over. I'll have more time for Will."

"I hope you're going to give yourself a break. Lay off the

worry-wart stuff. Believe me ..." Claire leaned in through the window and gave Jane's cheek a kiss. "You've nothing to fear."

"*Except fear itself*. I know."

Jane smiled.

Claire waved and departed.

Jane pulled away from the curb and started towards the end of the street, where she turned, went around the block and made for George Street.

He was still there.

"Hello."

"Hello."

"Do you remember me? You came to fix our phone line earlier in the month."

"Sure. On Cambria."

"That's right."

She smiled.

How many times had she rehearsed this meeting—carefully smoothing away every trace of eagerness—damping down every trace of desire—forcing herself to erase every trace of offensive interest? Nothing must show but her professional façade: *cool lady artist enquires about possible availability of someone who would be willing to ...*

"You never did tell me your name," she said, shading her eyes from the sun.

"No. I don't unless people ask, Mrs Kincaid."

Mrs Kincaid ...

Jane took a deep breath.

"So?" she said. And smiled again. "What is it? Your name ..."

"Milos Saworski."

"Milos Saworski." She put out her hand. "How do you do?"

"Fine, thanks."

His touch was still the same—strangely intimate, as though they had known each other for years.

"Can I help you?" he said.

"Well ..." Jane looked away and withdrew her hand. "As a matter of fact, yes. You see, I'm an artist. I work for the Festival."

"Yes. And your husband's an actor."

"That's right. So you see ... my job at the theatre is over for this season and I ..."

He began to wrap some wiring around his arm, bending his elbow and making a frame, sailor fashion.

"I have time now to go back to what I really want to do—which is paint and draw. There's never time for that sort of thing during the season, and so ... whenever it's over, every year, I get a chance to hone my talent."

She smiled and waved her hand as if her talent was inconsequential.

"Hone?"

"Perfect. You know. Bring myself up to scratch. You get rusty when you can't practise."

"Sure."

"So. Well. I ..."

She looked away from him and plunged.

"I wouldn't embarrass you—or anyone—for the world. But you must be aware that you have ... that you're ... that you have a fine body and I think you would make an excellent model."

She shaded her eyes again and watched to see how he had reacted.

Nothing.

He finished winding the wire, tied it with its own end and threw it into the back of the van.

"You mean naked?"

"Well—yes."

He took a pack of cigarettes from his breast pocket and matches from his jeans and lighted his smoke before he spoke again.

"I've never done that," he said.

Jane refrained from saying: *there's always a first time for everything.* She tried not to look too expectant.

Milos was gazing away down the street, as if weighing his answer.

Jane said: "of course, I will pay you. It's a professional job, after all."

"Yes."

"What is it that worries you, Mister Saworski? I hope you understand that there's nothing personal in this. I just need a model ..."

"Yes. Yes. I understand."

He knew she was lying. But he liked her.

"I would not want my wife to know."

"Why should she?"

He's married.

"She would not approve."

"I see."

"She is religious."

"Oh. Yes. Well. I understand. But ..."

"How often? When?"

"I don't know. In a way, that's up to you. I mean—you have a job. For me, it can be anytime."

"May I phone you?"

"But of course."

Jane got a card from her purse and handed it to him.

"The fax number is the same," she said. Then she laughed and said: "not that you're going to fax me."

"No."

He put the card in his shirt pocket.

"And so—I shall wait to hear from you."

"Yes."

"Is it ... is it likely you might say yes?"

"Oh, yes. I will do it. But I need to work out when."

Jane smiled—trying to show no more than professional pleasure and said: "otherwise I'd have had to find someone else."

Milos looked at her with remarkable candour.

"Be not worried," he said in his curiously formal way. "I would not want to put you to any trouble."

At last, he smiled. A child's smile. Someone had offered him a candy.

"Goodbye, then." Jane stepped forward.

"Yes. Goodbye, then. I will phone."

"Thank you."

They shook hands again. But he was already withdrawing into his other world and it was merely a handshake.

Jane went back to her car.

She felt dizzy.

Once inside and behind the wheel, she spoke inadvertently aloud.

"I did it," she said. "I did it."

arrivals
and departures

Disgraces to keep hidden from the world
Where rivals, envying his energy and brains
And with rattling skeletons of their own,

Would see in him the villain of this household,
Whose bull-voice scared a sensitive young child,
Whose coldness drove a doting parent mad.

W.H. Auden
A Household

1

Thursday, July 23, 1998

Stratford Beacon-Herald

A second killing has taken place in Stratford since the beginning of the month. On Sunday, July 12, the body of Margaret Miller was found by a neighbour. She had been raped and strangled. Her killer has not yet been found, though some of the evidence indicates her attacker was no stranger to our town. Clearly, he had a grasp not only of local geography, but of local custom—possibly even to the degree that he knew not only Mrs Miller's habits but those of her neighbours as well.

Yesterday morning, the body of Lenore Archer, a well-known Stratford hairdresser, was discovered in her home at 13 Blake Street by a visiting relative. She, too, had been raped and strangled.

Ms Archer was 38 years old, single and had lived in Stratford all her life but for a three-year period in the 1970s, when she studied professional hairdressing and make-up in Toronto.

The similarity between Ms Archer's murder and that of Margaret Miller has not been lost on the authorities. While exercising discretion in his statement to the press and television cameras at two o'clock yesterday afternoon, Police Chief Arnold Craig cautioned the public to "lock all doors at night and to keep an eye out for strangers in the area and others whose activities after dark are questionable." While advising that there is no immediate cause for alarm, only for caution, at the same time Craig stated: "it would be irresponsible of me in my duties as your Chief not to mention the possibility of a single killer being on the loose. Both Ms Archer and Mrs Miller met remarkably similar deaths under remarkably identical circumstances. A third as yet unsolved killing took place in Kitchener in June. We do not consider this to be coincidental. As a consequence, our forces are conducting a joint investigation."

When questioned by reporters, Chief Craig also said that he would "regret anyone casting unnecessary suspicion on their neighbours for negligible reasons such as loud parties, public drunkenness and late-night dog-walking. Such incidents, while perhaps to some degree could be viewed with suspicion, are not overly serious and must not be confused with violent behaviour, trespassing and loitering."

Ms Archer's aunt Mildred Cummings, who discovered the body, has said that Ms Archer's mother, who is Mrs Cummings's sister, is her only living relative besides herself. Mrs Archer, over 20 years a widow, lives in Kitchener. Funeral plans will be announced as soon as the police are satisfied that all the available evidence has been accounted for and the results of the autopsy are known.

Many of Ms Archer's friends and clients have already expressed dismay and regret concerning her violent demise. "She was an angel of consideration," said Mrs Violet Turner of Bridget Street, a longtime neighbour. "Such a sweet, dear woman—always such a pleasure to be with," said Allison Paget, a client. "And so talented."

It is expected that Mary Beth Anderson, Ms Archer's business partner, will continue servicing those customers who "expect and receive only the best of care at Cuts, Curls and

Colours," Ms Archer's salon on Erie Street. Ms Anderson, who declined to be photographed, expressed her regard for her late partner by stating that, while C.C.C., as it is known far and wide, will remain in business, it will be closed until a week from today, which will be July 30.

At 10:30 in the evening of the day following Lenore Archer's murder, Luke Quinlan unexpectedly appeared at Mercy Bowman's side door.

Mercy was opening a can of cat food in the kitchen, with all four cats in attendance.

The door was open, the inner screen door closed.

Standing on the stoop, lit by an unshaded overhead bulb, the figure was not immediately indentifiable.

"It's me, Mercy. Luke. Sorry to disturb you."

"No problem. Come on in."

"I hope you don't mind. I need to talk."

"Couldn't be more pleased. Haven't seen you for weeks. Just give me time to feed the mob."

She dished out the contents of the can, divided in four parts, onto the cats' plates—each plate with its own painted name: Rags, Lily, Gaby, Roly—and set them on the floor in their usual order.

"You hungry, hon?"

Why did I call him hon?

"No thanks."

He seemed restless, moving through the room to throw his jacket on a chair, take his cigarettes and lighter from a pocket, sit down, stand up and sit down again.

"Drink, then?"

"Sure. Anything."

Mercy scrubbed out the empty can with a long-handled brush, washing it clean beneath a running tap, crushing it, dropping its ragged lid inside and finally putting it into the blue recycling box by the back porch door.

"There. Always crush a can," she said. "One of my cats once stuck his head inside a can and would've died if I hadn't been there to pull it off. Never want to see that again."

She dried her hands.

"Beer? Wine? What?" she asked.

"A beer is always welcome."

"Help yourself. It's in the fridge. I know you don't like a glass. When you're ready, go to the back porch and I'll be there in a minute. Just going to open some wine."

Luke got two bottles of Sleeman out of the fridge and retreated. *Does she drink Sleeman herself—or ...*

Mercy opened a relatively cheap Chianti, found a glass, collected her own cigarettes and put them all on a small tray with two clean ashtrays.

Before going out to join Luke, she closed the side door and pulled the screen door open, hooking it to a towel rack under a smiling photograph of Tom. *First thing I see, coming in and last thing I see going out. My dear one ...* She kissed her fingertips and pressed them against Tom's smile. Then she locked the door. Now, the cats could come and go through the cat-flap and no one unwanted could get in. She hadn't always done this, but ever since the death of Maggie Miller, she had. *And now ...*

Don't think about it. Don't.

She took up the tray and went to the porch, where she toed off her shoes by the heel, set the tray on its table and sat back on the chaise.

"Lo-n-g day," she said—and poured herself a glass of Chianti. "You comfortable there?"

"Sure. Thanks."

Luke was sitting in profile, looking through the screen into the backyard.

Mercy drank and sighed.

"O merciful god of wine ..." she said, smiling and raising her glass to the heavens, "... whatever your name may be."

"Bacchus."

"Oh, yeah. I knew I'd heard it somewhere. Maybe school."

"God of wine and revelry."

"Just the wine, thanks all the same. I'm a bit too tired for revelry."

"Yeah. Me, too."

She lighted a cigarette. Luke was already smoking.

"So. You seem a bit upset, friend."

"I am."

"And ..."

"It's Runner. Gone now about three weeks. Not a word. Not a sign. Then today ..."

"Yes?"

"When I got home from work, round about 6:30, there was a message on my machine ..."

"From Runner?"

"Him? Never. He wouldn't have anything to do with any of that stuff. Answering machines—cellphones—he didn't trust them. No—it was someone else. Someone, I guess, who didn't know my cell number. Only my home number. It's in the book."

"Oh, yes. Of course. And ...?"

For a moment, Luke stared off to one side, drank beer, smoked and finally sat forward. Mercy watched him in the spill of light from the Saworskis' well-lit windows and side door. Agnewska could not bear even the thought of darkness, apparently. Every light in the house was switched on at sundown and not switched off until dawn.

Luke's face was haggard—old, almost sad. His jaw was clenched. His hair looked greyer than it really was.

She waited.

Let him do this in his own time. Whatever it is ...

"The message was from a stranger. A guy. I kind of think I know who it was—but if I do, it's someone I hardly ever see. I think maybe a dealer."

"Right."

"Well, you know Runner and his drug situation ..."

"Only what you've told me."

"On again—off again—every time longer, every time worse than the time before."

Mercy thought of her daughter Melanie, sighed and said: "yeah."

"So ... this guy said: *I know you're Runner's brother—and I know he's gone off the rails.* He said he didn't even know if I cared, but he said he'd seen Runner yesterday. Wouldn't say where, of course—not exactly—but he said: *I thought you might want to know he's in town and, if you do care, I'd suggest you look for him. He's in trouble, man. I mean—deep-shit trouble. Sorry I can't tell you more.* I memorized every word. Listened to it twelve—fifteen times."

"And ...?"

"And nothing. The guy hung up. No name—nothing. Just *deep-shit trouble* and rang off."

After a moment, Luke looked down at the bottle and cigarette in his hand and said: "I'm scared, Mercy. I'm scared. I mean ..." He looked stricken. "What was in today's paper—what if ..."

"Don't," said Mercy. "Don't say it. Don't even think it. It wasn't him."

"You don't understand," Luke said. "You don't understand. Before he left town, he'd been dating Lenore Archer for a whole week. For Runner, that's a record. Most of his women don't last a day, let alone a whole week. He never knew how to make or to keep them happy. In a funny way, he thought of women as *the enemy*. Maybe because all his early teachers were women. He was a tough kid to convince he wasn't stupid. At school they treated him as if he was, apparently. But he wasn't stupid—he was just afraid of what other people would think if he got things wrong—so he never offered any answers. He was a sad little boy, so my dad said. Little, like me. Small and sad. I even knew he was sad way back when I was first aware of him—when I was a kid and he was fourteen, fifteen years old. He always wanted to get people's approval, but didn't know how to get it. It was as if he thought he had to have permission to live."

Mercy listened to all this without comment.

Rags came and rubbed against Luke's shins. Then he sat down and started an elaborate washing process—chops, ears, paws, breastbone—all the feathery bits—the identity parts. Every cat's ruff—every cat's whiskers—every cat's ears are unique in the way they combine to make up its image. Having watched them for so long, Mercy had decided people have a lot to learn from the feline sense of self-presentation. A cat never lacks grace—it never lacks dignity. It displays a sense of self that, somehow, humans have either forgotten or never known. *All you have is what you are. All you are is what you were given. All you were given is the certainty of self.*

Luke leaned back at last, twisted the cap off the second bottle of Sleeman and drank.

"This man—this dealer—this person—whatever," Mercy said, "what makes you think you know him?"

"The voice. Kind of broken. Kind of rough, kind of mean. One of those *gonna getcha* voices you only hear after dark. What you might call a *midnight voice.*"

"Yes." Then Mercy said: "funny, isn't it—how voices like that only belong to men. I never heard a woman's voice like that—though a woman can put the fear of God in a person when she wants to. But it doesn't ... it doesn't ... what ...?"

"Kill," said Luke. He smiled ruefully. "*It can chill—but it ain't gonna kill.*"

They both chuckled.

"You think you've met him?" Mercy asked.

"Maybe. Could be. One of those weekend sidewalk types—only around on Fridays and Saturdays, when the cops are busy overseeing the heavy traffic. He runs something out of Detroit/Windsor, I think. More than pot. Far more, all the way up to crack."

"All the way down, you mean."

"Yeah, well ... He's some kind of big shot and well protected."

"What does that mean?"

"Oh—you know—knows somebody inside the law—has a few strong-arms—that kind of thing."

"Guns?"

"Sure. Some. But wouldn't carry one himself. Doesn't want to be caught with a P.O.F."

"What's that?"

"Possession of Firearms. So he just keeps someone off to the side somewhere, with eyes—and maybe more."

"It sounds like a bad movie."

"Well ... I guess. But they're not all bad." He grinned and hoisted the Sleeman. "I thought *Pulp Fiction* was terrific. Didn't you? Dealers, druggies and all."

Mercy gave a light laugh. "Oh, sure. I'm a sucker for John Travolta, I guess. Bruce Willis. Sometimes. I liked her, too. What's-'er-name."

"Uma Thurman."

"Yes." Another light laugh. "What kind of name is that?"

"German, maybe. Scandinavian. She's blonde."

"With help."

"They all get help. They're movie stars."

"Anyway," Mercy went on, "I thought it was ... You couldn't avoid admiring the way it was done—and the way the people were. It was all so ... all *too* believable. But, God, I can't stomach some of that violence. I mean—do people really do those things—kill like that—as if there was no one there but a store-window dummy?"

"Try Lenore Archer."

Mercy looked down into her empty glass.

"Yeah," she said in a whisper. "Sure. Try right here in town."

She filled the glass.

The words of the *Beacon-Herald* report—*a second killing has taken place in Stratford*—hung unspoken in the air.

Rags jumped up and lay against Mercy's thigh. She stroked the back of his neck until he began to purr. Then she stopped.

"What are you going to do?"

"I'm going to look for him."

"Jesus, Luke. Don't. Let him come to you. The others ..."

"The others are there, Merce. They aren't going to go away just because *I'm* on the street."

An owl spoke.

"Must be a lot of owls this year," Luke said. "I have one, too. Sits out nights on the roof. In the morning, those little round pellets they throw up—all the things they can't digest—feathers and mouse tails—teeth—claws—bones—lying on the lawn. I dig them into the flower beds."

"Why did you tell me that?"

"Because it's what I do. Bury things I don't want to see or know about."

"I'm sorry there's so much trouble in your life. I am. I sometimes wonder how you manage—all that time you were alone with Jesse and ... seems to me you're always alone, period. But you do. Manage. There you are. I admire you, Luke. A person could take lessons ..."

"No. Don't say that. To begin with, you haven't done badly yourself in that department. Everything you lost. Everything— everyone. Tom—your daughter—all that. But there *you* are."

"I have to be."

"Exactly. You have to be. So do I. God knows what would happen if we weren't here."

Yes.

"Look," he said—not looking at her. "Could I sleep here tonight? I mean—on the sofa. Even on the chaise, there. I ... I just don't ... I mean I can't ..."

"Go home?"

"Yes." Barely audible.

"I know it isn't fear," said Mercy gently. "But what is it? That he may come and you wouldn't know what to do?"

"Partly. And ..."

"Yes? Partly?"

"Partly that he might not come alone. And ..."

Mercy waited. She laid her fingers on the old cat's back. *Anything can be survived,* she thought. *Anything but being entirely alone—anything but being abandoned. Unless you find somebody—an open door somewhere—when every other hope is gone. All hope of anything turning out for the best.*

At last, Luke said: "I'm afraid he's going to tell me what he's done. And I don't—I can't bear to hear it."

Mercy said: "of course you can stay. The sofa's taken by the cats—and I lock the door between the house and the porch. So—you can sleep upstairs with me."

Then she smiled. "Don't worry," she said. "I have no designs. I'm beyond all that."

2

"So. What am I supposed to think? *We had a great love affair? We had a child—we took off into the wild blue yonder and headed out for that blue horizon we both used to sing about? And now we've crashed?* Is that it? Is that it? Done? Finished? Over with?"

"What makes you think it's over?"

"I haven't seen you in one whole week. *One whole week.* Not that I'm asking. Why would I ask? You'd only lie."

They were in the kitchen. Body sweat and sweating glasses—ceiling fans and broken promises—not to say broken lives. It was all in place. Every trace and every heartbeat. Eyes that will not lock. Hands that will not reach. Even the chairs refused to approach the table.

"Are you living somewhere else?"

"You know I come back. Most nights *I come back.* You're always pissed—so I ..."

"I am never pissed."

Finger-tapping. The shrug that said, without grace or pardon: *okay—you're never pissed ...*

"Something sure as hell knocks you out," he said.

"It's called *worry.* It's called *concern. Someone* has to do it, and I haven't noticed any offers from across the table."

Silence. Then: "you smoke too much."

"So do you. Does it matter any more?"

Nothing.

"Say something, for God's sake. Give me an explanation. *Anything.* Jesus Christ—why would I care who it is. I couldn't care less any more. I only want to know there *is* someone. I only want to know you're not lying in a ditch somewhere ..."

"Why would I be lying in a ditch?"

"There's been a murder, for Christ's sake. A woman was raped and killed. Second time in a month. Don't you ever read? Don't you ever hear what people are saying? Or are you living this secret life of yours somewhere so utterly devoid of other people, there's only one other—only you and *whoever*, while the rest of the world's off turning on its axis without you? Don't you ever see a paper, let alone read it? Witness a headline? Turn on the TV? The radio? Where—where the hell are you? *Where?*"

Griffin drank. And then: "I'm here. Right here. You just don't see me."

"You're goddamned right I don't. You could play *The Invisible Man* all by yourself without an ounce of computer animation. Who needs special effects? Who needs all that technology shit where you're concerned? *Lights! Camera! Action! A-la-ka-zaam!* You're a star! An invisible—ever-absent star."

More lethal martinis were poured.

Jane looked at her watch.

It was after midnight. "When?" she said. "Monday—Tuesday—Wednesday—Thursday—Friday—Saturday—Sunday. When?"

"Who gives a fuck?"

"I do."

"It's Thursday-going-on-Friday."

"Oh, yes. Thursday-going-on-Friday. Tomorrow's your day to play golf again—the way you did when I wanted you at the tech dress for *Richard*. You've come home to collect your clubs, including the goddamned putter I gave you for your birthday—home to get *that*, but not me. Damn you. Though why I call this *home* any more, I'll never know. But before the game—before you parade your *brilliant* Ferdinand in front of the evening audience, you need a comfy bed in which to sleep it off. Yes?"

"Sleep what off?"

"A twelve-day fuck! Or whatever it's been."

No response.

"Just tell me, for God's sake." And then: "*is* it Zoë?"

"No."

So what does a person do with that? What's a person supposed to do with no?

"Who is it, then?"

Again—no response.

"Looking at the floor isn't going to help you."

She even had to smile at this—at his childish inability to confess. *Did you steal that dime from my change purse, Griffy? Did you? Tell Mama.*

When that got said, a child's whole world became the floor, the back of a hand, a knee cap—a sudden interest in open doors and windows.

"Have you got nothing—absolutely nothing to say?"

A du Maurier box—red as only cardboard red can be—a lighter never seen before, initialled, gold and fingered with an unfamiliar, almost sexual caress, induced to flame and held to the tip of a filtered cigarette. And then a sigh—a finger-tap—a glass against the lip—a swallow—a shy, unaccustomed smile and then, with averted eyes: "I got the parts I wanted. Berowne. Mercutio."

Jesus. How am I meant to respond to that?

"Well. Congratulations. Good for you."

She felt ...

How? Suspicious. Leery. Bewildered.

What has he done? How has he got them back?

She looked at him.

Has he found a way to make it happen? Is that the reason for his absence?

And how do you ask a question like that?

You don't.

Then she said: "I'm glad for you. Really. Glad and proud. You deserve them."

"Well ... I'm pleased."

Pleased? After reaching for every suicide weapon in the house—after breaking my heart with tears while you crawl down the stairs and stumble-fumble across the kitchen floor—you're pleased?

"How did you find out? Nothing's been announced yet."

"I was told."

Oh, I see. Told.

"Who by?"

Shrug.

"Is she going to play opposite you again? In *Love's Labour's?*"

"Oh, for Christ's sake!"

"It was only a question."

"And the answer is—I don't know."

She waited. *Please say:* and I don't care. *Please say you don't care ...*

"And the truth is, I don't care."

Some prayers, at least, get answered.

"Do you know what changed their minds? About you, I mean?"

He gave another shrug. Drew another gulp of martini. Sat there, clearly so overtired he could barely move.

She took a breath—and then—"hon?"

He looked up.

"There's something I want to tell you. About a man I've met ..."

He sat forward.

"I beg your pardon." He gave a short laugh. "*A man you've met?*"

"Yes. He's ..."

"*You?*"

"Well—yes." She had to smile—he apparently found the thought of there being another man so unbelievable, he could not give her credit for it. *Well, well, well,* she thought. *Ridiculous incredulity—as practised only by unfaithful husbands.*

"What's his name?"

"Milos."

"He's Italian?"

"No. I think he's Polish."

"Polish!" He snorted. "*Well!* Get you! The Princess and the Polack."

"Don't talk like that. It's unacceptable."

"Oh, sure. Miss Southern Belle here hasn't a prejudiced bone in her white-white body. I'll bet!"

Jane drank and looked out the window at the dark.

"When did you meet him?"

"That's immaterial."

"Sure. Like someone left him standing on the porch. A total stranger. Was he gift-wrapped?"

"You're being ..."

"What? What am I being?"

"Funny, how—when the glove is on the other hand—you switch attitudes all of a sudden."

"That's *shoe-on-the-other-foot!* God, you're stupid."

Here comes the self-defensive rage. Turn your guilt into mine.

She had, in her way, only been teasing him with the notion of the other man. She had meant to say that Milos had agreed to model for her. But it helped, somehow, that he had jumped to the wrong conclusion. *Let him.*

"Is he coming here tonight? The Polack?"

"Of course not."

"Well." He stood up. "Neither am I. I think I'll just say goodbye and take my leave."

He gave an extravagant bow and turned towards the side door.

"I don't need anything," he said with an acid tone. "I have friends with clean beds—friends with razors—friends with fresh, clean underwear that fits—with toothbrushes, toothpaste, hairbrushes, combs, deodorant. Clean white beds with clean white sheets in clean, cool rooms. And ceiling fans. No women allowed."

He unlocked and opened the door.

"So—what am I supposed to do about all this? After all, we have a child. His name is *Will*—remember? Doesn't it interest you what *we're* going to do?"

"Frankly, my dear, I don't give a damn."

He had been waiting a long time to say that.

It made a perfect exit.

Except that Jane and Will did not have tomorrow, nor Tara to turn to, not being Scarlett O'Hara.

She locked the door.

I never used to be this afraid, she was thinking, *and now I can't stop. I guess it's a consequence of failure. No, goddammit! Not failure. Loss.*

Turning back into the kitchen, she found her fingers inadvertently reaching to pull her hair away from her face.

I had it cut—a week ago. Only a week. And now ...

Dear Jesus Christ.

Lenore Archer was everywhere that night.

3

The telephone rang.

Mercy answered.

"Mrs Kincaid?"

"No. This is Mercy Bowman. Mrs Kincaid is out. May I take a message?"

For a moment, the caller said nothing. Then he said: "Mercy?"

"Yes. Can I help you?"

"Mercy, it's me. Milos."

"Milos Saworski?"

"Yes. I'm your neighbour."

"Oh, I know who you are—hello. How are you? Is everything all right?"

"Yes. At the moment. I called because Mrs Kincaid asked me to."

"Is it about the phones? Is something wrong?"

"No. She just wanted me to call."

"I see ..." Mercy waited for an explanation, but none was forthcoming. "Okay, then. Is there a message?"

"No. Can you tell me when she'll be in for sure?"

Mercy looked at the clock. "Five-thirty, maybe. Six at the very latest. She's at the theatre. We're going out for supper. She's never late for that kind of thing."

"Could you tell her I called? And tell her I'll call back. At 6:00. Six on the dot."

"Absolutely. No problem. She'll be here."

"Thanks."

"Milos?"

"I'm here."

"How's the boy? Is he all right?"

"Not really, I guess. Agnewska's with him. She never leaves him ..."

He left this information hanging in the air—as if it was regrettable—as if he wanted to say more, but was unable—perhaps because Agnewska was there and listening.

"I hope she'll let you do something, Milos. It's wrong, you know, the way it is. He's in terrible danger."

"Yes. I know."

"I wish you luck, Milos. I'll tell Mrs Kincaid you'll call again at 6:00."

"Yes. Thank you. Goodbye."

He hung up.

Poor man, Mercy thought, the phone still in her hand. *He's trapped with a madwoman. I wish he'd take the child and run.*

But he won't.

He won't. If he was going to, he'd have run by now.

She set the phone in place and went into the sunroom to straighten things out. Will had finished the big puzzle and was working on a new one—round and pure white. Nothing but white—not even a shape within the shape. Just round.

Easy enough to fill in the outer circle. All those pieces were curved and Will had almost completed this. But the middle— the middle was a complete mystery. She knew that Will would solve it. It seemed that increasingly silence and mystery were all he was about: reading his books, solving his puzzles, falling into a well of silence—provocative and disturbing. He did not even speak to Rudyard, but only scratched the dog's ears as if to encourage him to listen, too. Their walks in the park were no longer happy times, but sullen times, Will often walking ahead or lagging behind, unjoined.

For some reason, the puzzle also made Mercy think of Luke.

Another mystery?

No. Not exactly. And not a puzzle, either.

At least, he's *not the puzzle. It's what's going to happen with us—that's the puzzle. What the future will be. All the pieces are there, I guess—but I don't know what kind of a picture they're going to make.*

Mercy sighed. She was a little surprised at how comfortable she felt about not knowing what would happen with Luke. She was humming as she went back to straightening up the room.

Just as Mercy was plumping the cushions, Jane arrived.

It was 5:15.

"Home free!" she sang. "God—what a day! *Richard*'s a smash and everybody's raving. Inside the company, that is. Today's dress rehearsal was the only chance some of the other actors would have to see it. You should have seen their faces! *Stricken.*"

"Doesn't sound too terrific to me," said Mercy. "Stricken? Sounds like some kind of disaster."

Jane laughed. "No, no, no. I mean *moved beyond words.* And I must admit, it was stunning. My windows, by the way, looked great. People talked about them. I was proud."

She threw her work-bag onto the kitchen table, got two glasses and went to the dining-room for a Yellow Label. "Let's celebrate!"

Mercy winced. Wine, wine and more wine. *Where is she going?*

When Jane got the bottle to the kitchen, she dropped the corkscrew on the floor.

"Look at that! I'm so excited, I'm shaking like an

earthquake. You'll have to open it. Please. And hurry. I'm going to explode."

Jane sat down, got her cigarettes and matches from her bag and pushed it aside, reaching for an ashtray.

"Here you go," said Mercy, filling the two glasses.

"Leave the bottle right there."

"Okay—but I hope we're gonna eat."

Mercy sat. They both lighted up on the same match—and Jane raised her glass.

"To *Richard III*. A triumph, all round!"

"To *Richard III!* Congratulations."

Jane drank. "Oh, the wonders of the theatre—the wonder of it all—corny, maybe, but it's true. There are moments—not a lot—but moments of pure magic. *Magic*—when everything comes together and the shivers happen. And when you're part of it ... I'm so proud, I could scream."

Jane refilled her glass and sighed.

"I won't sleep a wink tonight. Not one wink—but I don't care ..."

She clouded and leaned forward towards the ashtray.

"Griff wasn't there again. Oh, *why?* It was his last and only remaining chance—and my windows ... Now, all he'll see is the photograph. Damn it—and damn him."

"Yes. I agree. And I'm sorry."

"I haven't got a clue where he is. Not a clue. Or who with—or what the hell's going on ..."

She's speaking in speedo, Mercy thought, *as if she's on speed.*

"I know," she said, deliberately calm. "Don't think about it. Enjoy the success."

"Yes. Yes. Yes. Enjoy the success. It's all so brief. But—it's ..."

Nothing more.

After a while Mercy said: "you got a phone call."

"I did? Who from?"

"Someone I didn't know you knew. He's my neighbour, Milos Saworski."

"Oh, yes." Jane was guarded—attempting diffidence. "The phone man."

She looked into her bag as if searching for something. Mercy watched her.

"That's right."

"Did he leave a message?"

"Only that he'd call at 6:00."

"Six."

"Yes. And right now, it's 5:45."

"Five-forty-five ..."

"Five-forty-five."

They drank.

"How come you know him? Milos Saworski," said Mercy. "I didn't know you'd met. He never mentioned it to me. Neither did you, come to think of it."

"Well, I had no idea he was your neighbour. He came to fix the phone, that time Luke cut through the line with his spade. Three—four weeks ago—whenever."

"Oh, yeah. Then."

Luke.

Mercy smiled.

"You weren't here, I guess, when he came."

"No. I was walking with Will and Rudyard. You told me someone had come and repaired things when we got back. Interesting it should have been my neighbour, Milos. I know what he does—working for Bell and all—but it never even occurred to me it might have been him." She gave a laugh. "Well—stranger things have happened. So—why'd he call you—if you don't mind my asking?"

"No. Ask away. I was interested in him. I thought he might make a good model."

"Model?"

Mercy was cautious. *So that was it—the drawings ...*

"Yes. Posing. Didn't I tell you? Now that dear old J.T.'s gone, I'll be doing some life classes with Edna Mott," she lied, "me and five or six others. And Edna's found a woman, but she couldn't find a man."

"In a town full of peacock actors? That seems strange."

"Nonetheless ..." Jane shrugged. "So. Tell me about him. I only know his name. I saw him on the street the other day— and I thought: *perfect*. So I asked him."

"Just like that?"

"Just like that. Why not?"

"But he's a stranger to you. More or less. I mean—you wouldn't go up to some man in a restaurant and ask him if he'd like to be a model."

"I would, if he was the right man."

"Unh-hunh. My God—you're bold. Well. Nude, I suppose. Naked." *Of course. It's already happened. She's bluffing.*

"He has a fine-looking body."

"Unh-hunh."

"Well, he has."

"Unh-hunh."

"Tell me about him. He seems somehow mysterious. Odd. I don't mean scary. Quite the opposite. Innocent, somehow."

"Yes. Yes. I agree. He's like a child." Mercy reflected a moment and then she said: "it's not a happy story, I'm sorry to say..."

And she told it—all of what she knew—about Agnewska— about Anton the baby—about the doctors—about the religious war between them and about the likelihood the baby would die unless Milos found some way to rescue it. And about his growing desperation—and about his own fear he might do something criminal in order to save the baby's life. "It's a dangerous situation," she said. "Potentially."

Jane looked away.

When the story was over, she poured more wine and finally said: "as soon as he's phoned, we'll get in the car and go to Pazzo. I'm famished." This was a lie. She was not the least bit hungry. She was nervous—both of Milos and of Griff's absence. Part of her wanted to go out to all the restaurants looking for him—asking for news. *Has* anybody *seen him?*

"I hope you don't mind my telling you all that about my neighbour," Mercy said.

"No. No. Not at all. I'm glad I know. Maybe, somehow, we can help."

"Yes. It would be nice to think so. To help. If we can."

The telephone rang at 6:01. On the dot.

Nothing if not perfect, Mercy thought.

She answered.

"Yes, Milos. Here she is."

She handed the phone to Jane.

Jane put her hand over the mouthpiece and said: "could you make sure Will is ready to go? This will only take seconds."

"Sure."

Mercy moved towards the hall and the stairs, where she lingered long enough to hear the tone of Jane's voice as she spoke.

"Hullo ... Yes. Thank you ..."

Languid. As if ... what? As if something else.

As if ...

Rudyard was on the landing. Had he deserted Will, too?

She went on up, expecting to find Will in the sitting-room, watching television. But he was not there.

She looked in at his empty bed.

Where, then?

The bathroom.

No.

Where the hell ...?

He could not have gone out without their being aware. Although ...

He was getting almost too good at *sneaking*. Midnight forays in the kitchen. Videos he wasn't supposed to be watching, put in the living-room VCR without sound.

She went back down to the front door—out to the curb and looked either way along the street.

No. Not there.

Turning back to the house, she glanced up. Will was sitting on the roof with his back to her.

She had found him there twice before. The first time—about five weeks ago—she had asked him what the hell he was doing.

"Feeding my crow."

"Your crow?"

"Sure. He's my new pet," Will had told her. "He won't eat out of my hand yet, but there's a ledge up here around the chimney and I leave him some of Ruddy's kibble. He loves it. Sometimes he'll even come for it while I'm sitting here—'long as I'm still."

"Well," Mercy had said, "feeding a crow. That beats all."

Now, he was beside the chimney, off to the right—the west side of the house. Mercy went along the drive to the yard.

Will was staring at the crows in their tree.

Mercy counted them—five—and turned back to Will.

"You thinking of coming down?" she asked—with as much calm as she could muster.

"Why?"

He did not look at her.

"We're going to Pazzo for pizza. You wouldn't want to miss that, would you?"

"Did Mum ever come home?"

"Sure. She's been here over half an hour."

There was no immediate reply to this.

"I'm not hungry," he said at last.

"Of course you are. It's your favourite meal."

"Will Dad be there?"

Mercy said: "I doubt it."

"I want to see Dad."

"He's playing tonight."

"Who with?"

Sure. Too clever for words ...

"At the theatre. Where else?"

"I dunno. Could be off wherever else he goes these days."

"He'll come back."

"Promise?"

"Promise."

"Liar."

Mercy did not move. She froze.

Liar?

Yes. He's right. You are. You don't know if Griff's coming back. Why say he is?

Because he has to come back. He has to. Oh, dear God ...

"Whyn't you come down? We could use you down here. We miss seeing you—your mum—Rudyard—me ..."

"I'm learning to be like Dad. Out of sight. Gone."

"You'll freeze to death up there, if you stay till after dark."

"No I won't. We're in a heat wave."

"Your crow come to feed yet?"

"How can he—with you standing there?"

Could she—how could she command him? This kind of thing had never happened before.

"If you don't come with us, then what're you going to eat?"

"Dunno. Don't care. I'm not hungry." He looked away. "Maybe kibble."

Mercy watched him—Will not looking back.

"Mushrooms," she said. "Bacon-bits—onions ..."

He moved one hand, palm down, onto his knee.

"Not an anchovy in sight. Not even in smelling distance. Banned to the kitchen ..."

"Someone will have them."

"Not at our table, they won't."

"Mum likes them."

"No, sir."

"*You* do."

"You know damn well I don't."

There was a pause.

Pray God Jane has finished her conversation with Milos. I wouldn't want him to hear that.

"If I jump, will you catch me?"

"You have to be kidding. You weigh a ton."

"I don't even weigh a hundred pounds."

"So—you think I stand around catching sacks of flour all day?"

"I'm not a sack of flour."

"I didn't want to say *sugar*. I thought you might object."

She was smiling.

He did not smile back. "What's wrong with saying a sack of sand, or something?"

"Okay. I don't stand around catching sacks of sand all day. Come on, hon. We've got to get going. We're taking Rudyard out with us—we'll sit by the sidewalk. Your mum will be waiting."

"She's on the phone with her lover."

Jesus. Where did he pick that up?

"Well? Isn't she?"

"She doesn't have a lover, Will." *Pray God.*

"I thought maybe it was Dad. Doesn't she love Dad?"

So—mischief.

He was smiling. Not a lot. But some. Just at the corners of his mouth.

Mercy said: "you weren't so funny, I'd hide you."

"You never hided me yet."

"Time enough. But don't you make the mistake of thinking I wouldn't. I'm always willing. Depends on what you get up to."

"The roof."

"Very funny. Now you come down here."

He stood up.

"Okay. I'm going to jump."

"Go right ahead. I'm turning my back."

Which she did.

Will—please ...

There was a brief silence. Then she heard him scrambling over the shingles.

Don't burn your knees ...

She could tell he had reached his bedroom window. She could tell he had gone through.

She waited.

Maybe, she thought, *the best thing to do is not to mention this. Jane would have a heart attack.*

Rudyard came onto the lawn.

"Can he come, too?" said Will. "You said he could."

He was standing on the deck, brushing the seat of his pants.

Mercy turned.

"Sure. I'll phone ahead and get them to save us a table on the street. You, Mister Hawkins—go wash your hands. I can smell the tar from those shingles all the way over here."

He looked at her—not quite smiling.

She made a gentle *shooing* motion with her hand.

"You go on now. We're all waiting."

He went to the screen door, and looked at her over his shoulder.

"When I said I was going to jump—you turned your back," he said.

"That's right."

"What if I had?"

"I'd've caught you. Or done my best to break your fall. Thing is, when you're really going to jump, you have to sound like you mean it."

"I did. Mean it. For a minute."

"More like two seconds."

She beamed.

"Go get rid of that tar. I'll make the call. Two bits, I'm finished it before you've even put on the soap."

He opened the door and went inside.

Mercy looked up. Movement. The oldest crow of all—the alpha—left the tree and went to the chimney for his food.

She shook her head. *God bless all living things*, she thought. *And God bless Will for giving a damn.*

Making for the deck, Mercy could hear Jane saying: "where the hell have all you people been?"

"There's only two of us, Mum," said Will. "Two of us and Rudyard."

"That makes three," Jane said—and Mercy could tell she was smiling. Playing the game with Will, you had to know a lot about one-upmanship.

"Come on, Ruddy. Let's get your lead."

Mercy went in and Rudyard followed.

The roof was not mentioned. Mercy phoned Pazzo and booked a table on the street. "But we're going to ask if we can have a pizza brought from downstairs," she added. "It's really important."

4

Sunday, July 26, 1998

"You want one more?"

"Sure."

Jonathan and Griff were in Jonathan's sitting-room at the Pinewood. Griff had played a matinee of *Much Ado* and they had eaten afterwards in the Pinewood dining-room. More chateaubriand. *It's becoming standard ...*

Jonathan poured their second snifters of Grand Marnier, handed one to Griff and opened the windows onto the back lawns, the tennis court and the swimming pool.

"I've always loved the smell of the woods at the end of the day," Jonathan said. "The crossover from breathing in to breathing out that nature does. The trees, the flowers, the grass—everything exuding its individual scent. Which is like a breath, I guess. Like a person's breath. Except that nature never eats garlic." He smiled and sat down.

Griff had already taken off his jacket and was seated, open-shirted, with one leg over the arm of his chair.

"You shouldn't sit like that," said Jonathan. "It's too provocative."

Griff left his leg where it was.

They drank.

"I've been thinking a lot about *Love's Labour's*," Jonathan said, while lighting one of his careful cigarettes. *Careful*, because Griff had been watching over time how he fingered them, handled them, wielded them as instruments, as props. It was all controlled—*smoking as the manipulation of a sequence of gestures*, telling its own story while his words unfolded something else. All of this was an indication—a reflection, even an echo, of how Jonathan engaged his fingers, his hands, his lips in what he did to and with Griff in bed.

Jonathan's mouth, his tongue and even his teeth were extremely seductive.

Which he knew.

And his fingers, with their long, squared nails and their sensitive tips, were masters of seduction. With a cigarette, he could portray all of this—and, given the veil of smoke and the rolling of the ashes along the sides of ashtrays, any susceptible witness could become mesmerized by what had all the trademarks of an expert performance of every kind of sex imaginable. Jonathan had already done things to Griff that had no equal in Griff's imagination. And all without genital penetration. Other forms of penetration, yes, but never genital. That was where Jonathan drew and enforced the line. *We do not fuck.*

AIDS was the cause of this attitude, and for once in his life, Griff was glad of it. Jonathan's fear of it protected Griff from having to cross his own drawn line. He might have killed to protect himself from it, and this fact provided, from his point of view, perhaps the most curious aspect of his relationship with Jonathan. If Jonathan had tried or even said he wanted to *fuck* Griff, Griff would have battered him. But there they sat.

Here they sat.

"Tell about *Love's Labour's*," Griff said.

"To begin with, I'm moving it in time—and in space."

Oh God, not futuristic ...

"It will not take place in the King of Navarre's Royal Park. It will take place at Cambridge University in England. And when? In the summer of 1914."

Griff said nothing. He could already see it.

"All those beautiful young men—in their shirts and blazers, carrying their boaters, wearing their tight white trousers, holding hands in innocent comradeship—and the pedants, Holofernes, Nathaniel, in their scholar's black gowns and the Princess of France and her ladies in Edwardian garden party dresses, moving beneath the shade of parasols ..."

"Enchanting," said Griff. "Enchanting. Go on."

"And the uniforms ..."

"Uniforms?"

"Yes. The uniforms. First one, perhaps on Don Armado, *the fantastical Spaniard*—then two—then four—then five—then eight—then a dozen. A steady, subtle proliferation of young men in uniform. Europe—summer of 1914 ..."

Griff sipped his Grand Marnier and waited. He might have been drifting in a punt on the River Cam—with meadows all around him, leading downstream to Grantchester. It was idyllic.

"It's idyllic," he said out loud.

"It's meant to be. Everyone who's ever written of that summer says it was perfection. Sun, warmth, blossoms—the lot ... But there are clouds. It rains. A momentous event is waiting in the wings. And as the light, delightful playfulness of the whole play unfolds, the sky will darken, the uniforms and the military colours and the distant jingoistic music will become more prominent until—in a scene I'm still devising—Mercade will arrive with the news that the King of France has died. And we will understand that he has been assassinated, as happened to the Archduke at Sarajevo. And, as the young men and women prepare to part, with their promises of mutual fidelity and dedication to meeting again in one year's time, we will somehow—I'm working on this—understand that August the first, 1914, is upon us. Clearly, from that moment, all the young men are doomed—and consequently, the futures of all the young women, destroyed."

"It's beautiful, Jonathan. But why must it end with so much tragedy? Everyone?"

"Everyone. Because that is the meaning of comedy, my dear. It is also the meaning of all youthful stories. Nothing that is perfect lasts."

Youthful?

Young?

Us.

The end.

"So," Griff said. "What you want is the effect of ... I don't quite know how to say it, but you want to kill us all. To put us all away. Me—Nigel—whoever. To say: *if I can't have you, I will kill you.* Except that *you* don't kill. And you don't, do you. Of course not. Of course not ... Not with guns."

"Griff ..."

"I'm sorry."

"Don't be. I understand."

"I hate all masters."

"I am not a master."

"I know that."

"Don't walk away from me."

"I'm not about to. Walk? I couldn't creep. I couldn't crawl."

They laughed.

"Lie back ..."

"Yes ..."

"Just like that. One leg ..."

"Yes ... This one."

"Yes. That one. And ..."

"Oh ..."

"I'll just ..."

Oh dearest Jesus ...

Griff lay back.

Always the best kind of sex. To be had. To be done. To be so completely wanted that you ...

Stop ... Don't think.

"Mind if I make you utterly naked?" Jonathan asked.

"No. Of course not. No. No. No."

All of this happened.

At last, kneeling between Griffin's legs, Jonathan said: "there are places you need to shave, my dear. I can do it for you, if you'd prefer. Or you can leave them, as you wish. I and I alone will love them as they are."

5

Monday, July 27, 1998

Griff came back to the Cambria Street house on his day off.

No one was expecting him. Nothing had been said. There was no message, no phone call. Nothing. Just the Lexus pulling into the drive at 10:30 in the morning.

Jane was not there. She had gone to pick up some dry cleaning and to see Claire Highland. Mercy was in the kitchen preparing shrimp salads for lunch. In the living-room, the television droned on about refugees in Kosovo, Monica Lewinsky and Linda Tripp, while Mercy hummed the tune of "Stand by Your Man," which always made her smile—ever since she had seen Morey Henderson performing it at Marrat's on Cabaret Night a few months before. He had worn a "Monica" wig and a blue dress and changed the lyrics to "Kneel By Your Man" and ended the performance by hoisting his skirts and exposing his thong.

God. Had it been going on that long? Maybe not a year ago—but it sure as hell wasn't yesterday ...

Will was in the sunroom working on the circular puzzle—now having achieved about a third of its impossible centre.

Rudyard, who had been asleep under the table at Will's feet, looked up and spoke when he heard the Lexus come onto the drive.

"Shhh," said Will. "It's gotta be Dad." He recognized the car by the distinctive sound of its "superior" engine.

Mercy tried not to show surprise when Griff came to the side door. *One of those things that happens, every day ... the wandering husband and father drops by to say "Hi ... Just thought I'd pop in ..."* Sure.

What Griff actually said was: "oh—you're here. I was hoping the house would be empty."

Mercy shot him a look and went on peeling shrimp. "Come in anyway," she said. "We don't bite."

Will hunched over the puzzle. Rudyard yawned and stood up.

"Don't," Will said in a whisper.

Rudyard sat down.

Griff came into the kitchen.

Mercy did not look at him. She turned the cold water on and put the shrimp in their colander under its stream.

"Didn't you used to live here?" she said.

"Now, now," Griff said, going behind her and kissing her on the neck.

"Quit that," said Mercy. And meant it.

Griff backed away.

"I just came to get some stuff," he said.

"Yeah, well ... We were wondering. Maybe you bought a whole new wardrobe from the skin out or something. Where the hell've you been—as if we can't guess."

"Two bits you'd guess wrong."

"Two bits sounds about right—given what you've been up to. There's a boy in there hasn't seen his father for God knows how long—and not one word of your whereabouts."

"Good. It's meant to be a secret."

"So I gather." Mercy shut the tap off and began to dry her fingers. "Does she pay you?"

"That was unnecessary, Merce. It isn't like that."

"Isn't it? Seems like it, to me. Drop everything and run off with some drama queen. Maybe you pay her."

Will stopped his ears.

"Well," Griff said. "I think I'll just go and get my things, since we don't seem to be able to have a civilized conversation." He moved towards the hall door.

"Boy—you sure take the cake. You want a civilized conversation? With *me*? And I'm not even your fucking wife ..."

"Don't talk like that."

"Cake number two. You think Will hasn't heard all that language ninety times over? You must be deaf to your own words."

"Maybe I talk like that—but you don't."

"Damn right I don't, 'less I'm near you. 'Less I think the word *Griffin*—and worse than that, *Griffin Kincaid*. I have no need of words like that. It's you that brings them in here, hanging like a cloud of beasties round your head. Buzz—buzz—buster. *Buzz-buzz-buzz!*"

Griff started away into the hall.

"Aren't you even going to ask how they are?" Mercy called

after him. She moved around the island away from the sink into the centre of the kitchen. "Don't you even want to know if they're alive?"

Griff turned and tried to stare her down.

"We miss you," Mercy said. "You bastard." Her eyes were misted. "Just remember," she went on, "someone's here waiting. Someone's here, Griff. There are people here. This is home."

Griff turned away and went up the stairs.

Mercy returned to the sink—lifted the colander and dumped the shrimp onto a clean tea towel. Folding the corners over the centre, she stared down at the towel's design, which showed Griff dressed in his Ferdinand costume from *The Tempest*, with Zoë Walker kneeling at his feet.

Kneel by Your Man ...

I'll bet.

Will came up beside her and said: "where is he?"

"Upstairs."

"Is he leaving?"

Mercy sagged.

"Can't you get it into your head? He's *left*."

Will moved towards the hall, Rudyard at his heels.

Mercy looked after him—and put out her hand.

"I'm sorry," she said.

But he was gone.

Griff was folding underwear, socks and handkerchiefs into a suitcase lying open on the bed. Beside it there were polo shirts, trousers and one or two jackets on hangers.

Will stood in the doorway.

"Where are you going?" he said.

"Away."

"But where?"

"I'm fine. You don't need to worry."

Will thought this a curious answer.

"Don't you want to see Mum?"

"No. Not now."

Griff went on folding his clothes and laying them in the suit-case.

"Why not? She wants to see you."

"We've had an argument."

Will moved farther into the room. His father's clothes had all been laundered for him—dress shirts, underwear—every-thing. Griff never did any of that. Neither did Will. *Men don't, I guess ...*

"Have you and I had an argument ...?" he said.

"Of course not."

"Then why are you leaving? Don't you like us anymore?"

Griff closed the lid of the suitcase and snapped its locks. For a moment, he stared at it—not speaking—and then he said: "these things happen, Will. In marriages ... between friends ... even people who love each other. It's just ... something that happens."

Will said nothing.

Griff sat down on the bed and said: "come here."

Will went over to him.

Rudyard sat in the doorway, waiting.

"We need a rest," Griff said. "Same way you'd take a vaca-tion. You need ... I need ... your mum needs ... we need to get away for a while and be alone."

"Why?"

"Oh, dammit—stop asking *why*. I can't tell you why. There *is* no why. It's just ... it's just ... *we need to be alone.*"

"But—you're not alone. You're with someone else."

Griff closed his eyes.

This was a *farewell scene*. Surely he had watched it often enough over time to know how it went—know what to say. It's the *departing-father-and-son* thing—the *baffled-child-father-without-answers* thing ... the same old *goddamn-bastard-walking-out-on-his-family shit ...*

Say something, for God's sake. Even if it's not yours—even if it's just some lousy line from a lousy play or movie ...

Say something!

He knelt down and looked into Will's eyes.

He smiled.

"One day," he said, "you'll understand. Maybe when you have to walk away yourself from whoever it is you end up loving. For now—you can be sure I'm coming back. I love you, Will. It will take some time—I don't know—neither does your mum. But I will be back. I promise."

He put his arms around Will and hugged him, but Will did not respond.

Griff stood up.

He touched Will's head.

Will shied away. "Don't," he said.

Griff picked up the suitcase and the hangered clothes and went to the door.

Rudyard moved aside.

Griff turned and looked at Will.

"I love you," he said. "I mean that."

"No you don't," said Will.

Griff went down the stairs, said a cursory goodbye to Mercy and went to the Lexus, letting the screen door bang behind him.

Will came into the kitchen.

They heard the trunk of the car being opened and lowered, the driver's door slam and the motor start.

Rudyard was the only one who watched the actual departure.

Will picked up a shrimp and ate it.

"I'm glad Mum wasn't here," he said.

"Yeah. So am I. She's in the backyard. Saw the car and parked her own on the street. Whyn't you go and say hello. Take her this glass of wine and tell her there'll be lunch in half an hour."

Will picked up the wineglass and started for the deck.

"Will?" said Mercy.

He turned.

"Don't ask any more questions, honey. Give her a chance to take it all in. Maybe later. Now ... let's not say a word."

"Yes, ma'am."

Mercy smiled.

"Know something?" she said. "You haven't called me *ma'am* since you were three years old."

Will shrugged.

"It just came out," he said.

"I know. I know. But I thank you just the same."

"Yes'm."

"You go on now."

He left.

Rudyard gave a whine by the screen door, sighed and lay down beside it.

Mercy, resting her weight on her hands, hung over the shrimp—blinked two or three times—stood back and then said: "yes. *Go on.* I guess it's all a person can do."

When Will brought Jane the glass of wine, she said: "thank you."

Will turned and began to walk away.

Jane said: "aren't you going to say *you're welcome?*"

"Mercy told me not to say anything."

"Oh. I see. Well—thank you, anyway."

Will went into the house and back to his puzzle.

Jane drank—lighted the nineteenth cigarette of the moment—and lay back against the cushion.

She had heard everything Griff said to Mercy—everything Mercy said to Griff—and had cheered.

Then she heard the door—the Lexus—the departure.

Gone.

Done.

Over.

Well ...

It was all too familiar. All too reminiscent of her own departure from Plantation. Whenever that had been. *Nineteen-eighty-something ... who cares?* She left.

She had packed her bags at midnight, knowing she would leave by prearranged taxi at 1:30. Last train out of Plantation to New Orleans. Pre-booked hotel. Plane the next morning to New York—New York to Toronto—everything pre-secured from the local travel agent. *Far away north as I can get ...*

And the last meal—Jane on her own preordained side of the table—Maybelle at the far end. Joshua serving Creole shrimps and rice—green salad—strawberry shortcake, real whipped cream with brown—never white—sugar. Wine. Coffee. Cointreau—Maybelle's favourite. Orange.

"Mama?"

"Yes, chile."

"I'm thinkin' o' leavin' now."

"Leavin'? Leavin' what?"

"Plantation. Cloud's Hill. You."

"Aura Lee—my precious. You don' just stan' up an' walk away f'm Cloud Hill. F'm family. You just don' do that. All

them years o' history—Terry history—an' you the inheritor o'
all we stood for. You, the las' one o' your generation to inherit
the glory of the past. You jus' don' do that. Why, once you're
gone, precious, Maybelle won't have no one. *No one.* Not one
single soul. An' all my 'cestors dead 'n' buried. An' your sister
'Retta an' Harry, Lucius—leavin' already? I will have nothin',
Aura Lee. Not one jot 'n' tittle o' all my efforts to give you
lives! Nothin'. No! You will not be leavin'!"

Jane had set her fork aside at that moment. The shrimp on
her plate appeared to be staring back at her. *Look what
happened to us*, they seemed to be saying. *We perished.*

"Mama—I'm an artist," she had said—praying for the right
words. "There's nothing here for me. Nothing. I need to go
where I can function."

"You think I don' know you got tickets here to New York.
New York. Where you'll be one o' ten thousan' others all
wantin' the same thing? You think I don' know that?"

Jane said nothing about Toronto.

"What're you gonna do up there, 'sides starve?"

"I have my income, Mama. From Papa. I'll be just fine."

Joshua hovered.

"You done, Miss Aura Lee?"

Her plate had barely been touched.

"Yes, thank you, Josh. I ... tell Lorelei I had no appetite—
but tell her, too, how good it was."

"Yes'm."

Joshua lifted the plate and went to the end of the table.

"Mrs Terry?"

Maybelle's plate was spotless.

"Thank you."

Jane watched Joshua head for the kitchen. "Lorelei cooks a
mean shrimp."

"It's her job," said Maybelle efficiently. "Only reason I hired her. Don' care for them Creoles, but she knows what she's doin'. All that matters, in a kitchen."

She fussed with her napkin—folding—unfolding—folding it again and again.

"Why you wanta leave me?" she asked, accusingly. "Art—to be an artist is not an answer. Why you wanta leave everythin' you ever been?"

Jane laid her hands on the table and waited.

Then she said: "because I never been all that, Mama. I never was a Terry, heart-and-soul—an' I never will be."

Maybelle sat back and closed her eyes.

"I do not an' cannot believe that. You are Terry through and through."

"No, Mama. I am me, myself an' I. Nothin' more."

"You—yoursel' an' you. That it?"

Silence.

Then Maybelle said: "I shoulda got power-o'-attorney. Wish I had power-o'-attorney."

"Why, Mama? What good would that do you?"

"I could prevent you."

"What? From leavin'?"

"From *strayin'*. STRAYIN'. From leavin' the path!"

"I'm *on* the path, Mama. I'm where I need to be. I got the one an' only thing you never had—*choice*. An' I'm takin' this moment to exercise jus' that. *Choice*. I want *my* life, not yours. An' tomorrow—I'll be gone."

Maybelle's stricken face—the echo of her own—hovered over the moment—the memory. Now.

Is this what Griff has done? What I did?

I want my life—not yours? Is that what he's saying?

But what would that mean—in Griff's case?

She drank some wine.

Well.

Off we go into the wild blue yonder ...

Yes.

And there it is. Right over your head.

Mercy came to the door.

"You interested in rejoining the human race?" she asked.

Jane set the glass down.

"Sure," she said, and sat up. "Whatever *that* might be."

Mercy laughed. "Well," she said, "you got one of them standing right here and, in the kitchen, a boy named Will. Seems plenty human to me."

Yes. And the day after tomorrow—Milos.

Another member of the human race. But only just, as Jane remembered his other-worldly presence.

the kill

All goes to plan, both lying and confession,
Down to the thrilling final chase, the kill.

W.H. Auden
Detective Story

1

They had arranged to meet by the river.

Jane arrived in the Subaru, noting that Milos had parked the Bell van in the Tom Patterson Theatre lot.

He doesn't want to acknowledge this, either ... But, of course, he can't any more than I can.

"Hello."

"Hello."

He was wearing the same faded jeans—almost white with bleach—torn at both knees and along one thigh.

"How are you?"

"Fine. And you?"

"Fine."

He climbed in beside her.

She could smell the soap with which he had bathed or showered. She could smell the shampoo with which he had cleaned his hair. She could smell the detergent in which his shirt had been washed. She could smell his breath—cinnamon and cigarettes—and on his hands, the smell that comes from having held a piece of toast.

Jane began to drive, turning south on Erie Street.

"Where are we going to do this?" Milos asked, rolling down his window.

"In the country," said Jane.

"Outside, you mean?"

"Partly."

"Won't someone see us?"

"No. We're going somewhere private. A deserted farm."

"Oh."

Jane glanced at him.

"Are you nervous?" she asked.

"I just don't want my wife to find out."

"She won't."

The town slipped away and the landscape began to roll off to either side, displaying fields with cattle, fields with shoulder-high corn and fields where the second cut of hay was already being taken. Tractors—reapers—even men with pitchforks, spearing bales onto horse-drawn wagons.

"There seem to be a lot of people," said Milos.

"Not where we're going. Believe me." She smiled. "Tell me more about yourself."

"I am Polish."

"So I gathered."

He looked at her suspiciously, as if he might have made a mistake in telling her.

"Your name," said Jane—and smiled. "It could hardly be Italian."

At last, he grinned.

"No," he said. "It is Polish name, for sure."

"Have you children?" she asked—pretending not to know.

"Yes. I have one. A son."

"Like me."

"I see."

"How old is he? Your son ..."

"About six weeks."

"My son is seven. Years."

"Oh."

"Well—I'm older. It makes sense."

"Yes. You have others?"

"I'd like to—but I don't know. Time will tell. What about you?"

"I think no."

"Oh? Why is that?"

"My boy is not well. My wife is not ... it seems he might not get better. My wife is very unhappy. I think she will have no more children now. I am worried. Forgive me. Perhaps I should not tell you that. We do not know each other, yet. But ... he is not well. I am worried."

"I'm sorry."

They drove in silence for a moment. Then Jane said: "what do the doctors say?"

Milos looked away.

"It is difficult situation," he said.

"I see."

"My wife does not like doctors—medicine—hospitals. She is very upset."

Knowing what she had heard from Mercy, Jane said: "can you not take him to the hospital yourself?"

"No."

They passed another field being harvested.

For the next ten minutes nothing more was said.

And then: "here's where we turn."

There was a sideroad, its entrance almost obscured by trees and hedges. At the corner, there were the remnants of an old limestone wall among the elderberry and hawthorn.

Jane looked at Milos.

Dear God, she thought. *We've been talking about our children. How can I do this?*

* * *

Three years ago, or four—she could not remember precisely—
Jane had started taking classes with an elderly local artist, J.T.
Weatherbee, who had since died. She and the other students
used to accompany him on field trips, and one in particular
had been memorable. Its object had been to sketch whatever
could be found of old, abandoned buildings—houses, barns,
drive sheds—even outhouses.

There had been three vehicles—two vans and the Subaru. All
of the students were practising artists, one way or another—
commercial, architectural, cover artists, set designers—property makers, like Jane. J.T. was a superb teacher, and being
one of his students was a privilege—especially if you were
already a professional.

"I'm taking you out of town, this time," he had said, while
they fortified themselves with wine and sandwiches before
setting off. "I don't want to show you old town houses or
public buildings. I want you to explore the textures of ruin."

The textures of ruin. This was a phrase Jane had never
forgotten.

"When we come to people, when we come to life classes, I'm
going to ask you to explore the same thing. Not the beauty of
youth, but the beauty of age. Our models will all be over sixty-
five, and I've found a man and woman—a married couple—
who are what they call *naturists*. In other words, nudists. They
are eighty-four and eighty-five years old."

Jane remembered them fondly. They had posed seated, holding hands.

"But today, the beauty of age in weather-beaten wood and
brick—in limestone ... in collapsing barns and crumbling
houses. In abandoned rooms and rotting timbers. I'm not
going to tell you what to draw. As you know, I never do. I
want you to find what captures your own attention—no

explanations—no verbal interpretations. Only you—your eye—and your pens and pencils."

They had come to where Jane was taking Milos now—to a deserted house, an abandoned barn—an overgrown laneway, a ruined orchard.

Once, it had been a place revered by four or five generations of a single family. Now, the last of them had died, and for thirty years it had been emptied of all its former life. Broken windows, unhinged doors and windswept rooms were all that remained of the house—its porches falling, its chimneys crumbling, its wall-papers faded and its ghosts disbanded, leaving only the memory of shouts and whispers, voices in the hallways, laughter on the stairs. Even its mice had departed, so it seemed. It was as if, long ago, an emergency evacuation had taken place.

In the barn and drive shed, rusting, forgotten implements and traces of horsehair, cattle dung, pig manure and broken ladders—everything cobwebbed, the windows all smeared with age—harnesses and halters, water pails and curry combs scattered by playful, careless children who had come through the years to see what life was like "then"—"before"—"a hundred years ago."

She pulled off the road into a laneway, lined all the way to the yard with maple trees and fallen fences.

She could feel all the ghosts pressing forward to see who was arriving ... men, women, children, dogs, cats, horses, cattle ...

J.T. had called the barn *a cathedral in the wilderness*. Jane thought so, too. The whole compound—house—drive shed—barn—privy—seemed somehow holy.

She drove to the back of the house, where there was a wash shed and a hand pump—the wash shed lacking its door, the pump leathers rotted out, but a tin cup still hanging from the built-in hook.

They got out of the car and Jane went round to the trunk.

"I brought a blanket for you—and a robe, in case you get cold."

"I think I will not get cold today," Milos said. "It is hot. I perspire in spite of open windows and only a shirt."

He smiled.

Jane thought: *good. I want him to perspire. If he's wet ...*

She had considered bringing some suntan oil, knowing that a bit of oil was almost always used by models posing nude, especially for photographs. This way, the light had a better chance of showing off delineations.

She handed Milos the blanket and the robe and rummaged further in her work-bag. Finally, she produced a camera.

"Camera?"

He seemed alarmed.

"Yes. I'm going to photograph you."

"Pictures?"

"Yes."

"But who will see them?"

"Only me. Only you."

"I do not know. If my wife ..."

Jane laughed. "Milos! Please! How could you think I would send them to your wife? Why should I do that?"

"But if someone ..."

"*No one.* I absolutely promise you. These are for me—so that I can draw you. If you think about it, it will be easier for you. You will not have to stand still for so long." She waited. For a moment she was afraid he was going to say no. "All right?" she said.

"No one will see?"

"No one. But me. I will even develop them myself."

This was a lie. She had no darkroom. But she did not worry about that now. Now—she must get the pictures.

"So—will you?"

He waited, turned entirely away, finally shrugged—turned back and said: "if you promise—yes."

"I promise."

He came towards her, smiling, and shook her hand. "Good. Yes."

If she thought that he was nervous, which he was, she also knew that she was nervous—possibly more so.

I am a professional. He must never know this is anything but a professional encounter. I must not show a trace of desire—or of interest beyond the contours and the planes of his ...

She tried to think *physique*—but could only think of *body*.

Nude photography. *Old as the hills. Naked men and women—God! In their thousands—hundreds of thousands—populating every newsstand on the continent. Everywhere!*

"We should get started," she said. "We don't want to miss the best light."

"No."

He glanced at the sky.

It was 3:45.

"Where?" he said.

"I thought in the barn."

When they entered the derelict building, it was exactly as she had last seen it, barring the fact that more of its siding had dropped to the ground.

Streamers of dust-laden light fell through the open places—some of them keen as spotlights, others more theatrical, as if designed and manipulated.

Once past the horse stalls, they came to an area beside the stairs where there were traps through which the hay and straw had once been dropped. Thirty- or forty-year-old bales of each had been tumbled either by time or by design to the floor, where they lay as mute reminders of another age—of other lives and labour, other caring.

The supporting beams of basswood trunks, shaped to the needs of the architecture, stood up anchored in pits of old concrete, flaking away to show its sand and gravel. The rough-hewn horizontal ramparts for the lost siding were still fixed in place. All the work involved in the making of this barn had been done by hand. All the beams were pegged. The only nails in evidence were handmade and square-headed, used to fasten the siding—what remained of it.

Milos, perhaps overwhelmed by the size of the space in which they stood, gazed upwards and began absently to undo the buttons of his shirt.

Now, Jane knew exactly what she wanted. There must be somewhere for Milos to sit.

Two or three bales of straw, with the blanket spread across them, would provide precisely what was needed.

Having set down her work-bag, she began to pull the necessary bales into place—five of them, as it turned out. Two to sit on, three to lean against. She manoeuvred the latter into place against one of the uprights.

All the decisions had been made in the previous week, as she had thought about what she must achieve.

Milos was sitting on some rickety steps leading up to the loft, removing his shoes and socks. His shirt had already been hung from a peg. His belt was undone and the top button of his fly.

"It is very warm," he said.

Good, Jane thought. *The hotter, the better.*

She retrieved the camera from her work-bag.

Canon V, she read.

It was fitted with a lens that was designated by the figures 70/200, 2.8.

None of this meant anything to her. She only knew it was the camera she wanted, loaned to her by a photographer friend who specialized in portraits.

"You don't know enough about lenses to require anything else," the friend had said. "The one I'm giving you is perfect for what you need."

Where to begin?

How?

At least she knew the rudimentary aspects of picture-taking.

You're sounding more and more like a textbook, Jane—and this is not a textbook exercise.

What is it, then?

An exercise in lust. Admit it—you'd rather throw away the camera and kneel at his feet.

He was removing his jeans.

Jane had not imagined that he wore boxer shorts. Griff never did, and she had assumed all young men were the same—*binding themselves in clinging Calvin Klein,* as Claire had put it, after viewing a copy of *Vanity Fair* that seemed otherwise to be devoted to male nudity. *Except that they're never nude*—the way half the women were. *Same old story—Jesus,* Claire had said. *Even in the nineties, everything for them—nothing for us!*

"Where do you want me?" she heard Milos ask.

Looking up from the camera, Jane saw him hovering by the steps. He was still wearing his boxers.

"Sitting on the blanket."

Milos turned towards it.

"And, Milos ..."

He looked over his shoulder.

"Yes?"

"Without the underwear."

"Yes. Of course."

He turned away to remove them.

Jane saw that his back was perspiring. Also his sides, where the perspiration fell from his armpits.

He carried the boxers over to the steps, folded them and laid them beside his jeans.

The moment when Milos reached the bales was a moment Jane had dreaded, because she knew he was going to turn around and face her—and she would have to face him, too.

Nothing. Just another man. Just another model. Just another body. That's all.

But some bodies go so far beyond beauty, you feel ... What? You have to pull them back to earth ...

Milos could see her gaze and could not prevent one nervous hand from drifting towards his genitals. But, fixing his focus on hers, he pulled the hand back to the outside of his thigh—and smiled.

"And now?" he said. "I am where?"

Jane stepped forward. *Don't be so businesslike, for God's sake.*

"I want you on the blanket," she said.

You sound like an emasculated, prickish sergeant major. Loosen up.

Give me a chance. Give me a chance—a moment—just a moment. He is so ...

Milos climbed onto the bales.

"Lying down?"

"No." For a moment she had to look away. First, at her left hand—then at her right hand. Her elbow. Her wrist. There was straw on the soles of his feet. She wanted to pick it off—but dared not touch him. "Would you sit with your back to the beam?" she said. "You can lean against the bales. If that makes your shoulders itchy, we can adjust the blanket."

She was now about a yard from his dangling toes.

He leaned inwards.

"Yes," he said. "It is itchy."

Jane set the camera safely aside and crawled onto the straw beside him.

"You'll have to stand," she said.

This he did.

She grasped the edge of the blanket and began to pull it upwards.

Sinking back on her heels, she turned and found herself facing his groin.

His pubic hair glistened with sweat. Other sweat fell from his torso onto her cheek.

"I am sorry," he said gently—and wiped the drops away with his fingers.

"Not to worry," said Jane. "I'm sweating myself."

"Yes. It's very hot. Very."

"Very. Yes."

She climbed down.

Milos sat.

He seemed to understand at once where his legs should be for pictures—one knee slightly raised, his hands laid on either side of his thighs, the fingers reaching for his own flesh—one finger touching.

Jane picked up the camera.

She was shaking.

There would be forty pictures in all. Ten to each of four rolls.

This had been deliberate on Jane's part. *If there are more, I will lose him.*

She knew enough about life classes to know how boring it could be for the models and what happened to their concentration when they drifted.

* * *

#1: The line was liquid—just as she had wanted. *Not to begin—but to* flow ...

Someone—J.T. Weatherbee—someone—had said that. *Never begin on the page. Begin outside the page and enter already in motion—the way a dancer enters the light. Have you ever seen a dancer make an entrance? Never. They are simply there. Just there.*

Now ...

Let the line become itself.

Let the line become itself.

Let the line ...

She sighted him in the lens.

One line.

From his right earlobe to his right thigh.

He was longer in the neck than she had expected—ear to collarbone ...

Don't look away. Make a single line.

The camera tilted.

This was as she wanted it.

A black-and-white *line.*

The right arm faded away into the fall of sunlight—bleached by dusty brightness—nervous shadows—the shadows seemingly withdrawing, afraid to be seen.

Collarbone—curve of breast—nipple ...

Suckable.

Don't.

Make the picture.

Jane's forearm began to tense.

Don't move.

How odd.

Even the best-made men are flawed.

She remembered this from having watched Griff while he sat, having pulled on his socks, pausing before he stood up. A

crease—a demarcation—a line above the belly button—
navel—that line for which the pubic hair always seemed to be
yearning, rising to it, pointing always to the centre—to that
other line along the breastbone. Arrows—everything an
arrow, pointing upwards ...

Drawing with the camera ...

Yes.

I am drawing with the camera.

"No. Don't move. Be still."

Her own voice surprised her.

"Yes," Milos said.

Belly to thigh. Sweat pool. Hair.

Two lines. One dipping. One lifting.

Moisture.

Hair. The hairs glistening. If time had been stopped in that
moment, she would have paused to count them. But time continued. The hairs seemed tipped towards her—outward—towards
the camera—and downward towards the depths of the groin.

And the penis ...

Why is it suddenly the *penis—not* his *penis?*

Stop asking stupid questions and take the picture. *Carpe diem.*

Click.

One.

#19: Though the barn itself was dead—or so one might have
thought—there was still much life. No cattle, sheep—no
horses, chickens, pigs—but there were swallows. *Swifts.*
Wings. Dartings. Cries.

Their nests were tucked beneath the cross-beams—*wattle-
and-daub*—mud, spittle and straw.

Milos looked up towards the birds as they came and went.

Jane had asked him to pull himself forward, so that his body would be more attenuated—less foreshortened. More accessible.

The hairs on his legs and arms were glinting in the sun. The movement of his readjustment had caused a minor dust storm which disturbed the birds, who were in the process of hatching a second brood. Certainly they were busy enough mending their nests—chattering away like Chinese mandarins playing mah-jong.

Milos smiled.

"You like birds?" he asked.

"Oh, yes. And you?"

"Yes. Will you take a picture, please?"

Jane had only four more frames on the present film.

"Please—yes?" Milos added.

"Of course."

Jane shot two frames of birds—and then, barely knowing what she was doing, she went to Milos, touched his thigh with the flat of her hand—and took a photograph all at once of his languid penis, resting in its nest of hair like a brooding swallow with a clutch of eggs.

"Birds," she said.

Milos looked down at her.

He smiled.

"Yes," he said. "Birds."

As they neared the last of the frames, Jane asked Milos to stand.

He had been seated now for almost two hours—though he had gone, in that time, behind the barn to urinate.

Urinate.

That's right, Jane. He took a leak. He peed. Pissed. Wrote his name in the dust.

When he had come back, she went and did the same.

Only problem is, I can't write my name ...

Jane?

J-A-N-E? You can't write that?

God—you're a scream. Crawl back into your hole.

Just a joke. Thought you might need one, round about now.

Thank you, no.

Too much, eh? Too desirable? Is that the right word? Too goddamned gorgeous to live without ...?

Stop that.

Just thought I'd ...

Well, don't.

Sorry.

(A slight, mean-spirited pause.)

So. You made a puddle. Is that your signature? "My name is Puddle?"

Go away.

Can't. Stuck here. With you ...

Now he was standing above her.

All of him.

"Turn around."

"Yes."

"Lean your forehead—lean the left side of your forehead against the beam ..."

He did this.

"Let your shoulder rest there, too ... yes ... and ..."

She could not speak.

He was—literally—unutterably beautiful.

Oh, what do I do now?

Oh, God—what do I do?

Take the picture.

Jane stood back.

"Put ..." she said.

His body winced.

"Rest your right arm above your ..."

Bum.

"Like this?"

"Exactly."

He laid his wrist against himself, the wrist turned in, the hand open, its thumb rising ...

One long line, Janey—one long line ...

All the way from the neck to the crease between the cheeks and down the inside of his right leg ...

And along his bent arm, a vein that tracked the lifeline to his palm—sweat in every meeting-place, hairs flowing down his thighs—fingernails turned away, their blackened, work-stained edges—gentle reminders—silent exclamation marks—the soil of which he was a part.

There were two more frames.

"Look at me."

He turned.

The camera clicked.

She set it down.

"Done," she said.

They shook hands.

Jane turned away.

"No," he said.

He reached out and touched her shoulder.

"No," he said again.

She looked at him.

He was stooping, one knee resting on the bales, the other raised—all of him facing her.

He reached for the camera.

"It's not over," he said, lifting it so that he could see there was one last frame unused.

#40: Jane.

runner

Yet on the last page just a lingering doubt
That verdict, was it just? The judge's nerves,
That clue, that protestation from the gallows,
And our own smile ... why yes ...

W.H. Auden
Detective Story

1

Friday, August 7, 1998

You always know when a house is not empty. Not because of an unlocked door, an open window or a sudden noise on the second floor. You simply know you are not alone. It cannot be described any other way.

Luke felt it only seconds after he had entered the house on McKenzie Street, having parked his truck on the driveway. It was odd. He had almost gone directly from work to Mercy's house, but had thought it would be better to shower, change and have a beer first.

The only "abnormal" happenstance was that the light he always left on over the side door had either burned out or been turned off. Switching on the old bureau lamp beside the kitchen door, he tried to remember when he had changed the outdoor bulb last—but the fact was elusive. Maybe a month—maybe two months before.

He went to the fridge and got out a Sleeman.

Why not flick the switch and find out? he wondered—already certain of the answer. If the light had been turned off, then he was not alone. But he was not yet prepared to know this. He was content to pretend he was ignorant. *Let it ride.*

Why do we always try to appear nonchalant when we know we're being watched from the dark?

Interesting.

Luke took his cigarettes and lighter from a pocket, draping

his denim jacket over the back of a chair and sitting down
where he knew there could be no one behind him.

Sometimes he turned on the radio on arriving home. Not
tonight. He wanted every unusual sound to register.

Why don't burglars ever fart?

'Cause they never eat beans.

Grade Four—Lenny Gregson—quote, unquote.

This made him smile.

Silence. Not even flies.

I wish I had a dog.

No. That decision had been made after Danny had been
killed in front of the house by a truck. *Never again.*

Never.

He drank from the bottle and lighted a cigarette.

Maybe if I phoned someone ... Mercy.

He looked at the telephone across the room. It seemed to
look back at him expectantly. *Use me. I'm bored.*

No. Bad idea. Don't involve her in this.

The telephone drooped and pouted.

Luke wondered what Mercy was doing.

He glanced without expression at his watch.

Seven-forty-two.

She would be standing by the stove, finishing supper for Jane
and Will—unless they were going to Pazzo. Standing by the
stove, or cutting up a lettuce or putting the last piece in Will's
puzzle—a privilege the boy would offer her the way a man will
offer a diamond, if he has one, to the woman he loves.

Something fell to the floor. Inside the house, perhaps, or in
his mind.

*Turn on some more lights. Act naturally. Never let an enemy
see your fear.*

But it could be Uncle Jess ...

You think he's not an enemy?

Luke stood up. Two more lights in the kitchen. The back hallway.

Stairs.

He started to hum.

It's a long way to Tipperary,

It's a long way to go ...

That was the old family name for the john.

He veered into the room he used as an office—turned on the overhead green-shaded brass lamp and locked the cupboard door without opening it first.

If someone's in there, he thought, pocketing the key, *they'll need an axe to get out—and there isn't room to swing a cat, let alone an axe ...*

No one in the dining-room. Just the twelve empty chairs and the table with its rotting apples sitting on their plate.

No one in the living-room.

No one on the stairs.

Front door locked. He tested it.

Up to the landing. Light switch for the upper hall.

No one.

He looked in each of the bedrooms, turning on lights as he went and leaving them lit.

All that was left was the small two-piece bath, his own large bathroom—once his parents'—and his bedroom.

He checked the linen closet. Nothing but linen—almost a disappointment.

The suspense was affecting his back—his shoulders—his knees.

He reached along the wall for the lights in his bedroom.

They did not go on.

Darkness.

And someone waiting.

"I've turned the bulbs out," a voice said. "I can see you in the light from the door, but I don't want you to see me."

"Why not?"

"It's not a pretty sight."

"Are you hurt?"

"Sort of."

"*Sort of* doesn't sound like something I shouldn't see."

"Well ... maybe more than *sort of*. I just didn't want you to see it, that's all. They marked me."

"Jesus. You mean they cut you?"

"Yeah. On the face. It's the way they play the game. So's you can't go back for more."

"Are you in pain?"

"Aren't we all?"

"Don't get smart-ass. Tell me the truth."

"Of course I'm in pain, you cocksucker! You don't get cut without feeling it."

"Do you need a doctor?"

"Call a doctor and you're dead, Luke. Stone cold."

Luke knew this was true. Jesse made no threats he could not fulfil. There was always that knife. The switchblade in the back pocket.

"Let me do something. Come on. Get real. Let me at least do something."

"No, boy. No. I cleaned it up already. I just don't want you to see."

"Do they know where you are?"

"Probably." And then: "I'm sorry. I didn't want to get you in trouble, but there was nowhere else to go ..."

The old story. The same old story. *Nowhere else to go.*

"There's that light on the tallboy. You can turn that bulb on."

Luke moved to the tallboy and screwed the bulb back into place.

Jesse was half sitting, half lying on the bed—leaning back against the pillows, all the covers disarranged—his feet, in their stupid, childish running shoes, drawn in towards his bum—one hand holding a towel against his left cheek, the other hand holding a half-emptied glass of Luke's best whisky, Jameson's.

Luke could not see the cuts in the shadows created by the single bulb and by Jesse's raised and towelled hand, but he could see that both of his uncle's eyes had been blackened.

"Light me a cigarette, there's a good boy."

"Yes, sir." Luke had to smile. "You sound just like Dad."

"Why not? I'm his brother. We inherited the same voice. Just light me the cigarette."

Luke did this and crossed the room.

"No lookin'."

"Don't be ridiculous. I can't hand it to the wind."

Jesse set his drink on the bedside table and took the cigarette. He did not let go of the towel.

"Is that bottle up here?"

"On the floor. There."

Jesse indicated a place by his right side.

"Is there anything in it?"

"Sure. I only had one other drink besides this."

Luke went around the bed, picked up the bottle and went into the bathroom, where he dumped his toothbrushes from a heavy tumbler and filled it with whisky. The water glass had been in Jesse's hand.

It was only now that Luke noticed a bloodied towel thrown aside in a corner behind the toilet, and the bloodstains on the sides of the sink where Jesse must have gripped it in his hands while running the water to clean his wound.

Funny how it darkens down, blood, once it's spilled. Funny how nothing can disguise what it is. Must be some kind of atavistic survival instinct. Blood is flowing—beware ...

He went back into the bedroom and sat in the chair by the window, drink in hand. He lighted a cigarette and looked at the yard outside.

"What am I supposed to do?" he asked.

"You aren' suppose to tell no one I'm here."

"Okay."

"You aren' suppose to call no doctors."

"I won't."

"An', of course, you aren' suppose to tell no police."

"You're asking for a lot of silence, Jess."

"Yeah. And I'll 'cept the silence as 'greement, Luke. You already promise not to tell no one—an' *no one* include police an' doctor. Unerstood?"

"Yes."

"I mean it."

"Yes. I know you do."

"Otherwise, you're dead, bud."

"Sure. Yes. Dead."

"You got a woman now, I'm told."

"Oh?"

"Yeah. I heard it on th' street from some guy. Says you got a girlfrien'."

"I'm a little old for a *girlfriend*, Jess. I'm fifty, almost. She's even older."

"No kiddin'—you almos' fifty? I wouldn't'a pegged you more'n forty."

"Well ... here I am. Fifty."

"What's 'er name?"

"Marilyn Monroe."

"Oh, sure."

"I'm not telling. She made me promise. Just like you."

"Okay. Fine by me. Is she a good lay?"

"Are you?"

"Ho—ho—ho! Get the kid here! Talkin' back, already."

"It's none of your goddamned business, Jess. Besides, I'd rather hear about you than talk about me. What's been going on?"

As if you didn't know—or couldn't guess.

"I just been lyin' here, thinkin'."

"Oh? About what?"

"How all us kids used to come in here an' lie on this bed in the old days. How we'd make a pile-up Sunday mornin's, with Mum and Dad—Mar'beth an' Preacher—wearin' nothin' but their skin and we'd all come roarin' in, the ten of us, an' pile up all over 'em ... couple'a dogs—some cats—an' all us kids— an' we'd sing."

"Sing?"

"Yeah. We'd sing. Like 'Bicycle Built for Two' an' stuff. Like 'The Moon Comes Over the Mountain'—'Put on Your Old Grey Bonnet'—stuff like that. An' we always ended up with 'Tipperary,' 'cause one of us always had go to the john an' take a leak, 'cause we all got so excited, jumpin' up an' down an' singing an' all. God, but we had good times. God, but we had good times. Oh God ..."

Jesse started to weep.

"... Oh God, but we had such good, good times. Sweet times. Laughin' times. Always we had that ... always laughin'. Always singin'. Mum 'n' Dad."

Luke watched as Jesse manoeuvred the towel to his eyes to wipe away his tears.

"I done somethin' wrong, Luke. I just done somethin' real, real wrong. The worse a person can do."

"I know."

"You know? So how? You never got my call."

"What call?"

"I called you. At Kincaids'. Weeks ago—just after ... just after last time I saw you."

"You're right. I didn't get any call from you."

" 'Course not. Something wrong with the fuckin' phone. I couldn't get through."

"Oh. Then."

"Yeah, then."

"So? What did you want?"

"I d'know. I wanted ... help."

"What kind of help?"

"How the Christ should I know? I just wanted help. But I couldn't get through."

"And so ..."

"An' so ... I do be tired, Luke. I do be tired. An' scared. I'm scared. I don't know this man—this man I am. This man—I don't know—this man I don't know, who seems to be me, but I never met 'im, 'cept in the worse o' my dreams. I mean—like—I'm scared o' him. He scares me. Scares me. Scares the shit outa me. Oh God—I don't wanna be this man. I'm not this man. I'm *not*. I don't *know* him. Who the hell is he—who owns me? *Who the hell is he?* Where did he come from outa this ... outa this one-time happy kid? Where the hell did he *come from?* I don't wanna kill nobody. I don' wanna do that. How could I do that? How could I *do* that? Jesus. Jesus. Jesus. Help me, somebody help me. SOMEBODY HELP ME."

Luke stood up, his shoulders lowered, cigarette dangling, his feet like weights—cemented, incapable—and dragged the Jameson's off the floor.

Give him something. Give *him something. Anything. This.*

He went to the bed, refilled Jesse's glass and touched his uncle's forehead with the heel of the bottle. It would feel cool. It would feel connected—weight—like a hand—a finger— almost human.

Retreating to the chair, he refilled his own glass.

Luke looked at his uncle—recumbent on the bed, with his

killer's eyes and what they had seen—his killer's hands and what they had done—his childlike heart and all that it could not encompass. Jesse's only compassion, ever, had been for his own sad state. He had never understood there was something he shared with others. Only *he* felt sad—only *he* felt glad ... no one else ever cried ...

Sounds like the lyrics of a song.

Why not? You think a song can't tell the truth? And doesn't ...

"Jess?"

There was no response. Possibly a shift in the gaze from the end of his cigarette to the amount of liquor left in his glass. Nothing else.

"Runner?"

"Yeah, what?"

"Hey—don't get surly here, buster. You're lying on *my* bed. That's your blood on *my* towel—*my* pillow—your crappy shoes leaving dog shit on my covers. Don't fucking get short with me, Jess."

Luke knew Jesse would understand the tone of this. It was how he drew his own lines around his life. It was always *fuck off*—or *come in and be fucked*. There were no other rules. *Buy my act*—or *buy out.*

"So?" Jesse said.

He stubbed out his cigarette.

Luke winced.

Jesse had used the bedside table as his ashtray.

"What do you want to happen next?"

"Whad'ya mean, *happen next?*"

"Come on, Jess. You're running. I know you're running from the cops—but who else?"

"Them."

"I know, *them*. But who exactly are they?"

"You know 'em."

"I only know them because I've had some phone calls. And—maybe—I recognized the voices. But I can't be sure. Just tell me. Are they here? In Stratford? Kitchener? London? Or Windsor-Detroit?"

"Windsor-Detroit."

Jesus.

This was as serious as it could get. Windsor-Detroit was the hub. People died there. Were murdered. It was a gateway for illegal immigrants, prostitution and, above all, drugs.

"Are there guns? I know about the knives—but are there guns?"

"They don't need guns. Fact is, they never use 'em. There's other ways than guns. Other ways than knives, too. Like wires an' ropes an' plastic garbage bags as hoods. They got all kinds o' ways."

"Did you kill these women?"

Jesse lighted another cigarette ...

"Did you kill these women?"

... stared at the bloodied towel in his hand and threw it aside.

"Jess. Tell me. Just—for Christ's sake—say *yes* or say *no*. *Tell* me."

"I don't know."

"Come on, Jesse. Jesus! You did or you didn't."

"I don't know! I honest-to-God don't know. I know I was with Lenore Archer, but I was out of it. I know she said *no*. I remember that—so I hit her." Jesse blinked at Luke like a man trying to see through the dark. "I was there. She said *no*. I hit her—then I woke up down by the river. Next thing I know, people are saying Lenore is dead. She's dead. Murdered. Killed. By some guy who raped her. But she said *no*, Luke. She said *no*. An' I hit her—maybe real hard—but I don't remember the rest. Only the feelin' it musta been me. I mean—she's dead. So it musta been me."

Luke waited. Then he said, almost whispering it: "have there been others?"

"Yes. I think maybe—but I don't know. When you're out of it, you're out. It's worse'n bein' drunk, 'cause you're gone. Like *gone*, Luke. Like you died and come back—an' everythin's blank in the middle. The middle just isn't there. There's a beginnin'—there's an end and nothin' in between."

Luke looked out the window. Twilight was ending. It would soon be dark.

"I'm tellin' you true, Lukey. I'm tellin' you all the truth I know. Honest. That's all I know."

Don't call me Lukey, for God's sake—I'm not a child any more—and neither are you. Stop playing the goddamned fucking helpless child!

Tears of rage filled Luke's eyes. And dried.

He looked at Jesse—Jesse pushing himself fully into a sitting position, trying to light another cigarette without showing where he had been cut.

He *was* a child. A damaged child with an incomplete conscience—whose only pleasure had been pleasure itself—at all its simplest levels: *food—drink—drugs—sleep—and a good fuck, if you could steal one.* Never knowing how to be touched, he had never learned how to touch. Always shying away with a laugh, with a giggle, a smile when someone approached—or retreating, withdrawing in alarm—even, at worst, from his mother: *don't!* But never reaching beyond the desire to reach. Never understanding—never knowing how to send his fingers out into the air. Never, never saying *please*— or ever knowing what it meant to desire something beyond what you merely wanted—beyond what you considered yours by right.

For Jesse, the privilege of being wanted for himself had never been known. He was just one of *them—one of many—one of all*. Just someone on the street. No one had ever singled him out and said: *hey, wait a minute! It's you I want!* Which was why, perhaps, he had created his own unique world, where everything was taken because nothing had been given—or was likely to be given. Outside of Jesse's parents' love, and the grudging friendship of his siblings, there had been nothing. Nothing up close and not from a distance. A cruel person might say that Jesse Quinlan had *flunked all the desirability tests,* and moved on to gain remarkably high marks in hatefulness. To most, he was less than a rat and little more than a snake. But if you looked—as Luke was looking now through the dusk—you could see the man, a person whose suffering was incomprehensible to himself, whose agony of loss was founded on the fact that he had never owned anything. Not even dignity. Not even that.

"So, what're we gonna do now?" Jesse asked.

Luke had to look down at the floor.

What are we going to do now? Jesus.

"We could go out dancing," he said.

Jesse laughed. "Yeah, sure. Me dancin'. That'll be the day."

He gave a shrug. The last of the twilight reached for him.

Beyond the window, the birds called out whatever it is they call at dusk: *come home,* perhaps. Or: *take care, take care.* Whatever, it was loud and clear.

That dog that was always *down the street*, no matter where you were in town, began to bark. Suppertime? Strangers? Another dog? A rapist? A cat? A child stumbling home? Some-one arriving—someone's shadow leaning in towards the door. A murderer, perhaps.

No. The murderers are all right here.

All of them.

Messing up the bed.

Bleeding on the towels ...

Clinging—as if to Luke himself.

It's your blood, too.

Luke went down to the kitchen and made four sandwiches—ham and lettuce, some mustard—pressed between thick-cut slices of rye bread. He got out his knapsack, emptied it of his own possessions, put in a Thermos of hot tomato soup, the sandwiches, six packages of cigarettes and another bottle of whisky *to keep the cold away.*

He was done with Jesse—done with him. There was nowhere he could hide him, no way he could protect him, no one he could send him to. All his adult life, Luke had been his uncle's guardian. And his only friend. Now—no more.

There are limits, goddammit! There are fucking limits!

He got out his wallet and counted his cash. Luckily, a customer had paid him today at noon. Two hundred dollars in bills. There was always the notion that cold, hard cash had a value all its own. *Saves on taxes.*

So—I'm a crook.

And about time.

He would give it all to Jesse.

He would tell him never to come back.

He would tell him it was over.

And, in his heart, he knew that Jesse would understand this.

There are fucking limits, Jess: language—and a sentiment—Jesse would comprehend.

Otherwise, you have to turn him over to the police.

And that, no matter what, would never happen.

Never.

Luke went to the stairs, closed his eyes and went up.

He caught Jesse looking in the tallboy's top drawer—probably for money.

"I'm cold. I thought maybe there was a sweater ..."

Perhaps he meant it.

The truth was, it was hot—but a person in shock may not know that.

"Wait a minute. Stand away."

Luke went to the tallboy and got a thick black sweater out of the bottom drawer.

"Come on downstairs."

In the kitchen, Luke handed Jesse the knapsack, the sweater and the two hundred dollars in bills.

"What's all this?"

"You're leaving, Jess."

"Jesus, kid."

"Don't ask me to change my mind. It won't be changed. You're going—and you're not coming back."

Jesse folded his hand around the money and jammed it into his pocket.

"What am I gonna do?" he said.

"Leave."

Jesse heaved a few tears into his eyes and let them spill. He was good at that. He always had been.

"Goodbye, Jess."

Jesse fisted the tears away. The cut on his left cheek had been carved in the shape of a *D* for *Deadbeat*, which meant he failed to pay his debts. It was open still and livid. But he had forced himself to endure a washing of it and a dose of alcohol, so that at least it was clean, though it should have been stitched.

"Okay, then."

And that was all. He swivelled towards the door, pulled the knapsack onto his back, tied the sweater around his shoulders and—not even turning for one last look—he pushed the screen door open, shut it carefully behind him and was gone.

Darkness. The dog. And the owl on the roof. That was all. Nothing else. Not even traffic.

There was a dealer with the unlikely name of Melvin Plunkett. He lived above a warehouse in a loft.

Now in his sixties, Melvin had once been a promising entrepreneur in the early 1980s, offering the work of unknown artisans—men and women who made furniture and knew enough about antiquing methods to successfully transform a twentieth-century factory-made chair from Kitchener into a nineteenth- or eighteenth-century kitchen chair from Tuscany or Provence. Melvin had no talent himself for such things, only the talent to seek the talent out in others and to scoop up the money resting between the commission and the making. Then came the recession. Custom melted away.

Drugs were a godsend for Melvin Plunkett. The dealers came to him because he had a ready-made clientele of adventurous young millionaires and the climbing, clambering class of real-estate brokers who flourished in the 1980s and coasted into the 1990s with money still in hand.

Melvin knew many of these people from a shared childhood of impoverished genteel providence—private schools—upper-class neighbourhoods and dependence on an ever-promised family resurgence that failed to materialize. But sometimes it flourished briefly in the sale of a Rosedale mansion or a fleet of antique cars or paintings. In Melvin's growing years, a person survived not only on the moot inheritance of a good family name, but on dropping other names with the precision of a skilled bombardier.

Jesse had dealt with Melvin Plunkett in flush times—and

now, he went back to him at the end of his rope. He got through the door to the loft by flashing the bills that Luke had given him. Then Melvin saw the scar on his cheek.

"Jesus," Melvin said.

And that was all.

Jesse grabbed him by the shoulder, spun him round and hit him on the base of his skull with a convenient club of deadwood found in a pile of garden refuse by the curb, waiting for pick-up in the morning.

Melvin was wearing only his underwear—unattractive and olive-green—and fell to the floor like a stone. It would be hours before he awoke.

Jesse had been often enough in Melvin's loft to know where everything was: the stash, the needles and the spoons. He put the bills back in the breast pocket of his jean jacket, dumped his take into the knapsack and left. Only one word had been spoken: *Jesus.*

In the night, it rained.

Jesse went down to the river.

It was his favourite place. Ghost swans floating silent on the water—the rain falling sibilant from the trees—frog-song and worm-music—the Japanese curve of the bridges leading to the islands—the reflected lights on the current—and the distant sound of pianos from restaurants and bars.

The last he heard were the strains of Joni Mitchell's "Both Sides Now"—his lullaby.

In the morning he was dead.

Luke found him, as it seemed he must. He was slumped across a picnic table near the arena. His final act had been to shoot up everything in his arsenal. There was not a chance of survival.

For a quarter of an hour, Luke sat opposite him with his back to the river, holding Jesse's hand.

Runner.

Well. Now, he had gone the full distance. *The marathon to death.*

Oddly, at the very moment Luke had this thought, an early morning jogger passed by heading for the town centre.

"Morning."

"Morning."

A middle-aged counterpart to Jesse—but someone who wanted to live.

Luke watched him go into the mist and went round to inspect what remained of Jesse's possessions. Either his uncle had eaten, or someone had stolen the sandwiches. And the bottle. But not the soup. The sweater Luke had given him was gone, too, and Luke thought: *well—I'll keep my eyes open on the street. It may turn up and if it does, I'll know who the bastard was ...*

In Jesse's trouser pocket on the left side—the side he was slumped on—he found a wallet. Jesse's own was gone. But the thief might have been afraid to move him, and had failed to detect this one.

Luke pulled it free and looked inside. No money—but all the cards were there. A woman in Kitchener. Luke recognized the name from the newspaper reports. *Patricia Jackson.* Murder victim number one.

Well.

And so.

At 6:50, two policemen in a patrol car rolled past, headed for the far end.

Seeing Luke and Jesse, they stopped.

One of them got out.

"G'day."

"G'day."

"Everything all right here?"

"No," said Luke. "He's dead."

The other policeman left the car and approached with a cell-phone in his hand.

"Know who he is?"

"Yes. He's my uncle."

"And?"

"And ... I think you'd better see this. It was in his pocket."

Luke gave the wallet to the first policeman.

"Well, well, well," the officer said, and passed the wallet to his companion. "Well, well, well."

An ambulance was called. Luke was questioned. All the usual. An autopsy would tell what had happened. Clearly, Luke himself was clean. There was no suspicion. One of the policemen knew who he was.

In time—in a month—the verdict would be inconclusive regarding Jesse's death: *deliberate* or *accidental*. The point was moot. It hardly mattered. But the verdict about his three victims was positive—based on his relationship with Lenore Archer, and on a government cheque found in his room, made out to Margaret Miller, but never cashed.

And there were no more killings.

Whatever else could be said for Jesse, in his own sad way he had loved the fact of life—of being alive. *You know*, he had once said, *if there was no tomorrow, I don't know what I'd do.*

Let him pass. Let him pass, Luke had thought as Jesse's corpse disappeared into the ambulance. *Let him pass*—the way a breeze will pass. A whisper. A blink. And nothing more.

conclusions

In the burrows of the Nightmare
Where Justice naked is,
Time watches from the shadow
And coughs when you would kiss.

In headaches and in worry
Vaguely life leaks away,
And Time will have his fancy
To-morrow or to-day.

W.H. Auden
As I walked out one evening

1

Jane was still not used to waking up alone. Her hand still went out to find Griff, her eyes still looked for him, her ears still wanted the sound of his breathing, she still missed the smell of his skin and the touch, time to time, of his restless toes.

But. He was gone.

Now, there was another man—not her own, but someone else's—someone with a foreign name too difficult to speak, too indecipherable to spell. *Agnewska*. Jane could not say it—she could only hear it in the voice of a man she barely knew, but a man she also knew she loved.

She threw back the covers.

Will would be waiting for her.

No. He would not. He had given up waiting for her days ago. His survival now was entirely in Mercy's hands.

At the top of the stairs, barefooted but wearing her robe—what she had laughingly once called her *peignoir*—Jane listened to the sounds that were rising from the kitchen. She closed her eyes, drew in the scents of coffee, toast and bacon—Sunday-only food—and watched as Rudyard climbed up past her and went into the all-too-empty bedroom behind her, without a moment's pause to acknowledge her presence. He, too, missed Griff—but more than that, Rudyard still waited for him to come back.

Jane held the newel post in her right hand and made a curve around it with her fingers.

Hold on.

The wood of the steps was cool beneath her feet. There must be an open door. Someone had been cutting grass—probably Mrs Arnprior, who chose to have the boy come every Sunday at 7:00, just so she could be sure that if she could not sleep, no one else would.

Winter Sundays, the boy shovelled snow; autumn Sundays, he raked leaves; in spring, he hosed the driveway and rattled the garbage cans. Jane imagined he could not be normal. What normal teenager would willingly deprive himself of the only sleep-in he could hope for in the week? His name was Norman Fellows and twenty years later, so he dreamed, he would rival the names of Einstein and Hawking—and perhaps he would. But now, in Jane's estimation, he was strictly a pain in the ass. *And got paid for it!*

Still, the smell of cut grass was always a pleasure.

"Good for Norman," she muttered aloud. For a change, he had not been responsible for her early waking. That had been the empty place beside her in the bed.

In the kitchen, she took a cup to the counter and filled it with coffee.

"Morning," she said—and forced a smile.

Neither Mercy nor Will replied. As soon as Jane sat down, Mercy stood up.

"Jesse Quinlan's dead," she said. And went to the stove. "You hungry?"

"In a minute," Jane said—reaching out to ruffle Will's already tousled hair. "You ever hear the word *comb?*" she asked, smiling again.

"Not on Sundays. Only weekdays. Where's Dad?"

Sneaky.

Will was good at that. Start saying one thing, end with another—the other always a calculated surprise. A shock.

Jesus.

"You know he's gone, Will."

"Maybe. But where?"

Jane got out her cigarettes and matches.

"Off," she said. "Just *off*."

"You're not allowed to smoke inside when I'm here," Will said. And then: "you made the rule. I didn't. I don't care what you do."

Nevertheless, Jane set the cigarettes and matches aside.

Will said: "you really don't know where Dad is?"

"I really don't know."

"I saw him on the street. Other side of Ontario, by Bentley's. I waited, but he didn't look. Yesterday."

Jane refused to ask the obvious.

Will said it, anyway.

"He was alone."

"I see."

Mercy was turning the bacon in the pan.

"You want eggs?" she said to Will.

"One. Only one."

"Did the word *please* suddenly disappear overnight?" Jane said.

"I don't have to say *please* to Mercy. She's a servant."

Jane hit him.

Flat of the hand—stinging, but not harming.

Will hit her back the same way.

Jane was astonished. Speechless.

Will stood up.

At the sunroom door, he turned to her and spoke without nuance: "why don't you all fuck off."

Not even a question. Just the words. Six of them. *Why. Don't. You. All. Fuck. Off.*

He closed the door.

He did not slam it.

He closed it.

All of this happened in slow motion.

Jane waited—struck a match and inhaled.

"So," she said.

And that was all.

Then she stood up and went to the dining-room—retrieved a bottle of Côtes de Rhône, emptied her cup of its coffee in the sink, opened the bottle, refilled the cup and drained it. Then she filled it again.

"So—what are you doing today?" she said.

Mercy turned off the heat beneath the bacon and put the lid on the pan.

"If I didn't love Will, I'd be quitting."

"That's interesting. I mean—that's an interesting thing for a servant to do. A mere servant."

"I didn't mind that. I didn't mind it, because I knew he was saying it to you, not me."

"I only hit him because you were standing there and heard him."

"Does that mean you wouldn't've hit him if he said it and I wasn't here?"

"You know it doesn't mean that. If you hadn't been here I might've slugged him—knocked him flat. Jesus, Merce, I did it for your sake."

"Thanks all the same, next time, sit on your hands. Let me handle it."

"*He's* MY *son!*"

"Is he, now? Well—you could've fooled me."

Mercy came to the table with an empty glass.

"Any of that wine looking for a home?" she said.

"Sure."

Mercy sat down and poured for them both.

"You get drunk before noon, you'll miss that meeting," she said.

"What meeting?"

"Aren't you meeting someone? Elspeth someone?"

"Oh, yes. Thanks for reminding me. She's a photographer."

"You getting your picture took?"

"Very funny."

"Will you say *cheese?* Or *Pepsi?*"

"Neither. I say *shit*. Make a note for future reference. You can't say *shit* without smiling."

Mercy laughed—and stole a cigarette.

Jane pretended not to notice. "What're you going to do with all that bacon?"

"We're going to eat it. You, me and Will. He'll come back in. He's a boy, isn't he? A boy. You know—one of those young things needs a new pair of shoes every six days because he's growing. Called *a boy*. Not like a girl. We only grew on Sundays. Like today. Which is why we're going to eat the bacon. This is *our* day—yours and mine. And to think—it used to be my day off. Ah, well ..."

Jane reached out and took Mercy's free hand.

"Thank God for Mercy," she whispered. "Thank you, God, for Mercy."

She lifted the hand, kissed it and placed it back on the table.

There was a silence.

Neither woman moved.

Then Mercy said: "you hear me tell you Jesse Quinlan's dead?"

"No. Dear heaven. Poor Luke."

"Luke found him in the park by the river. Dead of an over-dose."

"Inevitable."

"I guess."

"Where had he been? I thought he'd run off."

"Well ... he came back."

2

Sunday, August 9, 1998

At two o'clock, as arranged, Jane drove to Ellie Benton's house on Mornington Street, which was also her studio. Unlike many of its neighbours, it was not greatly large but it was beautifully designed in an Edwardian style and was flanked by two others that must have had the same architect.

Elspeth Benton was not quite forty—a contemporary of Jane's who, on occasion, had shared classes with her under J.T. Weatherbee's tutelage. Basically a photographic portrait-ist, she also had a fondness—and some talent—for "portraits" of rooms and gardens emptied of their people. The people, however, *seemed* to be present. Jane had told her: *you photo-graph ghosts.*

It was true. One of Ellie's most famous photographs, which won both national and international competitions, was of a wisp of smoke left behind when Orson Welles had shifted from a chair at her request. Welles was famous for his cigars—among other things—and Ellie had debated asking him to give them up during her sitting with him, as Yousuf Karsh had done for his

portrait of Winston Churchill. But she disliked the thought of
the word *copycat* and had asked Welles to vacate the chair after
taking a mighty Wellesian drag on the cigar, and exhaling. The
designation of the picture was simply: *Orson Welles, 1982.*

Her first words to Jane on opening the door to admit her
were: "I was afraid you would get cold feet and fail to turn up."

Once inside, they went to the studio, where Ellie had set the
printed photos on the table, inside a large brown envelope on
which was written: *Jane.*

"Well ..." She smiled. "I certainly don't have to ask you how
you've been."

Jane shrugged.

"Not good enough, Aura Lee. A shrug says nothing. That's
its purpose. You want a glass of red?"

"Of course."

Jane set her bag aside and sat down.

She folded her hands in her lap. The envelope, filled with
Milos, had been stranded—perhaps deliberately—in the centre
of the table. The table was round. It had a green baize cover,
as if Jane and Ellie might be planning to play cards.

Ellie returned with wine already poured into giant balloon
glasses on thick stems. She set them down and plunked an
ashtray off to one side.

"Well ..." she said. "And I do mean *well*. Good heavens!
He's gorgeous!"

She raised her glass, grinned and drank.

Jane did the same. Without grinning.

Ellie leaned forward over the table.

"Okay, what's his name?"

"Milos. But he's not a model. Just a ..."

"Friend?"

"No. Acquaintance."

"Yeah, sure. Okay. I'd like to photograph him. With his clothes on."

Jane laughed.

Then sobered.

"You meant that," she said.

"Yep."

"It's not the greatest face on earth. In clothes, he's just ..." She scurried after a word. "He's just *there*."

"No. There's more."

Jane looked away.

Ellie reached for the envelope, opened it and spilled the pictures onto the baize.

She separated them—each photo facing Jane—using her finger-ends as if she was afraid of leaving her prints as evidence that she had seen them—using only her nails as traffic controllers.

"Aura Lee, my darling, these are not figure studies. These are love letters."

Jane did not look.

"Are they good?"

"Yes."

"Does that mean a whole new career is opening up before me? Photographing naked men? Sorry. *Male nudes*."

"No. But possibly a whole new way of seeing."

"Oh?"

"Yes."

Jane sat back.

"Can I tell you something?" Ellie said.

"Of course."

"All the time you thought you were shooting his butt, his shoulders, his cock—you were shooting *him*. There's a hell of lot more in these than just a naked guy. There's a person here.

Whole, but unconnected to the rest of us. Ethereal. Perhaps even an angel."

"Oddly enough, I thought of him as the *angel-man*. But angels don't take their clothes off for ladies."

"This one did."

Jane was silent. She drank.

"Why don't you look at them?"

"I'm afraid of them," Jane said at last. "Maybe."

"Look at this one," Ellie said, passing one of the prints through the air.

Jane glanced towards it.

"Take it. Take it ..."

The picture fluttered.

"Take it. *Look*."

Jane set down the balloon and accepted the photograph.

"Who's that?" Ellie asked.

Jane did not answer.

"It's Jane Aura Lee, hon. It's you. The you *you* never see."

It was just her face. Gazing upward, not quite smiling.

She was beautiful.

True. But something more than that. She was lost.

Ellie reached out and took her hand.

"None of us can see ourselves, Aura Lee. We can only see each other."

Jane bit her lip, set the photograph aside and looked up at Ellie. There were tears in her eyes.

"He's not even a photographer," she said. "He just snapped a picture."

"In the right moment," said Ellie. "He caught you. And that's what photography is about. It's about catching people unaware. Even a chair, a table, a lamp knows what it is when someone sits down, makes a six-place setting or turns a switch on. But the secret of seeing—truly seeing—is when the chair has just been vacated—when a glass is emptied and all the dirty utensils are lying on the plate and when the switch is turned off ..."

"When Orson Welles leaves the frame."

"When Orson Welles leaves the frame." Ellie picked up the picture of Jane. "I almost didn't give this to you. I thought ... *this isn't a good moment ... Maybe when she's old enough ...*"

Jane looked at Ellie, almost amazed.

"Old enough?"

Ellie smiled.

"I'm not going to explain that. *Never apologize, never explain.* Every artist's credo. But think about it. This picture broke my heart—and mended it in the process. As it began to emerge in the developer, dear friend, I began to weep. But by the time it was fully developed, I wanted to cheer. It's you, Aura Lee. And time you knew it."

Ellie was not *attractive.* She had another kind of beauty. Honesty. Her sense of presentation did not extend to herself, only to her pictures. Her hair was always the wrong length— too long, too short—she dressed in inappropriate colours, perhaps because she saw in black and white, like most of the best photographers. And she wore what she herself called *Greta Garbo shoes*—size-ten clodhoppers.

Looking up and seeing her across the table, Jane put her picture back amidst the others and, keeping it on top, she shuffled all of them like cards and placed them in the envelope. But her eyes never left Ellie's.

"There's a book about child abuse called *Our Little Secret*, El. This is our little secret—yours and mine."

"Understood."

"I'll look at these when I'm alone."

"Probably wise."

"You know Griff's left."

"Of course. Who doesn't. He made sure of that."

"Did he, now."

"Yep. Told everyone."

"Where is he?"

"You don't know?"

"Would I ask?"

Ellie looked away.

"It's none of my business," she said. "I don't know where he is," she lied. "And frankly, I don't care."

She did care—for Jane's sake, if nothing else. That had been the basis of their friendship—of all Ellie's friendships. There was no romance in her life. For her, romance was other people. All of them—if she loved them. There was little differentiation in her reflective attitude to those she was attracted to: men, women, children, dogs, cats, *things*—views, angles, daylight, moonlight, darkness. It was all a gift, if you knew how to accept it.

Jane opened her bag, put the photographs into it and got out her wallet.

"I want to pay cash, El. I don't want a record."

"Are you mad?"

"I hope not."

"Aura Lee, honey ... I will not accept a penny. All I want to know is how I can get in touch with him."

"I can't tell you that."

"Can't, or won't?"

"Can't. It's not his job. It's not what he does. For a living. I just can't tell you."

"Okay." Ellie smiled. "Just promise me one thing."

"Maybe."

"Next time you fall in love and borrow the camera, come back happier."

"Deal. If it ever happens."

"It will. I already know his name."

"Oh?"

"Yes." Ellie stood up. "His initials are G.K.—and he's coming back. You'd better believe it. I do."

Half an hour later, Jane was sitting in the park on a sequestered bench away from the path.

She had removed the envelope from her bag, but not opened it.

August 9th. In one month, her whole world had collapsed. She might have believed it could happen in a year—but in a month?

Troy. Griff's birthday party. The longing for the house. Luke's cutting of the telephone line. The arrival of Milos—not only on her doorstep, but in her life. Griff's mysterious behaviour. Tears of rage and impotence. The loss of his promised roles. His unimaginable disappearance from her life and his retirement into a privacy that, for Jane, was incomprehensible—that this most public of players should retreat from the scene, sending only his performances out in his place, was both mysterious and somehow sinister. And the effect of all this on Will, whom she was losing day by day in a now complete inability to communicate—he with her or she with him. *Why don't you all fuck off.* Jesus. And Rudyard grieving. And Jesse dead. And Loretta lost and gone. And Maybelle drifting. And Milos ... *What?*

Hanging in the mist. Seen, tasted, touched—but still unknown.

It had ended as swiftly as it had begun. *Do you?* Yes. *Will you?* Yes. *Goodbye.*

Goodbye.

She touched the envelope, where it lay beside her on the bench.

Look.

I can't.

Her hands were shaking.

What if someone saw her—looking at photographs of a naked man?

No one could see her. She knew that but she did not believe it.

Paranoia is every secret lover's companion—so at least you won't be completely alone ...

She took out the photographs and held them face down for a moment in her lap.

Milos.

Jane.

Turning them over, she set her own photograph aside, face down, on top of the envelope—so she would not have to see it. Herself ...

A flight of ducks winged past.

Mallards and teal.

She watched until they had disappeared downstream, where she could hear them landing in the water, claiming it with a clamour of voices—and a child's voice calling: *ducks, Mummy! Ducks!*

Ducks, Mummy—ducks. How often she had heard it in the same piping register from Will. *Ducks, Mummy. Ducks ...*

Birds.

She fingered the next photograph into view.

Milos seated, knee raised, head tilted back towards the beam, his flesh gleaming.

Dearest Jesus.

She lifted him higher into the leaf-filtered light.

What colour were his eyes?

She could not remember.

Dark.

Only dark.

Black—or seemingly so, the pupils distended because of the streaming dust-laden dimness that lit him.

Jane put the photograph back in its place, not looking at the others.

The memory of him was better than the record of it.

She closed her eyes and sat completely stilled.

When the last picture was taken and the camera set aside, he had led her up the worn-down steps into the loft.

They lay in the sun, side by side, both naked now—both dusty, both tasting, when they kissed, of red wine and self.

Their fingers met and touched. She led him to her breasts. He laid one hand on her belly and cupped her with the other.

Neither of them spoke. The swallows swooped and squeaked above them. A car went by on the road—an aeroplane over-head—a tractor moved through a neighbouring field.

She sank down the length of his torso, her hair streaming above her, fondled him, held him and put him in her mouth.

Milos flung his arms aside and spread himself like a feast.

How do we know these things, Jane wondered. *How do we know what to do? What can be done—and cannot.*

She possessed him as completely as a man more often possesses a woman. In a dream, while reaching for a glass of wine, she had found him. Now she drank him.

At the end, she rolled aside, her hand on his thigh, his hand on her shoulder. Still, neither spoke.

The birds fell silent. Everything stopped.

When they woke, it was moving on to dusk—not yet twilight, but the daylight fading.

In the car on the way back to Stratford, Milos said: "thank you."

That was all.

When she let him out on the corner of Erie and Ontario, Jane held onto his departing hand—pressing it until her fingers hurt. Then she let go. "Goodbye, Milos."

"Goodbye," he said.

He had never called her Jane.

Now, in the park, Jane lifted the photograph of herself.

Qui va là? Who's there?

Me.

Only me.

But all of me.

She fitted the pictures back into their envelope, placed the envelope in her bag, threw her cigarette aside, ground it into the muddied bank of the river, retrieved the butt and slipped it into her pocket.

Then she went home to Cambria Street.

That night, Jane dreamt that someone gave a party and all the guests, both male and female, were wearing Monica Lewinsky's blue dress with its stains.

No one thought this the least bit unusual or scandalous. The men and women inside the blue dresses were themselves, not disguised. Jane both knew and did not know who any of them were, in the way dreams have of presenting a cast of complete strangers as your closest friends.

Somebody sang a song.

Not a real song—a dream song.

It was sad and happy, beautiful to hear one minute, broken and distant the next.

It seemed they were all together on a boat—a ship at sea.

The sun was either setting or had just risen—Jane could not tell which. But knowing did not matter. They were on their way somewhere and the destination seemed not to matter. She was not afraid. No one seemed to be afraid.

She went to the side of the ship to look out to sea with a man who seemed to be an alien she did and did not recognize. They laid their hands side by side on the railing, but did not touch. The stars came and went. The sun—the moon—both darkness and light—and still they stood there side by side, alone, together.

Where are we now? Jane wondered in the dream. *Where have we been? Arriving or departing? Going home? Or leaving?*

The ship was childless. Nor were there any animals. Just all the men and women wearing the same blue dress.

Early in the morning, Jane went into her studio and put the envelope of photographs into a drawer.

For a moment, she stood there trying to remember if she was awake or not.

Locking the drawer, she held the key in her hand and the cold hard feel of it told her she had come home.

It also told her she had survived shipwreck.

Her nightgown was soaking wet.

Removing it, she threw it aside and climbed back into bed, still clutching the key.

She looked at the clock. Six. Two more hours to sleep.

3

At 2:30, Jane was standing in the foyer of Zehrs. In her hand was a plastic bag of lettuce, green onions, celery and two tins of tuna. Also a bottle of Hellman's mayonnaise. For a salad.

Behind her, there was a crowd of shopping carts and beside her, a woman who wanted to deposit one.

"I'm sorry," this woman said, politely enough, and smiling, "but could you move? I can't get by."

Jane stared at her.

"Yes," she said. "Yes—I'm sorry—but ..."

"Are you all right?"

"I ..."

"Ma'am?"

"Yes—I ... Do you know where there's a public ..."

What?

Public what?

Oh, God. Oh, Jesus.

"Toilet? You look sick."

"No. Public ..." At last it came out. "Telephone."

"In the parking lot. You sure you're all right?"

"Yes. Yes. Thank you."

At last, Jane made her way to the door.

The telephone booths were off to the left.

She entered one.

The door jammed and would not close.

Jane set her shopping bag on the floor and almost dropped her purse, fumbling for coins.

Inserting a quarter, she fought to bring Claire's number into focus.

At the far end, the phone began to ring.

Four—five—six times before Claire answered, out of breath.

"Sorry. Hello. I was in the garden."

"Cee?"

"Jane."

"I have to see you. *Now*."

Claire could tell she meant it.

"Okay. Hugh's off playing golf. Will you come right away?"

"Yes."

"Where are you?"

"Zehrs."

"Zehrs. You've lost your card and want to borrow thirty dollars ..."

"No."

"So?"

"I'll tell you when I get there. It's ... I can't."

"All right, kiddo. Just come. I'll be here."

Jane hung up.

Bag.

What?

Bag. Tuna salad.

Jane reached down, grabbed the bag—dropped it—grabbed it again and fought her way past the recalcitrant booth door.

Where's the Subaru?

She scanned the lot.

There.

Ten minutes later (it should have taken five but she made a wrong turn) she pulled up in front of the Highland house on Shrewsbury.

Claire was at the door.

"What the hell is going on?"

Jane went in and made for the kitchen.

"You brought me something?" Claire asked.

"What do you mean?"

"That bag."

"Oh. It's just some shopping. I guess I forgot to let go."

Claire had already opened a bottle of wine and set out two glasses.

"Sit," she said.

Jane sank into a chair.

Claire poured.

And waited.

Say nothing, she thought. *Let her do the talking.*

Jane slumped, staring at nothing, and then sat back.

"I've just been told ... I've just been told something I don't ... something I can't believe."

Claire closed her eyes.

Here it comes. What we've all waited for ...

"What?" she said.

"That goddamned fucking bitch Mary Jane Ralston was browsing in the ... browsing in the fresh veg area, when I went to pick up some celery and green onions ..."

"Oh?"

"Oh, yes. Oh, yes." Jane took a gulp of wine. "Our fingers brushed over the display of lettuces. And ..."

"And?"

"She looked at me as if she hadn't already seen me—which she *had*—and she said: *oh! if it isn't the late Mrs Griffin Kincaid.* So ... *what do you mean by that?* I said. *Well,* she said, *wellll ... we've all been wondering when the closet door was going to open. Now it has.* NOW IT HAS!"

"Jane—don't."

"SHE SAYS THAT GRIFFIN HAS BEEN SLEEPING WITH JONATHAN CRAWFORD!"

"Jane ..."

"JONATHAN FUCKING CRAWFORD, FOR GOD'S SAKE!"

Claire reached out and touched Jane on the wrist. "Don't," she said.

"WHAT DO YOU MEAN DON'T? GRIFF IS HAVING AN AFFAIR WITH ANOTHER MAN. GRIFF. GRIFF. GRIFF. MY HUSBAND. THE FATHER OF MY SON. WHAT DO YOU MEAN, DON'T?"

Jane subsided—got a tissue from her purse and blew her nose.

Then she fumbled a Matinee to her lips and tried to strike a match.

"Jesus—I can't even light a cigarette ..."

Claire lighted it for her.

"Oh, God, Claire. Oh, God. You have to tell me it isn't true. It can't be true. It *can't*."

Claire sat back. "Well," she said, "I'm sorry to have to say this—but it *is* true."

Jane stared at her.

"You've *known?*"

"Yes. For over a week. Well over two weeks."

"Why didn't you tell me? Why didn't you tell me?"

"Janey ... *how?* How could I tell you that?"

"You're my friend."

"Yes. I love you. And yes, I thought I should tell you, but rightly or wrongly—I thought: *she will find this out from Griff. One way or another, she will find out herself.* And I thought: *she won't want me to know.*"

"But you *do* know."

"Yes. But I haven't—and I'm not going to say a word. Not even to Hugh."

"How did you find out?"

"I saw them together once too often. I also know he's been

living with Nigel and Susan—and I knew there couldn't be an affair there—and I knew that Zoë Walker has been in hot pursuit of Richard Harms. And then ..."

"What?"

"And then I happened to see Jonathan kiss Griff at The Belfry—and Griff kissed him back. I've also heard of other sightings ..."

"Mary Jane Ralston said the same thing. She says she saw Jonathan ... *touching* him in the park. Stratford's Linda Tripp, for Christ's sake, had to be the one to see *that*."

Claire shrugged.

Jane swivelled and sat sideways.

"What am I going to do?" she said in the voice of a lost child. "What will I do?"

"Nothing."

"You're crazy."

"No. You'll do nothing The next step is up to Griff. If you challenge him with this, he'll slam the door in your face."

"Hasn't he already done that?"

"No. Because he doesn't know you know."

"I love him." Jane bowed her head.

"I know you do."

"And what about Will? What will become of Will? What if he finds out?"

"That one, as they say, is in the lap of the gods. But—you know? I cannot believe Griffin will not come back. I simply cannot believe it. And I don't."

"So—now what? Jesus—another man. Griff ..."

"Don't forget what he wants, Jane. And don't forget who he is. Griff Kincaid, alas, is one of those people you read about but think you'll never meet—the ones who'll do anything to get what they want."

"But he's ... he's *decent*."

"So is everyone—once. We've all done the unthinkable, one way or another. All of us. Everyone."

"Yes."

Milos.

Jane turned back and reached out for Claire's hands.

"Is it ... can we survive it?" she asked.

Claire tried to smile—but it was difficult.

"You've survived your mother, kiddo. And furthermore, you know who you are. And that's what it takes. It's what survival is all about. Knowing who you are."

"Yes."

"Why don't you take it to Doctor Fabian?"

"Yes."

"You want another glass?"

"Yes."

"If you don't stop saying *yes*, I'll come over there and hit you," Claire laughed.

Jane let go of Claire's hands and sat back.

"I've already been hit once today—and once, thank you very much, is quite enough."

"You want to come and sit in the garden while we finish?"

"Sure."

"We can listen to the birds. And I'll tell you all about the time I found an ancient copy of *Peyton Place* when I was twelve—and my mother came in and found me—only I'd already seen her very own name in the flyleaf! You know what she said?"

"No."

"She said: *oh, for heaven's sake—I've been wondering where that was.*"

Laughing, they took up their glasses and the bottle and retreated to a corner of Hugh's prized back garden.

"We're alive, kiddo. Think of that."

"Yes. Alive."

4

Tuesday, August 11, 1998

Doctor Fabian, as always threatening to spill over the sides of his chair, sat back and settled his hands in a gesture of prayer, fingers resting on his lips.

"Interesting," he said. "You told it very well. I could see it like a film—the ship, the people, the sea of blue dresses."

"It was vivid to begin with—but why does it strike me as sad? I should have thought it was comical," Jane said.

"No. Not at all. It is sad. Sad in the extreme. Sad—and in its own way, very wise."

"Wise?"

"Yes. Dreams have their own integrity. I'm sure you know that. And where there is integrity, there is most often wisdom. It is *us,* it showed you. *Let me show you,* it said, *who we all are.*" He looked away. "In this social masquerade we are all caught up in—here in North America especially— we have all been wearing masks and costumes for so long that we have begun to take it for granted that we, as we truly are, can no longer be seen. We have no need any more to fear being seen. But underneath the façade, we have been wearing the stained blue dress all along. No one is immune to scrutiny. No one. But we think we are. Not *me.* Not *I.* Not *us.* Why, *it's unthinkable,* we say. *How dare you question me? I have nothing to hide.* But those are probably the most dangerous words a person can say. To *think* you have nothing to hide is tantamount to an admission of guilt."

Jane was quiet for a moment. Then she said: "I don't like the word *guilt*."

"Tough," said Doctor Fabian. "I didn't invent it. The fact is, it's in all of us. What else?"

"Else?"

"What else have you to tell me?"

Jane lighted a cigarette.

"I've found out where Griff is," she said.

"Oh?"

"Yes. He's been living with two of our friends—the Dexters. Nigel and Susan."

"Oh, yes. I know who they are. Actors."

"They were at the National Theatre School with Griff, way back before I met him. My friend Claire told me. I think I've mentioned her. Claire Highland."

"Yes. You've spoken of her before. She teaches."

"Yes. History. Well …" Jane looked around the room and glanced at the Klee portrait of the tragic scholar behind Fabian's desk. "She knows what Griff has been up to."

"Oh? Is it her?"

"No."

"So?"

"I was standing in Zehrs. I was going to make a tuna salad …"

Jane kept her eyes on the portrait. It might, in that moment, have been a mirror image of herself … *Where has everything gone …?*

"A woman who works in the props department—a woman called Mary Jane Ralston—told me first. But her telling was cruel. Claire's was considered. And, I guess, considerate …"

She shifted her gaze to the window.

"Say it, Jane. Just say it. In either woman's voice. The voice is immaterial, now. Who is it?"

"Jonathan Crawford."

"I see."

"You seem remarkably calm—given what I've just said."

"Well. I'm certainly not going to pretend it's easy to comprehend. For you. But still ..."

Jane laughed. "What does that mean? *But still.* You've seen it coming all along?"

"No. But it doesn't particularly surprise me."

Jane stubbed the cigarette she had been smoking.

Fabian was silent.

"Aren't you going to tell me it's normal? Aren't you going to tell me it's just one of the conditions of ambition? That's what Claire said. *You have to remember who Griff is,* she said, *and what he wants.*"

"In some ways, she's right. Quite right."

Jane brushed the palms of her hands together and made a clapping sound.

"*Quite right. Just so. Fuck me—and I'll get the parts I want.* Yes? Why the hell not? What's a wife—a marriage and a kid? *Nothing. But I got the parts. I made sure of* that!"

"Did he? Get them?"

"Yes. Both of them."

"Well, then."

"*Well, then,* WHAT?"

"And you?"

"What does that mean? *You.*"

"It's a question about your own desires and motives. Have you never wanted anything so badly, you'd do anything?"

Jane looked askance.

"You appear to be nervous—unwilling to answer. May I

remind you of that young man? The man who works for Bell Canada?"

"You don't need to."

"Well, then."

"Well, then." Jane looked at Fabian. Fabian smiled. "Well, then. Well, then. Well, then. Is that it? *Shrug. Shrug. That's the way of the world ...*"

"It's the way of the world you chose to live in, Jane. And many other worlds as well. You think Ivana Trump ever really loved Donald? You think he loved her? Of course not. But they both got what they wanted. He got a beautiful woman—she got the money."

"The theatre isn't like that."

"I quite agree. But there are people in the theatre who are. When they need to be."

Jane sighed.

In a sense, she felt defeated by reality. In another sense, she felt—not knowing how, or why—somehow at peace.

"Did you get what you wanted from your young man?"

Jane waited. Then she said: "yes."

And please don't say: well, then.

For a moment, Fabian said nothing.

"How is Will?" he finally asked.

Jane turned and looked at him. "Will?"

"Yes. How is he?"

She looked away. "You're a clever man, Conrad."

"So. And the answer?"

"I'm losing him."

"Then get him back."

"How?"

"By showing him you're there. *There*, Jane. *There*. Not off in a wine-created fog—not drifting in this unbecoming self-pity.

Reassert yourself. To yourself. Let him know you're still *you*."

Jane prematurely put out the cigarette.

"Will he come back?"

"Which one?"

She looked at Fabian and gave another distant smile. *You bastard*, she was thinking. *But a clever bastard.*

"Either one of them. Both," she said.

"Yes."

"How can you know that?"

Doctor Fabian smiled his strange, conspiratorial smile, unclasped his hands, sat forward and said: "because I, too, have worn the blue dress. And I know the time comes when the wearer wants to shed it. Must, in fact, in order to go on living. And when you do, both you *and* Griff will be there waiting. Along with Will."

5

Wednesday, August 12, 1998

Sunday evening, on leaving Jane, Milos had walked down to the Tom Patterson parking lot, got into his van and sat there for half an hour. Two cigarettes. But silence. No radio. No tapes.

Then he went home. Agnewska said nothing but *hello* and did not turn around from the stove, where she was steaming cabbage rolls. Neither did they speak at dinner. Anton lay beside them in his basket on the floor. He slept, as he now seemed to do all the time.

When the meal was over, Milos had lifted the baby and held

him at his shoulder. The child smelled odd. Not that his diaper was fouled, but something else. He smelled as dying people smell while they lie and wait for death. It was almost benign—a recovered smell of self, when the powdering, perfumed cleanliness of daily living had been given over to the smell of life itself. Flesh and flesh only. Nothing more.

"Does he ever wake?" Milos asked.

"Little," Agnewska replied, still not looking at him. Increasingly, whenever she spoke, it was as though she was speaking to someone over his shoulder or off to one side—or possibly only to herself. Her voice was barely audible. She was removing the soiled plates and cutlery, taking them to the sink and submerging them in soapy water so hot that it startled her fingers.

Milos put Anton back in the basket and went upstairs.

On Monday, he returned to work.

He spoke to no one.

There was no one he could speak to. No one who would have understood; besides which, the only advice he wanted was unavailable to him—the advice of a doctor.

Agnewska had also gone into a decline. She had gone beyond her early panic about Anton—and far beyond her resilient hopes that God would intervene. She portrayed herself as a drudge, but she was not—in the truest sense. She was a woman who had given birth with her full enthusiastic consent, and a woman whose own decision it had been to have the life of a mother and wife. She wanted no other job beyond these. Her whole ambition had been to achieve the "independent" status that marriage to Milos had offered her. She was a *married lady*. In the traditional sense of both her culture and her religion, she had reached for and found her destiny. But she had little grasp of current reality—or of its consequences. Far beyond being ignorant, she had nonetheless made a pact with reality that if it provided her with security and surety, she would be obedient to its rules.

Now, she was paying for the pact in a situation she could barely comprehend. In Poland, where Witnesses had been persecuted and despised, her parents had promised her that life would be different elsewhere.

It was not.

The enemy took on a new face—that was all. Where the enemy had once been human ignorance and meanness of spirit, now the enemy was nature's ignorance of human emotion and its own random consignment of mismatched genes.

Not that Agnewska could have said all this. But she knew it through living out—or trying to live out—what was happening to herself, what had happened to her child and what had happened to Milos, who had turned away from her.

As for Milos, he was trying to deny the hatred he had begun to feel for his wife because of her denying their son the only help that could save him. And there was more. Her refusal to sleep with or comfort him or to let him comfort her with his presence, her increasing silence, plus her abject fear of God and her subservience to what she still believed was His will.

With all this, Milos himself felt a sense of guilt over his own inaction—but at the same time he could not help feeling—as most people do where personal guilt is concerned—that somebody else was really to blame.

Much of Tuesday had been spent in brooding. He had relatively few assignments and had spent hours sitting in a secluded corner at Bentley's, drinking beer. Not heavily, but constantly.

In all this time he had also been thinking about Jane and what they had done together—but she was gone now. The consequence of it was that he had taken one more step in the direction of his future and it had blinded him. The ultimate distance had now been seen and, for Milos, there was—just as he had feared—nothing there of substance. This certainty had convinced him to give up forward movement. The uppermost thought in his mind was: *stop*. This sense of hopelessness was not to last, but Milos did not know that.

In the night between Tuesday and Wednesday, he waited for Agnewska to fall asleep and, when she very quickly did, he got out of his own bed and put on his clothes.

Then he went to the bathroom, washed his face, brushed his teeth and used the toilet, which he did not flush. After this he lifted Anton from his crib and placed the sleeping child in the carrier that Agnewska kept for him on the table near the baby bath, with all its powders, oils and soaps.

He turned off the lights—except the night-light—and retreated with the carrier to the kitchen. There, he drank a bottle of beer, smoked a cigarette and wrote a three-word note to his wife.

Gone to hospital.

At the Stratford General, he parked the van, lifted the carrier, leaned in and kissed the child, locked the doors and went up the steps into the lobby.

It was 3:00 in the morning before a doctor came. His name was Scarlet and he was younger than the doctors who had examined Anton before.

Doctor Scarlet took them into a room where Milos explained everything as best he could. The doctor phoned the desk and asked for the file that had been set up at Anton's birth.

He then examined the baby.

"He is not asleep, Mister Saworski. He's in a coma."

There was a further examination to which Milos was not admitted. It would have been bootless, anyway. He would not have understood the language.

What he did understand was the verdict.

The child would die.

He was, in a sense, already dead. The combination of his natal flaws and of Agnewska's neglect had doomed him.

At 6:00 a.m., Doctor Scarlet took Milos aside and said: "however sad it may be, and however hard it will be for you and your wife to accept, the truth is that Anton cannot survive. His brain is incomplete. His motor instincts are hopelessly faulty. How he has gone on breathing is a mystery. Nothing propels him forward. At birth, he stopped living."

"May he die here?" Milos asked. "In your care. I cannot trust my wife—or her parents."

"Of course."

"When, do you think?"

"I'm afraid, today. If not—then, tomorrow."

"I see."

"Would you like to be alone?"

"Only if I can be alone with him."

In ten minutes, a nurse with tears in her eyes brought Anton wrapped in a white blanket.

"When you want me to return," she said, "ring the bell."

"Thank you."

Dawning.

Milos lifted his son in his arms.

How had this happened? What did it mean?

Nothing.

It was just the story of a life.

He carried Anton to the window.

It was to be a beautiful day. Not a cloud. Not a wisp of wind. Only the sky, its birds and the trees.

"Look," Milos said. "Can you see? This is the world, Anton. This is where you are."

The child's eyes had opened, but were still clouded with sleep.

Milos raised Anton's hand.

"See? Do you see? This is what we do. We say *hello*."

He waved their hands together.

Anton made a sound—deep in his throat. It was a sound that Milos would never forget—a sound that would reverberate from that moment all the way to his own death.

Milos held the baby as close as he dared, wishing that his own breath could revive the infant—wishing the early sunlight would give him back his life, the way it gave life to flowers and leaves and everything that crawled and walked and swam. And flew.

Sky. Birds. Trees.

The child waved both his hands. Just once.

Then slipped away into sleep.

Milos kissed Anton's forehead, each of his fingers and toes, his ears, his eyes, his nose, his lips.

He began to rock from side to side, gently—the way a boat will rock its passengers in a groundswell.

Someone should sing, Milos thought. But he had no voice for it. He was not a mother. Only a father—and fathers are helpless in such moments. They have no breasts—they have no milk—only arms.

He went and sat on the bed.

He sat there two more hours.

Then he rang the bell.

The child was dead.

When Milos gave him up into Doctor Scarlet's hands, he said only: "thank you." Then he went to the elevator.

In the lobby, others were arriving, others were leaving. Everything, as always after a death, seemed normal, ordinary—almost comically mundane. People still laughed—bought coffee and a doughnut at the counter, turned away to read the sports page and called out one another's names.

Milos went to the doors, passed beyond them, stepped down onto the path—could not remember where he had parked and turned back towards the hospital.

No. You have been there. It is done.

When he saw the van, he found that Agnewska was in the front seat. She wore the same blue coat she had worn when he brought her here for Anton's birth.

Neither of them spoke.

There was nothing adequate to say.

Two weeks later, Agnewska went back to her parents' home, where she was to remain for the rest of her life. In the years to come, Milos would see her now and then, standing with her pamphlets in hand at the corner of Ontario and Downie streets. But they never spoke. She would turn away and he would walk on by.

Mercy would see him, time to time, standing in his kitchen, sitting in his yard, polishing his van or cutting the grass. He bought a dog. A black Labrador. He called it Chops, perhaps for Chopin. Mercy did not ask. There was never another woman. Not that she could tell from what she saw—but there was music—music and laughter, and men who were older who came to play cards.

And there was a sense of peace about him, the sort of peace

that follows resignation—possibly reconciliation. Mercy knew it well. When Tom died ...

So.

Milos never said hello.

But he would wave.

And smile.

He would smile and he would wave.

Mercy needed no other sign—and no better one—to know that he would survive. More than likely because, above all, he wanted to. There was, after all, a whole new life to inherit—and inhabit.

6

Friday, August 14, 1998

Mercy had just fed Will his breakfast. Juice, toast and marmalade. He did not finish the toast and for the first time in her experience of him, he drank half a cup of coffee with milk in it.

Jane did not appear. Mercy did not worry, except for Will's sake. She knew exactly what was happening. When a marriage disintegrates, you fade. It would change.

"You want to go to the park?"

"No."

Will sat back in his chair with the cup still raised and banged his heels against the rungs.

Mercy knew she had to do something—rescue him, somehow.

"We'll go anyway," she said.

"So Mum can have her friend come over while we're gone?"

"What friend?"

"The man."

"What man?"

"The one she's fucking."

Mercy remained silent. She knew better than to protest the language. To protest at this stage would only produce more. Will had gone all the way over into wherever it is children go when they despair of adults. He looked ten years older—pale, thinning, ugly. His hair seemed to have died. It was lank—but he was only seven. *Lank* and *seven* do not match.

Mercy regretted what amounted to ugliness. Especially the thought of it. But it was there. A beautiful child was becoming unrecognizable. His eyes were slitted. His mouth turned down. His jaw clenched. Also his hands. They were either fisted or fussing—picking at everything, lifting utensils and laying them down in a clatter of noise, kicking with his toes, banging into rooms, slamming doors or leaving them inappropriately open, inviting flies and mosquitoes to invade the house. He had done no more puzzles and wanted no more books. He had never finished *Treasure Island*. Whenever Jane did consent to appear, Will got up and left the room. He had also started a war of resistance with Mercy. Not finishing meals was only a part of it.

He cut off his friends. He wanted none. The only time you needed friends was at school, where you could compare opinions, talk about hockey and deal in trading cards. Otherwise, children's games bored him. *All you do is lose and if you win, everybody says you cheated.* The only game he liked was croquet, but: *my stupid parents have ruined the lawn by putting in that dumb flower bed.* When Mercy had reminded him that the owner, not Griff and Jane, had asked for the flower bed, Will had said: *why didn't they refuse? At least they could have told them about the croquet.* Mercy had nothing to say to this.

Now, she went to the back door and told Will they were going to the park. She did not ask him—she told him.

"We'll rent a boat and row on the lake. I'll take some Pepsi."

Out on the water, she rowed and Will sat at the back with the peak of his cap pulled down so that she could not see his eyes in its shadow.

Rudyard sat in the prow.

"School starts in three weeks. Day after Labour Day."

Will said nothing.

"You'll be going into Grade Three."

"Yes."

"With all your friends."

"Yes, but I'm going to get a bike. Then I won't have to walk with anyone."

"We'll see what your mum says."

Will ignored this.

"It's gonna be blue," he said, looking off towards the gardens behind the houses on the opposite shore. "I've always wanted a blue bike. A ten-speed."

"Isn't that a bit risky?"

"Everything's risky. People on bikes get killed every day by stupid adults who don't know how to drive. You may as well get killed by a car as any other way."

"Why don't we talk about something else?"

"Why?"

"Because. I'm not in the mood for a lot of dead people. You shouldn't be, either. Look what a beautiful day it is."

Two swans came to inspect them. They were used to the presence of people on the river—the tour boat, rowboats, paddleboats and canoes—but they were nonetheless inquisitive. *Who might this be? Is there food?*

Unbeknownst to Mercy, Will had put half a piece of uneaten toast in the pocket of his shorts. He produced it now and scattered bits of it on the water.

The male swan came and tested it. *Good.* The female joined him.

"Swans mate for life," Will said.

"I'm not sure of that," said Mercy. "Geese do."

"Mum and Dad must be swans, then."

Mercy thought: *I'd rather they were geese.* And then: *I still don't think it's over. And I hope to hell, for Will's sake, it's not.*

An hour later, they were sitting on the sidewalk in front of Pazzo, eating pizza.

Rudyard was dozing at Mercy's feet.

"What does gay mean?" Will asked—seemingly out of nowhere.

"Happy," said Mercy. "Lighthearted."

Will looked at her suspiciously.

"I thought it meant something else," he said. "Something weird." He was slicing through his pizza and laid aside his knife.

Mercy waited.

Then she said: "it can mean other things."

"Like what?"

"Like ..." She sipped her wine and shrugged. "Why do you ask?"

"That man over there just told that woman he's sitting with he's gay. He doesn't look very happy to me."

Mercy glanced at the couple and recognized them as young actors in the company.

"So?" Will persisted. "If he isn't happy, what did he mean?"

"He meant he likes men instead of women." *Keep it simple.*

"Why?"

"He just does. There is no *why*."

"Why did he have to tell her?"

"Maybe she's fallen in love with him." Mercy smiled. "It happens."

"Is it wrong?"

"What?"

"Being gay."

"No. It's not wrong. It's just different."

"Than what?"

"Than men who like women."

"Like Dad."

"That's right."

"Do I know anyone who's gay?"

"I don't know. Probably. Why does it matter?"

"I just wondered."

Mercy looked at him. His expression was curious. Almost vacant, but not.

"It was fun in the boat, eh?" she said.

"It was okay."

"You want the rest of my pizza?" Will had finished his own.

"Long as there aren't anchovies."

"Don't ask," said Mercy. "You know better. This is good, though. Lots of mushrooms."

"Okay. One piece."

Mercy lifted the pizza onto Will's plate, and glanced down the street.

Rudyard suddenly sat up.

His tail began to wag.

"What is it?" Will asked.

The dog left the table and went to the railings.

Mercy said: "it's your dad."

Griff had just walked by with Nigel Dexter, who played

Caliban, heading for their matinee performance of *The Tempest* at the Festival Theatre. Neither man had spoken.

Will and Rudyard watched their departing backs in the way that people stranded on the shore watch the departure of a ship they have failed to catch.

Mercy poured another glass of wine.

"You want another Pepsi?" she asked.

"No thanks."

Will pushed his plate away.

Rudyard did not lie down again.

"Why don't we go?" Will said.

"In a minute. I still have to pay the bill."

"Can't we hurry? I hate it here."

"Will—*settle down*," Mercy said sharply. "They didn't see us, that's all. They were in a hurry. If they'd seen us, they would've stopped."

Will sat forward and stole a mouthful of Mercy's wine.

"Next time, ask," Mercy said, and drew the glass back towards her.

"If I had, you wouldn't have let me."

They were silent. Then Will said: "Mum told me Dad was staying with them. With Nigel and Susie."

"That's right."

Will thought about this and then said: "that's what friends are for, I guess."

"Sometimes." Mercy smiled.

The bill came. She paid—and they walked the long way home.

7

At 7:30, while Mercy was preparing the morning coffee and tea, Luke arrived. Will had not appeared yet.

"I'm on my way to the Sheppards'—could you afford a moment?" Luke said.

"Of course. Sit. Coffee in a sec."

Luke loosened his jacket and sat at the table.

"You okay?" Mercy asked.

"Sure. Just tired. The Sheppards want some new roses. I told them it wasn't the best time for planting, but they insisted. Maybe it will be okay. I've got them in the truck."

"The Sheppards?" She smiled.

"No," Luke laughed. "Thank God. She's a pain in the ass. No. Roses. Six of them."

"And of course, they'll blame you if they don't take."

"Whatever—they'll pay for them."

"I should think."

Mercy brought the coffee, milk and sugar and gave Luke a mug. Also a mug for herself.

"You been fine?" Luke asked.

"Not bad. Will's been acting up. I feel sorry for him."

"Yeah. Bad situation for a kid."

"The worst. I'm afraid it's doing him a lot of harm. I try— but there's not much a person can do, except try to reassure him. The saddest part of it is, he's begun to hate his parents."

"I suppose you never see Griff ..."

"Only on the street. Saw him yesterday."

"How's Jane?"

"Gone to earth, more or less. We hardly talk now."

"Too bad. She's a nice woman."

"Yes."

Luke stirred his coffee and then said: "I came because I wanted you to come to dinner."

"I'd love to. When?"

"Maybe tomorrow, if that's okay."

"Perfect."

"I make a great spaghetti sauce. That and a salad. That suit you?"

"To a T. What time?"

"Seven okay for drinks?"

"Sure. I look forward to it. I haven't been to dinner in some-one else's house for God knows how long. Can I bring anything?"

"Just you. And a bit of cheese, maybe."

"Sure. I'll be going to Sobey's later this morning. Perfect timing."

Luke finished his coffee, stood up and went to the door.

He looked around the room, empty of people but for Mercy.

"I miss them," he said.

"Join the club."

"See you tomorrow."

Mercy smiled.

Luke departed.

Mercy listened to the truck being started, watched it pull away and went back to the table.

Not even Rudyard had turned up so far.

In the garden, the crows flew off and would not return until evening. Mrs Arnprior threw open her windows. Mercy remembered with regret mornings in childhood when the milk and bread wagons used to arrive and the postman still came three times a day—people whose presence you could still depend on. Slowly, all that had been eroded. Now, there was no one.

8

Saturday, August 15, 1998

The heat was now oppressive beyond comprehension. *How can anything survive out there?* Jane wondered.

She was lying on her bed, wearing a cotton shift for fear Will might come in. Otherwise, she would have been naked.

An electric fan was turning to and fro on the dresser—humming what might have been an electronic tune. Something devised by one of those boy-wizards with no hair and thick glasses who kept turning up on television as *the next generation of genius.*

Mercy knocked lightly on the door and looked in. Seeing that Jane was awake, she entered.

"What?"

"Something I think you should see."

"Can't it wait?"

"No. Will is out blading with the Rosequist boy—and you have to see this before he comes back."

Jane sat up.

"What's he done? Killed Mrs Arnprior and pushed her under his bed?" She stood. "Which, sometimes, I wish he would. Of course you didn't hear her last night, but I did. 'Incantations to the moon ...'" Jane began to sing: "'Oh, moon, sweet moon, luna, luna, moon' ... She's crazy as a coot."

"Well, no wonder, in this heat. Come on."

Jane followed Mercy down the hall to Will's room.

"I was putting his clean clothes in the closet—and I found something I think you should see."

Will's bed, as always, was neatly made—with hospital corners and smoothed pillows. Mercy had taught him this, saying: *it's a matter of self-respect. How you treat yourself is gonna be how others treat you.*

"What?" said Jane. "Where?"

"In the closet. On the floor."

Jane crossed the room and looked.

"So?" she said. "Shoes?"

"No. At the back."

Jane rummaged.

It took only moments to find them—four ragged pieces of paper, stiff with paint. Jane's throat tightened.

"Oh God," she said. "Oh dear God ..."

She gathered up the pieces and, standing up, turned them over and over in her hands.

She looked at Mercy. "I can't believe it."

"No. Me neither."

The pices were the remains of a watercolour painting that Will had done at school. It had been awarded the class prize in the spring, and since then had been pinned to his bulletin board, in the centre of a collection of his other treasures.

Its subject was a family picnic. Jane could still pick out each figure—Will feeding something to Rudyard, while Mercy poured lemonade from a Thermos. Griff, his arm around Jane's shoulders, was laughing. Will had sketched in the faces with a pencil, somehow managing to give Jane an expression of utter peace.

"Well," Jane finally said, "at least he didn't throw it away."

"What do we do now?" Mercy said.

"I don't know. I'll keep these in my studio for now, and maybe someday we can glue the pieces to some kind of backing. But apart from that, I simply don't know. It's just ..."

She turned away.

"Dearest God, how have we come to this? How ..."

It was not a question that required an answer.

9

Sunday, August 16, 1998

St. Marys. The quarry.

"We used to come here all the time," said Will.

He was wearing a tank top and shorts. He was hoping to look older. Swimming was not good for that. You could not hide your age. His arms and legs were thin—but his ideal was Griffin.

Jane said nothing, though she knew all this. Seven, going on eight, was not a moment for comment. In time, Will would fill out and be what he desired—but now, he was still a child.

The quarry at St. Marys was a popular place for swimming parties—especially for people associated with the Stratford Festival. There had even been a death. Two, in fact, which gave the place a notorious, somewhat romantic aura—as if there were ghosts. The deaths had not been of actors, but—tragically—of the teenage sons of local farmers who never recovered from the loss and whose farms, side by side, had since become the sites of housing developments.

The two boys—fourteen and fifteen—had grown up

together. Their girlfriends, who were sisters, had lived across the sideroad. Born—bred—dead.

Late at night, summer of 1946, they had all gone out together to the quarry. The war was over. The bomb had fallen. They had missed it all. Too young. The world was theirs.

And so ...

Jane never told Will any of this.

Why would I?

There was still no lifeguard. A lifeguard could not be afforded. But there were multiple signs warning of the dangers—and there were ropes that separated the depths of the quarry from the edge. The quarry was rumoured—but who knew?—to have no bottom. *It goes all the way to hell ...*

It certainly was not heaven down there.

Nonetheless, the quarry at St. Marys was Will's favourite place.

Jane had said: "what would you like?"

Will had said: "corned beef sandwiches."

Now, they had finished eating and sat on the grass under the sun. There were tables, but Will preferred the grass. *I'm not a softie,* he had declared. *Only softies sit at tables.*

"We used to have picnics all the time," he said.

"Yes."

"Mum?"

"Yes?"

"Don't lie to me. Is Dad coming back?"

Jane looked away at the water and picked an ant off her left knee.

"I don't know," she said. *What else can I say?* "But I think so. And ..." She waited. "I really believe he will."

Will rubbed the toes of one foot against the toes of the other. He needed to cut their nails, but Jane had so far failed to teach him how.

"If he doesn't—what will we do?"

"How do you mean?"

"Will we have any money?"

Jane touched him on the forehead, brushing his hair away from his eyes.

"Hon," she said, "we'll always have money. I have my inheritance and—I wish you could take this in—I also have a job. I *make* money—every day—just like Dad."

Will looked away.

"Where will we live?" he said.

"Where we live now. Why not?" she said.

"But without Dad ... Will we move? I mean ... all my friends ... Grade Three .... my crow. Who's going to feed my crow?"

Jane took his hand.

"You are," she said.

"Is that a promise?"

"Yes. An absolute promise."

Will withdrew his hand and stood up.

"Now I know you're lying," he said. "You've promised everything and not one thing has come true."

After that, not much was said.

Finally, Jane decided they might as well go home. She asked Will to gather up everything that could still be discarded, shove it into the plastic bag that had held their sandwiches and take it over to one of the garbage containers near the picnic tables. Then she began to repack the satchel.

The picnic painting had not been mentioned. Jane had hoped the offer of a picnic would prompt Will to say something.

But ...

No.

Even their swim, earlier, had been silent—except for the

laughter of the few other families who had come to the quarry to cool off in its waters.

Pushing the cork back into the bottle of wine, Jane glanced over towards the tables to see if Will had found the right container for their non-recyclable debris.

He was not in sight.

Jane stood up.

No sign of him near the tables.

She scanned the groups of figures scattered over the grass.

"Will?"

Nobody paid any attention to her call.

Her eyes reached the water.

Jesus Christ.

Jane ran down to the water's edge and quickly checked the bobbing heads.

Please.

"Will?"

Nothing.

Here, the quarry walls went straight down. Jane dove into the water.

"Will!"

Still nothing.

Jane swam forward. She put her face down in the water and began to scan the depths.

Bottomless.

She surfaced and turned back towards the shore

I need help. Help. Help. Everyone!

Will was standing at the edge.

They looked at each other.

And, in that exchange, Jane guessed what he had done. He had wanted to frighten her—like Tom Sawyer. *Now, they'll all be sorry and I can go to my own funeral.*

When she emerged, the subject was not raised.

"I was hot," she said. As if she needed an excuse.

"Sure."

"I was hot. Go to the car."

That night, when Jane went in to kiss him, Will said: "thanks, Mum."

And Jane said: "what for?"

But they both knew. When Jane had stepped from the water, her expression had betrayed her. *I thought you were dead ...* But it never got said. Only shown.

10

Sunday, August 16, 1998

Luke's house on McKenzie Street was more or less brightly lit that evening at 7:00. Mercy had chosen to buy a Stilton cheese. The only problem was, it stank to high heaven—which she had tried to solve by carrying it in a maroon-coloured plastic bag she had set aside for gifts.

She wore a pale, patterned cotton dress with blue and yellow flowers on an eggshell background. It had long, loose sleeves and a scalloped neck. She also wore her fake pearls and had washed her hair.

She parked on the driveway and went back to the front door. The screened-in porch was set with chairs, a wicker sofa and some old tables.

There was also a pot of vibrant cyclamen. Red.

So, she thought, *he's planning something—proving he's civilized* ...

She rang the bell, remaining on the front step, even though she knew she could have walked straight into the house.

Luke came onto the front porch wearing a white shirt tucked into a pair of spotless tailored jeans.

"Good," he said. "Welcome." And opened the screen door.

At first they sat on the porch drinking wine and beer and exchanging mundane pleasantries. It was difficult to relax. They were both nervous of this new exploration of their relationship. They had shared a bed, but they had never shared a table—in the formal sense. It was odd and awkward, as though they were at the beginning of their friendship, not midway into it.

"Thanks for the cheese."

"I hope you like it."

"Yes." And then: "very much. I love Danish blue."

"It's Stilton."

"Oh, yes. How stupid. Stilton."

Then silence.

Some men walked past, carrying small purple sacks with gold tassels.

"Luke."

"Luke."

"Luke."

"Guys."

They walked on and Mercy said: "those sacks. What? They off to a party?"

"No. It's their bowling shoes. Crown Royal."

"Oh. Is that their team?"

"No." Luke smiled. "It's a kind of rye. You buy it like that and then you use the bag for something else."

"Bowling shoes."

"Bowling shoes."

Silence.

The subject of Jesse hung in the air.

Finally, looking out at the street, Mercy said: "are you satisfied it was accidental?"

"What?"

"Jesse's death."

"Yes."

"Have there been consequences? I mean, you mentioned dealers."

"No more phone calls. Nothing."

"And the police?"

"Why *the police?*"

"Well, they're involved, one way or another, in anyone's public death. What did they say? Were they satisfied?"

Luke scratched his face, to the left side of his lips. *Say nothing.*

"Yes," he said.

Mercy did not believe him—or at least, she knew something had been left unsaid, but she did not prompt him any further. It was clear that something about Jesse would remain a mystery until Luke chose to speak—and the choice, she knew, would have to be his.

"You got a light?" she asked.

"Sure."

Luke lit her cigarette and one for himself.

Mercy drank wine, crossed her legs and sat back in her chair.

"You come here often?" she said.

For about three seconds, Luke was confounded—and then, seeing her smile, he burst out laughing.

"Yeah," he said. "Pretty well every night." And then: "but I've never seen you here before."

"I work in another part of town."

"I see." Pause. "You married?"

"I'm a widow."

"Oh." Slight pause—then, looking down at his hands: "think you'll marry again?"

"Well ... I don't know. It would depend."

"On what?"

"My availability. From the past. There are ties I won't break."

"Like?"

"Man called Tom. Name of Bowman. Other things."

"Go on."

Luke refilled Mercy's glass and opened a new beer.

"I have kids."

"Some of us out here know that."

"Yes. But major kids. Not to be forgotten."

"Of course. Why would they be?"

"I don't want them to be a problem to anyone else."

"What makes you think they'd be a problem?"

"Some people don't appreciate other people's children. Especially people who've never had kids of their own."

"I had Jesse. Jesse and all the others—all the others, including my mum and dad."

"They weren't kids."

"Yes. They were. They were in every way but one."

"Which one?"

"Age. All my kids were fifty-year-old teenagers."

"Dead now? All of them?"

"Mom and Dad. Jesse. Huck. He died first, after Beth. She died at birth. And Mar'beth never really got over that, apparently. The birth had been hard—very hard—and then Beth died. Lived about four days, I guess. Long enough for Mar'-beth and Preacher to fall in love with her. Sad."

"Yes. Like my neighbours, the Saworskis. Their baby just died."

"Isn't he the Bell man who came to fix the phone when I cut through the line?"

"That's right."

"Seemed like a nice enough guy."

"He is."

"You ever know my parents? Mark and Abby?"

"No. But I heard about them. Everybody did, I guess. Back then, Stratford was still like a small town. Everybody knew everything about everybody else."

"What did you hear?"

"That they drank too much. Argued in public. Fought, I guess was more like it. How the police had to come time to time—and then, when they died, how their kid was left alone. Except I never heard your name. Not then. Sorry to say all this, but the battling Quinlans were public knowledge. You couldn't avoid it."

"That's okay. Best thing that could've happened, really, given what they'd done to their lives. God knows if they were ever happy." Luke thought for a moment and then said: "we don't know that many good marriages, do we?"

"Mine was good. With Tom. Not the other bastard. Stan. But Tom, yes."

"I thought you two didn't get married."

"We didn't. But it was still the best marriage a person could imagine."

"Did you love him?"

"Yes." She waited a moment. "Do you remember him? And all the cats?"

"Sure. I used to buy gas there way back when I started to drive—because he was way down on Lorne, south end of town, and my parents never went there."

"When did you start?"

"Thirteen."

Mercy raised her eyebrows. "But you didn't *own* a car, surely."

"Didn't need to. I had theirs. They got to a stage where staying in was better than going out."

"But they had to shop. They had to go to the liquor store."

"Yeah, but ..."

"But?"

"I drove them. Moved to the passenger side in the lot and they'd go in and do the dirty. Zehrs was a Loblaws back then, and I'd make up a list for Mum, who'd tell them she was nearly blind and would someone do it for her ..."

"Hah!"

"Yeah." Luke grinned and made a face. "*Poor me—I'm near blind—could you help?* Near blind drunk, of course. Clutching the counter just to stand up. Dad made his own list and would stagger around between the shelves at the liquor store and come back out with a cart full of bottles which I unloaded into the trunk."

"Who paid for all this? Neither of them had a job."

"Me, in the end. Before that, Dad's inheritance. He got the house and a fair amount of money."

"The house?"

"This house."

"Oh. But the money. All those other children ..."

"Preacher wasn't dumb. He knew the others could make it on their own. And they did—more or less. But Dad he knew would never make it and he didn't want to see him die of neglect."

"Some people call that *giving to the rich*."

"True enough. Dad was rich in what he didn't have. Rich in neediness. Neediness was his way of life. His excuse for quitting

the world. *No one never gave me nothin'.* 'Cept mother love—
a roof—food on the table—same as most kinds. For Dad, that
wasn't enough. He wanted more. He wanted shelter for life."

"Like Jesse."

"No. Jesse's excuse was fear of failure. Dad adored failure.
It added to his stature as a deserving drunk."

Mercy looked at the trees.

The leaves were lifting in a breeze, dry but vibrant. Green.

"Thank God we have them," she said, with a sweep of her
hand. "In their funny way, they tell us the story of our lives."

Luke smiled. "Yeah," he said. "I guess that's why I'm a
gardener."

They finished their drinks, stubbed their cigarettes and went
inside.

The meal was perfect—simple, blessed with flavour.

"You're a good cook," Mercy said, cutting into the Stilton
at the end.

"I've got a couple of good things. A frittata—a garlic shrimp
dish—stuff like that. I also do a pretty good roast of beef. But
I don't cook a lot. Not for myself, anyway. I'm always too
tired when I come back home, end of the day. I do a lot of
Campbell's Hearty Soups. They make a great meal for one
person. Also, of course, Kraft Dinner."

He laughed.

"What's a frittata?"

"Never had one?"

"Not that I know of, no."

"It's an Italian omelette. Fills the whole frying pan. It can
have onions, tomatoes, green and red peppers, sometimes
mushrooms. *Stuff.* With eggs. I love it. Also a *hearty meal.*
What you need at the end of the day."

Eating the cheese and salad, they were silent. Luke had opened two bottles of Valpolicella, saying: "you going to eat Italian, *drink* Italian."

Mercy had already studied the dining-room, with its long, wide table, its twelve pressed-back chairs, its Victorian sideboards, its mirrors, its sconces and its chandelier of ruby glass. And of course, its family motto passed down by Preacher and Mar'beth Quinlan: *Become Yourself*—decorated with shamrocks, oak leaves and acorns. Luke had told its story.

Now, Mercy said: "why am I here, Luke?"

He looked down at his plate and set his hands on either side of it.

"You're here because this house is too big for me to live in alone."

Mercy said nothing—drank some wine—lighted a cigarette and then said: "the ghosts aren't enough, eh?"

Luke still did not look up.

"No," he said, barely audible.

Mercy studied him, seemingly so far off down the table—his greying, grizzled hair, the sculpted shape of his ears, his muscled shoulders, his hands with their broken, impossible-to-clean nails, his forehead, eyebrows, cheekbones, lips. His chin, dipping down towards the plate, his eyes with their girlish lashes. His half-empty glass. The whiteness of his shirt. His posture inside it—bending, not slouching. He never slouched.

He's graceful, Mercy thought. Something too rare in men, except perhaps in some performers—actors, dancers, singers, hockey and baseball stars ...

"Is that all you have to say? *The house is too big?*"

"You're alone, too," he said, as if challenging her to a dual of conditions. He looked up.

"Yes," she said. "I'm alone, too."

"What's the point of it, when being alone is so futile?"

"I don't want to become a substitute for Jesse, Luke. Someone you feel you have to worry about—attend to."

"You should know better than that, Merce. It's the last thing on my mind." And then: "I like you."

"And you want a companion. So you won't have to rattle around in all these rooms. *Rattle, rattle?*"

"No. Of course not. It's just ..."

"You don't know how to say *I love you.*"

He looked at her.

She smiled, but did not sit forward. *Relax.*

Luke bit his lip and looked down. He moved his glass and moved it back again. His hands went down to his lap.

"We don't have to say we love each other," Mercy said. "I liked it when you said *I like you,* because I like you, too."

There was a moment.

"Is that a *yes?*"

"Possibly. With conditions."

"What?"

"I keep the name of Bowman. I go on taking care of Will until he doesn't need me. I bring some of my own things and lighten up the rooms. And I bring the cats. Also, we share the chores. I'll cut the grass and you can vacuum the rugs."

Luke smiled at her—but shyly—and it was then she realized how much and how deeply he wanted this to happen.

"Only thing is," Mercy said, "I hope you won't object to my going around telling people I'm living with a younger man. I'll be proud of that. *How young is he?* they'll ask—and I'll say: *he's fifty. Not bad for an old gal like me!* And they'll agree."

Luke stood up and went to her end of the table.

"It's a deal?" he said.

"It's a deal."

They shook hands.

That night, however, they slept in the same bed.

And later, on towards morning, Mercy woke and went to the bathroom.

All these rooms, she thought as she passed them. *All these rooms—and Will won't need me forever—and ... all these rooms ... I could repaper them, paint them ... put in two more johns ... something I've always wanted to be ... a house mother ...* The McKenzie House—Bed and Breakfast ... *Why not?*

When she returned to Luke's side, he reached for her again and the dawn slipped past without being seen.

11

Sunday, August 16, 1998

That same evening, while Mercy and Luke were eating their spaghetti, Griff, Nigel, Susie, Zoë and Richard Harms all had their dinner together at Pazzo. There were never performances on Sunday nights, only matinees, and so most restaurants were open only for lunch on Sundays. This evening, however, Pazzo had given over its front half to a busload of ladies from Buffalo, New York, who had just attended a matinee of *The Glass Menagerie*—and so the back half was open, as well, for local diners.

Since tomorrow all the theatres would be dark, it was a good time for actors to relax and burn the midnight oil, if they were so inclined. This night, it seemed they were more than inclined to do so. They were determined.

Over the first round of blue martinis, there was an air of celebration.

Zoë said: "I have made a decision, and I want you all to approve."

"Maybe they will—and maybe they won't," Richard said—and took Zoë's hand. He had turned up alone, saying that he preferred to spend the evening with friends *instead of that increasingly irritating harridan called my wife.*

Zoë, of course, had been delighted.

"Decisions! Decisions! But which one will it be? Zoë's thinking of giving up the theatre and starting a whole new life as a racing driver—that's my bet." Richard grinned, and winked at the others.

"So? What is it?" Susie asked.

"I've decided to change my name." Zoë beamed.

The others did not.

"Oh, Zoë darling, *no,*" said Susie. "Audiences are just beginning to know your name."

"Susie's right," said Nigel. "Never change your name in mid-career."

"I'm not mid-career, Nige. I've barely started."

"But it's been a hell of a good start. Leave it be."

"I thought of changing my name, once," said Griff.

"You never told me that," said Nigel. "What to?"

"Oh, I don't know. I thought maybe *Robert De Niro.* But somebody'd already taken it." He grinned.

"Oh, you punk!" Nigel said and cuffed Griff on the arm. They both laughed.

"Don't make a joke of this," Zoë said. "I'm serious. I want to do this—and I'm going to. I've already spoken to Robert. He's asked me to be in the company next year and I want to have it done by then. Robert agreed."

"All right," said Nigel, leaning back in his chair. "So what's it going to be?"

"Zoë."

"What?" the rest of the table said in unison. "*What?*"

"Zoe. Zoë without the diacritic."

"What the hell's a *diacritic?*" Griff asked.

"The accent. Those two little dots over the *e*. All I have to do is drop them."

"Why?"

This was Nigel.

"Because. Because I'm devoted to Zoe Caldwell—and she has no diacritic and look how far she's gone. All the way to the top and no looking back. I saw her in *Master Class* and fell instantly in love. She's one of the greatest actors of the age—this or any other age. She's a genius."

"Changing your name isn't going to turn you into a genius," said Susie.

"Nor an overnight success," said Griff. "That can take years."

"Wait and see," said Richard. "Give her a chance. I don't like it myself, but it's what she wants—and if it's what she wants, then it's okay by me."

Griff sighed. "Well—it's going to be hard to get used to ... But—if you want it that way, God bless." He raised her hand and kissed her fingers.

"Thank you, Griff."

"When do we begin?" Susie asked.

"Why not right now?" said Zoe.

"Okay," said Nigel. "This calls for a second round of martinis."

"Good."

Steve the waiter came to take their order.

Griff smiled at him and said, "Tell Jeff he's finally got it right. These were great."

Jeff, one of the young co-owners of Pazzo, was known to be proud of his martinis.

Steve rolled his eyes, said, "Yeah, sure," and hurried back to the bar.

At this point, Zoe looked nervous—but Richard squeezed her hand and told her to relax. "We'll get used to it," he said. "And in no time, we'll all forget it was ever different."

"Oh, I'm so glad. I was afraid you'd scream at me." She withdrew her hand and lighted a cigarette.

"When did you start smoking?" Griff asked.

"I only smoke after six—and then, maybe four or five of them. This is my first today."

They were an extremely presentable group of young actors. Anyone watching them—and people did—would know they were more than merely good looking. They were intriguing and beguiling. They had style and assurance and were relaxed—not putting on a show of airs. They also clearly had a great sense of fun and enjoyed being in one another's company. Nigel was as squared and craggy as Griff was smooth and sleek. Richard was counter to them both, having what is classically described as an *interesting* rather than a handsome appearance. These looks were advantageous to him as a character actor approaching a certain age. Susie was the dead opposite of Zoe—blonde, full-bodied and blessed with native and captivating charm.

"I love it here," Susie now remarked, looking around the large dining-room with its multiple tables and its busy servers—young men and women who all wore black and white. The Italian cuisine was excellent—the wines were top of the line and the clientele an even mix of theatre people, tourists and local citizens. And there were always flowers. And there was always music. And there was always someone you knew. William Hutt, who was having a year off because of his hip replacement, was sitting at a corner table with some New

York friends. His last performance before the operation had been a triumphant and definitive portrayal of *Lear*.

"Oh, dear," said Susie suddenly, looking across the table beyond Griff's shoulder.

"What is it?" Nigel asked.

"Jane," said Susie.

Griff froze.

"Who's she with?"

"Will."

"Well," said Nigel, "let's wait and see where they sit. It was bound to happen sometime, sooner or later. Sooner has always been my choice."

"Not mine," said Griff. "I could have waited. I'm not ready."

Only Susie, Zoe and Richard could see Will and Jane, who were following Larry, the other Pazzo owner, to a table diagonally opposite.

"Have they seen us?"

"Jane has. Will hasn't. His back is to us."

The second martinis arrived. Nobody moved or spoke while Steve distributed them.

"You ready to order yet?" he asked.

"No," said Griff. "We'll be having another martini. Give us a while."

"Sure. No problem. I should tell you, though—Dean has filet mignon tonight and if you want one, maybe you should reserve it now. We're filling up fast."

"Any takers?" said Nigel, looking around the table.

"Yes," said Zoe. Also Richard. Also Susie.

"I'll have one, too. That makes four. Griff?"

"No. No thanks."

"Four filets," said Steve—and went away.

"Are you sure?" Nigel said to Griff. "It's easy enough to get him back."

"Yes. I'm sure. I'm not that hungry."

There was a pause. The others looked away.

Having spent a moment with Jane and Will, Larry swung by the actors' table, humming "Buffalo Gals."

"That's a lively bunch out front," he said as he passed. "Not one under seventy—but *lively*." He stopped and looked at the silent table. "Well, have fun, guys ..." Larry smiled and moved slowly away.

For another moment, nobody spoke.

"So," Griff said at last, "let's raise a glass to Zoe Walker—soon to be a major motion picture ..."

He lifted his drink.

Richard said, "That was unnecessary, Griff."

"Was it? Isn't that what she wants?"

"No. And you know it. Straighten up."

"Richard, don't," said Zoe—and laid her hand on his. "Everybody calm down. This is not an easy moment for Griff."

"Yes," said Nigel. "Everybody lay off. We're here to relax and enjoy ourselves. I say let's drink to the next season, for which we have all been employed."

"Here's to that," said Susie.

"Yes," said Zoe.

Griff said nothing.

They drank.

Susie was watching Jane and Will.

They were ordering wine and Pepsi. Clearly, Jane had seen them. Susie wagged her hand and smiled. Jane nodded.

Susie thought she looked worn—not so much tired as burdened, but she was trying to be bright and easy for Will's sake. Sunday nights were normally a treat looked forward to by the whole theatre community, and clearly Jane was trying to create such an atmosphere for Will.

"Why doesn't somebody say something?" said Griff.

Susie flashed an urgent look at Nigel.

He glanced away and then back.

"Tell Griff what you said last night," she said, her voice lowered. "If you don't, I will."

Nigel hesitated briefly and then turned to Griff.

"Chum," he said.

Griff was watching his fingers turn the stem of his martini glass.

"Yes?"

"It's time." Nigel said this without emotion.

"Time for what?"

"Time to go back."

Griff lifted his head, gave a heavy sigh as if infinitely bored and said: "surely you must be kidding. Don't you understand? Haven't you grasped the plain and simple fact that I can never go back?"

Susie leaned forward. "Look," she said, "we don't know what's going on between you two—and we don't *need* to know—it's just ..."

Griff rapped the table with his knuckles. "*Never*," he repeated.

Zoe shifted closer to Richard.

"At the least, you could say hello," said Susie. She was watching Jane's face and it was a study in regret and longing.

"She's your wife, Griff," said Nigel. "He's your son. Don't turn into that kind of husband and father. That's beneath you. You're better than that."

"They don't know what's going on, either ..."

"Maybe not," Susie said, "but goddammit, Griff, they sure as hell know you've left them. Who the fuck *cares* why? *Why* is nothing here. Only the fact that you left. *Boom. Gone.* No husband. No father. No family. If you had—if you only had the guts at least to look at her, you might be shamed into crossing the room."

Griff turned the martini glass in a full circle and emptied it.

Nigel said: "you can't hide with us forever, chum. We love you—but we love the man who was, not the man who is. Susie and I—Zoe and Richard—have invested our faith in the man who was. We can't stay loyal forever to the one you've become. He's increasingly unknown to us these days. I'm your oldest friend around here, Griff. But friends are nothing if they don't expect and ask for the best."

Griff said nothing.

Finally, Richard said: "for Christ's sake! Stand up. Cross the room. Say hello. That's all you have to do. You're screwing everybody's evening to the wall and it's boring as hell. Get on with it. Go and be done with it."

Griff gave another sigh.

He fingered his glass.

"Where's Steve?" he asked.

"Waiting for you to cross the room," said Richard. "Everybody is."

This was true. All the other theatre people in the restaurant knew what was happening. None of them were unaware of what had become of the Kincaids' marriage. They, like Susie and Nigel, were one of the company's favourite couples. Everyone's affection for them was genuine, and had been shaken when Griff and Jane parted.

Griff pushed his chair back from the table.

"All right," he said.

Then he stood up, turned to them and said: "Look ..." He leaned his fists on the back of his chair. "I can't. I just can't. I'm sorry."

And left the restaurant.

Jane watched him go.

"What's the matter?" said Will.

"Nothing," said Jane. "Just someone I thought I knew—but I was wrong."

Richard said: "he's being a bastard. It's unforgivable."

"No, no," said Nigel. "He's not being a bastard. Whatever he's done, he's put himself in a corner and doesn't know how to get out. At home with us, he's like an overwound clock. It's a wonder he can perform."

"It's true," Susie said. She looked at Jane. "I feel sorry for them both. This isn't what was supposed to happen."

"Has anything ever been what was supposed to happen?" said Nigel.

"Yes," Susie said—and took his hand. "Us."

Nigel smiled and turned to beckon Steve.

"Third round of martinis—and then we'll order. Griffin has gone for a walk."

"I understand."

Steve left.

Richard said: "well, then. Clinton testifies tomorrow in the White House. The impeachment process begins. Poor bastard. Why don't they all shut up?"

"Good idea," said Nigel. "It's what we should all do."

the shining path

Across our sleep
The barbed wire also runs ...
Behind the wire
Which is behind the mirror, our Image
is the same
Awake or dreaming ...

W.H. Auden
Memorial for the City III

1

At 1:15 p.m., a chauffeur-driven Buick with American plates rolled up the drive of the Pinewood Inn in St. Marys.

Getting out, the driver went to the passenger door nearest the hotel steps. Opening it, he stepped aside for a woman of moderate height but of such immaculate poise that she seemed inches taller than she was. She wore an open, flowing summer coat over an elegant, simple dress of pearl grey silk. Her hair was relatively short and the very same colour as her Dior gown. A silk handbag, silk shoes, dark glasses and muted lipstick completed her image.

"Come into the lobby with me, 'Lonso, where I will find out what I'm to do."

"*Si, signora.*"

They went up the steps where Alonso removed his cap and opened the screen door to let his mistress enter. He followed discreetly after her and made sure the door did not slam.

In the lobby, the woman went to the front desk, told the manager who she was and for whom she had come.

"He is in the dining-room, madam. Shall I fetch him for you?"

"No. If you would simply point the way, that will be sufficient."

"Yes, madam."

As the manager moved away, the woman turned back to

Alonso and said: "wait until you see us pass and then go in for some lunch. I will let you know when I want you again."

"*Si, signora. Grazie.*"

The chauffeur withdrew. He was perfectly content to speak English, but he knew his mistress preferred to have him speak Italian. It added to her mystery and it also lent a certain cachet to her stature.

Though in permanent self-imposed exile from the public life of her past, his mistress was unable to go so far as to disappear from view altogether. Part of her still thrived on the wondering voices that followed her everywhere, whispering: *who is that? I know that woman—who is she?*

Removing her gloves, she followed the hotel manager— small and compact and unattractive as he was—who indicated the dining-room as if it might have been a ballroom and then went back to his duties.

Once beyond the portals, the woman removed her dark glasses, allowed her eyes to adjust to the light and walked to the farthest table beside the windows, waving aside the maître-d' as she went.

At the table, she stopped.

"Hello, Jonny," she said, her voice barely more than a whisper.

Jonathan Crawford looked up.

"Jesus Christ, Anne," he said. "Jesus fucking Christ."

"I thought we'd agreed that word was not to pass between us," the woman said. She smiled.

Jonathan rose. "I'm sorry," he said. "I'm sorry. But the shock ..."

"The shock?"

"Of your being here. You should have phoned."

"I didn't want to."

The woman removed her coat and sat down, laying her handbag and her gloves beside her on the tablecloth.

"I would like a glass of whisky," she said. "A large glass with no ..."

"No ice—and water on the side. Of course."

Jonathan beckoned to the waiter and sat down again.

He stared at the woman and fingered a cigarette.

She looked away.

"Beautiful as ever," he said.

"Thank you." She glanced at him and waved her hand. "So are you. Damn you."

"Well. What can I say to that?" He smiled.

"Just be glad I still think so."

"I am."

"Oh, yes. Of course. You always were. Glad."

The drinks came.

They drank without toasting.

Anne Churchill had married Jonathan Crawford in The Marriage of the Year, according to the *New York Times* and the *Post*, in May of 1976. She was the only child of Wylie Churchill, the multimillionaire inventor of Bran Meal, a cereal useful to both humans and to cats, dogs and horses. At her father's death, Anne had invested a good deal of her money in the arts, with a particular focus on the theatre. This way, she found Jonathan. This way, Jonathan was found.

Now she turned and looked at him, fingering her glass, deliberately swirling its contents until they spilled on the cloth.

"Clumsy as ever." Jonathan smiled.

"No. Trying as always to gain an anchor. If the cloth is wet, the glass cannot slip aside."

"Of course."

"Have you ordered?"

"Yes. I've eaten. Are you hungry?"

"No. I just wanted to be sure you were nourished."

"That sounds ominous."

"Perhaps it was meant to."

"Why have you come? All the way from Philadelphia, I presume. That's a long drive. Or did Alonso ...?"

Anne said nothing for a moment, gauged the distance between their table and the next—and said, almost diffidently: "I have something to tell you. But not here. We must find somewhere private."

"I have a room."

"No. Not a room. What I have to say, I can't ... I can't say it between walls. Is there somewhere else ...?"

"Of course. There's a garden."

"Then, in the garden. But not before one more drink."

"Certainly."

Jonathan ordered a magnum of red wine. It seemed appropriate.

"Who are all these people?" Anne wondered, looking around the crowded dining-room.

Jonathan smiled, waved his hand and took a deep breath.

"Stratford is a theatre town," he said. "Remember?"

"Oh, yes. Of course."

"They come from all over the world."

"Yes. I wasn't thinking."

"What *were* you thinking?"

She looked away.

"That I still love you," she said.

Jonathan sat back.

"Well," he said. "And part of me will always love you."

"Will it? Just a part?"

"You know me, Anne. You know there can't be more."

"But you're my *husband*."

"Yes. I was."

"Doesn't that mean anything to you?"

"It means I lied."

"Oh, God. Don't go back to that."

"But it's true. I lied. I had to. I loved you—but I knew I should not—could not be married. Simple as that. But you insisted. And I ..." He shrugged. "I was weak and I pretended ... I even pretended to myself that I could make it work ..."

"You did make it work."

"Did I?"

"Yes. You did. And you know you did. We were happy. For three whole years, we were happy. We even ..."

"Yes. We even ..."

The wine came. It was opened. The glasses were set beside it. Jonathan reached for the bottle.

"No," Anne said—and grasped his hand. "Outside. Outside. In that garden you promised."

"Yes. Of course."

"What lovely hands you have," she said. "Such lovely hands." She folded her other hand over his. "Golden fingers. Magic fingers. The fingers of the last aesthete. I always thought so. Long—delicate—tapered—beautiful, such beautiful nails. So few people have such hands, any more—especially men. I don't know why. I've never understood why ..."

She looked at him, still holding his hand. "And your long, mournful face ..." She reached up and touched his cheek. "Almost malformed ..." She smiled. "Which makes it all the more beautiful. Oh, my darling—oh, my darling—why? Why did it have to be? The way it was—the way it is. *Why?*"

Jonathan took her hands and laid them back in front of her. "We knew it when we did it," he said. "We knew. And we said: *it does not matter*. And we had—we had our time."

Anne looked down at her lap and said: "yes. We had our time."

"Shall we go out now?"

"Yes, please. Outside."

They sat on a bench beneath the trees at the top of the lawn.

There was a table with an ashtray—and a folded parasol which they did not raise. Where they were, it was not necessary.

Jonathan poured the wine, lighted their cigarettes, sat to one side and said: "and so—here we are."

"Yes," said Anne.

She looked at her skirts and smoothed them—lifted her bag and set it down and gazed across the lawn towards the rear of the hotel.

"How lucky you are," she said. "It's all so peaceful—graceful—what's the word?"

"Protective."

"Yes. It's all so protective. A haven."

"Yes. A haven."

"Is there anyone?"

"Yes."

"Do I know him?"

"No."

"Are you happy? I mean—together."

"It's possible."

"Only possible?"

Jonathan smiled and shrugged.

"Like me, he's a married man."

"I see."

Anne drank some wine, smoked her cigarette, looked at the trees to one side and said: "has he children?"

"Yes. He has a son."

"A son."

"Yes."

"I see."

Jonathan watched her carefully. She was tense. The public person was always there, no matter how she tried to be rid of her. Something was always in control—there was always something in the demeanour that would not let go. She had never been able to give herself over.

She turned to him, now, all her practised self giving way all at once before his eyes, and said: "I could not have to tell you anything worse than what I've come to tell."

Her eyes were filled with tears. She reached for his hands again and held them, burning them both with cigarettes, but still holding on.

"What?" Jonathan said gently. "What is it?"

Anne looked directly at him.

"Our son is dead."

2

Tuesday, August 18, 1998

Moonlight.

Two men lying naked on an unmade bed.

Open window.

Music.

"Must you play that?"

"Yes."

"It's so mournful."

"If it wasn't, I wouldn't play it."

Silence.

And then: "there's a lot I haven't told you."

"I'm sure. Sometimes in spite of everything, I think I hardly know you."

"It's been deliberate. I mean—that's how I've kept myself together. Being silent."

"You've hardly been silent, Jonathan."

"Yes. I have. I've hidden. Been hiding. It was necessary. If people know everything, they lose faith in the mystery."

Griff knew this was true. He had been practising the same thing.

This thought made him smile.

It's not easy being me.

This is news? It's not easy being anybody.

He listened to the music. Someone was singing.

"I had a visitor today. This afternoon."

"Oh, yes?"

"Yes. My wife."

Griff said nothing.

Wife.

"Does that surprise you?"

"Not really." Griff tried to sound diffident. "But I thought she was in Philadelphia."

"So did I."

Jonathan sat up against the headboard and lighted a cigarette. There was an open bottle of wine from which he filled a glass.

"You want some?"

"Sure."

Griff sat up and reached for a cigarette.

"Light?"

"Sure. Thanks."

They sat there—thighs touching—Jonathan's free hand grazing the hair on Griff's stomach.

"Extraordinary how potent cheap music is," he said.

Griff laughed.

"If I knew the next line, I'd say it," he said.

"*What exactly were you remembering at that moment?*"

"I don't know. I wasn't thinking."

"I just gave you the next line."

"Oh. All right. *What exactly were you remembering at that moment?*"

Jonathan looked away at the open windows.

"My son," he said.

"Jacob?"

"Yes. Jacob."

Jonathan removed his hand from Griff's stomach and wrapped it around his glass of wine. He fell silent.

"What made you think of him?"

"He's dead."

"Dead? Dear God. Oh, Jon. I'm so sorry. When? How?"

"Last week. That's why Anne came. To tell me. Drove all the way from Philadelphia. Well—was driven. She has an Italian chauffeur whose name is Alonso."

"She sounds moneyed."

"She is. One of the Philadelphia Churchills. Patrons of the arts. Lovely woman. Dear. But proud. Aloof. Still, she did well by him—our son. Very well. Gave him the education he wanted. Sent him out into the world and ..."

Griff glanced at the windows. *Moon.*

"What happened?"

"He was murdered."

"Jesus."

"Yes. *Jesus.*"

"What happened? Where?"

"He was in Peru. I think I told you. He was going to be an archaeologist."

"Yes."

Griff waited. His scrotum began to shrivel. He lowered a hand to cover it—warm it—protect it.

"In order to get his degree, he had to submit a report on a famous ruin and chose Machu Picchu." Jonathan took a drag from his cigarette and let the smoke out into the moonlight. "He loved the mountains," he said. "His name was Jacob."

"Yes. I know."

Griff looked at Jonathan, whose face was drawn and older than Griff had ever realized it could be. The long eyes were partially closed, the thin lips clenched. Griff reached out and touched his hand.

"Don't," said Jonathan, and withdrew. "Don't feel sorry for someone you didn't know. It's not a good idea."

Griff crossed his legs at the knee and waited.

"Tell me," he said.

There was a moment of silence and then Jonathan said: "they call themselves The Shining Path."

"Yes. I've heard of them."

Jonathan poured more wine.

"They're opposed to government. Seemingly any government ..."

"Marxists?"

"Possibly. Who cares. They kill. That's all that matters. To them. And to us."

"Yes ..."

There was a pause.

"He saw the same moon. The day he died—he saw the same moon we see—this moon ..."

"I'm so sorry," Griff said. "I don't care what you think or say—I'm sorry."

"I apologize," said Jonathan, and rubbed the back of Griff's hand. "I wasn't angry when I said that. I was just being ... *admonitory*." He gave a kind of laugh, ruffled Griff's hair and took a deep breath.

"Yes," Griff said. "You were being a *director*. *Ta—dah!*"

He said this gently.

Jonathan said: "there were conditions. Three hostages—Jacob one of them—all Americans. That was the point. The bargaining point. Because I'm Canadian—and because Anne is American, Jacob had dual citizenship. Damn it. That's what killed him."

Griff withdrew to an upright position.

"And ...?"

"And ... whatever it is they wanted—that American aid stop filling Peruvian coffers—whatever—whatever it was, it wasn't given. So they took them one by one ... One by one by one—three of them—and killed them, leaving their bodies in public places. Crossroads, village squares, garbage dumps—and retreating into the trees. Jacob was first. Thank God. If he'd been last, I cannot imagine the suffering."

He drank.

"He was twenty-two. Twenty-two years old ... Can you remember that? Being twenty-two?"

"Yes. Very well."

"Everything spread out before you ... the rest of life—the world ... Twenty-two years old."

"Yes."

Jonathan put his hand lightly on Griff's cheek.

"How good this has been," he said.

Griff waited.

"When I saw my wife today," Jonathan said, "when I saw her and remembered being in love—the only woman—the only woman ever in my life—and remembered Jacob—remembered what we had done—what we had created together, I thought ..."

He did not finish.

Griff said: "yes. I remember the same."

Jonathan smiled at him.

"Don't let this happen to you," he said. "To you and your family."

"No," said Griff. "I don't intend to. I won't. In fact ..."

"You know, when I married Anne, it was ambition. That and nothing else. Her money—her name—her beauty—the fact that she wanted me. So I said yes. Sound familiar?"

"Yes."

"I should not have done this to you, Griffin. I should have known better."

Griff was silent.

"I'm sorry," said Jonathan.

"Oh, no," said Griff. "Don't be. You've ..."

"Yes? I've what?"

"I've ..." Griff gave a rueful laugh. "I've discovered a lot about myself, lately. And ..."

"Yes?"

"I want to go back to the beginning. Of me. I was on my way somewhere—and ... blundered."

"We all do that."

"Yes."

"You said you've learned something about yourself."

"Yes."

"Will you be able to use what you've learned?"

"Yes. Onstage—and off."

"Will you go back? Eventually?"

"If they'll have me."

"Don't be an idiot. They love you. You love them."

"Yes."

"And I love you. But not ... not as a way of holding you. Not any more. I had that. It only made you hate me."

"No. I'm not good at hate, Jonathan. I don't know how. Not you, at any rate. Me, maybe. Myself. But not you."

"Well—you *can* be hateful." Jonathan was smiling.

"Yes. But that's different. If I do hate—what I hate is not being good enough to be who I am. And that's all."

Jonathan stood up and went to the open windows. He looked at the moon.

The moon. And the moon path out on the lawn. The shining path ...

Griff said: "I have something to tell you, too."

"Oh?"

"Yes. But I don't know whether you're going to think it's good or bad ..."

"Nothing could be worse than Jacob."

"Of course not. But I think ... I think this is the right time to tell you, nonetheless. Please forgive me. But I think ... I *know* it's the right time to tell you. In a way, *because* of Jacob ..."

"Go ahead."

Griff looked over at Jonathan, naked in the moonlight. Six-foot-three and taut as a wire. He glanced at Jonathan's flaccid penis emerging from its dark halo of pubic hair.

Sex. Women. Wives. Sons.

"I want to go home," Griff said. "Now."

Jonathan said nothing.

"I miss my son. Will. I miss Jane. I miss ... who I was."

Still nothing.

Griff stubbed his cigarette in the ashtray—as if it was a punctuation mark. The end of an affair.

"I wouldn't hurt you for the world," he said.

"I know that."

"But do you understand? Why I want to go back ..."

"Yes."

Jonathan turned and went back to the bed, stubbing his own cigarette beside the dying embers of Griff's.

Sitting down again next to him, he put his hand on Griff's thigh.

"You were—you are—and you will always be the most desirable man I'll ever know."

"I can't ... I don't ..."

"You don't have to say anything."

They drank wine. They lighted new cigarettes. The moon had moved from one window frame to another. The music had ended. It was 3:00 a.m.

"I'll always love you. In my way."

"Yes. And I you."

"And in March—we'll have Mercutio and Berowne."

"Yes."

They fell silent.

Then Jonathan said: "he was five-foot-ten. He weighed a hundred and sixty pounds. Trim. Lean. Serious. He wore glasses. Outrageously blind. Blind! But above all else, he knew who he was."

Like Will, Griff thought.

They sat for a moment more.

Then Jonathan said: "goodnight, Griffin."

"Yes. Goodnight."

Jonathan turned his back and lay, stretched out—sighing—holding a pillow in one hand—smoothing the palm of the other over Griff's chest.

For a time Griff lay still, finishing the wine, letting his cigarette burn to the bone—its smoke lying flat across the window frame.

Dead. A boy aged twenty-two. Full of promise. Gone.

The image of the corpse at the crossroads was too easy to conjure. *Anyone. Anyone. It could have been anyone. But it was him. It was Jonathan's son. His only child.*

Griff gently disengaged Jonathan's hand, sat up and swung his feet to the floor.

I'm lucky. Christ, I'm lucky.

Will.

Jane.

He stood up.

Tomorrow.

3

Wednesday, August 19, 1998

When Griff's car pulled into the drive behind hers, Mercy was standing at the stove preparing scrambled eggs for Jane, who was to take a class with Edna Mott later in the morning. It was 8:35. Will had not come down yet. Rudyard was in the backyard.

Mercy was humming the tune of "The Lady of Shallot" by Loreena McKennitt. It was her favourite song of the moment, possibly because it reflected her own decision "to look back out through the windows at life." Even though for the Lady herself, the glance had tragic consequences, for Mercy the tragedies were fading. Something new could happen. And was going to. Her decision to live with Luke and possibly to be his wife had brought the world into new focus. She could accept it now, in ways she had feared would never again be open to her.

The Lexus had an unmistakable sound to its engine—a low, contented way of dying into silence that told you it had arrived.

In the garden, Rudyard turned from the hedge he had been nosing and lifted his ears.

His tail started slowly to wave.

He raised his nose and drank in the scent.

It was him.

Rudyard went loping.

The familiar hand came down to greet him.

"Hello there, old friend."

Rudyard lifted himself onto his hind legs.

Griff carried nothing in his hands. He had decided to bring only himself to the door.

He mussed Rudyard's ears and went to the stoop.

Knocking lightly, he went in.

Mercy was already staring.

Griff smiled.

"Where is everyone?" he said.

"Right here," said Mercy.

"Of course."

Mercy turned off the gas burner, set the pan of eggs aside, covered it and laid down the spatula.

"You have business here?" she asked cautiously, wiping her hands on a tea towel.

"I hope so," said Griff. He could not stop smiling. Rudyard simply sat and stared, his tail still slowly moving back and forth.

"Do I get a kiss?" Mercy asked.

"Yes, ma'am."

They embraced.

"Oh, Lord," she said against his shoulder. "How I have prayed for this moment."

"Me, too," said Griff. "Much as you might think not."

"Yes."

Mercy stepped away, wiped the tears from her eyes with a Kleenex and said: "you want some coffee?"

"Yes, please."

"Sit."

"No. I can't. I'm too nervous. Are you expecting them? Now, I mean."

"Jane, yes. Maybe not Will. He's ..." She turned away to pour the coffee. "He's retreated."

"I'm sorry."

"You can apologize all you want—but it's been hardest of all on him."

"I guess ..."

"But seeing you ... You never know. With children, you never know. But I think you should be warned. It's going to take a while before he trusts you again. That's what he suffered most—the loss of trust."

"Yes."

Griff sat with the coffee.

Mercy joined him.

"The centre of every good life is the kitchen table," said Griff. He tried to laugh, but could not quite achieve it. "My mum used to say that."

"Yeah."

"How you been?"

"Living a new life."

Mercy told him briefly about Luke.

"Good for you," Griff said. "He's a wonderful man. I can't imagine a better. Not for you."

"We're going to be happy—that's a certainty. He's going to buy a dog." She laughed. "Me with my cats, him with his dog—what more could you want?"

"Sounds like perfect peace, to me."

Suddenly, Jane was there.

She stood in the hall doorway, wearing a pale blue dress, her hair falling over her shoulders. There was a scarlet ribbon in her left hand.

"Hello," she said. "I ... I heard voices. I thought maybe Luke ..."

"No," said Griff, and stood up. "Not Luke. Me."

He and Jane looked at each other, neither one moving forward, neither one retreating. Mercy watched her own hands move to smooth the tablecloth.

Then Griff said: "may I come home?"

Jane closed her eyes.

"Well, aren't you already standing there?" she said—opening her eyes and looking at him.

"Yes. It's me."

"Tell me your name."

"Griffin Kincaid."

"I thought so. There was something familiar ..."

Mercy stood up and went back to the stove.

"You want me to phone Miss Mott and cancel that class?" she said.

"Yes, please," said Jane.

She came forward and took Griff's hand.

"Please," she said. "Come now. Right now."

She led him from the room, followed by Rudyard, and they moved through the hall and up the stairs.

On the landing, Griff stopped and said: "Jane—I ..."

Jane laid her hand on his lips. "No," she said. "I don't want to know. It's over—whatever it was—and that's all that matters."

"I don't want to know, either. About you. The mysterious man. So it works both ways—what you said."

Jane smiled. "Three ways, Griff. It has to work three ways."

Then she led him to the top. Not letting go of Griff's hand, she went to Will's closed door and, knocking, opened it.

"Will?" she said.

He was sitting by the open window in his pyjamas, staring out at the garden. A minute later, he would have gone to the roof to feed the crow.

Jane said: "I've brought someone who wants to see you."

Will turned and looked at her.

Jane drew Griff forward and stood behind him, watching silently.

"Hello, Will."

Will said nothing.

Griff went forward and laid his hands on Will's shoulders.

"Well ..." he said. Just *well*—and that was all.

Will turned back to the window.

Griff dropped his hands and looked at Jane. She nodded towards Will. Griff reached for him again.

After a long moment, Will turned, looked up and said, very quietly: "Dad ...?"

They embraced, though Will's embrace was tentative—careful.

Time, Griff thought. *Give him time.*

Beyond the window, a breeze was lifting. The crows took flight. Mrs Arnprior came into her garden and began to hang a wash. A car went by. Jane patted Will's pillow. At last, he would be able to sleep. She looked across the room.

There they were. And here they were.

The three of them.

Yes. And Rudyard by her knee—and, downstairs, Mercy. And in a studio drawer, a painted family waiting to be made whole again.

swans

But time is always killed. Someone must pay for
Our loss of happiness, our happiness itself.

W.H. Auden
Detective Story

Two o'clock on a Sunday afternoon.

It rained, as it always did on this parade.

Not that the rain was depressing. Anything but. In fact, that morning Jane had seen Mrs Arnprior, in her nightgown, standing on her back lawn, arms lifted and face turned upward to the heavens. *Another answered prayer, Lord!*

There had been so little snow that year, the ground was bare half the winter. But this was farming country and townsfolk had gardens—vegetables, flowers and trees. Everyone depended on a generous water table. The rain was more than welcome.

Down by the arena, half the world—or so it seemed to Will—stood waiting under the cover of raised umbrellas, only one of these, black. Naturally, it belonged—as if you had to ask—to Mister Sissons, the undertaker. *Never say Si-ss-ons! Always say Si-zz-ens!* he would hiss at callers, even in their moments of darkest anguish. As for the rest of the *bumbershoots*—one of Will's new words—they provided a seeming cacophony of colour, shouting out *red! green! yellow! pink!* And even *polka dots! Blue.*

"When are they coming, Mum?" Will asked.

Jane said: "when they're good 'n' ready, hon. Don't forget, this is the most important moment in their year. They'll be nervous and excited as Dad is on opening nights."

Will looked at Griff, who was fending off the attentions of a talkative, clutching woman. He thought: *boy! Dad's getting mad—the way he does with me when I ask too many questions.*

He wanted to pee, but he knew it was out of the question. He was too old to pee his pants and there wouldn't be time to get to the washroom before the pipers announced the parade. He would have to tough it out.

Out of the question ... tough it out.

These were the latest parental admonitions. Jane had recently forbidden the purchase of a video game by saying: *it's out of the question*—and Griffin had said: *you've got to tough it out, kid,* when Will had fallen from his bike and painfully scraped both knees.

Rudyard pulled at his leash. He was bored.

Will looked up at Mercy. Maybe she would take Ruddy for a walk ...

Mercy read every corner of Will's mind—day in, day out. Looking down at him, she smiled. "*You* take him for a walk," she said. "I'm not about to miss this parade, same as I did last year when he wound his leash three times around a tree."

Luke, who stood beside her, allowed her to take his arm. His public reticence about having a girlfriend had begun to fade.

Will turned to Jane. He was eight, now.

"Mum?"

"Shhh. Be patient, hon."

Be patient. Tough it out.

He heard the wheeze of distant pipes—the initial exhalation that announced forthcoming music.

Everyone turned to the right.

Denser rain began to fall. So much more, it seemed to be prompted by the pipers.

Cameras—professional and amateur—were suddenly drawn, like guns.

Television crews and press photographers stepped into the middle of the road.

"Get out of the way!" people called.

"You're blocking the view!" others cried.

"Get out of the way yourself! It's our job!"

Mercy looked to her left. There was her young neighbour, Milos Saworski. *Still a mystery,* Mercy thought. *Still unreadable.* As always, he was wearing overtorn jeans and a child's expression. *That's his costume,* Mercy decided. *That's how he can be identified. Denim. Dreaming. Desire. His badges of survival.*

The dog was beside him. Chops.

Mercy smiled.

Claire and Hugh were standing on the far side beneath matching brick-coloured umbrellas. Jane and Griff waved. And Luke and Mercy. The Highlands smiled and waved back.

The pipers were coming abreast of where Will stood.

He strained against the rope.

Rudyard moved between his legs and burned Will's fingers where he held onto the leash.

Then he saw them, emerging from behind the veil of kilts.

A single white-faced goose.

A pair of black swans.

Two white geese with bright orange beaks.

Sixteen white swans.

"Sixteen, Mum!"

And they stepped. And they stepped. And they stepped again and stopped. And they conferred. Now, they became a regal procession—looking both left and right and then away, primly dismissing the human spectators. *We, after all, are kings and queens. We are above all this.* Besides, by then they had smelled the river.

Water.

The river Avon.

Lake Victoria.

Five months of living in a barn—of living in exile—or so it had seemed, even though it was an exile plentiful with hay and straw, with feed and warmth.

But it was not the river.

Not the lake. Not freedom.

Rudyard stirred and muttered: *kill.*

Will looked up at Griff, who went to stand behind Jane with his hand on her shoulder.

Jane reached back and wrapped his fingers in her own.

"So," she said. "Another year. Another swan-release ..." *We made it,* she was thinking, but left this unsaid.

The pipers and the crowd began to disperse.

"Heaven on earth," Jane said. "To see them all again."

"You almost forget how beautiful they are," Griff said.

"And how empty the river looks without them," Jane added. "Come on, Will—we're going home."

They began to break away from the others.

Going home, Jane thought. *Home.*

Maybelle had decided to give Jane the money to buy the Cambria Street house as part of her inheritance, the rest of which would come after Maybelle's death.

The only thing you have to promise is to light a candle once a week for your sister Loretta, she had written. *Never forget her. Never. And never forget your mama in your prayers.*

This was a promise Jane had kept, so that once a week she returned to the peace of St. Joseph's, where she began to enjoy a different kind of solitude—a sense of self-confident contentment she had never felt before.

Mercy took Rudyard's leash from Will and fell behind the others into what she laughingly called *the servile servant mode*. She loved her job, and would have died without it. It had given an otherwise emptied life the company of needful companions. Now, there was Luke—and the thought of the McKenzie House Bed and Breakfast she would create, and to which Luke had agreed. *No more empty rooms*, he had said. This way, for Mercy, there would be no end of something to do when Will was grown.

They came to the corner of Waterloo, where the swans and the geese were swarming beneath the bridge towards the dam and the waterfall. Will ran across the street so he could watch them coming out on the other side.

Above them, the crows were also returning, flocking in their tattered groups, calling out instructions—*you that way, we this*—just as Don Armado says at the end of *Love's Labour's Lost*, though Will did not yet know this. That would come later in the summer.

"Maybe our own crows are among them," Jane said, looking up. She waved—just in case.

Will looked, too, and smiled. *Alpha* was there, his voice the loudest.

"Pazzo is right there," Griff said, as they neared the upward-turning corner leading to Ontario Street. "Let's have some wine and salad. And we can all have a pizza to celebrate!" He turned to Will. "You like that?"

"Yes, sir!" Will beamed. "Yes, sir!"

Mercy let out more chain and said: "what about Rudyard?"

"I'm sure they'll make an exception on such an exciting occasion," said Jane. "Maybe he could wait in the back office. We can but ask. Jeff and Larry will understand."

"Pee," Mercy said to Rudyard. "Pee now, or forever hold your peace."

She and Luke hung back and took Ruddy to the nearest trees.

Wine—pizza—Pazzo. Peace.

As they headed for the side door leading to the downstairs pizzeria, Jane thought: *a year ago ... I thought I had it all. But I didn't. Not then. Then, I had only the promise. Now I have ... Don't say it. Don't even think it. Nothing is certain. So. But some things are possible ...*

After that, they all went inside—like the swans returning to the river and the crows to the trees.

Before she closed the door behind her, Jane turned for one last look at the river. The eternal promise of spring hung in the air and the rain that fell seemed perfumed with it—almost the smell of green itself.

Closing the door, she heard—before it shut—the distant sound of the water flowing over the dam, and she closed her eyes to watch the river in her mind, flowing downstream to continue its everlasting journey towards open water, open skies and the promise everywhere of life.

acknowledgements

My thanks especially to Iris Tupholme and to Lawrence Ashmead for their insight and extremely helpful editorial suggestions, and to Mary Adachi, whose copy editing was, as always, a formidable education. My thanks, too, to Beverley Roberts for providing the timelines of the war in Kosovo and of the events involving President Clinton and Monica Lewinsky. And to my agent, Bruce Westwood, whose enthusiasm and efforts on my behalf are unflagging. Finally, my everlasting thanks to William Whitehead for his steadfast sense of order, for his companionship and for his endless ability to keep our ship afloat.